GAMBLING ON MAGIC

Also by Christopher G. Moore

Novels in the Vincent Calvino crime fition series

Spirit House o Asia Hand o Zero Hour in Phnom Penh
Comfort Zone o The Big Weird o Cold Hit
Minor Wife o Pattaya 24/7 o The Risk of Infielity Index
Paying Back Jack o The Corruptionist o 9 Gold Bullets
Missing in Rangoon o The Marriage Tree o Crackdown
Jumpers o Dance Me to the End of Time o District #3

Other novels

A Killing Smile o A Bewitching Smile o A Haunting Smile
His Lordship's Arsenal o Tokyo Joe o Red Sky Falling
God of Darkness o Chairs o Waiting for the Lady
Gambling on Magic o The Wisdom of Beer

Non-fition

Heart Talk o The Vincent Calvino Reader's Guide
The Cultural Detective o Faking It in Bangkok
Fear and Loathing in Bangkok o The Age of Dis-Consent
Memory Manifesto

Anthologies

Bangkok Noir o Phnom Penh Noir
The Orwell Brigade

GAMBLING ON MAGIC

A NOVEL BY

CHRISTOPHER G. MOORE

Heaven Lake Press

Published in Thailand by:
Asia Document Bureau Ltd.
Monterey Place Condo 398
Soi Paisingtoh Rama IV Road,
Bangkok 10110, Thailand
Fax: (662) 260-4578
Web site: www.heavenlakepress.com
E-mail: editorial@heavenlakepress.com

Trade Paperback edition: Copyright © 2005 Christopher G. Moore
Second Printing, 2024
ISBN 978-616-7503-40-0

Author's web site: www.cgmoore.com
Author's e-mail: chris@cgmoore.com

For Michael ("Roxy") Roxborough

"Serious sport is war minus the shooting."
George Orwell

"Change is the nature of the universe."
I Ching, The Book of Change

30 September 1992:
in the Mojave Desert near Las Vegas

A strange yellow light flooded the Mojave Desert. The sunrays' hues ranged between barroom-nicotine and honey; the landscape painted a kind of tainted and corrupted longing, as the group walked through it at sunset. Going into the desert was Joey Balfour's idea. His eyes squinted as he surveyed the horizon. He remembered once having bet on a horse that was the color of that early evening desert sky and, although the odds were ten to one, the horse had won. An Indian woman with green eyes and gray hair studied the quality of the light as though she were studying the entrails of a gutted chicken, to divine meaning and purpose, to predict a man's future, a man whose life was in transition. Joey Balfour hadn't told her that this was the last night of his TV show.

Her old wrinkled eyes missed nothing, though. She looked melancholy. Her time had long passed. His mother, Jennifer, whispered something to the old woman which the wind coming off the desert smoothed to mutterings. Trenton, his father, walked ahead, inhaling the clean, pure air. They had walked ten minutes from the road where Joey had parked the car. The old shaman had brought along her grandson. Black Crow was eighteen years old but looked more like he was thirteen, with an Anglo-Saxon nose and mouth. Polite and observant, Black Crow knelt on one knee beside the sagebrush. Ahead of them along the desert floor were greasewood and pickleweed. On the other side of the mesquite, Trenton called out. He'd found a small Joshua tree half hidden by creosote bush. The others circled around Joey's father. As Joey was about to say something, Black Crow shouted, and everyone looked in the direction he pointed. Four or five feral horses ran through the light, kicking up dust and disappearing behind the saltbush. The shaman's face beamed as she cupped her gnarled hand above her eyes.

"Wild horses against the sun. That is a good sign," she said, turning to Joey.

Joey squatted down and plucked a desert marigold, put the bloom just below his nose and inhaled. As he rose to his feet, the shaman opened her leather pouch and removed a feather from the tail of an eagle, part of a shell from a tortoise, and a piece of rabbit fur attached to the hide.

"Place the flower you've taken from the desert with these things," she said.

Joey lowered the desert marigold into her birdlike claw of a hand.

The old woman explained that the quality of the desert light was an omen, as were the sighting of the wild horses, and choice of flower that Joey had picked from the desert floor. She read meaning into each separate thing, and into the collective whole as if they were equally important spokes in the wheel of fate. The rumor was that the old woman had the gift of prophecy, and Joey Balfour wanted his parents to witness her reading.

The old woman waited until her grandson had unfolded a blanket before she squatted down. She arranged the flower and things from her pouch into a small hole she dug in the sand with her bare hand. As the others gathered around, she chanted, moving back and forth for several minutes, occasionally stopping to scoop up a handful of sand and slowly passed it over the flower, feather, shell and fur until they were covered.

Joey's mother and father looked on as the old woman summoned Joey to sit beside her on the blanket. Black Crow unsheathed a Bowie knife and handed it to Joey. Light reflected from the blade, catching part of the old woman's face.

"See your reflection in this light," she said.

Joey saw a distorted image of his own face in the blade.

"The light is from the third cave in the mountain beyond. It rarely comes to the earth's surface. When it does, it is pulled out by wild horses. They bring this light to remind us of the time when an ancient tribe once left this land for another place, and how the world on the other side, a world we cannot see, swallowed them whole; when they awoke, they found themselves in harmony and balance with the universe, but in the quiet of their soul a voice whispered for them to journey to the place where they belonged. They never returned. But ever so often when the wild horses release the light from the third cave it is an omen. You will follow them to that magical place. And like them, you will not return."

30 September 2004: Washington, D.C.

"People often write to me and say, 'Shouldn't a casino ban a gambler who they know is betting the family rent and food money? Isn't it immoral for the casino to let him play?'

"And I say, 'The gambler has freedom of choice. That's what America is about: the freedom to choose even if it means smoking will kill you or eating junk food will make you fat. If he wants to play with that money, why should the casino stop him?'

"I think about casinos as a version of the gamekeeper's dilemma. A gamekeeper guards the last forty red barking deer left in the world. The species may collapse into extinction. An armed poacher sneaks through the barbed-wire fence. The gamekeeper recognizes the poacher as a man from a local village. His wife is pregnant. He has four children under seven. They don't have enough to eat. The family is starving. Does he turn his back and let the poacher bag one of the deer? Or does he challenge the poacher, and kill him if that is required? Let's take the story to another level, adding a couple more facts. This location where the rare deer are kept is the only place on the planet where they stand any chance of survival. And scientists believe that these deer have a protein that if isolated could cure cancer.

"We return to the gambler who shows up at the casino with his family's rent and food money. If he loses, they are in the street and have no money. How do the gamekeeper and casino decide what to do? Do they look to morality? Do they look to the common good? Do they follow what their boss requires of them? The gamekeeper shoots the poacher. The doorman at the casino lets in the gambler with the family's rent and food money. Why? Once the poacher kills and butchers a deer and feeds his family, what happens? The other villagers who are also hungry figure out the best way to a free lunch is to poach deer. They show up with guns and poach the rest of the herd. After the last deer is killed and eaten, their hunger returns and soon there is again starvation in the village. Nothing has changed except we no longer have a possible cure for cancer.

"If the casino turns the gambler away, I can tell you what will happen. He goes to the casino next door who are happy to let him in. You say, what if all casinos bar him, won't that fix the problem? No, it won't. He'll find a private game and lose his money in the basement of someone's house. He will in other words find a way to gamble. Unless you hog-tie him to his porch, he will get out and gamble the money. From the casino's perspective, this is a business. There's no percentage in letting someone else take the gambler's money. The family will be without a roof and food whatever the casino decides. It's the law of the jungle not morality that applies. What do we have at the end of the day? One dead poacher, a herd of deer that may save you from cancer, and one family in the street because the gambler believed Lady Luck would rescue him. Life doesn't deal out the same odds to every player. Morality has nothing to do with it. You make hard choices knowing that whatever you decide some people will always fail, be hungry, or live in total misery."

A showgirl in fishnet stockings and a low-cut top walks into the shot. She's carrying a long-stemmed martini glass with an olive floating on the surface. She stops, looks into the camera, then leans forward, smiling, offering the drink to the talk show host. She glances back at the camera. The audience reads her lips as she forms the words, "I love Joey."

"Is that martini shaken?" Joey Balfour, the talk show host, asks.

The showgirl nods, and forms her lips into a pout.

"Are you going to shake it?" he asks. He winks at the camera and chants, "Shake that bootie, shake that bootie, shake that bootie."

She rotates her hips into a perfect rhythm of grind and pump action, her breasts shaking above the drink, appearing about to pop out of her slinky top.

When she has finished her shaking, the talk show host takes the martini, salutes the camera, and takes a sip. "On our next show, we will have the greatest football player of all time back, Jim Brown. Until then, watch your odds and your ends."

Joey Balfour slaps the showgirl on the ass. She shakes her bottom and the screen cuts away to a commercial. The showgirl's ass dissolves to slot machines, lights flashing, cherries, oranges and apples spinning. Bells, sirens and whistles blare. Coins jingle-jangle as they fill and spill over the metal cup. Underneath the smiling faces of the man and woman who scoop up the coins is an advertisement for a casino on an Indian reservation in California, another in Arizona, followed by New York and Connecticut. A voice-over announces these casinos are part of The United Native Casino Association.

The giant plasma screen flatlines leaving a dark, dead blank hole.

In a small private office inside one of the inner rings of the Pentagon, the opposite side from where debris and body parts from the 9/11 crash site were recovered, the head of RCA sits forward in his chair and lowers a sleek black remote control like a gun he's holstering after the shot. He's killed the picture. He lays down the remote and picks up the telephone. He pushes his glasses onto his forehead, rubs his eyes, cradling the phone between his chin and shoulder. "I saw it. Let's get someone to Bangkok to take care of the problem. You are on the money. You have the go-ahead."

On his desk, he indulges himself, stroking the head of a porcelain dalmatian frozen in the sitting position in front of an old-fashioned gramophone, one ear cocked towards the horn. He smiles to himself. Sports teams understand the use of mascots. They build morale and purpose and mutual goals. He likes the dalmatian—ever listening, ever patient, ever in tune with the sound frequency beyond the range of human ears, the dog is the unofficial symbol of the unofficial agency. Lost in the fog of history, the dalmatian beside the gramophone recedes from consciousness. He has brought the dog back to life for an agency that doesn't exist on any record; there is no paper trail or unsecured database. Officially it has no working name or mascot. Officially it does not exist. Rendition Confirmation Agency, or RCA, is the internal name never spoken outside the basement.

The Annual
Canadian Thanksgiving Dinner:
Bangkok, Thailand

Joey Balfour was a late-blooming celebrity. Fame had arrived unexpectedly, long after the bonanza of riches might have drifted down like fine snow covering his entire life in blinding glory. Women, luxury penthouse, cars, travel and the rest of the loot that celebrities stash away had been Joey's for years. Fame after age twenty-seven is wasted. Twenty-seven years old was, for Joey Balfour, a distant memory, a lifetime ago, by the time a thirty-year-old tribal chief—a one-sixteenth-native fifteen-sixteenths-American millionaire—who goes by the name of Chief Black Crow, and who operates a casino in Northern California, paid cold cash to get the rights to Joey Balfour's old cable TV series. Chief Black Crow renamed the series *Gambling on Magic*. Just over twelve years had passed since the series had last been broadcast. The Indians released the TV series on cable, but not before an advertising agency devised a series of ads promoting Indian reservation casinos. Next the advertising boys launched a marketing campaign for the DVDs of the show. Thousands of DVDs flew out the door. A new generation discovered Joey Balfour. Every DVD had ads for the big, flashy offshore online gambling casinos; the ads carefully targeted hip kids who could steal some cash or their parents' credit card to play poker on the Internet. Chief Black Crow's one-sixteenth of Indian blood was enough to make him an Indian and no one in politics stepped forward to criticize the campaign to lure American teenagers to the Internet gaming tables.

Fame when a person reaches his fifties brings out the worst in others: envy, jealousy, and the feeling of a God-given right to share in the new wealth that fame has wasted on the old. They emailed or phoned and some flew all the way to Bangkok to find Joey Balfour and explain why he should give them money. He ignored them.

Joey reminded himself that Errol Flynn, the action adventure cult actor, had died at fifty years old. Flynn's feng shui personal number had been four: *Quatre, Quatro, Quattro, Cuatro.* Feng shui translates the number four as riches. But the Chinese also believe that this is the number of death. The scent of fresh cedar perfumes Joey's brain. Wood was the actor's element. And turquoise his personal color. Lessons from Sky and Ped into the art of feng shui had opened new portals on the life of Errol Flynn, and revealed secrets of how his chi had been blocked inside the room where he had lived at the time of his death.

As he read the invitation to the Annual Thanksgiving Ball, Joey had misgivings about attending. His sixth sense said a celebrity—even one by force of circumstances—should stay away from public functions. He decided to ignore this ripple across the surface of his existence; he would not let it ruin his life or restrict his access to the friends and functions he had always enjoyed. Besides, there were people at the Thanksgiving Ball whom he saw only once a year. Most of them would not have seen the original TV series and wouldn't have heard about the release in the States. This was, after all, Canadian Thanksgiving. He could just be Joey Balfour, Canadian expat and owner of the highly successful Feng Shui Flower Shop. Some of those in attendance would be his customers. They would expect Joey to support the Annual Canadian Thanksgiving Ball with his presence. Fame as a florist is what Joey had aspired to achieve since retiring to Bangkok. He refused to accept that his old life had been forever changed because an old series was back on the air. Joey calculated the probabilities and figured it was five to one someone would mention the TV series.

As a child Joey heard his mother calling out from the kitchen: "What's it going to be? Turkey? Or how about Spam for Joey?"

He had been old enough to recoil at the transparent jelly covering the rough combination of pork shoulder and ham inside a Spam can. It reminded him of mass murder and disposal units in a vast factory with assembly lines and workers in identical blue overalls, working silently except for the hiss of steam and the metallic sound of tin being cut, and the low growl of electric saws cutting through bone.

Trenton, Joey's father, had looked up from his table stacked with books and research material and smiled. "Joey'll have the Spam. We can share the turkey."

When you are the only child of a professor and the heiress to a small fortune, the experiments in child rearing can turn a kid into a guinea pig. Joey was a carefully studied specimen in the family lab experiment. His parents were Sixties beatniks, free spirits, anti-war, anti-government, passionate and idealistic, believers in the love and peace slogans. They secretly admired Joey's decision to run away from home at seventeen years old to work for Eugene McCarthy's presidential campaign in New York City. No one raised an eyebrow when Trenton had a chance to take a university position in Canada. It was assumed they would leave the United States. People make lots of assumptions. For instance, an only child is supposedly spoiled rotten, deformed in expectations, robbed of a grounded reality in the world of hard knocks, unable to understand that the entire world isn't designed to love him. Like all assumptions, Joey's family tested them, digested them, and retooled them before coming up with a variation that had others scratching their heads. Like all assumptions, Thanksgiving dinner was a lesson that one should not expect turkey. Trenton taught Joey that all events in life were based on probabilities and the smart people learned how to calculate the odds of something happening, or not happening. One year Joey's mother served the family Spam to teach him the lesson that a long shot does sometimes win.

Joey Balfour shot pool the day he decided to take Sky and Ped to the Annual Canadian Thanksgiving Ball, as in the previous years. The best course of action was to continue his life as if nothing had changed. He remained the same Joey Balfour in the company of two beautiful women. The Joey Balfour who appeared in *Gambling on Magic* only faintly resembled the Joey Balfour who would attend the ball. He could be the father of the young Joey on the TV series. But the probabilities of that event happening could easily be calculated as zero.

Men in dinner jackets and women in ball gowns sip red wine from long-stemmed glasses. They hover in the shadow of an ice sculpture. Guests circle the sculpture positioned on a table against a mirror; the lighting from the base is a ruby red, and small candles have been placed around the perimeter. Bowls of nuts have been placed in front of the candles. The effect is dramatic, a voodoo ritual, a blood sacrifice, an offering to the gods. What doesn't come to mind, though, is Thanksgiving. The chairwoman of the organizing committee explains as several guests listen that the hotel catering staff had been told to make an ice-sculptured turkey.

The hotel staff had smiled, nodded, and said in English, "Turkey. No problem. We make a very beautiful turkey."

What's a turkey? The question lurked behind those whiter than white teeth smiles. Silent, brain circuits rattling, bouncing through images from childhood recollections without settling on anything specific, until a picture slowly came into focus.

Joey believes the staff knew nothing of Spam.

The symbol to set the tone of the evening for the guests to the Annual Canadian Thanksgiving Ball is an ice-sculptured duck, the back feathers sweeping back into a sweet upturned tip. The pièce de résistance is a top hat. The carver's idea of a turkey was a duck wearing a top hat cocked to the side. The image had filtered through a lifetime of huge blocks of ice and sharp tools and cold hands and goose-skin flesh, and was agreed in a five-minute conversation with two phone call interruptions—one from her boyfriend wanting to borrow money and one from the manager wanting to know the cost of fifty kilos of ice—between the ice carver and the hotel catering manager and two junior staff. The consensus being this turkey was a work of art. They did not charge enough for the job. They had no idea of the work that went into getting that beak to resemble a bird's bill.

During the cocktail hour water drips from the duck's beak, splashing into a silver birdfeeder. The chairwoman calls the manager who sends the assistant manager to examine the duck carved out of ice. All attempts to point out that a turkey and duck are different breeds are futile. Nothing is getting through. The assistant manager hears what she wants to hear.

She responds with a haughty confidence as if this white woman is missing the entire point, "Same, same. You eat turkey, you eat duck. I think duck is more beautiful."

With that reasoning the chairwoman who had lived in Thailand for many years is aware that any further complaining is pointless. What if today were the Canadian Annual Easter Ball and instead of a bunny the hotel expected the guests to accept an ice carving of a hedgehog with a long spiny tail? The thought trails through her mind like a jet that has taken heavy cannon fire and streams of smoke flowing out from the wings, the fuselage tumbling like a cartwheel. She wants to say this but she's falling through a hole in the blue sky. She sees herself spinning towards the earth as she stares at the slowly melting duck—half bird, half fountain.

The ice duck faces a stage where a middle-aged man stands between two Thai women in evening gowns. The chairwoman knows him well, and knows his mother. But Joey Balfour, who calculated the odds of a smooth, uneventful evening as five to one, has no idea of the surprise this night holds for him. She waves at him but he's distracted, smiling, feeling good that something special will happen this evening. The ice duck will spoil nothing.

Joey, Sky and Ped stand under the Annual Thanksgiving Ball banner; light-colored drapes hang down from the ceiling and along the borders are ears of corn, squash and pumpkins. The faces in the crowd wear formal bow-tied smiles but on closer inspection, Joey detects a subtle cloud hanging behind their eyes; some hint of discontent, grief or disappointment. Photographers read the emotions in their eyes. You can tell which ones are on painkillers or tranquilizers or thinking about killing themselves. Boiling behind the eyes are the hidden worlds. The photographer speaks to Joey in Thai, telling him to smile. If Thanksgiving could be erased from the banner, any generic word would fit: think of jewelry, punting, and hockey, and blue jays, or Alberta pig farmers. Any one of the events slides so easily into the generic one-size-fits-all ambiences. The men in dinner jackets and the women in ball gowns are surrounded by corn and under the direct gaze of an ice duck.

"Look at the turkey, smile and say, 'Vancouver'," says the photographer. He doesn't know a turkey from a duck and appears to be related to the ice carver. And he doesn't actually say the word Vancouver. He is unable to say "v" so asks Joey to say "wancower" which is not a place you will find on any tourist map of British Columbia. But it does make him smile.

This is the second year running that Joey has appeared with these two flower shop employees. No set of women has ever appeared with Joey three years in a row. The insiders who know Joey exchange glances, placing side bets that this Canadian Thanksgiving Ball will be their swan song. Joey is sensitive to gossip going on around him. Most of his relationships have elapsed at hyper-speed not unlike a traffic light changing from red to green. What the people around them don't understand is that this time it is different; the numbers add up to the right sum. Joey's personal number and the numbers of Sky and Ped produce a winning bet, and, to add another layer, their personal colors produce a perfect harmony. Sky and Ped have nothing to worry about. Turnover stops once the *Book of Change* delivers the right combination to unlock the feng shui code that birth has bestowed on each living person, and provides a guide to maintaining harmony and balance.

Joey cheers the women up with a light banter about the other guests and the way the reception room has been laid out. He tells them that five-star hotels should have a minimum of one star removed unless their ice carver is capable of distinguishing between twenty-seven kinds of animals. Another star trashed for the staff photographer who calls a duck a turkey.

Confusion hangs like a fog, misunderstanding and miscommunication multiply until it is unclear what will emerge from the block of ice. No two Canadian Thanksgivings are ever the same. In Las Vegas or Vancouver, lawyers would be called, lawsuits issued, but in Bangkok they were lucky that duck hadn't been carved with a twelve-inch anatomically correct penis. Or unlucky, whispers one of the girls.

The man smiling into the camera, peering through his glasses, his arms wrapped around the waist of two women, waits for the flash. Joey is squinting as he stares at three men standing near the ice duck with their backs to him. Joey can't see their faces except in the mirrored wall opposite. From the stage he sees their dinner jackets worn over broad, middle-aged frames, two of the men have graying hair, the other man's head is shaved and he is wearing brown loafers. Men in dinner jackets bear a strong tribal resemblance and these three tribal members seem familiar. Like the ice carver, Joey's mind floods with a memory so real and vivid that it takes his breath away. He's seen this scene before. He was in Las Vegas, and in 1972. He was driving at eleven at night and his mind was thinking about the odds on a Yankees game when three old-time mob guys in dinner jackets suddenly appeared in the middle of the street. They were walking. But the street wasn't anything like Sukhumvit Road in Bangkok. The mobsters walked down a side street. Joey slammed on the brakes. Another two feet and his Buick would have mowed them down, plowed them into the cement, and wiped them out like a rookery of penguins. Joey looked up at the last minute, and saw them, hit the high beams, his heart in his throat, beating like a tom-tom drum. What were those guys doing in the middle of the street? It only occurred to him later. They were talking business and this was the only place where the cops couldn't listen. The technology was already advanced in 1972. Their hotel, a restaurant, a club, it didn't matter, any confined space had a listening device in the wall, ceiling, table, floor, chair, ashtray, toilet seats . . . the possibilities of planting devices even then were endless. So if they wanted to talk over some mob business they walked side-by-side down the center of the street. They could talk, make deals, decide who should be whacked, who should be paid off, and the cops and FBI couldn't listen in on their conversation. Somehow it never entered their heads that someone might run into them. They were gods and gods were immune to civilians crashing into them. Maybe they were right. People were born hard-wired with an instinct for danger and obstacles. Mob guys sent out radar signals so that anyone from Iowa to Maine knew to steer away.

The only thing you need less than a felony record is to run over a mob guy in Vegas. Make that three mob guys. Three strikes and you are out. You were the ball and you were high above the fence, out of the park, in a cement barrel dropped into the deepest part of a remote lake.

The man with the shaved head turns in profile; his jowls and head have the same even stubble leaving only the contour of the bone structure to define their boundary. Joey wonders what it is like for a *ying* to wake up in the middle of the night and see this living death mask on the pillow next to her. Disturbing. The man smiles and waves at Joey. His name is Paul; he is a partner in an international law office on Silom Road, and Feng Shui Flower Shop supplies plants to Paul's office. The staff has a detailed chart that describes the position of each plant, the color and type of plant and how to position it near sofas and conference tables to get maximum power in negotiations. According to the *Book of Change*, Paul, like Joey, has by birth been assigned a personal number, the number nine. Each number calculated using the *Ba Gua* scheme carves a portal into the prevailing winds of fate, preoccupation and luck that shape a person's life. Each number is divided into a matrix, each assigned a place. Nine falls inside the fame square. Or call it a box with a label attached. Paul's life is squeezed inside this box. Joey also lives in this box; all number nines live in this box. Paul's element is fire; his color is red. He wears red: a tie, a button, a handkerchief, a watchband. Red is the color of life and luck. The Bird of Paradise, streaks of red in the bloom, is positioned beside the receptionist's desk to lull waiting clients. Twice a month the old plants are rotated out, replaced by new plants. Business has been up twenty percent since Feng Shui Flower Shop delivered their first plants. Paul, like other clients, swears by the feng shui readings. Word of mouth has brought many new clients. They often compare charts, colors, elements, and whisper about the *Book of Change* as if it were a holy book.

The photographer waits for Joey to leave the stage. A queue forms on the left, snaking back around the quintet and hill tribe silk vendors sitting behind folding tables. Couples want immortal memory in the well-crafted annual Thanksgiving photograph, proof that one more year of their life outside of Canada can never be reclaimed.

The woman on Joey's right whispers, "He's taken our picture twice. He wants us to go. We must go now."

Ped works in the flower shop. Her background was in design, and she had already made her mark when Joey hired her. She is sensitive to the feelings of others and to her own sense of face. According to Ped's chart, her personal number is six, her personal color is blue and her feng shui is linked to the sky. Number six makes her a patron, whose task in life is to help and protect others. Her father, a serious student of the *Book of Change*, used his knowledge, belief and devotion to rear his daughter. When Ped was six, her father taught her how to make a feng shui chart. Her nickname corresponds with her feng shui. The name Ped, along with her place inside the *Ba Gua* octagonal, intrigues and comforts Joey Balfour; a name in harmony with one's nature is a rare thing. Ped is a rare person. Blue is the color for a person who is careful, deliberate, calm and self-absorbed. Two years before meeting Joey, Ped left her boyfriend of five years. His color was gray and made him fearful and depressed. Balance and harmony had eluded them; the stormy relationship had left each of them doubtful, angry, and empty. After six months the clouds lifted, and the sky turned a rich blue once again.

Joey stares dreamy-eyed at the ice duck which is drawing increasing attention from the other guests in the queue. They are mumbling whether Joey is okay. His face is chalky and he is squinting as if in pain. Is Joey having a heart attack?

The woman on his left gently tucks her knuckles into his ribcage and tickles him. "Enough, I am hungry."

That's Ped, and, in Thai, her nickname translates as duck, making her the one guest who feels the ice sculpture is a work of art, and the perfect touch to an evening of glamour, high-society people, ambassadors, generals, lawyers, and businessmen. The same people who order from the flower shop. The chairwoman of the organizing committee has a deep suspicion that Ped had something to do with the ice sculpture but she can prove nothing. Just a trail of association: the flowers for the event are from Joey's flower shop and Ped is the person who appears to be the true organizational brains behind the flower business.

Sky knows flowers. Reading her chart reveals that southeast is her direction. Sky, like Errol Flynn, is a number four, and feng shui places her destiny on the prosperity square. Her color is the color of passion—violet. She feels the personality of the flower shop's customers and claims they have music and tone that she hears. She worked as a top DJ before being snatched away for Feng Shui Flower Shop. She knows people as she knows characters in books, and most of all she knows Joey is not really a florist. With delivery boys, office staff, counter people, sales and management, Feng Shui Flower Shop has thirty-five employees.

Ped's reading is legendary in her family. She's a book junkie, a book john, a book collector. As a child she read books under the sheets with a flashlight. Some women take books like men take prostitutes, and for the same reason, for the drama, to explore, to find hours of stimulation. Often at night, Ped will read to Joey; sometimes when the three of them are together in the bedroom, she reads until the other two drift into sleep, hearing her voice, floating down a tunnel of unconsciousness. She has read all of Jane Austen, loves George Sand, and has a picture of Iris Murdoch on her desk. Joey is drawn to her bookish ways. Once she looked up from the book she was reading and said, "Editors, literary agents, and publicists are pimps. They hawk their wares to the rest of us. They never tell you this one is a street harpy, this one is an old pro, this one I guarantee is a high-class geisha. They often lie. You can only tell by reading a few pages. Then you can tell whether it is a pancake recipe thrown together quickly, or whether it is a samurai sword, an instrument that will exist forever." She cleared her throat and continued reading from *Great Expectations*. Even though Dickens was a man she had been seduced by his voice, and he held her in the palm of his hand, toying with her, putting ideas in her head. Joey and Sky exchanged a glance.

Inside the ballroom the band equipment is on stage but there is no one from the band. A dozen or so tables stand in a semi-circle around the stage. His party is booked at table number eight where there are settings for ten people. Number eight translates as knowledge. Joey's table has a good view of the stage. They are facing northeast. Joey's Feng Shui Flower Shop logo and name is on the curtains to the side of the stage along with Air Canada and Scotiabank. The chart Sky had made took into account the feng shui of herself, Ped, and Joey. Satisfied with the results, she shares a smile with Ped. Joey's a silver sponsor. They had had many discussions about this: gold is too much exposure but bronze is too distant. Joey has taught them to think of the best set of probabilities. In horse racing, Joey always knew when to make a place bet. Silver is often a smart ticket if you have some doubt. Bet to place is a doubting man's default bet.

The surprise card off the bottom of the deck is dealt when a stranger pulls up an empty chair at the table. He has a hairy body which at first glance appears as a unified whole, one set piece. His neck is demarked by a freshly shaved straight line that separates the mangrove of chest hair from the higher elevation of his beard-less head. There are two kinds of middle-aged strangers that Joey Balfour dreads. One is the stranger who looks like he's just been pulled behind a pickup on some bad Texas road and cut loose to find his way back to town, and the other has the look of the stranger who has been behind the wheel of the pickup. The Rev. Joshua Cecil looks like he's just stepped out of the pickup having dragged someone for ten miles over hard dirt roads. His white hair is combed straight back from his forehead. No one had told Joey that this stranger would be joining the Feng Shui Flower Shop table.

Joey's suffering a Spam moment.

The Rev. Joshua Cecil hands Joey a business card that shows an address in Dallas. "You're probably wondering why I am at a Canadian Thanksgiving?" From the moment he sat down the man has never stopped smiling. His fixed smile has the disturbing quality found on the face of true believers, mugs, or drug users.

Joey stares at the business card, making the little noises that Japanese people make when reading the title and address of the giver. "Are you visiting or living in Bangkok?"

"I'd say the Lord has sent me as a visitor to this great city, Mr. Balfour. There are many in the city seeking to know about the good book. It is my mission to spread the word of our savior and lord."

He hasn't told the reverend his name. Nor has he given him a card. This isn't a good sign. "How do you know my name?"

"You are being very modest, Mr. Balfour. Your name is on the lips of many. They say you were a player. A man who had the power to move the point spread."

He has seen the TV shows, thinks Joey Balfour, and he wants a donation to his church. The shakedown from charities is one of the first things a celebrity learns. The second thing a celebrity learns is that the need of such charities is limitless. It is all making sense.

"I memorized what you said on one of your shows. Perhaps you remember saying it," says Rev. Joshua Cecil. "Professional gamblers never fall in love with a horse, a pair of dice or a deck of cards. They don't pray to get an edge or inspiration. Mugs fall in love with baseball and football teams. This happens all the time at the college level. They bet their feelings. Gambling is not about faith. It is about numbers. Counting. There are good decisions and bad decisions. Most people don't know this and that is why they lose their shirts. Love and faith is a guaranteed way to lose your bank. Emotions skew the calculation of odds. A professional's take on chance is based on an objective, factual look at past performance and the current competition. Fall in love with a film or a book. That is where love belongs: inside the head. There is no God to help you in a casino. Taking out your wallet and betting with your heart means you are throwing away your money.'"

A glimmer of that show returns to Joey as Rev. Joshua finishes. He finds it chilling that this stranger has gone to the trouble of committing to memory what he said on a TV show years before. Joey has no memory of this speech, though it sounds like something he would have said.

"What do you want?"

The reverend's eyes narrow, his eyebrows meet in a ridge over his nose. "Cancel the TV show and the DVDs."

Joey leans back in his chair, arms folded around his chest. "I don't own it."

"Condemn it. Repudiate it. Cast it down to the depths." The preacher's jaw juts out.

Joey laughs until he has tears in his eyes. "The show owners might wanna take my scalp, and hang my hair on the wall of one of their casinos."

"Find a way." He no longer sounds like an ordinary preacher.

Joey wipes away his tears. This isn't a joke played by one of his clients. The man across the table is serious. "Why don't you and your fundamentalist pals go after the Indians. Burn 'em out like in the old days. Give 'em blankets with smallpox. Wasn't it someone like you who invented biological warfare?"

"You're going to be very sorry, Mr. Balfour."

The sound of the pickup fills Joey's head and he thinks of Joshua and his friends tying him to the back fender. This is not a good feeling. Nor is it intended to be.

"Is this a threat?" asks Joey.

Sky and Ped have said nothing. They quietly study Joshua Cecil's face.

"We are at war, Mr. Balfour. The forces of good and evil are aligned everywhere in the world waiting for the final confrontation. In these days, faith and belief are our weapons to smite our enemies. Our faith tells us that good will prevail and evil will be vanquished. The true believers of our Lord will rise into heaven and take their seat by His side."

"His side, my side. Your way, my way. Big band, the blues. Ray Charles, Keith Jarrett. Charles Dickens, Iris Murdoch. Shake that bootie."

"Their eyes will boil in their sockets and their faces will melt into the earth. They will be lost forever."

Joey taps his knife with his finger. "I don't really know how you got a ticket at this table. I can help you find another place."

Before the first plate of turkey arrives Rev. Joshua Cecil pushes his chair back and stands. He nods to Ped and Sky and then to Joey. "You can run to your godless theories, Mr. Balfour. But God is watching." Looking over his shoulder, Joey notes the preacher stops and stares back at their table with a terrible wrath and hatred in his eyes. His face trails a perpetual smile as the default setting thickens, goes cloudy, stabilizes for no more than a second into a glower before roiling into the final mask of malice. He leaves through a side door as the emcee explains the rules of the silent auction. He turns, looks back, like someone squinting through a crack in a circle of covered wagons, Indians shooting arrows. *Crazy bastard,* thinks Joey. It is as if the preacher looks into the Sunday collection plate, finds a steel slug, and confronts the sinner.

As his father taught him years before, you can never be certain about getting turkey for Thanksgiving dinner. Once in a blue moon you may get Spam. Other times, you may get nothing at all.

22 December 2004:
Bangkok, Thailand

In the distance, the bedroom alarm clock rings—not an ordinary bell, mind you, but the sound of a soft hum, a roulette wheel spinning; the spin enters the sleeper like a worm burrowing slowly through Joey's brain where he's in the midst of a nineteenth-century-style duel. Only it isn't Russia but Cuban countryside surrounding the field of battle. On the table is a copy of *Anna Karenina* with a gold bookmark sticking into the halfway mark of the book. He's been living inside Tolstoy's mind for many nights since Ped began reading it aloud.

Joey turns over on his side. The alarm clock soundtrack continues—a roulette wheel morphs into the sound of old-fashioned pre-digital slot machines, a whirl of levers followed by the clinking of cherries and apples and oranges lining up, finishing with a wailing horn so real that one can see inside the sleeping brain the flashing lights that announce a winner. Waking up in the morning, opening both eyes and finding everything still works is winning; it is the jackpot of getting one more day to play a new hand of cards. His best friend, Marty Gage, who he had met while still at high school, has programmed the alarm with the actual sound of an old-time slot machine. Casinos use these soundtracks with the new digital silent-as-funeral-parlor slot machines. The casino floor men reported that the absence of noise spooked the punters. Silence disturbs gamblers, breaks down their self-confidence and makes them fearful. Noise reassures and comforts them just as it brings Joey Balfour to consciousness in the morning. No one can win in silence; noise celebrates victory.

From the alarm clock on the nightstand the soothing, familiar sound registers deeper and deeper into the tissue of his sleep. The cracking of gears and wheels as the slot spins its tune of chance pierces his mind, sweeps aside the curtain of rest, and finally drops the guillotine blade on Joey's REM sleep. He holds the dueling pistol out as the face of Frank Costello dissolves into nothingness. The jackpot sirens wail; Joey slaps a pillow over his face, rolls over in bed, and pulls the sheet over his head. He fights like a long-distance swimmer out of energy to reach the far shore of his dream. Joey Balfour dreams of the past—1958 and Cuba and revolutionaries winding their way down the paths of their jungle stronghold in the mountains, storming through the streets of Havana. Fleeing ahead of the young Castro are the old gang, including the usual suspects: Fulgencio Batista Zaldívar and Meyer Lansky. These gang members are blood brothers. And the men who trail behind them are familiar American faces: Frank Costello, Vito Genovese, Santo Trafficante Jr, Moe Dalitz, and Lucky Luciano; all of them are fleeing the rebels.

The gangsters, tough guys, wise guys, are fearful; the rebels are driving them out of Havana, smashing the old order—casinos, brothels, the hotels; inside his dream, Joey sees on their faces that they know that their cause is lost, and they don't need an odds maker to tell them that sticking around is a losing proposition. Fidel Castro stops in the street, raises his rifle, and takes aim at his target. Errol Flynn who is running shoulder-to-shoulder with Batista turns toward Castro. Roulette wheel and rifle fire merge. Joey's brain triggers the smell of cordite, rum, and dust—old memories scattering through gateways of his consciousness. Joey noses deep into his pillow. He wants the camera to keep rolling but all he hears is the alarm clock. Sometimes in this dream Errol Flynn is dressed like Robin Hood. Other times he has a movie camera and he's recording Fidel Castro's entrance into Havana.

Joey stretches out his right arm and finds the space normally occupied by Ped empty and tentatively reaches out with his left hand, slowly marching up toward the pillow only to confirm that Sky has also vanished. They have already gone to Feng Shui Flower Shop.

Coffee-milk light slants through the windows across his bed. On the wall above are three framed original movie posters. A 1948 poster from *The Adventures of Robin Hood*, a 1938 poster from *The Dawn Patrol* and a 1940 poster from *The Sea Hawk*. Joey has an original poster from every Errol Flynn film. The collection is his hobby, his passion. In most of the posters, there is the familiar face: Errol Flynn, a sly penciled moustache above his wolfish smile stares out through the portal of dead time. Each poster is costly, precious, rare. Joey blinks off the sleep and looks up at Robin Hood in a funny hat and tights and knows that he is still alive. None of the girls he brings back to his penthouse have any idea of the value of the posters. Value is hardly universal, for example Ped collects first editions and Sky collects modern music and fashion magazines. Each collection is valued highly by the owner.

Joey stretches his arms, and slowly lowers his right arm and then his left as he looks at his watch. Marty's flight from Vancouver should have landed at Don Muang Airport and with some luck he should have cleared customs and immigration. Even with the arrival of his best friend, Joey keeps to a regime of reversed banker's hours. Vampire hours. He sets his casino soundtrack alarm clock to nudge him from another round of REM sleep thirty minutes before the bank closes and then rushes out of his penthouse and drops into the back of his chauffeur-driven BMW. He deposits dividend checks, exchanges money, transfers funds, and pays his bills. Most people hire others to do the day-to-day transactions but Joey insists on queuing up with motorcycle messengers, office clerks, and maids because he lets no one else get close to his money. Standing in line, he looks terrible, his eyes rimmed with dark, blackish skin the texture of bubble wrap, his stubble of a beard gives his cheeks a reddish hue, and his hair is uncombed, unwashed. To the others in the queue, Joey Balfour is another semi-insolvent and lackluster *farang* who has fallen on hard times. His appearance—and in Thailand appearance is everything—invokes tongue-clicking registering feeling between disgust and disapproval and a warning not to get too close. Once, a bank teller opened Joey's bank book, saw all the zeros after the number nine and briefly lost consciousness. An inhaler stuck into her nostril revived her, and all around thought it was his appearance that caused her to pass out. Now the tellers know him and gossip once they spot him. One teller hinted that Joey's accounts are a sly front; he has too many millions on deposit in too many accounts. Too many regular cash deposits on Wednesdays and Fridays. That teller is no longer employed by the bank. The bank manager, who fired her, gives Joey a little wave from behind a bulletproof enclosure, and remembers Joey from the Annual Canadian Thanksgiving Ball when he had been trolling for business among the Canadian expat community. He comes out and leads Joey to the front of the queue as the others grumble and verge on the edge of open revolt.

"Khun Joey, have you eaten?" asks the bank manager, a young Thai with an American accent. This was a common greeting among Thais who constantly monitored their bellies like moped gas tanks, and assume the highest compliment is to ask a friend whether his belly is running on empty or has recently refueled. He wants to say, yes, four boiled potatoes, two fried yams, and a medium-rare two-inch yak steak simply to judge if the manager is even vaguely interested in what his intestines are dissolving. The bank manager is angling for a tip on a game. *A Joey tip is money in the bank*, he jokes.

He has several papers for Joey to sign. One of these papers is an official-looking document. Joey signs and returns the document without reading it, and says, "I'd say Man U over Arsenal this weekend. My local odds maker says Arsenal has more chi." Joey knows what the banker has screamed out of his swank corner office to obtain—information to bet on the match. Joey understands the value of information. He never bothers to clarify that Ped is his local odds maker. She's more of a sounding board than odds maker, a risk manager who looks deep into the possible unknowns. She does the charts on all of the English premier league teams. This includes the managers and key players, the situation of the stadium, and the color of the uniforms. She calls it science. Joey calls it voodoo.

The banker, a punter, is appreciative of this tip as he guides Joey to the teller's window. The gentle pressure at Joey's elbow shuttles him along to the next stop. There is something disturbing when your banker takes more than a few seconds mulling over whether to bet feng shui or a probability theory generated outcome.

After his banking is finished, Joey returns to his penthouse, showers and wanders into the kitchen and opens his fridge to find something to eat. He refuses to call the stuff in plastic bowls breakfast. His maid rushes in and takes the plastic bowl, opens it, smells the contents, and usually dumps the contents in the garbage. She cooks him bacon and eggs with fried tomatoes and toast. The coffee is brewing. He eats in front of his computer. A spy camera installed by Marty during his last trip to Bangkok is concealed in the ceiling of the flower shop. He downloads the footage of Sky marveling at the hundred-dollar bill. He replays the scene where Bill Hunt comes through the door of Feng Shui Flower Shop. Joey sips from his cup. Then he opens the *Wall Street Journal*. He nibbles at the toast and eggs. Food ingested at four in the afternoon doesn't have a meal time tag attached except in England and certain gated communities in the commonwealth where the inhabitants call such a meal by the absurd name of "tea." Strange, the English and their meal time names. Strange are the Thais who chart the invisible forces of earth, fire, metal, water, wood before deciding upon choosing a career, entering into relationships, the monkhood, changing jobs, cars, women, monitoring their health and hedging their bets about the future. Bill Hunt is after an old Las Vegas thief named Jim Pauley, a bad apple who fell far from the tree. A hundred dollars folded into Sky's hand is not a good sign. He studies the perplexed look that comes over on her face as Bill says, "One hand washes another."

On the table lay printouts from a dozen websites. Sports schedules: horse races, boxing, college football, English premier league football, professional baseball and college basketball. He checks the odds before going online to place several bets, including a sizeable sum on Arsenal. His table clutter includes a messy, well-fingered stack of high-resolution color printouts of Hollywood movie posters with captions and prices. Joey's circled an Errol Flynn poster from the movie: *Cuban Story.* The details of the offer include an important feature for a collector Errol Flynn has signed the poster. The seller is asking fifteen grand as the film is obscure (it showed only once in Moscow) and only two or three posters were ever made and no one knows if all three, or two, or even just one have survived. Like a rare Liberty Dollar the value comes from scarcity.

Howard Boggy, the owner of the poster, is an eccentric, cranky and cunning twenty-seven-year-old and a Harvard dropout, who runs an ISP in upstate Maine, near the Canadian border. He has a history of sending computer viruses to enemy websites and flooding email accounts with spam. He also has a checkered history of accumulating different nationalities and identities. Joey figures that Howard has a separate nationality for each of his multiple personalities. Boggy is by turns, tricky, brilliant, resourceful, determined, bent and spiteful. His feng shui color is purple—the color of a heroin addict's dreams. And Howard Boggy, among other things, is the world's leading expert on Errol Flynn memorabilia. It takes a forger to spot a forgery. Boggy has never passed off one of his fake Flynn 'original' movie posters on Joey. Although he would never admit it, he's afraid Joey has enough juice in Las Vegas to track Boggy down in a snow-covered hut in the Ural Mountains and have his balls cut off and fed to the mountain goats. Howard Boggy has sold original Errol Flynn posters to Joey before (including the ones over his bed); and he knows how much Joey lusts after this poster. Boggy holds to his price, sending cryptic notes: *Pitcairn Island trials reveal dark secrets*. The British had seven islanders in the dock on multiple charges of sexually abusing minors. Boggy had his finger in many pots, stirring the witch's brew of Errol Flynn's legend. One of those pots, it seems, is boiling over. Boggy feels that Joey's reaction comes from a primitive sexual need for dominance and control. That is how Joey understands the Pitcairn note from Boggy. Game theory, though, depends on reading the information from the other side accurately, and Boggy has his own agenda, his own problems, and his desire for the money grows by the hour.

Meanwhile, Joey scans the printouts for information. He knows that Sky will phone. She will have a message for him. One of those old Las Vegas shadows is drawing closer.

Feng Shui Flower Shop

Air bubbles rise to the surface as goldfish circle inside the aquarium. Gills open and close. Goldfish (if you are a true believer) create positive chi in an office or shop. They also work wonders for shut-ins, the insane, prisoners, and the lonely. It is more than common sense. It is a science, a mystical practice that looks to balance harmony in the universe.

Feng shui (straight from the *Book of Change*) is Sky's bible. And Ped is another believer in that good book. To the left, Sky positions a green porcelain dragon, which she bought at the weekend market and on the right, a large white marble tiger with a painted red tongue and predatory eyes painted black. Out of sight, in the back of the shop, is a black tortoise—not a real tortoise but a striking example of what can be rendered from teak wood. Just outside the entrance, a discerning customer will notice a red phoenix as if in flames, its beak open crying to the gods above. Each day, before Sky opens the shop, she inspects the protective animals, dusts and polishes them, talks to them as if they are feeling real needs, wants and desires, and then sets out offerings of fruit and tea and rice.

The real genius in sourcing the right kind and color for each animal is Ped. She has the same quality of understanding that the old Indian shaman showed years ago on the desert floor outside of Las Vegas. As an interior designer and fine literature addict, she knows the craftsmen, those with the ancient art, who create with the necessary ritual to invest each animal with the precise disposition needed for its role in a room. Ped loves to place garlands of flowers around the marble tiger. That the white tiger is her favorite animal is no surprise: Ped was born in the year of the tiger. White is for seduction. Black is for money and power. Joey Balfour favors the tortoise in the back of the shop. It captures the true nature of a professional gambler. Or so he says. Joey has been overheard saying to a friend: *In Thailand you have two choices in making a bet—probability theory or a version of feng shui.* In truth, though, it is the unqualified nature of luck that descends like a fog on a poker hand, a roll of the dice, on marriage, taxes, and death. *In Las Vegas our best customers were those who made their bets based on feng shui,* says Joey. Whenever he watches Ped or Sky making an offering, he feels but never expresses his feelings that feng shui is an old-fashioned Chinese superstition direct from the most primitive part of the brain. Even the communist purges failed to stamp out the belief. All of the employees of Feng Shui Flower Shop are true believers, even the ones without a recent drop of Chinese blood coursing through their veins.

Ped has walked up Sukhumvit Road to Starbucks to order coffee to go. Sky works alone at the counter as a stranger comes through the door. This is a slow time of day. All of the delivery vans are on the road. There is rarely any walk-in business. It is peaceful in the shop and Sky is happy to sit behind the counter sheltered by the guardian animals listening to music with a deck of tarot cards. 'Baby Come to Me' is the song, and she's thinking of Joey as she listens to the lyrics, *Baby, come to me, let me put my arms around you.* She's moving her foot to the ballad and looking dreamy, losing herself in the song. The door brushes against a wind chime and the tingling of blades of glass announces a customer. She looks up from the cards, having just turned over the "hangman" and watches a farang in a suit and tie walk into the shop and close the door behind him. She's never seen him before. Sky, like Ped, knows most of the customers by sight; they rarely have strangers wandering into the shop. It is a highly personal business. The stranger examines a funeral spray—clusters of forget-me-nots and yellow carnations—that is scheduled for delivery in the afternoon to Wat Thong. He turns his attention to a dozen poinsettias, the brilliant scarlet color overpowering the other flowers. Each Christmas she debates with Ped where to place the poinsettias so as not to upset the delicate feng shui balance of the shop. A messenger walks into the shop, nods at Sky and picks up the funeral spray. He's early for the delivery to the wat. As she deals with the messenger, she observes the farang—the suit isn't a designer number, it is ordinary in cut and cloth. With a flick of her wrist, she lays down the hangman card, snapping it, which makes a sound like the breaking of a neck.

"Can I help you?"

Her English is near perfect and clearly not what he expects to hear. The flicker of surprise registers in his eyes as he wipes beads of sweat from his forehead and nose. He looks at the handkerchief and laughs. "It is so hot. You don't sweat. Why? Look at me. I am melting. At Christmas it shouldn't be this hot."

Like an ice duck, she thought. "Can I help you?" At university she studied English but coursework bored her; her passions were fashion, trends, music and friends. Her English shows an educated woman whose heart rules her head, and at five foot seven she has some head to rule. Conversationally she appears to be close to a native speaker. Being with Joey and listening to Ped read has improved her English over the past couple of years. Before, her English had been constructed on a customized vocabulary—mainly from an old textbook tutored by Indians, Australians, and backpacking refugees from America. Bits and pieces of slang from foreigners who haunted high-society discos when she was a DJ. A foreigner can still make her nervous and self-conscious. When she panics she goes mute, uses her hands, and if possible flees, disappearing like a ghost. So far with the stranger she is safe inside the illusion of fluency.

"Is your boss here?"

Sky grinds her teeth. Unless she stops before she turns fifty her teeth will be ground down like an elephant's and she will die of starvation. "I am the manager. What flowers do you have in mind?"

He smiles the way a sweating man with much on his mind smiles. Distracted, annoyed, wheezing, and agitated. "Nice flowers. But what I need aren't flowers. I want to talk to Joe Balfour. Tell him I want to buy him a Christmas drink. He knows me from Las Vegas."

No one she could remember ever called Joey by the name Joe. Her cool smile, steady and defined, ever so sensual at the corners, discloses none of the suspicion roiling inside her skull. She turns down the music. She's being asked to do something outside the daily formula, beyond the master plan, the danger area where the only recourse is thinking through the options and possibilities. This is not something she likes. Her anxiety level prepares her to escape into the back room and out the backdoor. She freezes, wondering whether to pick up another card. Abandoning the shop, the cash register, and leaving the stranger alone would cause a problem. She thinks of the word, the one that humbles and distresses: the word is "problem." How she hates that English word, the edge of conflict and confrontation it promises, leading her to spend most of her waking life avoiding the perimeters where problems live and die. This is what makes her Thai to the core, Joey tells her. Don't think of a problem but of different paths, each with a different outcome, and before starting on the journey, know where you want to go and if you are brutally honest with yourself, then you will know which path is the one to take.

"If you leave me your name and phone number, I will give it to Khun Joey," she says.

"Coon what?"

He is fresh to Bangkok, she thinks. The new ones are the greatest threat. They know nothing and such ignorance makes them confuse all women with bargirls. It is so easy to lose face with the new farang. She cuts him a long piece of rope. Will he tie himself up in knots? Will he hang himself? Or will he do something unexpected?

"The word 'khun' is like the title 'mister' in the English language," she says. "It is a polite form of address. It shows respect. We use it in front of a first name. That is our culture." One day perhaps he will be like the others and know these basic things. For now, it is childlike wonder.

The stranger sighs, his face flushed, a slight twitch around the corner of his left eye. "Bill Hunt is my name. And I've come a long way to see Joe. Tell him that Bill Hunt's staying at the Grande Sheraton Hotel on Sukhumvit."

Though he has trouble pronouncing Sukhumvit, mispronouncing it as "Skunkvent," he can be forgiven and she suppresses a laugh. She thinks the road smells like a skunk. Anyone who makes her laugh is on his way to winning her affection.

She hands Bill a piece of paper and a ballpoint pen. His writing is a childlike combination of print and discursive script. Mentally deranged people write in this mixed up fashion. He finishes, folds the paper and hands it to her. But he's not finished. Not until he removes a hundred-dollar bill from his wallet and slides it over the top of the note.

"One hand washes another," he says. His hands make a washing motion. He wishes her Merry Christmas, leaving her perplexed, confused.

She doesn't understand the meaning of this slang phrase. It is not one she's come across before. Is it a sign language she should understand? It is one of those moments where she looks at the picture of Ben Franklin and then at Bill Hunt, wondering if he is laundering money or changing money or propositioning her. She feels upset, as if she's been insulted but continues to hide her discontent behind a smile as she nods, and the wind chimes once again tinkle as he leaves the shop.

She waits until he has left the shop and unfolds the note.

Dear Joe,

I am staying in room 1819 at the Sheraton. We need to talk about Jim Pauley. He's in Bangkok and the casino knows that you've seen him recently. You can understand that old debts are never retired. They only gather interest. Jim's debt is long overdue.

Bill Hunt

Thumbing through her Thai–English dictionary she double-checks the meaning of "debt", "interest" and "overdue" and then she phones Joey and asks him why he's not paying his bills, and why Jim Pauley is defaulting on his debts as well. He asks what has inspired her interest in the mortgages and loans of his life, and that is when she mentions Bill Hunt's visit.

"Remember the Thanksgiving Ball?"

How could Joey forget? In the couple of months that have passed, they've talked about that evening many times.

"Bill Hunt reminds me of the farang in the brown shoes. The one who was stealing the cashews," Sky says. She says nothing about the hundred-dollar note that she massages between her forefinger and thumb, and she turns over another tarot card: the black queen. Later she goes into the back of the shop and rubs the hundred-dollar note across the shell of the black tortoise. This gesture is for good luck.

Joey knows Bill. He is a ghost from the past, an old-time Las Vegas hand; he came from a time before MBAs, business plans, floating point debt ratios, and 401-K plans. Bill Hunt is one of the few left in the business from the late Seventies. Very few guys of that generation are still around. Time passes, but locked somewhere in a casino back-office database is Bill Hunt's name, and when all the scenarios are run through the game theory, once in a blue moon, Bill's name flashes on the screen. He's the code-red guy of last resources. He trails a history of the old days that few can match.

As Joey puts down the telephone, pieces of information start to fall into place. What is Bill Hunt doing in Bangkok, showing up at Feng Shui Flower Shop and asking for him? Joey takes a deep breath and looks out at the city below his penthouse. The newspapers are on his lap. A cup of coffee on the table has gone cold. The warmth of the sun is on his face. Memories of the old days are always a nanosecond away. Now they filter back like a sudden storm, blowing wind and rain. He calms himself, eyes half closed. He repeats his old mantra: *There can be no probability analysis without information.* Finding and analyzing information takes time, resources, experience, and an appreciation of the volatility and uncertainty of the universe where nothing stays still. Las Vegas is like Bangkok, everyone has a past trailing behind at ten paces, and one day that past crashes against the wall of the present. A dozen years have passed since he last thought of Bill Hunt and Jim Pauley. The past never really leaves us, it lurks like an old melody drifting into consciousness between a cup of coffee and the morning newspaper. Not all songs are ones people want to hear again. They bring memories of an overhang of tooth and claw, of those who wish to avenge a loss, of those whose menace accelerates with age.

It was the kind of pure recognition that Errol Flynn must have felt in the end, Joey thinks.

Sky puts down the phone and stares at the goldfish swimming. Oxygen is the lifeblood of an aquarium; gossip is the oxygen of an office. She can't wait to tell Ped about the stranger named Bill Hunt and the hundred-dollar bill.

Bangkok Reunion:
High School Bootleggers

Marty steps from the lift directly onto the penthouse floor. He carries two suitcases, which he lowers to the marble floor as he rings the doorbell. A moment later, a maid opens the door and Marty enters. Putting his suitcases inside the hall, he steps out of his shoes and accepts the glass of water. He likes this Thai tradition. Door opens and a glass of water is on a tray offered by a smiling maid. It's a nice welcome, thinks Marty. The old gag from Joey's TV show plays in his head as he eyes the maid and the tray: "Shake that bootie, shake that bootie."

He drinks the entire glass of water and puts the empty glass back on the tray. He's glad to be back in Thailand and in Joey's penthouse. The entrance opens into a huge ultra-chic sitting area. Chrome and polished glass bookshelves, and movie posters, large vases filled with every imaginable tropical flower, a large wet bar wedged in one corner, and chrome and white leather sofas and stuffed chairs. There is a ninety-inch plasma screen on one wall. The room, polished and immaculate, is as germ free as an operating room in a five-star hospital.

"*Nai* wait you on the balcony," says the maid. Jell is in her early forties, wears jeans and a T-shirt. She has worked in the household for years and knows Marty from his annual visits. Everyone has been expecting his arrival.

Marty understands only a few words of Thai but he remembers that *nai* means boss. Wherever Joey has been, he's always been the boss.

He follows Jell down a long corridor to the end where the master bedroom sprawls with a one-hundred-and-eighty-degree view of an angry gray-yellow sky. In the distance, Joey tracks the activities inside an old Christian cemetery: the tombstones are largely destroyed, graves are half dug up, a worker stands in an old grave, changing the oil on a new silver-gray Camry. The sunlight reflects off the tinted windshield. Joey puts down his binoculars and sips his coffee laced with a shot of rum before he opens a folder and fingers through a stack of documents. The maid slides back the glass door and Joey looks up from the paperwork. Old friends exchange an affectionate hug.

After Marty sits down, Joey hands him the binoculars. "The Camry is getting an oil change in a cemetery," says Joey. "The man working on the car is sweating. Is he hot or is he afraid of ghosts below his feet? Commerce overcomes all."

"I bet he clears out before nightfall," says Marty.

"That is a safe bet, Marty."

"Something on your mind?"

Joey hands him the preacher's card. "I want you to check out this Rev. Joshua Cecil."

"Thinking about joining a church, Joey?"

Joey grins, reaches over and gives Marty a fake punch on the shoulder. "Let me know what you find."

They are friends from Joey's teenage days in Vancouver and pick up exactly where they left off since Marty's last trip to Bangkok one year ago.

Joey was a senior in high school when he first met Marty. The year before, Marty had graduated and got his first job driving a taxi and had enrolled in technical school. He had been scouted by the Yankees and was waiting for them to call him. Meanwhile, he pretended to go to class at the technical school and killed time driving the taxi. Joey had finished his runaway year living on the Lower East Side of New York, where he had joined as a volunteer worker on the presidential campaign of Eugene McCarthy. He had hitchhiked from Minnesota to New York, leaving a note to his mother. "I won't be home for dinner tonight, or any dinner in the immediate future. Don't worry. Eugene is *the* man." His mother had read the note several times wondering if this were her son's way of coming out. It wasn't that simple—nothing in Joey's life had been simple. There was no way Joey would have imagined that, after running away from Minnesota to New York, one year later he would be going to high school in Vancouver, British Columbia.

The second day Marty told him about the Yankees. "You really going to play for the Yankees?" asked Joey. "I lived in New York. I saw the Yankees."

"You lived in New York?"

Joey told him about handing out fliers for Eugene McCarthy and attending rallies and smoking dope and hanging out with people with long hair, tattoos, and dark rings under their eyes. "I paid sixty-two dollars fifty a month rent for a fifth-floor walk-up in the East Village," said Joey as if this was a normal thing for any seventeen-year-old kid to do.

Marty eyed him wondering why such a kid attended this school in the West End on Denman Street. Joey was the only kid there whose parents weren't divorced or separated, or the father in prison, or the mother on drugs or hooking two streets over from the school.

"You don't sound like a Canadian," said Marty.

"Because I'm not," said Joey. He explained that since his parents were Americans, he was an American.

Marty rolled his eyes. "They are going to draft your ass and send you to Vietnam."

"I don't think so," said Joey.

They watched the TV news over lunch and the images of Vietnam combat, rice fields, peasants, water buffaloes, dead bodies in body bags, helicopters and tired teenagers in combat fatigues filed across the screen. Marty looked at Joey and said, "That's your future."

"Not a chance," said Joey.

Glued to war footage on TV, Marty wasn't convinced. "They are sending everyone to the war. Once you register they will send a letter, and next thing I'll be going home after pitching for the Yankees and turning on the TV to watch you getting shot at as you stumble along a jungle trail."

Marty had an unusually evolved imagination for a baseball jock. "I've already registered at the American consulate. The consul told my mother that as far as he knew no kid had ever been drafted who had registered for the draft at a foreign consulate. Not since World War II. Registering outside the country wasn't exactly American. They didn't want to give a rifle to someone who had registered at the embassy in Paris or London. Or Vancouver. Who knew what such a guy might do with the rifle? He might just take off for another country other than Vietnam. How could they find him? Send the army after him? Besides, think of all the bad press and the political cartoons in the newspaper."

"Who told you this?"

"My mother." He added as if that wasn't quite enough to convince Marty, "The American consul told her."

That did the trick. "You know an angle or two," said Marty.

Joey showed him his draft card. As Marty examined the card, Joey wondered if Eugene McCarthy had known about this loophole? If everyone had just gone overseas and registered for the draft, there would have been only people who didn't know how to get passports left to fight the war.

Marty toyed with the card, held it up to the light, squeezed his jaw like he was waiving off a signal from the catcher behind the home plate. "If we changed the birth date on your card, that opens up some interesting business possibilities."

The draft card which listed Joey as eighteen was altered that afternoon and suddenly Joey turned twenty-one. After looking at his work, Marty blew on the card. "Congratulations. You're an adult. And we are in business."

Not only would Joey never get drafted but his draft card opened up a whole world closed to high school students. It became his salvation, his opportunity to go into business. In those days there were no photo IDs. Marty waited in the taxi and Joey walked into a government liquor store and the cashier, a government employee, carded him. The guy at the cash register stared at the draft registration card, sucked his teeth, shook his head—this was at the height of the Vietnam War—and he squinted at him, long and hard, "I hope you don't have to serve, son."

"Me, too," said Joey filling his cheeks with air and nodding his head trying to look sad, frightened and anguished.

Joey bought a large amount of booze: three bottles of vodka, five Johnny Walker Reds, six Captain Morgans. Marty stood outside with the trunk of the taxi open. They drove straight to the school where a group of students were waiting. They sold the bottles for two and half times the amount they'd paid. They sold the booze out of the trunk of the taxi Marty had rented from a Hungarian immigrant who drove it six hours a day, five days a week. Marty had the taxi eighteen hours a day, seven days a week. With the profits, they drove to the horse races. The thing with driving a taxi was you could park it any place. No cop bothered you in those days. Marty parked right in front of Exhibition Park. They climbed to the top of the stands, poured Captain Morgan into Coke until they ran out of Coke and then passed the bottle between them. They'd split two-dollar bets, and won a twenty-two to one bet. They agreed to use the proceeds to buy more booze to sell at hugely inflated mark-ups. After the last race finished, Joey and Marty left in the stream of people piling out of Exhibition Park. Marty climbed into the taxi, put on the vacant light and waited a minute for a fare. There was no fuss, no wait, and Marty always got a fare on the way out. Sometimes Joey would get in the driver's side and passengers would climb in.

"Hey are you old enough to be driving a taxi?"

"I am twenty-one years old," Joey said. "And I've got an American draft card to prove it."

Just like at the liquor store, the passenger would go silent for a moment, "Hope you don't have to go, son." Such a passenger would always fold an extra couple of dollars into his hand. "Good luck to you, son. Watch your head over there."

They drove straight to the government liquor store to buy a carload of booze to sell at the school the next day. After a couple of months, Marty confided he had decided not to go with the Yankees. The money in Vancouver was too good. Besides, with all the drinking over the past dozen weeks, no one, including Marty, could distinguish his fastball from his change-up. Marty had stopped working, stopped going to practice, and signed on with Captain Morgan and Joey Balfour as the winning club.

The Mysterious Death of Errol Flynn

As they sit on the balcony looking out at Bangkok, Marty is thinking he has two more years before retirement and he can spend them full-time in Thailand. He is a senior computer programmer for the provincial government. Most of the working days, though, Marty does jobs for Joey Balfour. Most assignments are small things—following up a movie poster deal with Howard Boggy, or checking on Joey's parents, or tinkering with the latest revised version of feng shui software for the shop. They can't fire him. He is in the union. In two years he will have a pension.

What is inside Joey's head isn't the cemetery auto maintenance. He's thinking about Mr. Errol Flynn; one of those life-long obsessions. And Joey silently leans back in his chair, thinking to himself, *Love is a dick-trick* a saying that one of Errol Flynn's ancestors had according to legend scrawled into a stone wall on Pitcairn Island. Hardly anyone younger than fifty remembers the age when this adventure actor from Australia was taking over as the American action role model, as a warrior model, as Don Juan and as an icon for America's boys. He is no ordinary A-list actor. Errol Flynn is Johnny Depp, Brad Pitt, Mel Gibson, and Harrison Ford rolled into one legend. Errol Flynn had been the ultimate A-list action adventure actor; now he was largely forgotten except for a handful of classic-movie fans. He was the ultimate action hero who played at the casinos in Havana. Flynn, like most professional gamblers, had the hunger for action forever roiling in the gut. And a bottle in his hand to dull the pain of always being one step away from the real action.

"Why does Boggy want all that money for a *Cuban Story* poster?" Joey asks.

"Boggy says he needs the money to disappear for awhile. You know, like a kid running off to New York to work for Eugene McCarthy."

Joey sighs, wondering what scam has caused Boggy's flight from justice. The police just don't decide one day, *Hey, we can fill our quota by arresting Howard Boggy. Let's bust Boggy. Watch him bellow and moan, pull out his hair and beard behind bars.* Why do this? Just because they feel that he's an asshole with an attitude? Joey simply does not believe the system in America is that corrupt yet.

Marty reads his mind, "It's not the police. It's some agency. Maybe the FBI or the CIA or a third, unofficial outfit. You can never nail them down. Boggy's vague on who's after him."

"What'd he do to get on their radar screen?"

"Nothing that is listed as an actual crime."

"Then why do they want him?"

"It's possible that he made a connection between two events that weren't supposed to be connected."

Joey finishes his coffee. He looks through the binoculars and fiddles with the focus.

"You're talking in code, Marty," says Joey. "Boggy is a conspiracy freak. He always thinks that someone is out to get him. That's why he lives on coffee, aspirin and works eighteen hours a day. He gets into a person's face. That isn't a real reason for the Feds to bust his balls. It does explain something. If you think someone is after you, sooner or later someone will come after you and you can have the satisfaction that you aren't crazy."

"Boggy says he has evidence that the FBI rubbed out Errol Flynn. He says he can prove this happened. He has a handwritten letter, the rare kind that sometimes surfaces in an underground emporium where such items are hawked. It fell into the hands of a specialized collector. Boggy traded rubber-plantation shares for the letter."

"Have you seen it, Marty?"

He says nothing and looks at the traffic below.

"Boggy has been known to say and do wild things. And get himself involved in strange schemes, taking matchsticks for durians."

"Someone went to a lot of trouble to put a bomb inside Boggy's computer, using highly specialized technology developed by the Israelis. They used a phone to trigger a kilo of C4 hidden inside his computer. Fortunately for Boggy, he was away. The people who did this knew Boggy lived beside the computer. This wasn't a warning. Boggy was lucky. He had pre-programmed the computer to automatically log into a secret cyber-location. One of those places where all kinds of information and gossip are traded. When the computer logged on, the explosive charge detonated with sufficient force to demolish his living room and wreck the kitchen. He could look down and see a family of Latinos sitting under debris. Pots and pans scattered everywhere. They cowered under the dining table waiting for God's wrath to finally finish them off."

"Okay, I give up. I'll pay his fifteen grand for the poster," says Joey.

Marty does his pitcher neck roll, staring out at an invisible batter. It is one of the two out and three walk counts in the bottom of the ninth inning neck rolls, full of stress, twitching, not taking a signal, waiting and finally winding up.

"He's sold it already, Joey."

At first nothing registers as the pitch goes knee high over the plate. Joey does not immediately recognize that he is out; that the game for the last Errol Flynn poster he's been plotting to buy is now beyond reach.

"Sold it? Who bought it?"

"Boggy said it was a John Doe purchase. An agent bought it for a buyer who is the brains behind an offshore company with nominee directors. You can never track down these people. Their transactions are untraceable."

Joey's cell phone rings. He lets it ring five times before he reaches over and picks it up.

"Bill Hunt wonders why you haven't phoned him," says Sky.

The evening before, he overheard Sky describing Bill Hunt to Ped as an *u-baht* farang. In Thai *u-baht* means ugly and it also means evil and sinister. A bad omen. Joey thought, *You gotta love a culture where surface looks determine the capacity for goodness and evil.* Sky's description had made him smile. Bill Hunt wasn't ever going to win any beauty contests.

"I was just about to phone Mr. *u-baht.*"

A burst of laughter loosens her up and she blows a kiss into the phone. It is their deal: every time Joey makes her laugh, he gets a kiss.

The call terminates. Joey turns to Marty, "You remember Jim Pauley."

"The guy who ripped off the casino sports betting bank. He got away with mega bucks."

"That's the guy. Pauley said he lived by two rules. First rule is you never pay more for the girl than the cost of the room. The second rule was the perfect woman was half your age plus seven."

"He stole the last rule from W.C. Fields."

"The problem is he stole big time from a casino in Las Vegas. It burns them up. They've been sniffing around for him for years. Now Bill Hunt's in town because he thinks he can get their money."

"What is Pauley doing in Bangkok?"

"Living by his two rules. And trying to stay alive by making a couple of exceptions."

Marty shrugs his shoulders as Jell sets down a fresh mug of coffee on the table. "What does this have to do with you?" He drinks the coffee and stretches out his legs. He aches from the long-haul flight. His muscles are tight, his throat feels sore, and the skin below his eyes is puffy like burnt marshmallows. Marty isn't following the conversation all that well. He's just stepped off a plane and the last thing he wants is some weird conversation about a crook from years ago.

"I figured the casino hired Bill Hunt to track down Pauley. And he's got it in his head that I know where to find him."

"Do you?" His head is killing him. He rubs his neck just behind the base of his skull.

"I have no idea where Pauley is hiding."

"Then what's the point? Tell Hunt you don't know. Finished. Over. The betting window is closed."

"I get the feeling it's not going to be that easy, Marty. Either Bill's gambling on the fact that I know something or someone behind Bill's placing a bet I can help them."

Joey looks over and Marty is fast asleep. His chin resting on his chest, his coffee cup on the table a few inches away. It bothers him that Sky took the hundred dollars from Bill Hunt. It upsets him that he has to deal with Bill Hunt. And he was just getting his head back from the confrontation with the preacher Joshua Cecil, who like a breath of hot, stagnant air, had ruined his Thanksgiving dinner. Then Howard Boggy sells the *Cuban Story* poster to a John Doe.

Joey reminds himself how people get stuck in a hole when they hear the word "gambling" and it makes them concentrate on images about card sharks, slot machines, lotto plays, underworld figures, and Las Vegas. The problem was the movie images of gamblers distracted them from understanding the fundamental truth behind any gamble. Everyone handicaps the possibility of something happening. Take the first election of George Bush. None of the Republican heavyweights wanted to run. Their advisors thought the odds of winning were stacked against them. No one wanted to run against the Democrats. So George Bush slipped into the void. They thought he'd lose. But he won. Jim Pauley took a gamble when he walked away with half a million dollars from the casino. He worked at the sports betting window a couple of years and one night took a walk with his bag stuffed with cash. The odds of getting away were stacked against him. Like George Bush, he knew he could turn a losing situation into a win. All he had to do was disappear into paradise, keep his head down, blend into the crowd and let time erase the memory of his gamble.

Bill Hunt showing up in Bangkok and going to Feng Shui Flower Shop sends a message that the ball is once again in play. Casino amnesia isn't working in Jim Pauley's favor. If Joey has to handicap the odds, he will likely put money on Bill Hunt. Jim has broken too many rules of the game. One rule, okay, but the two rules he lives by, that is not okay. As Sky would frame it, after the theft, the chi is out of balance. With Bill coming to restore harmony and balance, earth and fire are converging, and Jim Pauley is the fall guy who'll play the role of "wood."

How Jim Pauley Walked Away with Casino Money and Sports Betting Chips

Jim Pauley worked behind the betting window of the casino sports book cage on the day of the sixth game of the World Series. The odds were in favor of the Atlanta Braves over the Blue Jays. Joey, who after high school had become a Canadian citizen, had bet on the Blue Jays winning the series. None of the odds makers liked the Blue Jays. No Canadian team had ever won a World Series. But Joey liked the odds, feeling a certain nationalistic irrationality in Las Vegas had been worked into the spread, and, besides, Joey felt the time had come for a Canadian club to win the series. The game had started in Atlanta and the punters watched the play-by-play on casino TV sets.

Jim worked alongside Holly Crewman, who had once been a professional wrestler, and traveled on the circuit as Miss Armed 'N Dangerous. She watched Jim and Joey talking at the betting window halfway through the last game. It was being played at Atlanta–Fulton County Stadium, long since demolished. Joey had bet five grand on the Blue Jays. Behind the window, Jim watched the game on the casino TV. He stretched his arms over his head, yawned; his shoulder-sleeve shirt slipped down to reveal part of a tattoo. A red heart with a name underneath. It happened too fast. She couldn't read it but a subliminal image was branded into her brain. It was a woman's name, she'd swear that it was an American woman's name.

"Dave Winfield never did anything for the Yankees," said Jim Pauley. "That's why they traded him." But the conversation drifted away from the World Series after Jim took a personal call. It was a long-distance collect call from Thailand. Pauley had been going back and forth to Thailand for about a year; he had started making frequent trips after his last divorce. He could hardly talk to Holly or any other woman. He warmed to Holly because of the honesty of her professional wrestling name. "Jackie took the house and car," he had told her. "Even without a gun, a woman is a dangerous thing."

"Better stay single, Jim," she said, pausing as a thought crossed through her mind. "Aren't you seeing someone new, honey? I hear you've a mysterious girl."

"You believe everything they say about you?"

She thought that Jim had a good point. "A man's got his needs. Only thing is those needs sometimes make him say and do things he regrets. You know what I'm saying? When you're dealing with a woman, you've got to give her the odds up front."

"Holly, I am doing fine. Thanks for your advice."

Whatever the rumor mill said about Jim Pauley, one thing was for sure: he was already a goner, and head over heels in love with a twenty-something girl who had been raised in a village which was within sniper-rifle range of the Cambodian border. She was a Surin province ying who drifted to Bangkok for work. Toom worked as a cashier in a department store, and Jim had been sending her money to help her go back to school. In August, he had proposed to Toom, and she had accepted. His divorce had just become final. He was broke and in love with someone who lived ten thousand miles away. He ran up huge phone bills phoning her every night. At the end of August, Toom's application for a visa to the States was rejected. The American embassy official who interviewed her believed that she was a bargirl and would do a runner. Toom broke down in tears.

When Jim put down the phone, the blood had drained from his face, and he looked uneasy on his feet. "You okay?" asked Joey.

"Toom's gone to the doctor. She's pregnant."

"You're going to be a dad," said Holly, listening in to the conversation. "That's great news, honey." But she was thinking, *If this other woman finds out about the pregnant Thai woman I don't want to be around.* She'd been in the ring enough times to know a fake punch for the real thing.

"Yeah, great. I am here, and she's in Bangkok. After alimony payments, you know how much money I've got left a month after rent and car and ex?"

Joey shrugged. "A grand or two."

"Three, four hundred dollars. And that goes on phone bills."

"You'll figure it out, Jimmy," said Holly. "Luck turns up in some pretty funny places. But you gotta be fair to the woman. And fair to anyone else if there is anyone else. Not that I am saying there is. Just in case someone else is hanging around for you."

By the top of the eleventh inning, David Winfield hit a double, driving in two runs. In the bottom of the eleventh, with a man on third base, the Blue Jays' relief pitcher, Mike Timlin picked up a bunt from Nixon and threw him out at first. Joey jumped to his feet and thrust both arms into the air and did a little victory dance in a sea of punters holding Atlanta Braves bet slips, smoking cigarettes, looking sad and defeated. Holly had arranged to leave early and with the Blue Jays' victory there were not a lot of punters coming to collect their winnings. "Honey, will you take over my bank?" she asked Pauley. "I've got some private business to look after so I'd like to leave a little early if that's okay with you."

"Sure, I'll take it to the cage. Consider it done."

He counted his bank: he had two hundred grand cash and one hundred and twenty-five grand in casino chips. Holly's bank came out to one hundred and ninety-five grand. He then added her bank to his own after double-checking that the math was right, and Holly signed off. When Joey came up with his betting slip, he slid it across the counter to Pauley. Joey had won twenty grand betting on the Blue Jays. Pauley counted out the cash. His good-natured banter had dried up. There was none of the usual, "Hey, Joey, good payout."

Joey understood that with an ex-wife to support and a young pregnant girlfriend in Thailand Pauley's life was not a bucketful of laughs. He peeled off a hundred-dollar note and gave it to Jim Pauley just as the phone rang again. Another collect call from Thailand, and he said into the phone in front of Joey, "I can't really talk. I'll phone you later."

Joey was not only the last person to talk to Jim Pauley, but he was the last person to see him before he walked out of the casino.

Pauley's supervisor sat behind his desk in the back room doing paperwork. The head of security, romancing a hooker in another back room, failed to see Pauley walk out the door. Pauley closed the last betting window. He didn't want to risk any more big payouts from the bank. Pauley knew that one of the security cameras was broken, and there were no cameras in the cage. He dumped his bank and Holly's bank into an old New York Yankees' duffel bag and covered the cash with a pair of jeans and a T-shirt with Angkor Wat on the front. He worked alone in the cage. Pauley sucked in a deep breath and strolled the hundred feet to the main door, carrying the bag with him. No one saw him leaving. A half an hour later, a punter from California walked up to the betting window, wanting to cash a bet. He saw the cage was empty and phoned security, asking when the cage was going to open. The sports book supervisor looked up from behind his desk as security arrived.

"Did Pauley say he was going out?"

"No, Pauley hadn't said anything about leaving. Has he gone?"

Joey spent three hours being grilled by casino security, by the management of the casino, and by the police. It had been his lucky day. He'd won twenty grand betting the underdog team. He had an idea why Pauley had run. He had family problems, including an ex-wife making him crazy. There was no percentage in getting into the drama of the pregnant girlfriend in Thailand. Let the police find out about his domestic troubles from Holly and Pauley's ex-wife. The casino knew Joey was a professional and begrudgingly believed his story: he had the bad luck of being the last person to see Jim Pauley but overall he'd had a good day. The guy who took the blame was Bill Hunt, who had been head of security and had let Pauley walk out of the place. After the casino finished with Joey, he went downtown with the police. At the station, he was led into an interrogation room. The door closed behind him and a plainclothes detective.

The detective leaned over the table, his nose two inches away from Joey Balfour's face, "You must have some theory, Mr. Balfour."

There was no way he was going to get out of there without giving them something. "There is something but I don't know if it's helpful."

The detective rose up, paced to the end of the table, lit a cigarette. "Let me be the judge of what is helpful."

"Pauley was a big Yankees fan. Dave Winfield played for the Yankees before he was traded. George Steinbrenner paid a snitch to get dirt on Dave. He wanted to ruin him. He belittled Dave, all six foot six, and two hundred and forty-five pounds of the man, because he didn't get enough hits in the Yankees World Series a few years ago."

"What's this got to do with Pauley running off with the casino's money?"

"Dave showed him how you could always turn things around. You wait for the right ball at the top of the eleventh inning and you take your swing. When Dave won that last game in Atlanta, I saw a light go on in Pauley's head."

The detective coughed and spat a smoker's gob from deep in the lungs, "That's too intellectual, Joey. Guys like Pauley don't think like that. They just see a bunch of money and take a chance. He was up to his eyeballs in debt. And he had an ex-wife driving him nuts."

"You're right. Dave Winfield had nothing to do with his decision."

"You got a smart mouth on you, Joey. One day it's going to get you into serious trouble."

Dave Winfield had once got into serious trouble when he was still playing for the Yankees. The Yankees were playing the Blue Jays in Toronto. During the pre-game warm-up, Winfield threw a ball and, in a freakish accident, the ball struck and killed a seagull. The Toronto police marched onto the field and arrested Dave and someone threw a towel over the dead bird and carried it off the field. Cruelty to animals was the charge against Dave Winfield. George Steinbrenner said, in Dave's defense, that Dave lacked the criminal intent, the killing of the seagull wasn't intentional. "No way," said Steinbrenner, "could Dave intentionally hit anything with a baseball." *Now there was a guy with a smart mouth*, thought Joey.

How Twelve Years Later Jim Pauley Came Back on the Radar Screen

Bill Hunt stares into his glass at the bar where he's waiting for Joey who is half an hour late. It is early evening and a couple of farangs in business suits huddle together a couple of feet away, talking business and stock markets. An early bird high-class hooker cruises in and she looks into Bill Hunt's cold blue eyes, the eyes of a security man, and sees some reflection of terror and hurt that makes her move quickly down the line to the businessmen. His looks give her a chill the way that ugliness and evil can do. Hookers have a sixth sense about dangerous men. They search for the easy mark. They scan a room for the mugs with too much money and too little brains to hold on to it. It is as if Bill Hunt has x-ray vision. He can see through the hooker, make her feel cheap, naked, and dirty in pursuit of easy money. She has no secrets from him. Her job is to fake the girlfriend act and move herself up in the world from a lifetime of third-rate cheap-hotel performances to the big time.

When Joey walks in, he's immediately met at the door by the manager who smiles and *wais* him. They exchange words but Bill Hunt is too far away to pick up what is being said. Marty is half a clip behind. They find Hunt at the bar, sipping a gin and tonic from a tall glass. It had been Hunt's idea to meet at a trendy bar on the ground floor of his hotel for the hometown advantage. Only it seems the local bosses know Joey and pay him respect. Hunt notices their attitude. That's Joey Balfour moving straight to the top, getting the best table, the best service, the best women. Not much had changed in the way Joey entered a room over the years including the way Marty Gage tagged along one step behind Joey, just like in the old days.

"Hey, Bill. How's it going?" says Joey.

Bill Hunt straightens himself up. He's a head taller than Joey and his imposing figure is an asset in the intimidation business; only Joey is on home turf and Bill's size or blowfish swelling-up routine cuts no ice. This isn't Las Vegas where Bill Hunt has half a mile of backup. *Bill Hunt just can't let go of the past*, thinks Joey. The casino must have long ago forgotten about Pauley, but not its head of security the night of the theft; he took Pauley's crime personally as if it was his money that Pauley had looted.

Joey introduces Marty as his partner from Vancouver. "I remember you from the old days," says Bill Hunt. "I saw you a couple of times in Joey's show."

Marty remembers the burly security chief, too.

Marty and Bill exchange a nod like two prize fighters at a weigh-in, TV cameras rolling, cameras flashing. Then Joey sits down, leaving Bill standing at the bar and orders his usual, a double eighteen-year-old single malt whiskey and tells the waiter in Thai to add the drink to Bill's tab.

Bill Hunt overhears the order and says, "Aren't you gonna order a martini? Get her to shake that bootie."

Joey turns to him. Over the years, Joey's lost count of the number of people who have ordered him a martini. He's not surprised that Hunt is someone who believes everything that he sees on TV.

"You thought that was a real martini?"

Hunt blinks, looks away. The thought of a fake martini had obviously never occurred to him.

"I hate martinis. It was the producer's idea. He loved martinis. James Bond loved martinis. I stick to single malt whiskey. You don't need to shake a whiskey."

"Fake or not, 'Shake that bootie' will be on your tombstone," says Bill Hunt, trying hard to recover some dignity.

"What can I do for you, Bill?" Joey gets straight down to business.

"Any idea why this wing nut Pauley sells fifty grand worth of chips twelve years after his theft?" Bill Hunt has a rough streetwise

New York accent from somewhere between Brooklyn and Queens and half a dozen wise-guy movies.

"I'd say he needed the money," says Joey. He's smiling as the double-shot glass appears at the bar.

Bill Hunt doesn't much like the grin. "No one at the casino thinks this is a funny situation, Joey." His eyes don't blink as he waits for Joey to lower his glass.

The eighteen-year-old malt whiskey swirls around his mouth as he's thinking that Bill Hunt is someone who can't let go and wants to make up for his lapse that night twelve years before. It is killing him that Pauley has got away with the money and never paid a price. Bill's one of those old-fashioned Las Vegas types who never forget, never forgive—vengeance is mine says the Lord. Joey swallows his whiskey. But dismissing Bill Hunt would be a serious mistake. Those who survive in the gaming business avoid serious mistakes in judgment. "You go to my shop and you give my girl a hundred-dollar backhander. I get phone calls of great urgency and what this comes down to goes something like this—you want to tell me the casino doesn't have a sense of humor when it comes to Jim Pauley. That's not a major piece of new information. But if I had to guess, no one working there has given a thought to Pauley in ten years. Except for you. The back office? Those guys don't give a second thought to Pauley. You, I can understand. It happened on your watch. That still sticks in your throat. After all these years, you've got to move on, Bill. You and I don't have a beef. For what I know, you could have emailed me from Las Vegas and saved yourself a trip."

"I figured you had a hidden camera in the shop," says Bill Hunt.

On his last trip, Marty had installed the cameras—three state-of-the-art spy cams—the year before.

"You can take the man out of the casino but you can't take the casino out of the man," says Joey.

"Joey, you gotta understand something."

"I am listening."

"We know that Pauley's here."

Bill Hunt reaches into his jacket pocket and fishes around, his knuckles bulging against the cloth. His clenched fist emerges like a claw in the cage of an amusement park game with prizes lodged inside. He sweeps his hand across the counter with the skill of a professional dealer. Sports betting chips in denominations of five hundred, a grand, and five grand encircle Joey's glass of expensive malt whiskey. Joey looks up at Bill Hunt and smiles. He recognizes the casino sports betting chips. In the old days, he did a segment on his TV show about casino chips. It doesn't take a genius to figure out the chips around his glass were part of Pauley's haul in sports book chips.

"I haven't seen these for awhile," says Joey.

"Let's say they've been out of circulation for many years."

Not that many years ago, high rollers used the chips to avoid the mandatory reporting requirements for cash bets of ten grand or more. Chips were not cash, and they were a way around the reporting requirements. In 1992 gamblers figured out that the casino chips were a free ride to cheat on taxes or to launder drug money. The sports betting chips were as good as gold—with one minor exception: the chips on the bar counter are stolen property. Joey picks up a five-grand chip and shows it to Marty.

"Do you remember the five-grand chip?" asks Joey. This had been the highest denomination sports betting chip when Joey Balfour's cable TV show had had its peak audience.

"You had one on your show," says Marty.

Joey Balfour nods, sips the single malt whiskey and lets himself remember.

Marty rolls the chips between his forefinger and thumb before handing it back to Joey.

Joey turns to Bill Hunt, dropping the five-grand chip into the ashtray. "I heard that after the theft, the casino called in all the sports betting chips. And the word was the casino claimed they got them all back."

"What else could they say?" says Bill Hunt.

They understand each other. There is always comfort in knowing the shorthand code that underlies a complex history. Hunt is right. What was the casino going to broadcast: they didn't know how many chips were still spinning around in lockers, drawers, and Pauley's duffel bag?

"I always figured they didn't get them all. What did they have, Bill? There was another couple of hundred grand of chips floating around in the world. Pauley stole some of them. But there are other reasons for chips to go missing. Pauley's theft didn't explain all the lost chips. And that creates a problem. The casino doesn't know how to get the non-stolen ones back. So how did these chips find their way back to Mama?"

"Pauley cut a deal. A high roller named Spira took fifty grand's worth of Pauley's chips. Spira was wise and understood the play. He knew Pauley had been holding on to them since '92."

"Waiting for a chance to make good," says Joey. "You gotta admire his patience. He waited a long time, Bill."

Bill Hunt admires nothing about Jim Pauley. He carefully collects each of the chips. Joey sees this isn't the direction Hunt wishes to go. Leave sympathy for the mugs. "If you got to Spira, then you know more about Pauley than me."

Bill Hunt shrugs, and exhales in frustration like a troglodyte who misses the next branch of the tree he intends to swing on.

"Pauley knew Spira from the old days. He thought he could cheat the casino one more time. The management knows that Spira is a good customer. He's a regular. He bets a lot of money on college football. Ten days ago Spira rolls into the casino with the gym bag and dumps out the chips, and gives the cashier a bullshit story that he found them in the bottom of his drawer. Some fucking bottom drawer. The cashier calls the supervisor and he calls over the on-duty manager. They take Spira to the back office for a private talk. Spira sticks to his story. He said he'd forgotten all about them. Would you forget that you had fifty grand in sports betting chips for twelve years?"

"The casino refused to cash them," says Joey.

"Of course they fucking did."

"And Spira must've known they wouldn't cash them."

"He figured the odds."

"He's a high roller and understands the casino will cut him special privileges. It's how the system works."

A smile spreads across Bill Hunt's face. "We had a little talk with Spira."

"Meaning you threatened him with a conspiracy and accessory to grand theft," says Joey. He visualizes Spira in a small back room with some heavy men in his face. If any of them were smiling, they would have the Bill Hunt smile: full of wordless menace and pulsating anger. No police department is as efficient in the art of personal intimidation as casino security personnel—mostly ex-cops and military who love that they no longer have to play by the old rules.

"We didn't want to hurt the relationship. Lean too hard on Spira and he takes his business across the street. That fifty grand, along with the rest of the chips, was written off years ago. But no one has written off Pauley. We made Spira a deal."

Joey finishes his single malt whiskey and orders another round. Marty is talking to another hooker with a velvet smile and a blue silk dress with a plunging neckline. She slides onto the chair next to Marty, crosses her legs and smiles a thousand-megawatt smile, all white teeth, shining and perfect.

"You got him to rat out Pauley."

"He told us that Pauley is in Bangkok."

"So are twelve million other people," says Joey.

"But not all of them had a triple by-pass in the last month. Spira gave Pauley twenty percent of the face value of the chips. Ten grand covered the operation."

"You cashed the chips?"

"We gave Spira twenty percent in new chips which he turned around and lost on a Boston Red Sox game. He moaned and we gave him another five grand of new chips. That's how things work. One hand washes another. Spira's happy. We treated him right so he will keep coming back and losing in our casino. And we have information Pauley is still alive and kicking."

Joey slides the last of the remaining chips back as if he is asking to see Bill Hunt's hand in a game of invisible poker.

"What is it you want from me?" asks Joey.

"The casino can't quite forget you were the last one to see Pauley in Las Vegas. You end up in Bangkok. Pauley ends up in Bangkok. You can't blame the casino for thinking there is a connection. And we'd hate to find out that you know where Pauley is and that despite our request we find out that you won't help your old friends settle a score. That would be a bad thing, Joey."

The casino's head of security is still sore after all those years. The anger comes through in Bill Hunt's posture, his words, his presence; Jim Pauley is a flesh-eating virus he's been unable to excise. Hunt stacks the chips in neat rows on the bar counter. The waitress eye-balls him as he is on his third stack of casino chips. She *smells* the whiff of money as sure as she would smell the flowers as she walked into Feng Shui Flower Shop.

"He's retired," says Marty who leans forward.

"I am in the flower business. You've been to my shop."

Bill Hunt nods, eyes the stack of chips. "You know, the casino retired these chips. But that didn't stop them from still being in play. Old gamblers are the same. They are always in play. It's in the blood. The professionals' constant need for action, Joey. You remember that. You said it on TV. And, by the way, your show is back on the air. A lot of people are talking about it. But I guess you knew that. You always were a bit of a celebrity in Las Vegas. I heard a rumor that you run some high-end action here. You'd be the man to do that. Right, Joey? But you shouldn't think that means anything as far as finding Pauley is concerned. This is an old score and it needs to be settled."

For those operating on the inside, it was an open secret that Thailand attracted many gamblers from Las Vegas. Joey ran into them from time to time, in a bar, in a restaurant, in a shopping mall. They had different stories. Some were young; most were old-timers who cashed in their bank long ago and buried themselves in young Thai wives. Every so often one would say hello and want to talk about old times; others would look away, increase their speed, and slip into the crowd or the dark. Bill Hunt speaks a larger truth and Joey knows this. What all these men have in common is a large hole in their heart once they turn their backs on professional gambling. Strip away the glitter of the showgirls and neon lights of Las Vegas, and you're left with what gambling is really about: negotiating around obstacles and coming out on top, winning, and getting around those dead-end warning lights that say: *You can't go any farther, you have to stop.* Joey liked that defining moment when he had to find a way of getting around the blockage and there is pride in finding that opening.

"If I get any information, I'll let you know," says Joey.

"You do that, Joey. Make it a Christmas present to your old friends in Las Vegas."

Marty has his arm around the waist of the hooker. "I'll catch up with you later," says Marty.

Joey knocks back the last of the eighteen-year-old single malt whiskey.

"I'll come around for some flowers tomorrow afternoon," says Bill Hunt. "That will give you time to find this information."

As an old security chief, Bill Hunt knows a thing or two about how gamblers think. It is his business to know how they react to a challenge.

People who gamble needed stimulation. The casino went with Freud rather than feng shui and the *Book of Change*. The bosses understood the needs of people. That's why they kept the rooms cold. They blended and weaved subliminal messages into the piped music: *Bet. Be happy. It is a sure thing. Bet more. You can do it.* They knew how to spin the dream. *Success. Victory. Happiness. Bet. You are a winner. They can't beat you today.* One of those Sunday-inspiration church messages promising the afterlife to the hopeful, faithful, and the loyal. Casinos, churches, and political parties, like all product advertisers, promised a version of paradise. They climbed onto the celebrity train—all of them—smiling and reading other people's lines and the train would sooner or later slam into a wall. One day the true believers would no longer believe in them. Until that day, Joey told himself, people were content for their idols to tell them how to feel, to dress, what was right and what was wrong, and what to do. They let others place their bets and make the odds. Maybe it is a blessing for most. They are too frightened otherwise. The color of the room must be bold. No pastels they put people to sleep. And behind the happy-face messages of salvation and cold room and loud colors is the cellar door where people like Bill Hunt stay until called to bring home one of the sinners.

Joey knew enough security guys like Bill Hunt to know that none of them ever understood the true nature of professional gamblers.

He did a piece on his TV show about casino security. He got a lot of mail from that show. It is as if he were looking in the camera again, as he looks across the bar at Bill Hunt.

Security guys by their nature lived far away from the edge. Professional gamblers searched for the edge. They inched closer and closer, until they hung all ten toes over the side and peered down into the void. Like casino security, gambling was a full-time job. Bill Hunt got a monthly check for just showing up. There was no check in the mail for gamblers; without brains, information, people working to feed in fresh data, they fell into that void and were never heard of again. Some died. Some were murdered. Those who won had people working for them to challenge their assumptions, but even with that extra edge, they still lost close to half of their bets. Nerves of steel were needed to watch the money flow down the drain. They made the money on a thin edge. A win had to cover the five losses and make a profit. Some broke under the full weight of all that pressure. In their minds, they are action heroes. Players like Errol Flynn, sword in hand, taking on the overwhelming forces and defeating them.

Joey filters the old show transcript through his memory. He forgets nothing. Watching Bill Hunt collect his chips, he figures that Jim Pauley broke under the sustained pressure of the losses: money, ex-wife, and pregnant girlfriend. Bill Hunt comes to town to squeeze Joey for information about a thief who disappeared twelve years ago. Some guys never can accept that the team they believed could never lose went down in defeat. Joey Balfour in the old days spent hours handicapping a horse race. He laid all of his bets before going to the track. At the track he'd watch mugs poring over the race forms between races, and running down to place their bets two minutes before the window closed. Not one of those guys was a professional. The bet-by-the-seat-of-your-pants gambler always lost his ass. It was like getting into a sword fight with a fencing master. The blade passed through the heart in the time it took to breathe in and out. The professionals went to the track to socialize and make contact with other pros, trading information, and making friends with money people. Bill Hunt was like a mug at the track. Now he wants to trade information with a pro but he has nothing to trade.

Bill Hunt follows Joey to the door.

He stops Joey with a hand on his shoulder. "One more thing you ought to know, Joe. The casino has an Errol Flynn original signed poster. It's from the movie *Edge of Darkness*. I have it in my room. It's a very special poster. Let's say the casino, as a token of its appreciation and support, wants me to give it to you. But I need something in return."

Joey Balfour spins around, smiling. "Free posters like free love are expensive prizes."

Hunt has Joey's attention. He knows about the World War II movie and the movie poster. Errol Flynn played a secret agent in a village in Norway. It is interesting that of all the posters, this is the one that Bill Hunt shows up in Bangkok with. It doesn't make sense to come all this way with *that* poster.

The First Time Marty Gage
Saw Errol Flynn's Bedroom

During his lunch period, Marty's taxi stopped in front of the school on Denman Street and Joey climbed into the passenger's side. Marty drove to Joey Balfour's apartment house at Broughton and Davie. They could have easily walked from the school but Marty insisted on using the taxi. He pulled up in front of the building and switched off the ignition. The apartment house had five floors. Most of the units were ordinary apartments, and there was nothing special about them. But the penthouse, well, that was a different story. No other apartment house on Broughton and Davie or in the West End had a penthouse like the one on the fifth floor of this building. Joey led the way into the lobby and pushed the button for the elevator.

As they walked into the elevator, Joey removed a key from his pocket and inserted it into the keyhole next to a small bronze plate that read: penthouse.

"You need a key in the elevator?" Marty was impressed that first time.

"Only for going to the penthouse floor. Everyone else pushes a button."

Along the polished chrome panel, all the other floors had a standard elevator button. The ordinary buttons carried a message for all passengers: these floors were open, public access to one and all. But the penthouse floor where the Balfour family resided required a key—it was a private, privileged, exclusive area.

"Your parents must be really rich," said Marty. His mouth hung open as he walked into the foyer of the penthouse that first time.

Joey's father, Trenton Balfour, was a leading marine biology professor at the University of British Columbia and his mother came from an old, wealthy New England family who had made their fortune in timber, mining and shipping.

Marty stood in front of the elevator as if frozen, as he stared straight ahead into the foyer. "We're not going to get in trouble or anything?" asked Marty.

"Marty, I live here."

Marty smelled a trap. How could a kid going to a rotten school on Denman Street live in a penthouse? What was wrong with his parents? Didn't they know what kind of school they had put their kid in? Didn't they know they had choices? Joey Balfour could be sent to a really good school where he might meet kids just like him with keys to penthouses and staffed with teachers who weren't just crowd-control specialists or lunatic-ward goons.

"You want to look around?" asked Joey. He looked over his shoulder and saw that Marty, having stepped out of the elevator, wasn't budging. "Okay, how about I pour you a drink. Scotch? Beer? Gin? My dad has just about everything that has alcohol in it." Trenton Balfour had converted the foyer into a wet bar so when someone stepped out of the elevator, they walked straight to a large wet bar with a counter and stools.

"I'll have a beer," he said.

Joey walked behind the counter, opened the fridge, used an opener to pop the cap off a bottle of Molson and poured it a little too fast into a tall, fluted glass, the foamy head spilling over the edge of the glass and sliding down the side. "Sorry about that," said Joey as the beer dripped over his fingers. He handed it to Marty who guarded his territory in front of the elevator. He licked the beer from his hand and grinned. "Cold enough?"

Marty held the glass of beer, nodded, and took a tentative step forward. He was like a man with a fear of heights.

"How about I take you on that tour?"

Marty sipped beer from the glass, wiped his wet knuckles on his jeans, and wondered whether one day, if he made the Yankees starting lineup, he too could aspire to such a pad. "You sure it's okay?"

Joey opened another beer and drank from the bottle. "Come on, I am on my lunch break. I don't have all day."

Drinking beer for school lunch, they wandered through all five bedrooms of the penthouse; each bedroom had a private terrace and bath. Joey saved the master bedroom with its double terrace for last. He opened the sliding glass door and stepped out. He looked up finding a grayish sky that threatened rain. Toward the horizon, the sky roiled with thick black clouds moving in over English Bay. Joey shivered and drank from the bottle. He turned and walked back into the master bedroom and told Marty the story of the building.

A Hong Kong Chinese merchant named Samuel Eliot Wong had designed it in the 1950s. The developer had an intuition that one day the British would betray Hong Kong to the mainland. Politically he was nearly fifty years ahead, a visionary. Wong also anticipated the type of modern interior that one day would be a feature of luxury urban living. Wong lovingly labored over every detail of construction. The penthouse had a purpose; it was intended as Wong's rabbit hole (the Chinese always keep three) to dive into once the British showed their true colors and played their hand, ordering armored divisions of the red horde from the mainland to overrun the colony, slitting the throats of anyone wearing glasses, speaking English and with an education. Wong had ordered lavish double sinks, a separate shower and bath, a separate toilet and dressing area. He also had a sewing room and a freezer room. Supposedly the penthouse had built-in secret vaults and safes, but no one had been able to find them. In the 1950s when Wong had predicted the English would betray Hong Kong everyone wrote him off as paranoid and crazed by angst and conspiracy.

A squall from English Bay brought a sheet of rain and Joey backed away from the sliding glass door, closing it against the rain.

"Someone famous once died in this bedroom," he said.

Marty settled onto the edge of a chair at the foot of the bed. "Who?" His voice sounded doubtful but so far nothing that Joey had told him had been false.

"Errol Flynn," said Joey, watching the rain against the terrace window.

"Didn't he play Robin Hood?"

"That's him."

"He died here?"

"On that bed." Joey pointed at his parents' bed. Of course, the bed probably had changed over the years, but metaphorically it was that bed or one very much like it.

Marty stared at the bed, drinking his beer. He thought about the movie and tried to remember the actor's face. Some images started to come back. Errol Flynn wearing a green top with silver eyelets and leather drawstrings around the sleeves and neck. He had a wispy goatee and mustache. His pageboy haircut flipped under at the ends, and he wore a black cape that made him look like Merlin the Magician. Not the Merlin from English folklore but the drug dealer who hung around after school. Marty thought of Robin Hood sprawled out dead on the bed.

Joey walked past Marty and stood beside the bed. He pursed his lips, and a serious expression tightened his brow as he pushed his knee into the bed. "I reckon he died just about here."

Marty stood next to Joey and looked at the bed. "Sounds like bullshit. If someone that famous had died in Vancouver, why didn't I hear about it? And besides, what was Robin Hood doing here?"

"It happened almost ten years ago. You would've been nine. Were you reading the newspaper at nine? I don't think so."

"I don't believe it," Marty said, finishing the last of his beer.

"You want another one?"

Marty shrugged. "Sure."

As they walked back to the wet bar in the foyer, Joey told him about some of the other tenants in the building. "Most of the people living in this building are crazy," he said. "Like the Faragos. They live on the third floor in a crappy one-bedroom unit. And they are very weird."

"What's weird about them?"

"My mom says they have no visible means of support, no job, and no visitors. The rumor in the building is they have sub-par IQs. At night you can sometimes find them wandering like beggars in the hallway on the third floor dressed in old dirty robes that smell. They have this blank expression on their faces. Some nights they spend hours riding the elevator up and down like it is an amusement ride. Twenty times a day they check their mailbox and ambush other tenants in the lobby. The Faragos never receive any mail. Have you ever heard of someone not getting *some* mail?"

Marty confirmed that was a new one to him. "That is weird."

"I feel sorry for them. I am the only one who ever talks to them. I think I am the only friend they've had in years. They told me about Errol Flynn and how he had died in the penthouse while a seventeen-year-old girl was with him. He was really old. You hear what I am saying, Marty? Naked. Seventeen. No clothes. She sat on my parents' bed with Robin Hood."

"But your parents didn't live here ten years ago," said Marty.

That was beside the point. For Joey Balfour, when you were eighteen years old and registered for the draft, carrying an altered draft card that says you are twenty-one, and your best friend is next to you, then you deserve to have point of view about the importance of a naked seventeen-year-old sitting on a bed accepted without bringing up irrelevant points. Joey had first heard the Errol Flynn dying-in-Vancouver story in a different way, from someone who'd heard it after hitting middle age with the layers of worldly-wise knowledge to recast the image of a young girl and an old actor. The Faragos had seen all of Errol Flynn's movies. They might have been crazy but they knew Flynn's movies better than anyone alive. It was their passion. He was their action hero; the only person who had brought a wisp of dignity and meaning to their lives. And Errol Flynn's movies may be what made them a little, well, nutty. They had invited Joey to see their posters of the films. Mrs. Faragos gave him a poster for *Cry Wolf*, a 1947 film starring Errol Flynn. His mother let him keep it on the condition that he got straight As at school. Even one B grade and the poster would go back to Mrs. Faragos. He left that piece of information out of what he told Marty that lunch period in the penthouse in Vancouver. Before Joey said it was time to go back to school, he showed Marty the poster.

"Wipe your hands," said Joey. "This is really valuable."

Marty wiped his hands on his jeans. "Wow. Is this something else."

From that day on, Marty thought Joey had the talent to become a first-rate horse race handicapper. Joey lived in a five-bedroom penthouse where a famous actor croaked in front of his naked girlfriend who was young enough to be in the class behind him in high school. It cemented their partnership. They shook hands after finishing the second noontime beer on their decision to go into business. After that day, Marty bought day-old racing forms at a steep discount, which was only fair as the race was already over. The old racing forms were piled up like junk ready to be returned for cash and Marty worked a deal with the newsagent; he gave him fifty cents for each expired racing form. It was free money for the newsagent. The forms were going to be returned anyway. So what was Marty doing with the old forms? The idea to buy those forms and start on the long road towards learning the art of handicapping horse races was Marty's stroke of genius.

During Joey's lunch hours, in line of vision where Errol Flynn died in the arms of his teenaged honey, they'd handicap the horse races from the day before, and then find out right away whether they had picked the winners. It was perfect because they didn't have to wait to know if they were right. It was cold blooded, and that was the best way to learn a profession and make no mistake about it, gambling was a profession. Just like acting was a profession. Both required the suspension of disbelief and fed upon the appetite for adventure and action and risk.

The race was already over, and they didn't have any money on the line. Marty would walk out of the elevator and go straight to the fridge behind the bar, then open a beer with the racing form under his arm. They would lay out the form on the floor and study the horses with the passion of youth. It was Joey Balfour's school lesson, Marty and him poring over the stale forms, making the calculation about each horse in every race. Marty might not have made the best pitcher the Yankees ever put on the mound, but he was the best teacher ever when it came to handicapping horse races. George Steinbrenner would have hated him, caused him grief and traded him after one season. Marty was that smart and that good.

Joey's Birthday 23 December 2004:
Bangkok, Thailand

The pavement is cracked, broken, divot-sized chunks missing as if a giant had been trying without success to blast his golf ball out of a sand trap. The stretch of wrecked pavement runs for kilometers along the odd number sois from Soi 23 to Soi 35. This is also the last of the line of buildings from old Bangkok: a string of three- and four-story shop houses hawking everything from bamboo furniture to rice and eyeglasses. Most of the daytime pedestrians are schoolgirls in uniform, running, jostling and giggling; at night those on foot are shiftless, solitary figures in sandals walking fast towards Soi Cowboy. None of the daytime or night-time pavement walkers venture into Feng Shui Flower Shop. Joey's clients, discreet and rich, drive inside the grounds in the back of chauffeur-driven expensive cars; their drivers park in a large lot hidden from the street, where they wait for their master or his wife or minor wife to finish choosing fresh flowers. Set thirty feet off from Sukhumvit Road, the narrow driveway passes between a glass and steel building on the left (housing a real-estate shop selling luxury condos) and another box-shaped glass, cement and steel building on the right (an ultra-modern furniture shop). Joey thinks the location is perfect. The feng shui balances all the elements and adding flowers completes the harmony. Money flows in and stays. At night, no one expects to find anything behind the darkened real-estate and furniture shops.

Moving through the driveway, the headlights of Joey's chauffeur-driven car swing over the front of Feng Shui Flower Shop. The low-rise building is sandwiched between a travel agency and an organic restaurant. As he gets out of his car, Joey instructs his driver to wait. He strolls through the parking lot remembering that, not that many years before, a single-story house rested where the organic restaurant had been built. In front of the small single-story wood house was a nursery. In those days, the owner, a middle-aged Thai woman, would come out of the house to sell wilting flowers in black plastic pots for fifteen baht. It was only a matter of time before the real-estate developers sucked the owner from her house with a vacuum cleaner of money, and leveled the house and nursery, recycling the land into a vast assembly line of chrome and glass. They had left the enclave in the back, waiting for the right time to raise a thirty-story building. Meanwhile, Feng Shui Flower Shop, Joey likes to think, is a tiny ember from the large bonfire of the old days.

The entrance of the flower shop is a plaza of swept, polished flagstone. Directly in line with the front door is a lit water fountain. The water pressure is low so it comes out more like the gurgling of a drowning man. Sky says the water fountain is good feng shui; the movement of water brings harmony and ensures the chi flows into the shop. The small enclave delivers a new age, peace is with you, health and love, a higher level of consciousness. Joey's parents, approve of the shop and location. They are hippies at heart. Secretly, Joey also believes it is a perfect location for a flower shop. He bets that Sky, whom he loves in his own way, will stay put for a very long time in such a location. The old saying in real estate is: location, location, and location. The same with a woman, Joey says inserting his key into the front door of the shop. Each time he arrives late at night, he marvels at his cool, isolated, and peaceful sanctuary.

The organic restaurant is closed, as is the travel agency. A night watchman lingers on a bench near the parking lot. He's watching a small portable TV. He looks like a thief who could break into any locked car inside two minutes but would take an hour if he were being paid by an owner who had locked his keys inside. Joey's driver eyes him. They are not alone. Half a dozen new, expensive cars are parked side by side in the parking lot. Other drivers sit inside their air-con cars, waiting. The cars and drivers are familiar to Joey and his driver.

Joey finds Sky in the back of the shop where she's watching a cable TV fashion show called *Bare Skin*. She's huffing and panting, eyeing the screen and lifting dumbbells. She curls a five-kilo dumb-bell in each hand, slowly raising them to her chin. Her biceps bulge and the carotid arteries on either side of her neck rise bluish and swollen under the surface of her translucent skin. Beads of sweat swell like raindrops on her forehead. In the shadows lurk dozens of green feathery-leafed plants, some in giant pots, others in modest holders, carefully and lovingly arranged in a variety of pans and dishes on the parquet floor. The large plasma TV screen flickers like a magical eye from deep inside a tropical jungle. All elements reflect perfect feng shui ensuring strength, power and health.

Sky wears a low-cut, skimpy, sleeveless T-shirt with no bra and a tight-fitting pair of shorts. Her nipples are clearly outlined against the damp T-shirt. Her outfit goes well with her white Nikes, which she wears without socks. Joey admires her breasts. She's particularly proud of them. She chose them from an American model that she had been eyeing for months on fashion TV. The Canadian Thanks-giving Ball was the first time she'd been able to display her new breasts in public. Not exactly a full display but they attracted atten-tion at the table and later with Joey on the dance floor. The singer watched her as she looked out into the audience, missing notes as she struggled over the lyrics to "Fool for Love". Sky understands that pirating breasts isn't an intellectual property violation. Her eyes belong to a French fashion model, and her nose to a German model; the chin is from a model from the Czech Republic. While Sky retains an Asian look the foreign landscaping has muted the flat nose, small breasts, and weak chin, fusing together an ultra-modern face and body that people seem to find vaguely familiar but as a whole the package fits everywhere and nowhere. With a catwalk face and body, Sky proclaims to the world that she is a member of the new fashion species, a specimen that synthesizes the best of races, body parts and features.

Her latest round of silicone inserts cost one-hundred thousand baht. Joey paid the full amount in cash, counting out each one-thousand-baht note at a time on the surgeon's desk. On the day of the operation, Joey followed her into the operating room dressed in a surgical gown and mask so that he could hold her hand. He watched as the surgeon cut slits under each of Sky's armpits and carefully, with gloved hands, inserted the silicone. During the pre-surgery conference, the surgeon let Sky hold one of the silicone inserts. She turned it round in her hand like it was a small lifeless jellyfish, her fingers tracing the edges, gently squeezing it. The doctor handed another silicone insert to Joey who held it in his open palm, shaking it to calculate the amount of elasticity. To Joey, silicone looks like a kilo worth of giant oyster. Sky hands her silicone insert to the surgeon. Once inside, they would give Sky the illusion of a supermodel's breasts. *It is a kind of masquerade,* thought Joey. *The giant oysters will forever dwell beneath her skin. Sleeping giants buried in her flesh, and I shall touch them over and over again knowing their true nature.* The doctor sensed from the way Joey massaged the silicone that he was unhappy and assumed it must be the price. What the doctor didn't know was that Joey was factoring in the first editions that Ped would demand as her compensation for Sky's latest round of cosmetic surgery.

She could have saved twenty thousand baht by going for the cut-rate boob job but that would mean scars under each breast and no one could guarantee exactly how long that inferior grade of silicone would last before the first leak sprouted. Sky and the doctor looked to Joey for an answer. He was thinking that Iris Murdoch's first novel, *Under the Net*, and a first edition at that, is far less than twenty thousand baht. Ped would look up the price on the Internet, so there was no point in lying.

"The odds are to bet another twenty thousand," Joey finally said. He would make it right by Ped. Sky sighed and the doctor smiled. The farang had done the right thing. Everyone smiled. No one would lose face and the feng shui of breast alignment favored an early morning operation.

Sky's new breasts came after Joey had invested twenty thousand baht for her nose jobs, another thirty-five thousand for the eyes, and forty thousand baht for the new chin. As Joey goes into the back room, he sees most of Sky's best features are marching down the catwalk on Chic Fashion Channel. On the upper right-hand corner of the screen is the pink stylized flower that Joey says is a magnolia. Sky's not sure if it is a magnolia or a daisy. Sky doesn't look as Joey comes in; she is too busy scanning the models on the TV screen, looking for additional features. Joey says he will pay for dimples, skin sanding, liposuction, or whatever she finds is the latest trend.

Joey knows how to treat a woman, gain and maintain her loyalty. It is a simple formula: pay for her beauty maintenance program.

Joey asks her for a favor as he stands behind her and raises his hands, helping her do a set of curls. They watch Naomi, hips in motion, smiling, head cocked to the side, gliding down the catwalk. He changes the screen to a remote camera. A group of men are playing cards. They seem to lack energy. He switches the TV back to Fashion Channel.

"Let me check out the game room," says Joey.

"You don't stop working. Not even on your birthday."

He shrugs his shoulders. "I won't be gone long."

"Ped plans to read again tonight."

Joey turns, smiles. "Yeah, that's good."

He loves the sound of her voice making characters come alive, the story, the setting, the way she pauses, like a trained actress, building the mystery and suspense, her eyes bright and clear and full of joy.

At the end of the corridor, Joey stops, pulls out his key and opens an outer door. He continues down a short passage to another door with a guard posted out front. "Everything okay, Khun Mongkol?" The security guard's Feng Shui Flower Shop uniform is freshly pressed, the collar open. The guard nods, and unlocks the door. Joey steps inside where eight men sit at a large table, playing Texas Hold 'em. They are all smiles. "Happy birthday, Joey," says one of the players, then the others join in and sing him a round of off-key "Happy Birthday".

"If you need anything, let me know," says Joey.

Around the table are wealthy businessmen, politicians, fixers, and officers. Men who play golf together, invest in each other's ventures, and play poker twice a week in this room. Four women in ball gowns carry drinks on silver trays. Orchids and roses fill the corners of the room. The women wear flowers in their hair. The players are treated like high rollers. They are also some of Feng Shui Flower Shop's most loyal customers. Protected by the chi of the place, they all feel like winners.

When Joey slips back into the workout room, Sky, perched on the exercise bike, is scanning every catwalk model with intense concentration. The TV screen is positioned in front of a mirrored wall; that way Sky can study the TV and her face and make instant comparisons. She is studying her reflection and trying to ignore Joey's face behind her in the mirror. He knows by now that with Sky it is better not to sign any blank checks.

She looks at him in the mirror. "Hi."

"Hi, yourself," he says.

The boob job is still being paid for in installments without interest. Tonight Sky is reducing her debt. Joey has an appointment. She's prepared as her foremost creditor marches in close quarters inspecting, sniffing around his collateral. It is also Joey's birthday so she wants the evening to be something special.

"I need your help, Sky."

The sweetest words a woman ever hears are a man's call for help.

"Of course, Joey. Whatever you want."

He knows she's thinking this is about some kinky sex trick. "I need information about a farang who had a triple by-pass operation a month ago. I am thinking it might be the same hospital that you use. That hospital is used by most foreigners."

"I don't see how I can help," she says. Her voice is thick with disappointment. It is so much easier to grant a sex wish than to find information.

He uses the back of his hand to wipe the sweat off her brow. "Sweetheart, you've built a good relationship with your doctor. I've paid him a lot of money. He will help if you ask him. I'll give you a picture of the guy. His name is Jim Pauley. But that might not be the name he used at the hospital. So it won't pay off to search the database. He's got to look at the photo and show it to the doctors who perform heart operations. Are you following me?"

Sky is absorbed in the TV image as one of the models, tall, young, with full lips and dark auburn hair stops, turns and smiles into the camera, revealing her naked belly under a skimpy top.

"That's the belly button I want for my Christmas present," she says. "Look quickly, Joey. There. That one. See it?"

"You can't just pick a belly button after seeing it on TV for three seconds. You have to live with these decisions. Not to mention all the medications you have to take each time you go under the knife," says Joey.

"I guess I could ask my doctor, Joey." She looks away from the TV and examines his face wondering if he understands what she means. It isn't clear from his expression.

"Good. Ask him to check with his buddies in cardiology if they have seen this guy. It's no big deal. Either they've seen him or they haven't."

"And I can have *that* belly button?"

Joey tries as hard as he can but he can't recall *that* belly button. Put it in a line-up of belly buttons and stick a gun to his head and tell him to pick the right one. *Might as well pull the trigger*, Joey thinks to himself.

"Yes, baby. You can have a new belly button but only after I get my information."

Joey has a reassuring tone like Johnny Carson. His voice is like a TV personality, full of wisdom and confidence. This troubles Sky because most of the time the sound masks competing distractions that filter into the consciousness, pumping puzzling, unsettling, and dangerous images.

The chances are if Jim Pauley is in Thailand then he's living under a new identity. New nationality, age, address, but he can't change his blood type or eye color. The chances are Bill Hunt, if he spends enough time and money, slows down and remains patient, will sooner or later find Pauley. *It is hard to hide from anyone with resources and determination who wishes to find you*, thinks Joey.

Bill Hunt's resources with the casino backing him extend beyond Joey Balfour, the last man to see Jim behind the cage before the act of grand theft. Going to Joey is one of those old-times-sake's gestures, like the guy who goes back to the same woman even after leaving her for the third time. Or pre-sleep masturbation sessions. It becomes a habit, and one that is nearly impossible to break because it is linked deep down to faith that somehow in the universe all past connections continue uninterrupted through to the future. Joey factors all this information into calculating the probability of Bill Hunt tracking down Pauley. In his mind, there's no reason why he, Joey Balfour, should allow a signed original poster of *Edge of Darkness* to slip back into the void when it could be hanging on a wall of one of his bedrooms. In fact, he tells himself, that poster would go quite well in the back of the flower shop, the room where

Sky exercises, and the room where they make love. Sky makes the first move, snaking her arm behind her back and finding Joey's zipper. She sees his eyes become larger in the mirror in front of her. "Come closer, birthday boy," she whispers.

On the catwalk, a Victoria's Secrets model is wearing some black-laced fuckware. A little shiver goes down Joey's spine as the model whose breasts are exactly reproduced on Sky stops at the top of the catwalk, hands on her hips, and pouts her lips directly into the camera.

Sky asks in her tiny I'm a debtor offering an installment voice, "Is Temperance Hill running tonight?"

Like most couples they speak in a private code, part erotic, part bits and pieces of old conversations, convoluted, disjointed symbols of desire, fear, anger and pain, break-dancing into a language only they can understand.

Joey groans with pleasure as her hand touches his flesh. His underwear knots under his scrotum and her long red fingernails tap dance on his erection.

"What are the odds of that horse finishing first?" She leans her head back and whispers in his ear before using her teeth on the flesh of his earlobe.

His voice is in slow motion as the blood headed for the vocal chords is sluicing through the gateway of veins in his penis. It is a throaty, raspy croak of a voice.

"His odds are forty to one. Just like the Belmont Stakes," replies Joey with a little cough.

"Temp, temper, Temperance," she whispers. "He's out of the gate. Bring him home, baby. Make him a winner. Win the big prize. You can do it."

Sky moves off the bike and onto the floor, bending forward on all fours. Her clothes are heaped in a rumpled, wet pile next to the bike. She glides him inside, a sound launches in her throat, something in the mid-range between a sigh and a cough or a distant cry. She breathes in deeply, then arches her back, bucks and throws back her head, exposing her neck. Joey is a stallion, also her jockey. Joey, the jockey, as if standing with the balls of his feet on the stirrups, rides her for all he's worth. The Victoria's Secrets catwalk gushes with long-legged fillies, black net stockings, white feathery wings like an angel's, and painted lips, gorged and seductive. The back room smells of orchids and sweat. The mirror fogs until their shapes blur into indistinct movements, roiling inside a cloud like the one that rolls over English Bay from the balcony of Errol Flynn's penthouse. Feng shui experts agree that all bedroom mirrors must be covered before the occupants turn in for the night. This is not exactly a bedroom, though Sky sometimes dozes off here. Tonight, neither Joey nor Sky has any intention of going to sleep.

One of Sky's best attributes is she's been well trained. She knows the track. She knows her jockey. She knows her horse. Sex, after all, is mostly ritual, a passionate sprint, a leisurely stroll, or an adrenaline charge for the finish line.

"Temperance Hill," she whispers. "Ride me. Ride me hard. Ride me long time."

Sky may not understand the universal formula for all gamblers but she knows what Joey needs to get out of the gate, and once out of the gate he belongs to her. He is predictable like most men: he runs the same track, same speed, same conditions, and she knows how he likes to storyboard each race. She calls their coupling with the same soundtrack as the announcer who called the race on the day that Temperance Hill won at Belmont. She knows that the soundtrack of that race excites Joey beyond anything she has in her grab bag of tricks. *Thank God for the Google God*, she says to herself. She located a man in Nevada who had the transcript of that race. It only cost her one nude photograph in exchange. Once she had the transcript, she surprised him, she addicted him. Sky knows full well how to stay secure and safe inside Joey's life. She might not be able to read aloud *Anna Karenina* or *Madame Bovary* like Ped but she knows the script of the Belmont Stakes takes Joey to heights that no book cover ever touches.

One thing is for sure: Joey never tires of hearing that race called by Sky; Joey knows that he will win. There is a reason for his confidence. There was a racehorse named Temperance Hill, son of Stop the Music, mother was Sister Shannon. When Temperance Hill won the Belmont Stakes the odds were forty to one. Joey walked away with forty grand after the race. He loves Temperance Hill for the same reason he loves the Blue Jays; these were underdogs, chasing after a dream with the heavy money against them, finding a way to defeat the odds and enter the winners' circle.

Temperance Hill sired many winners. That stud managed to get around, siring foreign champions, stake and individual winners. Temperance Hill was the father of six hundred and two starters. And where did such a stud finish up his life? A retirement with only one requirement: screwing mares and eating the sweetest grass. The horse went to Thailand. Temperance Hill, the horse that returned forty thousand dollars on a thousand-dollar bet, followed Joey to Thailand. Like Jim Pauley. All of these long-shot winners travel to Thailand. *Why is that?* Joey asks himself. *Is it karma?* But karma is another way to express hindsight bias. No one could reasonably predict that Temperance Hill would end his years in Thailand anymore than that on the night Joey scored on the Blue Jays, the usually reliable man behind the sports betting cage at the casino would steal half a million dollars and flee to Thailand.

Temperance Hill's half brother, Across the Channel, eats his heart out, forever stuck in the States. Temperance Hill is the icon for all old studs that looked for one more season to produce a winner. In his last season, the old horse could no longer cover his mares, and the decision of what to do with a stallion who could no longer cover his mares was obvious. The owner could only do one thing. Call it old age, lack of usefulness, absence of purpose, call it whatever one wishes, Temperance Hill was put down. He got a lethal injection at a farm outside of Bangkok and Temperance Hill passed onto the final pasture. Joey heard several days in advance from an old Las Vegas hand of the owner's decision to euthanize the horse. Joey arrived at the farm outside of Bangkok on the morning of the appointed day and watched as a vet slipped a long needle into the winner's vein. Temperance Hill shuddered, slipped into unconsciousness, and after a few minutes, his breathing stopped. Instead of last words, there was a final whimper before the long void of silence. On the day of services for the horse—and there were services befitting a hero—Joey conferred with Sky and Ped, and they organized the flowers for the ceremony, hundreds of white carnations individually hand picked, which Joey personally delivered.

As Joey reaches the final stretch there is no hindsight bias, no horse, no Las Vegas, no Blue Jays, Bill Hunt or Jim Pauley. His eyes are tightly closed and he tries to cry out but the sound is caught deep inside, nowhere near emerging from his throat. Sky is still calling the race. Joey is in the middle of a Temperance Hill moment of darkness, which erodes in a couple of seconds into a twilight of consciousness.

"Happy birthday, Joey," says Sky.

He collapses, exhausted, onto the floor.

His legs are wobbly as Sky reaches down and wipes his face with a towel. She kneels beside his head and smiles. "You won big time, Joey," she says. Her head tilts to the side and a cloud of doubt crosses her face. "Do I read as well as Ped?"

"You read just fine," he says.

She studies his face searching for any hint of irony and, finding none, she rewards him with a flurry of kisses and hugs.

Joey Balfour is covering his mares for another season in Thailand. Sooner or later, he will see that Temperance Hill's arrival is no accident; the old stud comes with a message for him. The old-time winners, past their prime, arrive in Thailand not for a new start but for their final coverage of mares, before they, too, will go the way of Temperance Hill. Their new Thai owner will one day be forced to make the same cold, calculated decision and come to the same conclusion. The only question each birthday is the probability of Joey making it through one more season. One more Christmas season spent in Thailand. He opens his eyes and looks at Sky. But he is thinking of Temperance Hill as he slipped into the big sleep with the assistance of a lethal injection at age twenty-seven. In horse years, he was an old man.

"You beat the odds, darling," Sky says, running the cloth over his neck.

"Most of the time, the odds are right. You must remember that. It is only in the freakish cases that a high-odds horse beats the favorite."

"But it happens," she says, her tongue running over her upper lip.

Temperance Hill's life is a living testament. It does happen. That's what creates hope and legends and opens the world of possibility so that it looks like a large door rather than a keyhole. Joey explains that horse racing has its own class system every bit as harsh as anything invented by the Thais, Chinese, Indians and English. Every horse is assigned to a certain class of racer. And if you put him in a race where he is far better than any other horse, he will win. He will always win. It is a given. It is like a Yankees pitcher who shows up to pitch a Triple A game. His skill, talent, and ability will in all probability show through. He is that good. The gap isn't one step, it is nearly a universe in time and space. Yet in any given game, even the best, he can have bad luck, pitch like he doesn't belong, run like he's in another class. It happens. Talent without luck comes to nothing. Luck without talent can be made to work. With both luck and talent Ped says the world is able to embrace the likes of Jane Austen and George Sand.

Sky raises her hand and brushes her long black hair from her face. She understands luck. She appreciates talent when she sees it; talent inspires her and makes her envy someone who has more than her. Unless it is, as Joey says, another universe away. That isn't simple talent. That is a supernatural gift.

"Life is about matching up like with like. That is the nature of making odds—making certain that oranges and apples don't get confused," says Joey. "Except on the racetrack in Thailand, where what you get at the starting gate is a mixed bag of oranges, apples, pineapples, durians, and the occasional grapefruit." His post-coitus state of mind is relaxed and in the mood for figuring the odds. "I figure the odds are Jim Pauley shopped for his triple by-pass where most farangs shop for one. He's a nobody. I figure he stopped looking over his shoulder years ago."

He turns to Sky and pulls her face closer to his own. "I need you to do me this favor, baby. You gotta help me out."

"Was sex okay tonight?" she asks.

"It was great, baby."

"What I am asking is whether you think that I am really good."

He sees something in her eyes. A flash of concern as if she's questioning herself. She's asking if she's as good as Ped.

"Not just good. You're the best," he says.

"Promise that you're not just saying that."

He smiles, leans forward and plants a kiss on her forehead. "Promise."

Mostly the competition between Ped and Sky is left unspoken as they are friends but neither can stop wondering about their place in Joey's heart. Each believes the way to his heart is to tell him a story, one that calms him, excites him, allows him to leave the cares of his past and his present far behind, stories that hold him still and in their power.

Sky's holding a photograph of Jim Pauley; her head tilts to the side, her eyes wide, bright, non-blinking. He has a long, horse-like face, only his lips are big like an African's, and his eyes are huge like headlamps. It has fallen from Joey's trousers. She wishes Pauley were more handsome. It is so much easier to throw one's heart into the search for a handsome man. "Okay, I will ask my doctor but no promises, Joey."

Joey finds his eyes tearing up. The fight between the head and the heart is clearly over once his eyes tear up. At this point, he is unable to stop. This doesn't mean, though, that he's certain of the exact cause of the tears that spill down his hot cheeks. Is it because today he turns double the age of Temperance Hill and no one in his immediate circle except Marty and Sky seem to have remembered that it is his birthday? Or is it because Sky clutches Pauley's photograph and promises to deliver it to Dr. Suporn? Or, applying Occam's razor—if presented with a complex, elaborate explanation and a simple, elegant one, always choose the simple, elegant one—from his side vision, Joey leans up on his elbows long enough to glimpse a fleecy-haired, lissome, pre-menstrual-like Victoria's Secrets model marching like a drum majorette down the catwalk. That is a great body. If it were humanly possible to do so he would place money on such rare, natural beauty. He is crying because there is no way he can lay down a bet on this surefire winner on his birthday.

A Lethal Injection to Put Down
a Twenty-Seven-Year-Old Stud

Boggy sits on the edge of the bed, head bowed, as he waits for Jennifer Balfour to find her cigarette lighter inside her Gucci bag; the lighter is resting deep within an inner fold. "I can't remember where I put it. I am having a senior moment," says Jennifer. A senior moment is a moment of remembering but instead of recalling a memory, the mind flips over to the frequency of white noise.

One of Boggy's arms is heavily bandaged and in a sling. He looks like someone who fell off a cliff or out of a tree, addled, confused, sad, and miserable. She performs this procedure with the professional hand movements of a gynecologist. Boggy looks terrible; he has raccoon-like rings beneath his eyes. He has flown twelve hours in steerage class in the flight from Vancouver. Jennifer flew in the super-business-class sleeper. She is alert and rested, smiling and calm. Her inner peace is a source of strength for Boggy who personally has none to spare.

It is three in the morning when Joey unlocks the door and slips into his five-bedroom condo. He switches on the hallway entrance light and goes straight to the wet bar and pours himself a double shot of an eighteen-year-old single malt scotch whiskey. He opens the fridge and pulls out a plastic tray of ice and dumps the cubes into a silver bucket. He drops three ice cubes into the crystal glass, raises the glass, admires the amber color, and allows himself a cool sip, his eyes scanning his room. He freezes, glass to lips, ice on his upper lip, turning his head one way and then the other. Joey walks closer to the wall behind his white leather couch. He blinks, sets down his glass, and rushes over, his knees in the soft leather, his nose an inch from the glass. His heart races as he lifts his hand and touches the frame. It is real. He's not caught inside the web of a strange birthday hallucination. Hanging on the wall is the only known original movie poster of Errol Flynn's homage to the Cuban revolution—*Cuban Story*. In a swirl of black ink, the poster is signed on the lower right side—*to Woodsie, with love, Errol Flynn*. Joey's forefinger traces the signature. It has the feel of an authentic Errol Flynn signature. For a moment, Joey is unable to breathe; his knees fold under his weight on the couch. He continues to look up at the framed poster with a little boy's awe. Today he's turned double the age of Temperance Hill. Nothing in the day has prepared him for this mysterious gift. He reaches over and finds his glass of expensive scotch whiskey.

"Happy birthday, Joey," Jennifer Balfour says. She is standing twenty feet away, having watched her son's face turn into the little boy's expression she remembers so well; she has allowed him to have his moment in front of the Errol Flynn ultimate must-have poster.

Joey takes another drink. "Mom?"

He's afraid to turn around. It is the second time in an hour that a woman's voice, after a moment of immeasurable pleasure, has whispered, "Happy birthday, Joey."

"How? I mean, where?" Joey runs out of steam.

His mother closes the distance and edges next to him on the couch. She gives her boy a hug and a kiss on the forehead. "You are still drinking too much, darling. You will have a liver like a duck, the kind they feed until the liver is so large that it is suitable for pâté."

"A crazy American named Howard Boggy tried to sell me this poster. He wanted an outrageous sum of money and had an even more incredible story."

Boggy slowly appears around the corner as he hears his name.

"Hi, Joey. I didn't know it was your birthday. But Happy birthday anyway." He's shy, stoop shouldered, his full bushy red beard giving him the appearance of a logger rather than a computer genius. He looks like he's walked back from the frontlines of a civil war. Arm in a sling, his hair uncombed and wild, his eyes rheumy and shifty.

They have never met before. All correspondence has been through email. As far as Joey can remember, he has never seen a photograph of Howard Boggy. He stares at Boggy. His eyes running over every one of Boggy's features. Joey takes in the sight of this pale, young, plump, out-of-shape, bearded man without a single gray hair in his beard or head. He looks at his mother, then back at Boggy. His eyes glance up at the movie poster. It is all too confusing.

"Howard, this is my son, Joey. I understand that you two have never met but that you know each other very well."

"He came here with you?" Joey, mouth open, looks at his mother again. He's babbling. Obviously Howard Boggy is with his mother, under her care, and, he speculates, deeply in her debt for reasons soon to be disclosed.

She takes his amazement in her stride. "He didn't break in, if that's what you mean, Joey. I used the key and security pass you gave me last time. "

"You might have phoned," says Joey.

"And ruin your birthday surprise?"

His mother has style, determination and a single mindedness. Her lipstick is also smeared and her dress wrinkled from the long-haul flight. He looks behind his mother at the figure of Howard Boggy who remains at the far end of the room. Boggy looks like someone has poured tequila on his hair and set it on fire; his shoulders hunch forward in an awkward position, and he's all left hands and feet. His clear blue eyes don't match all that puffy blackness around them, but fail to age him out of his twenties. A tight-skinned, pale, haunted young man holds a nickel-plated .38 handgun in his good hand. He'd been hiding it inside the sling. Joey recognizes the handgun as his own. It is a matter of opinion as to whether Boggy is pointing the gun at Joey. Arguments could be made on both sides. His right hand with the gun rests at his side. It seems his guest has been snooping around. Joey's mother has no idea that the young man that she has invited into Joey's penthouse is holding a handgun. She is a woman for whom violence of any kind is repulsive and when she sees the handgun, she reacts immediately with total focus and concentration.

Joey says, "Howard give me the gun."

Joey is aware this line is not original but it is highly appropriate given the circumstances. Jennifer Balfour turns her full attention on Boggy who wilts under her gaze. She rises from the couch and marches over to Howard Boggy and takes the handgun away from him like she would firmly take her favorite bra from the mouth of Mercury, their Labrador retriever. Boggy even has the same guilty, tail-wagging look of Mercury and he makes no effort to resist as Jennifer takes the gun, shaking her head in disapproval. Naughty dog, her head shaking says. She gives the gun to Joey.

"Mother, you might begin by telling me what Howard Boggy is doing in my condo. And why his arm is in a sling. He's got one good arm and what does he do with it? He uses it to stick my own gun in my face. What is that?"

"You're being overly dramatic, Joey. The boy is dead tired from the flight. His arm hurts and he's on strong medication. To make matters worse, the poor boy was wedged between two very large-boned people, one of whom had a gastric problem."

At a moment like this, Jennifer Balfour transforms herself into Olivia de Havilland in *The Charge of the Light Brigade,* leading lady, feminine, heroic, and vulnerable. She leaves no room for doubt that Boggy is her charge and under her maternal influence. She treats him like she would a child; the old motherly instincts from Joey's childhood flash like hot spots across her memory.

"I told Jenny that I would sell her the poster on the condition that I could meet you," said Boggy.

Joey's ears ring. Jenny. No one in thirty-five years has called his mother, Jenny.

Her Olivia de Havilland smile continues on her lips. "He said that he had always wanted to go to Thailand. But he needed an excuse. I thought, why not? You two should meet. You've been buying original Errol Flynn movie posters from Boggy for a long time. It would be a good thing. People should have more face-to-face time. All this Internet and typing messages I am afraid is not the way to conduct a normal, meaningful social life. Everyone needs to look someone in the eye. One look is more valuable than a thousand emails can ever be."

"The Feds want him in a bad way."

Jennifer Balfour leaps to the defense of Boggy who stares at his bare feet. "Howard was very honest, Joey. I know the authorities are giving him trouble. Look what they did to his arm. They tried to murder him. But that is their job, isn't it? It is not like Howard committed any crime. To make selling Errol Flynn posters a federal offense is beyond common sense."

His arm looked bad but it didn't look like anyone had tried to kill him.

"They know that I know what they *did* to Errol Flynn and that's why they blew up my place," jabbers Howard Boggy. "They don't want to arrest me. They want to kill me. In cold blood they murdered my cat. I almost lost an arm. Don't you understand, I am afraid?" Boggy blubbers and folds his splayed fingers over his face, his body shudders. Twelve hours seated next to a passenger playing a non-stop duet of bowel trumpets has reduced Boggy to a slobbery kid.

"There, there, Howard," Jennifer comforts him, cradling his head. "He saw Marty in Vancouver. Marty phoned me and said Howard was scared. Someone did blow up his apartment, Joey. That is not the way to serve an arrest warrant. Look how they kidnap and torture people these days. The boy was at great risk. It is just like the old days when your father and I ran an underground railway for boys escaping the Vietnam War."

Joey thinks about Marty, across town in a cheap hotel with the hooker he took from the bar in Bill Hunt's hotel. He thinks about phoning him. Then decides it is pointless. This doesn't stop him from being upset with his friend. He should have told him that he had delivered Boggy into his mother's custody. She is back in her old business of saving the political refugees flowing over the border from the United States.

Joey also wonders how much of Boggy's performance is jet-lag induced, how much is personal theater, and what residue of these raw emotions results from genuine fear of harm by the Feds. The picture of Boggy in Vancouver, however, is coming together. Boggy flees to Vancouver, and first hunts down Marty Gage, and it is a short step from Marty to Jennifer Balfour who shares the nightmarish vision of Federal agents and their long history of dirty tricks to silence critics.

"Stop for a moment. Think of the odds. Boggy is in danger. Give him the benefit of the doubt and say someone tried to kill him. He crosses the border into Canada, and then flies to Vancouver. And my mother brings him to my condo in Bangkok. What are the odds that Boggy is safer here? What are the odds that all of us are now in danger?"

"I got new ID. My New Zealand passport says I'm Gunnar Brogge. Customs and immigration hardly check wounded people. It's a good thing to know."

"Errol Flynn played that character in *Edge of Darkness*."

For the first time Howard Boggy manages a wisp of a smile. "That's very good. I thought of Morgan Lane from his role in *Montana*. But I thought the name was a little too cowboy like." Boggy seems proud of himself.

Joey slumps down on the soft leather couch, pulls his legs up and rests his chin on his knees, looking at Boggy's large, disheveled head leaning on his mother's shoulder. Bill Hunt is sleeping across town with a movie poster of *Edge of Darkness*. These are Temperance Hill-type odds.

"But of all places to run to, why choose Thailand?" asks Joey.

Boggy shrugs his shoulders. "It is as good a place as any to start over," he says. "I mean, you started over here. And you didn't even have to run away. And everyone is watching your old reruns on TV and wondering whatever happened to Joey Balfour."

"How old are you really, Howard?"

"Gunnar. Please call me Gunnar."

"How old are you, Gunnar?"

"Gunnar's twenty-seven," he says. "Do you know a doctor who could look at my arm? There's something not right with it."

Joey closes his eyes and whispers one word: "Sky." He wishes for an instant he was still with her, that he had never left Feng Shui Flower Shop. He should have slept there with her at the shop, or brought her back to the condo. She asked him, more than once, but, no, Joey Balfour had his driver waiting outside and decided to go home. It is her reward for forcing him to promise that she's the best.

Temperance Hill was Howard's age when Joey watched his eyes go wild with shock and fright as he received the lethal injection. This was a bad age for a horse to start over; but a good age for a man who decided to change his name to Gunnar and planned to grab a second or, in Boggy's case, third or fourth chance at winning.

"Until Gunnar gets his feet on the ground, he could always stay here, Joey. You have five bedrooms. You wouldn't even notice him. And you could help him find a doctor."

Joey likes Boggy more as the depressed, paranoid kid. But this is a new Howard Boggy. A boy-man free falling, in a deep funk of a mood, and training a small nickel-plated handgun on him. He can deal with the problem of a handgun situation. What all gamblers seek to do is to avoid disaster. The chances are one cannot survive a disaster. Joey turns and looks up and stares at the new Errol Flynn poster. He is happy to have it. This ends the search for one more of the Errol Flynn posters. But nothing is solved. Bill Hunt floats into Bangkok with a special-item poster. Somehow it devalues what Boggy has sold to Joey's mother. At a minimum it opens a new volume Joey would rather shut and leave on the table. Jennifer Balfour waits for her son to say something. She knows there is no point in rushing Joey. His mind is working through the probabilities and assigning the risks. Is this good luck? The poster on the wall suggests that it is. Is it bad luck? He stares at Boggy and how his one arm in a sling seems to cause him pain. That is how her son's mind works.

Howard reaches with his good hand into his pocket and at first Joey thinks this might be medicine for the pain or another gun. He's not sure and keeps the nickel-plated .38 aimed at Boggy. If he wasn't half crippled, Joey would have pistol-whipped him. No one pulls a gun without either using it or having it used against him. That's the rule of the street. Bangkok street, Vancouver street or Las Vegas street, any street in the world. Beating up someone with an arm in a sling takes a certain mentality. *Bill Hunt would have beat the shit out of Boggy*, thinks Joey.

"Easy, Howard." Joey watches the hand come out of his pocket.

"Gunnar. The name is Gunnar. And you can relax. It's only a piece of paper," says Boggy, looking hurt.

"Joey, please don't point the gun at Gunnar." Jennifer says this as if it isn't the polite thing to do to a guest.

"I only want to show you that I am not crazy. That I have something that *they* don't want me to have," says Howard Boggy. It is the madman's *they* Boggy chooses to use as if UFOs are pursuing him.

He drops the handgun on the couch as Boggy steps forward with the paper. It is a photocopy of an old letter, one written on a manual typewriter and the letters look rough like a child's handwriting. Joey puts on a pair of reading glasses. Even with the glasses it is difficult to make out all of the words.

"That letter was written in 1959 by someone who worked with J. Edgar Hoover. It quotes Hoover as saying that Errol Flynn was an Aussie pinko faggot. It says Errol slept with James Dean and a thousand women, most of them in their early teens. Hoover believed that Errol Flynn was not just an actor, but also an icon. An influence on mid-western farm boys. The fighting force needed to fight communism. Errol Flynn had to be stopped. And he must be stopped by all means at our disposal. That's what it says."

Boggy's display of drama impresses Jennifer Balfour.

"There you have it in a nutshell," she says.

"The FBI killed Errol Flynn and covered it up."

Boggy blubbers. A long, deep sniffling sob comes to the surface, from exhaustion, the pain shooting down his arm, the memory of his dead cat. He's reached the end of an emotional road and if he had the gun back he would turn it on himself.

"Put the letter on the web. Then everyone will know."

"They'll say it is a forgery."

"Is it?"

Both Jennifer and her son look at Howard Boggy. An old conspiracy to murder Errol Flynn could pay handsome returns for someone in the business of selling old movie posters. Where there is motive and opportunity, there is a balance in weighing the probability of criminal and non-criminal intent.

"It is real. I swear it." Boggy makes the sign of a cross over his heart. "They didn't blow up my place and kill my cat because I was running a scam. They wanted to blow me and this letter up. I have the original. But they don't know where I've hidden it." From under his T-shirt, Boggy takes out a gold chain and there is a key on the end.

The badly injured arm supports his side of the argument that something has happened. A bomb, falling off a motorcycle, a mugging or tripping over his own feet and going head first down a flight of stairs. Joey plays with the image of a bomb exploding. Meanwhile, Boggy shows him a key he claims is to a safety deposit box where he's stashed the original letter. The pieces of Boggy's story fit together unless the possibility is entertained that he planted the bomb himself, knowing that if he exploded a bomb in his own apartment no one could question the authenticity of the letter or his interpretation of the contents. The problem with deciding the truth of his story is partially sabotaged by the deceitful and sharp way in which he runs his business and life. All kinds of strange, random events continue to happen to him. He attracts chaos. In Boggy's universe the pieces of a story are in flux and could fit naturally in an infinitely appealing number of ways.

Joey stands in his living room with the black sky of Bangkok beyond the windows. His mother to one side of the *Cuban Story* movie poster. And Boggy under the assumed name taken from an old Errol Flynn movie on the other. It is like turning over a coin: heads, tails, and then heads again, tails, tails, on and on until the end of time. A fifty-fifty chance with each flip. What is it with Boggy? A black-bag operation has been put in motion to silence him? Or is the entire, elaborate scheme nothing more than a cleverly devised plan to raise the price of his Errol Flynn movie poster inventory? Each is a possibility. Each connects together like Siamese twins, and what separates evils and lies from good and truth is a knife-edge of belief in who has the most to lose. And who has the most to gain.

"Gunnar, explain to me, in your own words, why, of all places you could stay, you've decided that you want to stay here?"

"That's easy. I Googled your name and it gets more hits than a well-known Japanese general who was a war criminal. All that war fame was nothing compared to Joey Balfour. That tells me that the brutality and torture of evil government people don't always finish in the money in the fame game. That's the game I am in. You are the Errol Flynn of gambling. Everyone says it. Who is going to touch you? I mean, you are famous. I have a better chance of surviving if I stay close to the king of sports betting than staying on my own.

I worked out the odds. Staying with you is a good bet. I will be in the money."

This sounds like something Boggy heard from one of Joey's old TV shows. It just doesn't sound like Boggy. The words don't seem to belong to him; he's borrowed them without knowing exactly how to use what he's borrowed. Besides, his explanation doesn't ring true for Joey who thinks this is from the imagination of someone who only knows the digital world of the Internet. Someone who is twenty-seven years old projects the weighed value of fame is equal to the number of hits on Google.

"I have to look at it from my side. Here's how I call the odds, Gunnar, Howard, or whatever you want to be called. You and your story are a long shot for winning the truth stakes. What I can do is give you three days. Then you disappear. Got it?"

Boggy awkwardly reaches out with his hand.

Jennifer, hands on her hips, smiles. "Go on, Joey, and shake on it."

Joey extends his hand wondering how the old-fashioned hand-shake interfaces with the weird fusion of fame. To Boggy, Joey's old. Ancient. A Las Vegas sports betting legend with one foot in the grave. He decides there is no answer; Boggy's mind is as opaque as a skylight in the roof of one of those million-dollar houses on Point Grey Road.

"Tell me where the letter's hidden," says Joey.

"If they torture you, you'll tell them." Boggy's mouth tightens as if bamboo has been slipped under his fingernails. "They can use torture. It's unofficial government policy. They can make you talk."

"But if I don't have the information, they don't know that. They think I am holding out, and then they have no choice but to torture me to death."

"They know when someone is telling them the truth," says Boggy with utter conviction that he knows what he's talking about. "They have secret truth serum. You can't lie once they inject you with it."

"I've had a hell of a lot of fun and I've enjoyed every minute of it," says Joey.

Boggy balls his hand into a fist and slams it into the wall. "Yes, Errol Flynn's last words. Brilliant. Your mother said you were brilliant. Straight As in high school."

Joey and his mother exchange a glance. "You told him about my high-school marks?"

"In Vancouver, you exceeded all expectations in that high school, Joey."

"She also saved your life." Boggy seems to have harvested an entire crop of family lore from Jennifer Balfour.

Like generations of troubled men before him, Boggy flees his bombed-out apartment in Maine and makes his way first to Vancouver and finally lands in Bangkok. Joey credits Boggy with a sign of genius for having invented a foolproof rescue operation. What better person other than Joey's mother to help in his great escape; that is a fabulous stroke of luck, putting the whole bank on a long shot. Rescue is a trait that runs deep in Jennifer Balfour's genes. This time Jennifer is up against a different kind of operation. Officially the people who work for RCA are on the payroll of other agencies. They are seconded to RCA where they manage operations authorized to kidnap, transport, and deliver suspects to Third World countries where old-fashioned means of persuasion are used to extract information, confessions, and retribution. They get what they want when they want it. Like a Dalmatian dog in front of a gramophone, they hear the music.

There are voices in the outer hallway. Joey recognizes Marty's. "We're in here," he calls to Marty. No one expects Marty to arrive at three thirty a.m. When he comes into the living area Marty's not with the woman he had picked up in the bar of the five-star hotel where Bill is staying. She has dumped him. And he's gone out to find a replacement. Only this time he's not chancing taking her back to his dive of a hotel. Joey figures he's told her that he lives in a penthouse. This woman is taller by a full foot—she is almost as tall as Marty—her hands are larger than the earlier pick's and her feet are huge. There's a slight rasp in her voice. Her arms wrap around Marty and they stop dead in their tracks as Jennifer Balfour bolts forward and gives Marty a big hug.

"Marty, what a pleasant surprise to see you."

At first he cannot speak. "Mrs. Balfour. What are you doing here?"

"Well, it's . . ." Jennifer Balfour says, breaking off as she sees Marty isn't paying any attention to her or to Joey.

He is unable to concentrate because all that he sees in front of him is Boggy who turns away from the poster and faces him, chin down. Marty's jaw drops and his mouth moves but no sound comes out. His companion nudges him in the ribs with her skinny elbow.

"Boggy, what the hell?"

"I'll explain it all later," says Joey.

There is a long silence.

"This is my friend Star," he finally says, his eyes way too open for three thirty a.m. Marty is locked in Star's embrace. He glances over at Boggy who shrinks into a soft chair as if he is trying to disappear. Jennifer and Joey are fixed on Marty's companion.

No question about it, Star was born a different kind of 'sun'. Perfect eyebrows, an oval face and wide smile with straight white teeth. But Joey's eyes concentrate at breast level where Star's curvature presents a crossword puzzle. He judges the angle, the arc, the size, the distinct outline of the aureoles and the answer comes to him. He's seen enough plastic surgery as Sky has gone through major realignments, refits, hollowing out, suctions, and Botox injections to know the work of a good surgeon.

"Tyra Banks," says Joey, winking. He recognizes those breasts immediately; it is like recognizing a signature tune for an old situation comedy. Sky, like Star, has pirated the breasts from the American model. He's not making a judgment on her womanhood. The breasts are a point of admiration for the skill that has gone into turning the perfect upturned nipple, hard and rippling through the transparent silk blouse.

Star blushes, a coy turn of the head, her lips go into a little pout. She squeezes harder on Marty's arm to the point where he winces from the pain. She definitely has muscle tone in places Marty had when he was a possible Yankees starter. Her message is clear: *Why didn't you tell me the place was going to be crawling with your friends*, Star whispers in Thai to herself. Her entire assessment of the score with Marty is tumbling over and over in her mind and she questions her own ability to judge a trick. She is shaken by the event and Joey's comment. How does this man in the apartment know that her tits come from Tyra Banks? Whatever hormones she's eating day and night they've kicked in and her face shades red and pink from the mouth to the eyes like a neon sign in a Las Vegas casino as the slot machine announces a grand winner.

Marty pulls Boggy up by the back of his collar and frogmarches him to the new poster hanging on the wall. Boggy leans forward, his uninjured hand in his pocket, and reads the inscription from Errol Flynn. Star, Marty's *katoey* friend, stands a few feet away, pumping from leg to leg like she's making butter or cheese, under the watchful eye of Jennifer who is of this world but whose experience of transgender beings is limited. Star is unable to decide what her trick intends to do with the young, bearded scared-out-of-his-mind farang.

"He called her Woodsie. But in Cuba he sometimes called her Eldora," Marty repeats after Boggy. His tone registers no hint of a question mark but a soft sign of recognition.

"Beverly Aadland." Howard Boggy's face is a couple of inches from the poster. "She was with Errol Flynn when he died in Joey's bedroom."

Actually he died in Trenton and Jennifer Balfour's bedroom almost ten years before the bedroom was the Balfour master bedroom. A mere detail but one that Boggy gets wrong, opening up the possibility that other details are also flawed, inaccurate, suspect, including the letter pinning Flynn's death on J. Edgar Hoover and his knowing the identity and affiliation of the people who supposedly set a bomb in Boggy's apartment. Star and Jennifer sit together on the sofa talking like they've known each other for years, and Jennifer is asking where Star goes for her hair and for the secret of who tailors her clothes. Marty's pickup settles in like a regular guest, meeting the friends and family. Boggy sneaks more than one glance at Star. The connections between Boggy and Marty and his mother circle around, misfire, then start again inside Joey's mind. An hour later and the exhaustion has caught up with everyone but Joey. He loves Bangkok because, like Las Vegas, it is possible to keep gamblers' hours. At four thirty a.m. he has his second wind and is feeling, well, not exactly good, but in far better shape than anyone else in the room. Boggy curls up in a chair in a corner, fast asleep. Marty and Star disappear into the guest room. The crack of light under the bedroom door vanishes into darkness. The apartment is quiet.

Joey and his mother are on the balcony looking at the cars on Silom Road.

"This has been the ultimate Spam moment," he says. There is no need to distinguish the Spam that comes out of a can and the spam that comes from the Internet. Jennifer knows the Thanksgiving dinner game. "Bringing Boggy here is a lifetime of Spam."

She takes a deep breath, her forefinger draws a circle on her knee.

"I saved your life once, Joey," Jennifer Balfour says. "You might have been killed in Vietnam. And now I am saving it a second time."

She tells her son that bringing Boggy to Bangkok has a larger purpose; it is all part of her master plan to save his life a second time. "I bought the poster from Howard and listened to his story. I am not certain that at first I believed all his wild flights of conspiracy, death threats, bombings. Clearly he had had a great personal adventure. But what did it all mean? Our family has maintained solid political contacts after all of these years. I decided the best way to test Howard's story was to tap into these old friends and find out whether an agency had received a court order to read Howard's email—and if, in doing so, they'd been reading the emails he's exchanged with you. What I found out is that it was more than emails they were reading. Someone had accessed his bank records, and recorded his telephone conversations. A court order was issued as part of an investigation into Howard Boggy's child porn racket. Or, as Howard says, they were using that as cover for removing him from the Errol Flynn business. The FBI has a long rap sheet on Errol Flynn. I am certain that you are aware of Flynn's 1943 statutory rape charge. Howard certainly made it easy for them. He's been posting nonsense on chat rooms about the injustice of the Pitcairn Island child molestation convictions. Since the first day of the arrests of the men on Pitcairn Island, Boggy has launched a one-man crusade accusing the British authorities of injustice. But he didn't stop there. Boggy posted long rants on several forums claiming he'd uncovered evidence that J. Edgar Hoover had ordered Errol Flynn's murder. It's no wonder that someone in the government made it a private project to chase him out of the country. I believe he has done nothing wrong. He holds strong views and he's young. That doesn't make him a criminal."

"Listen to what you just said. Boggy has a death wish, Mother."

Jennifer Balfour wraps an arm around her son's shoulder. "And you, my son, are once again on the radar screen of the agencies who have you in their collective memory from your Eugene McCarthy days. The TV shows are becoming a cult in America. People are saying terrible things about that showgirl shaking her bootie in front of the camera. That's not a good thing, Joey."

Tolstoy Rules for Dueling

He closes the bedroom door as Ped looks over her reading glasses and smiles, "Happy birthday, Joey." In her hands is a dog-eared copy of *Anna Karenina*. "Where's Sky?"

"She staying at the shop tonight."

He has the look in his eye that says Sky has banished herself for the evening.

"Why don't we save the next reading for another night?"

Joey shakes his head as he undresses and climbs into bed. He props up two pillows and folds his arms over his chest. "I'd like it very much if you read to me." He knows the passage about dueling from years before when his mother had gone through a Tolstoy phase.

Ped clears her throat, opens the books and reads, ". . . challenging him to a duel would be dishonest behavior on my own part. Don't I know in advance that my friends would never permit me to engage in a duel—would never permit the life of a statesman needed by Russia to be placed in jeopardy? Then what would happen? What would happen would be that I, knowing in advance that things would never get so far as real danger, simply wanted to acquire a certain false glamor by means of such a challenge. That's dishonest, it's hypocritical, it would be deceiving both others and oneself. A duel is unthinkable, and no one expects it of me. My aim is to safeguard my reputation, which I need in order to continue my career unhindered."

Sneaking Out:
Vancouver, Canada

Marty, wearing a windbreaker over a sweater, stands outside in a light, driving rain holding half a dozen small stones he's collected while walking along English Bay. He looks around in the darkness; Marty is alone, though in his mind, he's on the mound and fifty thousand Yankees fans watch as he winds up that golden pitcher's arm and delivers the first stone high into the sky. It doesn't matter that he will never throw a hardball in the big leagues or ride in a ticker tape parade down Wall Street or wear a World Series ring. Marty is already there, at that moment as the stone finds its target: the fifth-story balcony window of Joey's bedroom. It is a few minutes past one a.m. when a small stone picked up from the beach strikes the balcony window. It takes two more stones striking the window before Joey goes out onto the balcony and looks down. Marty waves a bottle of Captain Morgan and does a little victory dance.

"You want a drink?" shouts Marty.

"Not so loud," says Joey, but his voice is lost in the rain.

"It's fucking raining. Can't you get your ass down here?"

"Coming. Give me half a second."

Marty throws another stone, which catches Joey between the eyes.

"Hey, that fucking hurt."

"Good arm, hey?"

"Yankees starter's arm."

Someone comes out on the balcony on the third floor and looks up and then down and shouts for some peace and quiet. Joey looks down and sees old man Faragos, his hair wild and his eyes bulging with a crazy sense of curiosity. Joey would have thought Faragos would be angry. In his old, tattered dressing gown, Faragos leans over the railing. Joey backs away. He's afraid Mrs. Faragos will demand that he return the *Cry Wolf* poster if he's caught causing a disturbance that might lead her husband to have an Errol Flynn heart attack. She says the building has been cursed ever since that day in October 1959.

"Then why," Joey's mother had asked, "do they stay here?"

And his father, Trenton, replied, "They have no other place to go, Jenny."

As Mr. Faragos stands in the rain doing his search under the dark sky, Joey's already pulling on a sweatshirt and stepping into his jeans. His teeth chatter as the rain strikes his bare feet. He goes back into his bedroom for a jacket and scarf. He knows that it is impossible to take the elevator, as the doors open into the foyer. His father would sleep through the groan of the cables and pneumatic sound of the doors opening. But not his mother; her head would rise from her pillow and she'd be in the foyer in less than twenty seconds carrying a baseball bat to knock the burglar senseless. The Hong Kong merchant understood that betrayal was the most common element in the universe and knew the foremost architectural feature in any building was the best means of escape. Half of the construction is spent on perfecting avenues of escape; the other half is spent on tolerable living quarters as he waits for the day when he must flee. He made certain he had a quick, non-mechanical way to reach the ground. Joey turns out the lights in his room, slips out to the balcony, swings a leg over to catch the top rung of the fire escape ladder and climbs straight down to the ground.

As he passes the third floor, he waves at Mr. Faragos. "Don't worry, Mr. Faragos, I am going down to find out who is causing trouble. I'll handle it. You and Mrs. Faragos aren't to worry."

Mrs. Faragos, unstable on her feet, leans against her husband, smiling, pushing back a thicket of rain-matted gray hair from her forehead. "Joey Balfour you are such a sweet boy." They've both been into the booze for a number of hours. He smells the cheap rum.

"Thank you, Mrs. Faragos. But I better go now."

"Throttle the blackguard," says Mr. Faragos.

"I will, sir. I'll use both hands, Mr. Faragos."

Joey disappears down the fire escape ladder and at the bottom jumps to the ground. Marty hands him the bottle and Joey takes a long drink, wiping his mouth on the sleeve of his jacket. He nods at Marty. "Now." And Marty groans and moans, "Stop. You're killing me. I won't come back. Let me go."

They both look up at the third floor and Mrs. Faragos is applauding.

"We can go now," says Joey.

"Your mom is right. Those two are crazy," says Marty. "And I am starting to have my doubts about you."

The streets and pavements are deserted as they walk over to Thurlow Street, passing the bottle of Captain Morgan between them. They fall in with a group of homeless men who are standing around fires lit inside old garbage drums. Shirts loose, worn outside of their jeans, and wearing old unlaced boots they look like they've been out in the open for some time. Flames shoot from the open drums. A couple of the men warm their hands. No one has an umbrella. They seem to accept the rain without complaint. One of the men has the *Vancouver Sun* classified ads perched like a tent over his head. The rum feels good inside. Marty is shuffling a deck of cards, watching the red embers spark out of the drum. One of the men asks Marty for a cigarette, and he produces one from his jacket pocket.

"What are you kids doing out this time of night?" the bum asks, lighting the cigarette from a piece of fire passing over the lip of the burning drum.

"Celebrating," says Marty. "He's just finished high school."

Marty points to Joey who looks embarrassed.

"I am twenty-one and can prove it."

Joey takes his draft card out of his wallet and shows the bum.

"Twenty-one is bit old to be finishing high school. You got a problem upstairs?" The stranger taps the side of his own head.

Marty smiles. "Nah, he's not really twenty-one."

The stranger nods, taking in the two young men warming their hands over the fire. "The draft board in Ohio wanted to draft me. And they would've got me, but I came to Canada. They can't touch me here," he says. He looks like a bum because of his shabby clothes but from the way he talks he sounds educated, not at all slurring, bum-like.

Marty hands the bum the Captain Morgan and he takes a long pull before handing back the bottle. "If you go back they'll put you in jail," says Joey.

"But I ain't ever going back."

"I'll drink to that," says Marty. "And I ain't ever gonna play baseball for them. I made up my mind."

"Why don't you throw your draft card in the barrel?" asks the stranger. "If you are against the war, then throw your card into the fire. Or are you for the fucking war?"

Joey fingers his draft card. This small document is a lifeline to sustain their illegal liquor business. Without it, they are doomed. *What is it going to be?* Joey thinks. Solidarity with a semi-bum draft dodger meaning he burns the card or a continuous revenue stream meaning he keeps the card in his wallet. This is the first moment of consciousness for Joey and he knows that his decision will haunt him his entire life. He stares at the fire. Marty has a large lump in his throat, his eyes tearing up as he looks into the fire as if he sees his whole life from Yankees pitcher to illegal booze salesman in the flames.

"I want to see some action," says the bum. "What are you gonna do?"

"I am registered here. They can't touch me. I need this card to spread the word that there is a way out. I found a legal way not to go to Vietnam. I am living proof. I need the draft card to spread the gospel. I can save hundreds of lives. That is my mission."

The bum's smile grows large, the red flames reflected in his bloodshot eyes. "Man, I wish someone had told me. You have a mission. Go forward and spread the word."

Both Joey and Marty know their mission. It is to go to Granville Street and hustle money at the pool tables from the clerks and office workers in the financial district and then go out to Exhibition Park with their bank and bet on the ponies.

On the way back to the apartment, Joey tells Marty how his mother had managed to save his life. By now, Joey's feeling the rum and his legs are a little wobbly. He knows that he has to climb the fire escape ladder five floors in the rain. The building is in total darkness as they stand in the grass along the side. Everyone inside is asleep. "Aren't you gonna tell me how your mom saved your life?"

"I told you that I ran away from home when I was in eleventh grade."

"You were living in Minnesota, I remember that."

"I went to New York City and worked on the Eugene McCarthy campaign. I helped print posters and leaflets. I was out getting other kids to quit school and join the great movement. I did drugs. I had great sex. I got drunk every night. Vomited every morning before printing more posters. I nearly overdosed twice. I caught the clap once and crabs twice."

"Yeah, yeah. And she rescued you. That's what you mean. But that's not really saving your ass."

Joey finishes the rest of the Captain Morgan and throws the bottle across the street where it breaks against the curb. "Later, she found out that the FBI had me on a list."

"What kind of a list?"

"The kind that says when this person registers for the draft, he's to get an immediate call up and he's to be sent straight to Vietnam. It was their way to fuck with you if they think you are fucking with them," says Joey.

"How did your mother know?"

"Her family's connected to people in Washington. They give all this money to politicians and politicians tell them things they need to know. That's why my father took the job at the university. My parents had no choice. They came here to save my life. If I'd stayed in New York or gone back to Minnesota, do you have any idea what would have happened to me?"

Both of them are so drunk they are finding it difficult to stay on their feet.

"Tell me. What?"

"I'd be carrying an M-16 through rice fields. Me, Joey Balfour, high-school graduate, would be a moving target. Those are bad odds, Marty. You handicap those odds and you come up with a bet that I wouldn't finish the race. I would fall face down in some slime shit ditch running along a rice field. I don't even like rice."

"Your parents did that for you?"

"Fucking awesome," says Joey. "And this is how I reward them. Getting drunk. Climbing down the fire escape and getting drunk."

"But you graduated. That's something."

"Did I tell you that my mom negotiated with Mr. Clancy that I could skip the eleventh grade if I got straight As in the twelfth grade? And I said, 'Mom, at least you could have tried for a couple of Bs.' She didn't know; and I didn't know that just showing up at school and filling out the examination guaranteed straight As. I didn't tell her that I'd have to be dead drunk or in an ICU to get Bs at our school. And I didn't tell her that my school was so lame they had to disband the football program because the coach couldn't recruit enough people to turn out for practice. You didn't even have to try out for the team. If you showed up in street shoes and without a uniform you were on the team. But he couldn't get eleven people to fill all positions. I am a total shit. I didn't tell her any of this, and now she thinks I am a genius. She saves my life and I get straight As and I feel I've let her down. Maybe I should enlist and go to Vietnam just to show the bastards that Eugene McCarthy's frontline volunteers aren't afraid of anything."

"You should sleep on that one, Joey. Remember tomorrow we're going over to the races. But we're tapped out. We'll hustle fifty bucks from the stockbrokers on Pender Street. I'll come around ten thirty a.m."

The pool hall is in the basement of an old building and opens at eleven a.m. because it is in the financial district, and it never occurs to anyone that kids would go anywhere near the area so they think it is safe to open early. It is that sort of thing that Marty is good at finding out. The wedge of opportunity opened by the ignorant assumption of grown-ups who assume, they understand kids. But they understand nothing about how kids think. The stockbrokers all believe they are Minnesota Fats; it is the easy way to bankroll a day at the track.

Joey is already one floor from the ground on the fire escape ladder. Marty cups his hands around his mouth and calls up, "Hey, Joey."

Joey stops climbing and looks down. "What'd you forget?" He can barely make out Marty's form in the darkness below.

"Nothing. I wanted to say I am glad you didn't burn your draft card. After the races we'll stop and buy another load of Captain Morgan and Jim Beam."

"School's gonna be over in a few months, Marty."

"For the kids in that school, it never started. So how can it be over? Besides, they know we keep on sellin', school or no school, and they got nowhere else to go. Were you serious about that mission thing, telling people how to get out of the draft?"

Joey Balfour looks up at the sky, feeling the rain on his face. "If I did that, they might come after me. Make an example out of me. Put me in the front of a platoon sent on a suicide mission. I think we ought to stick with what we know. Horse races, pool, and selling booze."

That speech cheers up Marty.

Reliability is the first virtue in selling anything, Joey thinks. And he's also glad he didn't burn his draft card. It was so good feeling twenty-one in the rain climbing up that ladder past the balcony of the Faragos who were asleep clutching knives and hammers in their tiny room lined with Errol Flynn posters. He feels as he reaches his own balcony that no summer will ever be like this one will.

Trading an Errol Flynn Poster
for Jim Pauley

Bill Hunt, his collar wet from sweat, rolls into the courtyard of Feng Shui Flower Shop. Mopping his brow with a fist of hotel tissue, he approaches a thirty-something Thai woman, her long dark hair held by a clip away from her face, and a garland of white lotuses weaved into a bun on the crown of her head. She's singing to herself. She has a nice, clean voice that carries through the courtyard. Her serene face is without makeup: no lipstick, eyeliner, or rouge. She presents the anatomy of peaceful contentment as she sweeps the flagstone in front of the shop. The door is open behind her and the flower shop looks empty of customers and staff. Fresh flowers and plants are lined up in front of the shop and displayed inside the window.

"Hey, miss, you working here?" Bill Hunt nods at Feng Shui Flower Shop.

Ped stops sweeping and looks up, smiling. Customers come from miles away to be in the presence of Ped's radiant smile, one that draws megawatts from an invisible power plant. "What can I do for you?" Her English is perfectly grammatical and, at first blush, Bill Hunt reminds himself this is Thailand and not a shopping mall in Los Angeles.

"I am looking for Sky. Is she around?"

Ped holds on to the broom with both hands. "We call her Madame Bovary. She comes in later. If you come back around five she should be here."

Sweat drops from his nodding chin. He's impatient. She can see that waiting is not something that Bill Hunt does well. Not only is

Bill Hunt ugly he's obviously not a reader. The Madame Bovary reference draws a blank expression.

"Do you know where I could find her?"

"She's at the hospital," says Ped.

He registers some surprise. "Nothing serious I hope." Bill Hunt watches the small gush of water from the fountain.

"Sky will be fine. Is there anything else I can help you with?"

Bill Hunt picks a bouquet of flowers. "Any chance Joey might be inside?"

"He's across the street playing pool. I can phone him, if you like."

He hands her a thousand-baht note. "No, that's not necessary. I am an old friend. I'd like to surprise him."

"Let me get your change," says Ped.

"Keep the change," he says. "What's your name?"

"Ped. It translates into English as 'Duck' like in *Duck Soup* the Marx Brother's film."

"Where'd you learn all this American cultural stuff?"

"Why don't you ask Joey?"

"I'll do that."

He's about to turn and leave, when he pulls out a red rose and hands it to Ped. "This is for you, Duck. And you let Sky know that Bill came around asking for her."

Ped takes the rose and runs it under her nose. "I'll tell her."

Bill crosses Sukhumvit Road at Soi 22 intersection and walks straight into a three-story pool hall. Not far from the door, Marty racks the balls on a table near a window overlooking Sukhumvit Road. Joey is at the other end of the pool table, chalking the end of his cue. It is early afternoon and the room is almost empty. The *katoey* Marty had brought back to Joey's condo is still wearing the same set of clothes. She's perched on a stool at the bar sipping a half-full bottle of Heineken beer. Joey leans over the table and sends the cue ball crashing into the tightly packed rack of balls, scattering them across the table. The three ball drops in the side pocket. Joey's one of those nervous players who concentrates himself by constantly chalking the end of his cue. The six ball falls into the corner pocket and the cue ball rolls back, as Joey walks around the table looking at the four ball.

"You always were pretty good at pool," says Bill.

Joey looks up from his shot and sees Bill Hunt standing at the end of the table. His face is expressionless as if Bill Hunt normally parachutes down at the end of a pool table. It is the kind of face genetically engineered for poker, displaying no hint of what cards he is holding. "Marty and I grew up shooting pool in Vancouver. Marty would beat me two games, I'd beat him one or two. Sometimes I'd beat him three in a row. It was the others who came around who had a hard time beating either one of us."

"I went around to your flower shop. I had a little talk with Duck. And I bought these." Bill Hunt held up the flowers before walking over to the bar and handing them to Marty's *katoey*. "Why don't you have these, sweetheart?"

The *katoey wais* Bill and then glances over at Marty, who is standing with his hands on his hips and not looking happy about the interruption or the fact that Bill Hunt is romancing his love interest.

"My name is Dow. It means Star," says the *katoey*.

"This place is like the Sixties with all these hippy names. Sky, Star and Duck," says Bill Hunt.

"I don't remember anyone in the Sixties named Duck," says Marty. He's holding hands with Dow.

"You Canadians don't know shit. In the Sixties, if you were in Vietnam, you'd hear guys yelling duck every time they were in the field." Bill Hunt is one of those guys who laughs at his own jokes until he looks around and sees no one else thinks it is all that funny and then he looks pissed off.

Joey lines up the cue ball and sinks the four ball. "Good shot," says Marty.

"I came around to see . . ."

"If I've found Pauley," says Joey not letting Bill Hunt finish.

"Bingo. You are fast, Joe. Always were fast off the mark. So what have you got for me?"

Jim Pauley's been off the radar screen for twelve years and Bill Hunt somehow expects that Joey is going to turn him up in twenty-four hours. "You remember D.B. Cooper?" asks Joey, missing an easy shot on the two ball, which skitters off the bank and misses the side pocket.

"He was that crazy guy who jumped out of a plane with about two hundred grand in the early Seventies." Hunt sits on the barstool next to Dow, and leans back with his elbows on the counter. "Missed your shot."

Joey nods and watches as Marty goes to work on the striped balls. "Who'd they have looking for D.B. Cooper?"

He looks up to find Bill Hunt staring at him. "Who?"

"Half of the fucking State of Washington, highway patrol, FBI, private investigators. And what did they come up with? A few shreds of a parachute and some singed hundred-dollar bills. No one knows whether he's dead or alive. He vanished, Bill. Right in America he disappeared."

"D.B. Cooper didn't go around selling stolen sports betting chips twelve years after he stole them either. If Pauley had stayed lost or dead, then that's one thing. But he's rubbing our noses in it. He's selling stolen chips."

The D.B. Cooper story isn't working. But it was worth a try. "I've got people working on it," says Joey.

By now Marty has sunk four of the striped balls and Dow is applauding each of his successes.

"In the casino, the floor manager, one of those new breeds with an MBA from Chicago, told me he spent more than a hundred grand to learn one important thing about managing a business and people. You got to give them the right incentive or they won't be motivated to do their best. And if you can't get the best out of the people who are working for you then your competitors will eat your lunch. Because they are smarter and give incentives that make their employees hungry to bring in the business."

Joey rolls his eyes as Marty calls the eight ball in the side pocket, lines up the cue ball and, in a quick flick of the wrist, sinks it. "What are you saying, Bill?"

"I am giving you another forty-eight hours."

Marty looks up from the table and exchanges a glance with Joey.

"And then what?" Joey is expecting to hear a threat of violence. He is half right and half wrong.

"That Errol Flynn poster I have in my room? I am gonna torch it. Watch it burn to ashes, stuff the ashes in an envelope and send them around to your flower shop, and then I'm getting on a plane and flying back to Las Vegas."

Bill Hunt has, and he knows this, a one-of-a-kind poster.

He's unaware that Sky has been to the hospital and talked to her doctor, and phoned Joey to report that none of the surgeons recognized Pauley from the photograph. This is discouraging news. Those doctors opening the chests of farangs to fix their faulty valves at the leading expat heart surgery center in Thailand aren't able to identify Jim Pauley. Joey's thinking of backup and wondering if Bill Hunt is bluffing or whether he would really burn the Errol Flynn poster from the movie *Edge of Darkness* starring Errol Flynn as Gunnar Brogge, and he's also thinking of Howard Boggy playing the part in his new undercover role at Joey's penthouse.

"I don't get it, Bill. You guys at the casino have got all kinds of resources. Why come around and buttonhole me? At the time the theft happened, I told you and the cops what I knew and what I saw. I was a bystander who wholly by accident happened to be the last one to see Pauley before he did a runner. And that was more than twelve fucking years ago."

Hunt's beer arrives and he takes a long pull listening to Joey Balfour.

"I've got a theory about you."

Joey shakes his head. "Did this theory also come from your Harvard MBA?"

"It was Chicago, not Harvard. And no, it didn't come from anyone at the casino. The theory comes from the school of hard knocks where you watch how the same few people have a knack of witnessing certain events. There's Joey Balfour, the last man to collect his bet, and a twenty-grand bet. This happens minutes before his buddy Jim Pauley peels off formation and gets lost in the clouds. And there was Joey Balfour as the last man who saw Eddie the Knife before the cops found him next to his car. You are a man of coincidences in time. And I am betting you might just have one more coincidence in the next forty-eight hours that leads me to Jim Pauley."

Eddie the Knife Doesn't Get to Testify

Everyone in Las Vegas referred to Edward Deavers as Eddie the Knife. Given that he weighed in at three hundred and fifty pounds, Fat Eddie would not have been out of line for a street name of a Las Vegas bookie. Except Eddie the Knife carried a knife in his boot and had once stabbed a black man from Los Angeles by the name of Washington. No one ever got Washington's story, but according to Eddie, Washington jumped him in the parking lot of a casino one night, high as a kite on cocaine. His attacker turned out to fit the common profile of a mug down on his luck. Mugs, and it makes no different what their color is, get desperate, and they convince themselves they have no other way out other than to rob someone to get money for the next bet or fix or both. Eddie reached into his boot, whipped out the knife and cut Washington real good. He didn't die but he didn't look too good either with a cut running across his face making him look like some freak from a tribal initiation ceremony that had gone wrong. The police called it self-defense and Eddie the Knife established an instant reputation on the Strip. This happened at the beginning of Eddie's career as a bookmaker in Las Vegas, and the nickname stuck with him. He kept an apartment in the Vegas Tower where Joey had a place. Eddie always parked on the third floor of the building. One afternoon, after work, Eddie pulled out the summons and showed it to Joey. Eddie the Knife had been summoned to testify before the grand jury the next day.

Joey read the summons calling Edward Deavers to testify on 1 November 1992 for unspecified grievances that the State of Nevada had against certain unnamed individuals. "Hey, Eddie, what's that grand jury going to ask you?"

Eddie the Knife shrugged his fat shoulders and stuffed a candy bar into his mouth. "Fucked if I know, Joey."

"You must have some idea. They just don't pick a name out of a hat and invite the winner to come around and talk to them," Joey said.

Eddie chomped on the candy, his mouth a mush of crushed peanuts and chocolate. "They don't give you a list of questions."

"I guess they want to surprise you," said Joey. "So what are you going to tell them?"

It sounded like Eddie was being honest when he insisted that he didn't know what he was going to say because he didn't know why they wanted him to testify.

Joey liked him and had invited him onto his live TV show at the casino a couple of times. The viewers liked Eddie as well and called in asking him the usual mugs' questions like how they should figure out how much to bet; Eddie would come back with, *You meet these university guys who come to Vegas who tell you to bet the square root of pie or x percentage of your bank divided by the opening price of IBM. That's all garbage. Let's say your rent comes due tomorrow and it's a grand and what you've got is one grand. What amount do you bet? You bet the grand. If you win, you pay your rent and you've got the other grand in your pocket. If you lose, then you find another place to live.*

After one show, Eddie the Knife said, "Hey, you wanna try the best Chinese restaurant in Vegas?"

And Joey said, "You're on, Eddie."

They got into Eddie the Knife's red Caddy and drove over to the restaurant, which was nowhere near the main Strip. The blonde waitress who came in at about two hundred pounds came to their table and said, "The usual, Eddie?"

And Eddie nodded, "Make that a double order. The same thing for my friend."

While they waited for the food, Eddie kept saying, "Joey, wait for it. This is the best Chinese food in Vegas." After a few minutes, it became the best Chinese restaurant in Nevada, then the best Chinese food in the United States and finally the joint was better than any fucking restaurant in China. Eddie the Knife had been on a roll on the set and Joey cut him more slack than he would normally consider cutting someone like Eddie.

"It's that good?" asked Joey secretly hoping that now Eddie the Knife had exhausted all possibilities of a better Chinese restaurant on the planet, that he might go to some other place in the universe.

About the same time, and before Eddie the Knife could take Joey on a Star Trek tour of Chinese restaurants in the Milky Way, the big-boned blonde waitress came around with Eddie the Knife's usual: two dozen egg rolls and two large bottles of Pepsi. That was Eddie's idea of the best Chinese food in the world.

Someone must have known what they were going to ask him and had a pretty good idea of Eddie the Knife's answer because they shot him. Joey Balfour was the last person to see him alive and, for five minutes, was a suspect. Eddie the Knife booked sports bets. In other words, that was what he did for a living. His father had been in the furniture business in Indiana. Eddie the Knife got his start in high school basketball in Indiana. This was the biggest sport betting business in the state and Eddie the Knife owned it. It was a better business than furniture. He didn't have to go around dusting and polishing furniture all day long, which left a lot more time for eating.

The day Eddie the Knife got popped, he closed up his shop at five minutes past four p.m. Joey saw him going out, "Have a good one, Eddie."

"You wanna go for Chinese food later?"

"I'll pass. Another time, Eddie."

"I wish your show was still on. I miss it. You get another show, you let me know."

"I'll call you."

Joey never had a chance to call. At four thirty-five p.m. Eddie was dead on the third-floor parking lot beside his red Caddy. He'd been shot seven or ten times. They never got a right count on the number of entry and exit wounds. The point is, it had taken a lot of lead to kill him. Though someone said two shots had killed him. The rest were an advertisement. What mattered, though, was that Eddie the Knife had seen Joey and then he had seen the hitman. And the cops were thinking maybe the last one to see Eddie the

Knife was also the guy who pulled the trigger. Like with Jim Pauley, the police took Joey down to the police station and put him in the same interrogation room and with the same detective who had grilled him earlier about Pauley running off with the casino sports betting bank.

The detective spent the first five minutes looking at the report and shaking his head. "How does one wise guy manage to say goodbye to Jim Pauley and Edward Deavers and then tell me it is all a big coincidence? What are the odds of this happening? You do the odds for baseball and football games. You tell me the odds. You're the bookmaker."

Joey's lawyer came into the room and advised Joey that he didn't have to say anything to the cops. And if the cops wanted to press any charges then they should press them, otherwise let his client go. As it turned out, Eddie the Knife's murder was never solved. No one ever found out why someone was afraid of Eddie the Knife going before the grand jury and spilling his guts. Given the way Eddie failed to tip, it could have been the big blonde at the Chinese restaurant or just about anyone else except for Washington, the mug who was responsible for Eddie's nickname. Washington was in a rehab center in Seattle trying to clean up his act one more time.

Errol Flynn's Premonition of Death

Joey calls Bill Hunt's bluff. "There's nothing all that special about an original poster of *Edge of Darkness*. I have one. Come to think of it, I have two. You can order them like candy bars off the Internet. An original is maybe a grand or so. Burn it, hey? That's not exactly a tragedy, Bill." There's no need to let some half-assed, ex-security chief who screwed up his job at the casino think that he's holding a better hand than he's actually drawn.

A creepy smile appears at the corner of Bill Hunt's thin lips. "Is that so? Errol Flynn signed the one I have 'To my comrade and friend, Fidel Castro.'"

He's good, thinks Joey. "No one's ever heard of such a poster. If it existed, believe me, I'd know."

"What if I told you that all along it was right under your nose? Only you didn't know it."

Joey shoots Marty a look as if to say, *what do you think?*

"Joey's an expert on Errol Flynn posters. He's been collecting ever since we were kids. He'd know if this poster existed."

Bill Hunt takes another pull on his beer, looking at the breasts of Star who is stretching back her elbows on the bar. There is a hint of recognition, thinks Joey. Bill must be a fan of Fashion Channel. He's seen the breasts before only not on a *katoey* in Bangkok. Distraction is the art of deception and Star is an artist.

"I bought it from a man named Faragos who lives in Vancouver."

Marty misses his shot, sending the cue ball off the table and bouncing across the floor. "How do you know him?" His hair stands straight on the back of his neck and he feels a chill as he breaks into a sweat.

"Let's say, I did some checking. Joey, it seems, lived in the same building as the Faragos. He knows the people I am talking about. I tracked them down to Errol Flynn's old apartment house and offered them a bunch of money. They took it. And why wouldn't they? They were living like trailer-park trash. The money meant something to him and his wife. The poster with that signature I figured would mean something to you. Though if you ask me, Errol Flynn was trash compared with Clark Cable. Or Humphrey Bogart. Bogart was a class act."

What would Bill Hunt know about class? thinks Joey. His cheap suit, lousy haircut, and moron forehead mark him as someone who parrots what others tell him is class. *Here's looking at you, kid.* But Errol Flynn is the actor who died in his penthouse.

Bill Hunt drops a photo of the signed poster onto the pool table. Joey looks at the photo without picking it up. There is a blow-up of the signature and inscription to Fidel Castro. Marty comes around the table and picks up the photo.

"Is the signature real?" asks Marty. "In the age of Adobe Photoshop is anything real?"

There is no clear answer. Only gradual shades of doubt.

"If experts can manufacture diamonds that fool the gatekeepers on 47th Street in New York, reproducing Flynn's signature isn't a big problem."

Joey considers whether it could be a good forgery. But he knows by looking at it that this isn't the case; he recognizes Errol Flynn's signature. He also knows that the Faragos are incapable of forgery not so much from a moral position but as two persons with just about enough technical skill to work a can opener. He stakes his professional reputation on it being the real thing. All the time Joey and his parents lived on the fifth floor, the Faragos had this poster stashed in their tiny, smelly, messy apartment, hidden away in a closet, waiting for the day when someone like Bill Hunt would come around with a lot of money and offer to buy it. According to Hunt, the Faragos had done odd jobs for the actor. Joey knows this information. The mention of their name brings back the reek of spoiled food, cigarette smoke, stale beer and heavy, motionless air.

What he doesn't know about the Faragos comes from the swine-like lips of Bill Hunt: A couple of days before Errol Flynn's death, Errol had gone down to the Faragos's apartment with a number of posters and asked them to hold on to them for safe keeping, including the one intended for Fidel Castro.

"The old man Faragos said that Errol Flynn made him swear that Fidel would get the poster, should anything happen to him," says Bill Hunt, his pig eyes the size of pinholes. "It seems Flynn had a *premonition* about his heart attack. Otherwise why give the poster to the Faragos?"

Where in the hell does someone like Bill Hunt pick up a ten-dollar word like premonition? His brain is incapable of remembering three syllables. Like his name, Bill Hunt is definitely a one-syllable man.

Joey watches as he picks up the photo and has it half stuck in his pocket before some idea misfires in his brain and he changes his mind and stuffs it in Joey's pocket instead. "The Faragos still remember Joey Balfour. They speak well of you by the way." Bill's smile has a cruel hint of repressed violence.

"They didn't think much of Bogart," says Joey. "Errol Flynn could play a tough guy but you knew inside he wasn't tough. He had a certain smile that lit up the screen. You couldn't say that about Bogart. He promised violence when he smiled. Flynn smiled and women got weak in the knees. The Faragos thought Flynn was superior to Bogart. He'd seen bullets fly in real life."

He's investing more time in Bill Hunt than he's worth. Something nags at Joey. Call it boyhood memories of the Faragos. Hunt's talked with them; he's been in their apartment, sat in the chair Joey remembers. There's a connection from his past running straight through Hunt.

"So they told me."

Joey leans against the pool table and stares over towards the bar. In the mirror behind the bar, flashes of traffic from the street streak past. He wishes Bill Hunt would fall under a bus. He knows people who could help Bill Hunt find a bus to fall under. What's his game? What motive brings Hunt all the way to Bangkok with *that* poster? Does Bill Hunt know that Howard Boggy is sitting in his penthouse along with Joey's mother? The same Howard Boggy who is traveling on a forged New Zealand passport under the name of Gunnar Brogge. Only in *Edge of Darkness* Gunnar didn't walk around Norway with one arm in a sling. Like the cop in Las Vegas observed, as Joey was leaving the interrogation room with his lawyer, "There's something spooky about the way crime and violence whisper a quiet *hello* before moving to rip through your life, and we get the call to go in and clean up the mess. Most of the time we find guys like you hanging in pieces from the shower rod. A perfect crime leaves no trail, no prints or mark. On the surface no crime has been committed. It is an event within nature and the law. That's what makes it perfect. That doesn't mean people don't know who did it. They just don't wanna talk about it. But one day when the whisper becomes a shout, it is too late; there is no time to escape the evil as it slowly saws through their body and soul."

Joey Balfour never liked cops who talked too much. This one had a sharp edge like an old-fashioned straight-edged razor. Hunt is making him see the glint of light reflected from that blade and he doesn't like what he sees.

As far as Joey is aware there is no such poster. If such a poster had existed Howard Boggy would have mentioned it, found it, and put it up for sale. He'd have been flooding Joey's mailbox with offers to sell it. Over the past four years, Boggy had been preoccupied with Errol Flynn movie posters. He knew the history of every Errol Flynn movie and the whereabouts of every original poster, and had a database with all the major collectors and collections. Nothing about Errol Flynn could escape his obsessive desire to gather all information about the actor, his love life, his movies and the posters.

Through a series of emails, Boggy established that his all-time favorite movie had Errol Flynn in the lead as Fletcher Christian in the 1933 *In the Wake of the Bounty*. Howard Boggy runs to the hills with cat blood smeared on his hands. An agency dispatches people who follow in hot pursuit. Joey doesn't immediately see how to draw a connection between these facts. Maybe Howard Boggy hasn't told him everything. Withheld information had the same effect as misinformation—it changed the odds. Fletcher Christian and Fidel Castro made strange bedfellows. One inhabited Pitcairn Island and the other Cuba. Both were island men and both were revolutionaries.

Both men found that legendary tales had overshadowed their real lives. Action heroes are all legend. These were real, flawed lives smoothed out and polished up for resale.

Bill Hunt is holding some good cards after all; the old casino security chief has found something worth further inspection. Marty runs the quality control. If he says it's real, then that is good enough to broker a trade.

Boggy Goes Undercover as a Norwegian Fisherman

Boggy wakes up in a strange bed, a strange city, rubs his eyes and opens the blinds and looks out from the seventeenth floor. He carefully puts his bandaged arm in the sling before he goes to the sliding glass door, which leads onto a balcony; he slides the door open and the rush of thick, hot air sucks his lungs into the back of his mouth. He quickly closes the sliding door, pushes his nose against the glass and looks down. He has no real idea where he is and as he pads down the hallway he hears nothing. It is too quiet and he glances at his watch. It is six thirty in the morning. No one else is up, he tells himself. He goes into the kitchen, opens the fridge and drinks half a liter of orange juice from the carton, burps, puts the empty carton back into the fridge, opens the lid of a long-shaped piece of Tupperware with his teeth and sticks his nose inside until the whiff of durian makes him gag. He seals the lid, shaking his head, his tongue lolling like a panting dog. "That stuff is rotten," he says to himself. He wants to puke as he slides the Tupperware into the garbage under the sink.

The condo is full of unexpected booby traps. Under clear wrap he finds a plate of sliced watermelon and eats until the plate is clean. Jell appears in a new green maid's uniform with the words Feng Shui Flower Shop stitched over the pocket. She's been watching him from around the corner. She flashes a ferret-like smile as if to say "I've caught you in the act. I found you licking a plate like a dog." But she says nothing, takes the plate and washes it in the sink. Next she reaches under the sink and takes out the Tupperware, empties the contents and makes certain Boggy sees her washing it, too.

It is a small defeat. Boggy retreats to his room and puts on the same clothes that he had worn for twenty-three hours (door-to-door) on his journey. The clothes smell musty with damp sweat but nothing like the durian he accidentally stumbled upon in the fridge. He creeps out of the condo, passes Jell in the hallway, ignores her, and then rides the elevator down to the ground floor. Walking out onto the street, he stops and looks back at Joey's building. It is pyramid shaped. Boggy feels he recognizes the building; he pulls out his wallet and removes a one-dollar bill. He turns it over and looks at the pyramid on the back, and then up at Joey's building. Joey's condo is below the eye level on the pyramid. Why isn't he surprised that Joey Balfour lives in a building that is an exact replica of the dollar-bill pyramid? The Latin over the pyramid on the bill—*Annuit Coeptis*—is from Virgil and translates as "providence has favored our undertaking." And at the base of the dollar-bill pyramid it reads *Novus Ordo Seclorum*—more Latin from Virgil—meaning, "the beginning of a new era." Boggy wonders if the gambler from Vancouver has any idea what this building means. Providence has shone on Joey. He has his own TV show. He has the best Errol Flynn original poster collection in the world. Why wouldn't he live in a building from the American one-dollar bill?

One of Boggy's hobbies is to search the Internet for information about hiding places, disguises, safe houses, black-bag operation field manuals, trailing people, losing people who trail you, and disappearing. He remembers that the first thing you do when on the run is to secure your hiding place. How do you do that? The professionals recommend you walk the perimeter of the building you are using. Memorize all the access points in and out of the building. Plan your escape before you need to know where to run with first, second, and third options. Those are the main points Boggy has put to memory. The Internet escape manual stuff, however, neglects a few minor practical points: the searing heat of the tropics multiplied tenfold by a city covered in concrete and steel, the fences and vendor stalls, garbage and rats, howling dogs, and a fog of pollution, not to mention the gated parking lot and underground passageways. Real life is all too confusing. It dawns on Boggy that there are many ways to get in and out of Joey's dollar-bill pyramid. Gunnar Brogge, played by Errol Flynn in *Edge of Darkness,* teaches him the art of the disguise.

With all those Nazis buzzing around Flynn found an easy way to blend in. If the building has a zillion exits and entrances, then fall back on disguise. Blend in. As he seems to be the only one leaving a trail of sweat, he isn't going to be difficult to track.

Frustrated and exhausted, and once again hungry, Boggy strolls in his lopping ape-like walk down a side lane and, even this early in the morning, street vendors are setting up shop, putting out their wares, tables and plastic chairs, cooking food, chattering among themselves in a strange language. *Joey lives inside a milk and honey vat of money*, Boggy thinks to himself and feels slightly upset that over the years he has sold posters to him at too cheap a price. *He never drowns; he rarely looks over the top. He doesn't have to.* The idea puts Boggy in a rotten mood of self-loathing. He glances back at the pyramid as if afraid his jet-lagged mind is playing tricks and to see if he's being followed by one of those dreadful private investigator types in dark glasses with a wire sticking out of his ear. In a street vendor's tray, Boggy looks for a pair of sunglasses. Black shades look suitable for Gunnar Brogge, he tells himself. Shades help a man blend in. It takes the edge off his heavily bandaged arm hanging in a sling. He finds a table covered with all kinds of sunglasses and a mirror and chooses a pair. The vendor punches a number into a cheap calculator.

"Three hundred dollars for these, you must be fucking nuts," says Boggy.

He is unaware that the vendor wants three hundred Thai baht, which comes to about eight dollars. Boggy shows him a dollar bill from his wallet. The vendor waves his hands like a puppet whose puppet master is suddenly slipping into an epileptic seizure. Boggy tries speaking to him in dollar-bill-type Latin and gets no response. He tries French and Spanish and some German. Nothing in his language bag is working.

A Thai man with two plastic bags filled with rice and chicken stops beside Boggy and says, "This man is mute. He uses sign language. Can I help you?"

The interruption startles Boggy who starts to back away until he sees this kindly, thin man doesn't look anything like a secret agent or any other type of agent. "He wants three hundred dollars for a pair of sunglasses. He might be mute but he's not dumb."

The Thai explains that he is asking for about eight dollars but will likely take six dollars; in Thailand, he goes on, vendors expect everyone to bargain on a price. Boggy takes a five-dollar bill and puts it with the one-dollar bill and offers them to the vendor who stares at the money. The Thai, who wears an old shirt with the sleeves rolled up and baggy bags and sandals without shoes, interprets for Boggy and after the vendor is convinced the money converted into Thai baht is the usual local price, he takes the cash, grins and hands the sunglasses to Boggy who slips them on.

"My name's Howard. I mean Gunnar." He's now wearing a pair of cheap plastic wrap-around sunglasses.

"Mine is Daeng. It is a nickname and means red. Are you Norwegian?"

"I come from a small fishing village." He tries using the accent Errol Flynn had used in the movie.

Daeng stares at him for a moment. "I sometimes bring fish for the cats."

They walk together for a little distance and Daeng stops, leans down, unfolds a sheet from a newspaper and scoops out two cups of rice and chicken. A moment later three cats creep forward, watchful, one foot cautiously in front of the other, until they set on the food as hungry as wolves. Boggy kneels down beside Daeng, watching the cats with ribcages showing through their mangy fur.

"Are these your cats?"

Daeng strokes the back of one of the cats. "They are ownerless cats."

"Why do you feed them?"

"It is a way to make merit."

Boggy's bushy red beard has flecks of watermelon and several black watermelon seeds embedded in it like war journalists, evidence of his recent breakfast. He's wearing black shorts with his stubby, hairless, ivory-white legs disappearing into a pair of sandals and a T-shirt with a tiger's head on the front.

"Are you a boy scout leader?"

"You are new to Thailand, aren't you?" Daeng looks at his arm in the sling.

"Why do you say that?"

"Is your arm all right?"

Boggy takes this as a trick question. The men looking for him must know of his injury.

"It's from a fishing-boat accident," he says.

Daeng smiles. "I see. You see, I am making merit because that is what all Buddhists should do and if they make enough merit then they are not reborn again."

"Then what happens?"

"They are released from the cycle and find genuine harmony and peace."

Boggy tries to digest the meaning of Daeng's words. He follows the Thai on his neighborhood tour of feeding stray cats. "I had two cats at home," says Boggy who suddenly feels homesick. "One was named Caesar and the other is Octavian. I named them both after Roman generals. But Caesar is dead."

"I am sorry to hear that," says Daeng. He pauses as he looks up from the cats. "Is that common for Norwegian fishermen to name cats after Roman generals?"

Boggy blushes beneath his wrap-arounds. Errol Flynn as Gunnar Brogge would never have made such a cock-up and he wonders if his cover is now blown and he must either flee or strangle the interloping feeder of stray cats. "In my village nothing is as it seems," says Boggy. He knows that is from a different movie, like *The Village of the Damned*, but it is the first thing that pops into his head.

Daeng kneels beside one of the strays, one with a nasty, open wound festering on its leg. "Then you've come to the right place."

"What do you mean?"

"You'll feel right at home in Bangkok, Gunnar. I must go."

As Daeng hurries down the pavement Boggy calls after him, "Will you be here tomorrow?"

"I come every day to feed the cats. It is my duty."

After the Thai man disappears into the crowd, Boggy breathes a sigh of relief. He likes a man who thinks cats are his way to salvation. In a time of crisis, when all the avenues appear blocked and going forward or backward seems equally dangerous, that is the time one needs to have the comfort of a stranger who loves cats. Someone who doesn't ask a lot of embarrassing questions.

The Sweet Perfume of Money and Power

Joey pulls his thick wad of cash from his pocket, peels off a crisp thousand-baht note, and, smiling, folds it into his hand. "We need my usual table. There are seven of us tonight. We want to be close to the band."

"Yes, Khun Joey. Of course, Khun Joey. That is no problem, Khun Joey." The host is dressed in a dinner jacket and has the grave, kind and comforting face of an undertaker helping the bereaved choose an appropriate coffin. The host's white teeth reflect off Joey's shoe tips; the Thai barks at a couple of the women who immediately ascend the stairs. The moment he thinks Joey's not looking, his face looks more like that of the foreman of a crew of slaves hauling ten-ton stones across a desert to build a pyramid.

The rest of Joey's party sweeps into the entrance behind him. In his formal white shirt and wearing the same gold cufflinks he wore in the Stardust ballroom twenty years ago—the letters J.B. are raised in small diamonds—Joey's black suspenders with calf-leather supports disappear inside his black evening trousers. His black patent-leather shoes, so bright and shiny like dual mirrors, bend and twist the overhead light from the large chandeliers. In these clothes he's the definition of action and stardom. The host continues to bow and *wai* Joey. The manager stands on the red-carpeted stairs, smiling with his arms out to embrace him.

"Joey, we miss you too much. Why don't we see more of you? Where are you hiding? You see over there, Feng Shui Flower Shop. And there. And there." He points to flower displays around the large ballroom.

For an instant it is as if Joey Balfour has never left Las Vegas. Bangkok can be what you want it to be if you have enough money. Like all gamblers who drift into and out of the city, he loves the feel of the outrageous, over-the-top luxury. It knows no bounds. It fights but never quite escapes the gravity of full-blown, unashamed vulgarity.

The manager takes a long, slightly disapproving look at the *katoey* next to Marty. Though she is wearing one of Sky's ball gowns, Dow—who insists that Marty and everyone else call her Star—appears insecure, shuffles her feet, and wrings her hands together in an uneasy fashion. She feels out of place. She looks like the showgirl on Joey's old TV show. All that is missing is the tray with the ice-cold martini. Marty tries to make small talk and leads her over to a large, roaring bronze lion. "It's a Las Vegas kind of place," he explains to her. She's heard of Las Vegas.

The foyer is lined with bronze lions, a bronze swan in the middle of a fountain, and red velvet curtains. The decoration is ornately carved rosewood or teak. Half a dozen young women (pulled from the fish-bowl viewing area), in ball gowns much like the one worn by Star, form an honor guard. The yings are beautiful enough to be high-fashion models with their perfect makeup, two-hundred-baht hairdos, and cream-colored skin, the type that makes the Chinese and Japanese men pant like Labrador retrievers watching a bouncing ball. They have bodies that big money lines up to buy. The Saks Fifth Avenue private members' counter quality. As if creating a necklace of flawless five-carat diamonds, the manager knows never to put in this greeting line-up any ying who does not have class, charm, and beauty. Joey inspects them in the way a foreign leader should inspect, but never does, the honor guard sent to meet his plane. None of them look distracted. Expectant and professional, their duty is to await the command to turn up the pilot light until the kettle reaches boiling. They stand around smiling in their gowns waiting to get fucked for money; there are no dreams attached to what they do.

Sky has phoned ahead to make certain everything is the way Joey likes it.

Both Ped and Sky know the private club manager and staff. They have his private cell phone number. The club is a good customer of the shop. Sky, in the old days, before Joey hired her, worked as a top DJ at the disco behind the club. Everyone still remembers Sky, although it has been three years since she last worked at the disco.

The last person in the entourage is Sully, an American from upstate New York, who looks like he has just come off a crowded Southern Jersey beach: short-sleeved cotton shirt and department-store sale trousers. Joey reeks of money and Sully carries the scent of someone who's getting by on a tight budget.

Joey, freshly showered, hair parted, eyes bright, leads the way, slowly climbing up the stairs, examining each of the yings in ball gowns, who are bowing their heads and *waiing* him, giving each of them two hundred baht. When he's eighty years old he intends to be doing do this ritual. It is a slap in the face of death to give money to smiling, hungry, greedy, beautiful women. Sky is on one arm and Ped on the other and the manager is now at the top of the stairs, smiling, looking down at this procession as the pinnacle of his evening. The whole purpose of the exercise has been to bring Sully, an old-time Vegas gambler, into Joey's world, as a taste of the old times when it seems even Sully was a winner. Over the years, Joey's run into Sully, usually in a retail, mugs' bar in Soi Cowboy, drinking a rum and Coke and watching a football match on the bar television. Years before, Eric Sullivan—who everyone called "Sully"—had an apartment across the hallway from Eddie the Knife and, once or twice, Sully would go with them to what Eddie the Knife called the best Chinese restaurant in the world.

Sully lives in Bangkok now in a one-room apartment that Joey visualizes as a replica of the one he had in Las Vegas, and he's married to a bar ying from Surin province near the Cambodian border. In all the years that Joey's lived in Bangkok, this is the first time that he's invited Sully to his club. Joey is a star from the old days. Sully never amounted to much. Las Vegas was full of guys like Sully who had youthful dreams long after middle age set in, rolling along, sure that their day was just around the corner. The ritual greeting is not lost on Sully who knows the tribal ways of the Las Vegas crowd. Sully is surprised that Joey invites him out and is wise enough to know there must be a good reason. With Joey Balfour, ex-Las Vegas, high roller, TV personality, and odds maker par excellence, there's always a reason; and Sully figures he's being romanced. All professionals know the script: the mug is there to be romanced, made to feel safe, wanted, admired, respected and then relieved of his earthly goods. Until he walks out of the room wearing nothing but his smile. It is the way the system works.

The table is covered in white linen and the singer who fronts a Filipino band blows Joey a kiss. The head waiter and two assistant waiters seat the ladies and one wannabe lady. Candles are lit. Sully sits on Joey's left. A silver bucket filled with ice arrives with a bottle of champagne. The head waiter pulls up the silver wrapping like he's removing a condom and pops the cork. Joey's glass is filled first. He drinks, wrinkles his nose, and finally nods as everyone who has been holding their breath sighs, blowing out two of six candles. Joey judges a two-candle anxiety by staff as a success. The other glasses are filled and Joey rises. "I'd like to make a toast."

The others rise to their feet.

"To my good friend, Sully. May your luck flower and may each new bloom bring riches and happiness, and may you walk only on rose petals along a path leading to a long, happy life."

Marty is wondering if that comes from an Errol Flynn movie or if Joey heard it from one of his high-rolling friends, or made it up on the spot. He knows Joey better than anyone but is never certain of the source of his material; though he is certain he never is without a graceful, elegant line. Everyone on the TV show said that Joey Balfour was the best.

Sully closes his eyes and he's in the Stardust. He remembers the night that he was so far back in the showroom that the third chef was making salads at the far end of his table. He catches a glimpse of Joey sitting at one of the front-row tables with a tall blonde in a low-cut dress. Wayne Newton—Mr. Las Vegas—microphone in hand, is singing and looking straight at Joey, walking slowly toward his table. Newton, with his hair coifed and wearing an Errol Flynn mustache, goes down the stairs and walks straight to Joey's table and reaches out and shakes Joey's hand then leans over and kisses the classy six-foot blonde on the cheek. The showroom spotlight lingers for a moment. A thousand people erupt into applause. They love Joey Balfour. It is surreal, dream-like as Joey Balfour waves like a heavyweight boxer dancing around the ring and the crowd loves him. They love anyone in the front row. Perfumed with money and power, the front row in Las Vegas always smells and looks good.

A private nightclub connected to a disco off Sukhumvit Road is a long way from Las Vegas, but, for Sully, it is as if that night at the Stardust is happening again—only this time he's at the ringside table; he's seated next to Joey and the limelight spreads across the entire table. The singer comes down to sing for Joey. He has that much power, and everyone in the room knows it. Joey enjoys all the benefits of being a celebrity with none of the drawbacks. No photographers lying in ambush or tabloids printing lies to destroy his personal life or strangers stopping him on the street for loans, autographs, or simply to touch the sleeve of fame. *For guys like Joey Balfour, it is Christmas every night of the year,* thinks Sully.

After the singer goes back to the stage, Joey turns to Sully.

"It's not Vegas."

"You should know, Joey," said Sully.

Joey's crooked smile hangs like a glider about to hit a cliff. "Sully, I've always liked you."

Sully nods. *Sure, you do,* he thinks. "What can I do for you?"

In Las Vegas, it was always a question of how much a player needed before the house gave him a complimentary room and drinks. It was called show money. Sully is no fool, he knows the score, that he never had any real show money. What he had in his pocket was more like what Granny carried in her purse after she cashed her social security check. Anyone who couldn't show seventy-five dollars was kicked off the free bus to Atlantic City. Gambling was a business. The big casinos handed out tickets to all the big shows. Where a man sat said who he was in the language of a casino showroom. All the mugs and small-timers got stuck in the back of the room. The free seats were reserved for players who showed the big money. The people who actually shelled out money for their seats got the bad tables. They sat down all confused trying to figure out why their money got them such crappy tables. They had no idea how the system worked. Tom Jones or Wayne Newton didn't necessarily recognize the faces on the equivalent of the fifty-yard line in the main showroom, but when they went out into the audience and smiled at the women sitting at those tables, and shook hands with the men, the singers knew they were close to money. The real money was around those tables. Free tables. The real money is next to Sully at this table.

"Sully, I'd consider it a personal favor if you would help me find Jim Pauley."

Sully's jaw drops far enough to show the gold crowns on the back molars. "The guy who blew off the casino with . . . what was it? A half a million in cash and chips? It was hardly worth his risk and effort. He must've been stupid."

"That's the guy."

"That was years ago. The casino must have written that off last century."

"The casino can write off bad debts but the people directly involved still wonder what happened to Pauley and that money."

"I can understand that. But why ask me? I never knew the guy in Las Vegas. I saw him once or twice, yeah. I knew him to see him. That was a lifetime ago. I wouldn't know him today if he were sitting at the next table."

Half a dozen Hong Kong Chinese men in dark suits and ties maul some yings in ball gowns. Unlike Las Vegas, money here buys the good seats. The Chinese are having a great time grabbing ass, their barking laughter rising over the music as they chase the yings in ball gowns around.

If the object is to find a farang in Thailand—especially one who doesn't want to be found—start by looking for his woman, do a background check on her, and that starts with finding another ying from the same village. It is the ying convoy—a conga line of yings—that will take you to him.

"A couple of years ago, I heard you were at Pauley's wedding."

"Christ, that was five years ago," says Sully. "I wasn't invited. I happened to be in the village the day of the wedding. His wife and my wife are from the same village in Surin. Pauley nearly had a heart attack when he saw me. He pretended not to remember me and I pretended not to remember him. I didn't see another farang at the ceremony."

Sully knows one of his Saturday-night poker club members must have said something to Joey, who had filtered away that piece of information for a rainy day. Whatever clouds were gathering over Joey's head Sully can't say, but he knows one thing: Joey Balfour must be hearing claps of thunder in his ears to press Sully on a five-year-old wedding.

"Tell me about the wedding."

"It was an upcountry wedding."

"Come on, Sully. You can do better than that."

Joey's right, thinks Sully. The man has good instincts. Always had, and that explains why someone from the casino is leaning on him.

"It was an upcountry wedding. A happy day for the family. They had scored a farang. So they celebrated like it was an end-zone victory dance." Pauley's upcountry wedding left an image branded in Sully's consciousness forever, a vibrant and hallucinatory image: the bride's aged father in a freshly washed blue shirt and matching trousers dancing barefoot on the damp, cracked earth. Dogs and chickens scattered as he danced in front of all the relatives in a circle near his wooden house on stilts. Pauley's father-in-law had two teeth left on his uppers and one sticking up at an angle from the bottom. On his head, tilted to the side, was a Rastafarian wig—a toothless Bob Marley, his skinny arms and legs a blur of motion. Sweat rolling down his chin, the man laughed until the tears started. His eyes on fire, his mouth open, breathing hard, guttural and raspy, like a dying man in the final throttle before pushing off to the next life. His skin was leathery from the sun and elements; his face frosted with lines and craters, and cheap whiskey and long-term worries, softened as he waved at his daughter. This was, he said, the happiest day of his life. He wanted to die this day because whatever came next would be something less: a smaller, and a narrow, shallow life. He didn't know his son-in-law was a hunted man.

"Pauley had a triple by-pass operation."

"I didn't know that," says Sully.

"That's not an easy thing to go through alone, Sully. You'd need someone to look after you. A caring *Isan* wife for a start. That's what I am saying. Your wife is from the same village as Pauley's wife."

"I know who Pauley's wife is. There's no need to get my wife involved."

"You can reach his wife?"

"If I have to."

"I am asking for a little help here, Sully. Nothing you can't live with. Nothing that is going to put you in an awkward position."

"I can give you an address in Surin."

Joey smiles. "A cell phone number, Sully. She will have one. Can you see I get her number?"

"No problem, Joey. Whatever. But I don't think it's going to be all that useful."

"What are you saying?"

"Pauley's wise. If he feels someone from the casino is in town, he'd cut his wife loose. He'd go to ground. That's what he did before. They didn't find him. I don't think it would be any different this time."

"The yings are wise as well. She knows where her boy would run. Just like your wife would know how to track you down, Sully. She'd find you no matter where you tried to hide."

Pauley knows this, they both are thinking. Pauley would cut his wife loose. Or maybe he would cut her loose to protect himself. "My wife and Pauley's wife go to the same witchdoctor," says Sully.

"Shamans, witchdoctors, are a national sport," says Joey.

"After Pauley's wife got out of jail on a gambling charge, she saw the witchdoctor. My wife says she asked the witchdoctor for the voodoo needed to get him back."

Ped and Sky are out on the dance floor slow dancing. Marty and Star are holding hands under the table and whispering. Joey watches Ped and Sky dance. Something is happening to Marty that he's not seen before. He turns around and stares in disbelief as Sully's opening up as the band plays "Feelings".

"Pauley's wife did time for a gambling rap? That's rich," says Joey. "How'd she manage to do that?"

"Running numbers in the wrong neighborhood."

Joey nods, "She didn't do her homework. How did Pauley ever get married to someone that sloppy?"

"Gambling is like wrestling a drunken alligator. If it is a baby alligator, then you got a good chance of winning. If it is a big, world-class gator, then the moment your concentration goes you lose your balls," says Sully. He's been in the health food business for a couple of years but still makes ends meet by playing with locals who think they know the game. He knows his level, Sully does.

A bottom feeder stays where the leftovers are easy to find. Playing poker with even second-tier Las Vegas players and Sully would be sweating to break even. Bump up a level or two, he loses his ass; the competition gets tougher and the chances of getting wiped out greater. Staying small time is the best option for a guy like Sully. *He's happy enough to live on the scraps*, thinks Joey. People who know their place, know their level, stay happy and get on with their lives. Those who try and jump the next level, like Sully says, get their balls eaten. Pauley made a big jump and he's still watching every shadow waiting for the day that gator goes for him.

"Gators is a good way of putting it, Sully. But I can't relate to it. What I can relate to are cats. I love cats. And I'll tell you why: Cats are a gambler's animal of choice. Cats give reasonable odds of doing or not doing something. It's something you can handicap. Dog behavior is too predictable. You never get good odds for betting on dog behavior. Dogs are love sluts, food sluts, cuddle sluts. You know what they will do. But cats, unless starving, circle and survey. Love, food, and cuddling needs are unpredictable. Pauley's a cat, Sully. And I want to find what tree he's climbed to hide in."

Caesar Dies and
Boggy Escapes to Canada

Octavian vomited half a can of tuna. A rusty gray sludge with flecks of blood covered the unwashed dishes on the kitchen table. He didn't know that Octavian was sick. Not right away. Boggy had been working behind his computer in the bedroom; he'd logged into a chat room under an alias, this chat room was devoted to people seeking to expand civil liberties for tribal minorities in the South Pacific. Steam rose from his head as he corresponded with a woman in New Zealand about the trials going on in Pitcairn Island where the mayor, postal inspector and four or five others were on trial for various sexual offences going back forty years. Boggy was multi-tasking. Living alone in the apartment in rural Maine gave him hours and hours for his various activities. When Octavian puked in the kitchen, Boggy was in his eighteenth non-stop hour of work: he was chatting, he was buying e-gold for one of his accounts, bidding for an apple orchard in Penang and negotiating with Joey Balfour in Bangkok for the sale of an Errol Flynn poster. He planned to sell the poster and invest the proceeds in the Penang apple orchard, mortgage the orchard to a customer in Qatar (where they were crazy about apples) and buy more e-gold. He had a tentative deal with a graphic artist in Russia to joint venture a comic-book series. The hero was a cat-loving bearded genius unraveling secrets and conspiracies of evil corporate plutocrats seeking to take over the world.

Only Joey Balfour was balking at paying what Boggy even though he knew in his heart of hearts this was a giveaway price. Joey knew the real value of the original Errol Flynn movie poster;

he was, after all, the most important collector of Errol Flynn posters in the world. When a man has a true passion, there was a duty to explore what trip wires activated such a response. He had files on Errol Flynn—all the Freedom of Information Act stuff on Errol Flynn, three biographies, and most of the actor's films. It was useful in his arguments with the thick-headed, unreasonable woman who attacked him in his role as chairman of the International Civil Liberties for Tribal Peoples in the South Pacific (ICLTPSP or, as the chat room monkeys called it, ICETITS) for defending this bunch of child molesters and rapists. This was the state of Boggy's mind and business activity at the time of Octavian's food poisoning attack.

It was three in the morning—a prime time to be in contact with the rest of the world if you live in rural Maine. Boggy slumped back in his chair, lit a cigarette, and sucked on the last piece of ice floating on the top of his sixty-four-ounce plastic bucket of Coke. He sipped the Coke through a straw, long, sucking sips followed by lip smacking and some owl-like hoots. His mind was on the apple orchard. It was easy to ignore the snow outside his window. At first, he didn't hear Octavian down the hall in the kitchen. It was usually very quiet that time of night. The mewing only gradually entered his consciousness. He wrinkled his nose and took the straw into his mouth and took another pull from the Coke.

He typed a reply to the woman who called herself H24Me: "The British have no legal jurisdiction over Pitcairn. Show me any international law that allows them to try them? Besides, show me what the British have ever done for those people? They have their own customs. They've done nothing but ignore Pitcairn Island. Except now they want to build a prison. Give me a break. Not a school or a hospital or a library but a FUCKING prison. How sick is that?"

"You are disgusting, insensitive and obviously very fucked up. You have no sympathy for the poor girls, who were used, raped, controlled, raped again and again. They were children, only twelve years old, when they were forced to have sex. That's criminal. They deserve more than time in prison. They should cut off their filthy dicks and feed them to the seals and sharks. That's what I think, asshole. And I wish I'd never helped you with that passport, dickhead."

He heard the faint sound of Octavian moaning. This wasn't the noise the cat made when it wanted to go outside. It wasn't the sound of Octavian wanting to fuck.

"My cat's sick," he wrote. "Got to go."

"Sure, you're losing the argument and now your cat's sick. And you have to go. How pathetic. How typically male, running away when he's beaten but can't admit he's WRONG."

Boggy didn't bother to answer. In any event, before she logged off, H24Me gave him one of her special emoticons: a raised, long, shapely, feminine middle finger with a highly polished red fingernail. It slowly rose like a monster from a giant cracked egg nestled in a cool, foggy river bottom. The bitch had made it herself, he thought. Boggy had been willing to offer her some shares in the Philippine chicken processing plant ten clicks out of Angeles City and a lifetime free subscription to the new comic books, but now he was angry. H24Me was an asshole. He moved her email address into his blacklist file. Then he got up from his computer, lit another cigarette and went into the kitchen for more ice. Octavian wasn't a complainer. As he walked down the hall, he heard the cat moaning and rushed into the kitchen to find Octavian sprawled out on his chair, panting, eyes rolling into the top of its head. He inspected the vomit and the blood drained from his face. Octavian had never coughed up blood.

The vet lived four miles away on the edge of town. No doubt he was sound asleep. Boggy gently wrapped Octavian in a blanket and rushed outside and started his motorcycle. He wasn't thinking straight at this point. He trundled through the snow, the wind biting on his face. Turning on the headlamp, there was nothing before him but white. He cradled the basket with the cat inside between his legs and set off. Halfway to the vet's house, Boggy reached for his cell phone. He'd left it in the kitchen. An investor—someone from Boston, so he said—had made an appointment for a telephone conference at four a.m. to discuss a fishing boat in Halifax that was going cheap. He had been willing to trade the fishing boat for an old letter in which J. Edgar Hoover had said some mean, nasty things about Errol Flynn. Boggy knew the letter had value. He'd thought of selling it to Joey Balfour but the idea of trading it for a fishing boat had the possibility of quick profits, which could be rolled over into other ventures.

Boggy made a hard decision. He had reached a crossroads, one of those defining moments of life. What would he choose to live with? Octavian dying for lack of medical care or missing out on the possibility to buy a thirty-five-foot fishing boat at a fire sale price. He took a deep breath. As chairman of ICETITS he knew that the value of all life (not just human life) was their guiding principle. He sucked in his breath, and chose to save his cat.

When the vet, with sleep-matted eyes, opened the door and stared at Boggy in the doorway, he shook his head, then sighed, nodded and let him in. Boggy stomped the snow off his boots and tried to yawn to thaw out his face. The vet sighed as he looked at the cat and then at Boggy and, without a word, Boggy followed him into a small surgery where he laid Octavian on the table. "Doc, Octavian's power vomited blood and tuna all over the kitchen," said Boggy.

"Let's have a look." The vet gently unwrapped the cat and inspected his eyes, tongue and stomach. He went to a cupboard and gathered a bottle of medicine and a needle. "This ought to help," he said.

"Is he going to live?"

"Howard, your cat is going to be all right. But feeding him spoiled tuna isn't the best thing. Be more careful in the future."

Boggy felt guilty. "I promise, doc."

The tuna had been out for a couple of days. Well, less than a week, he was sure. He'd forgotten the tin only to discover it on top of the fridge. It looked okay. Octavian could have chosen not to eat the tuna. Cats are smart. They normally don't eat bad food. The vet agreed that Octavian must have been very hungry. Boggy checked his watch. He figured that with a little bit of luck he could get back home in time for the phone call from Boston. The vet waived off his fee and showed Boggy to the door. Getting the semi-knocked-out Octavian squared away on the motorcycle wasted a few minutes. Once he had the groggy cat balanced in the basket, he set off for home in the chilly stillness and total darkness of four in the morning.

Boggy switched off the ignition and gently lifted Octavian off the motorcycle. Two steps in the snow from the bike, an explosion ignited a fireball, illuminating the gentle mounds of snow as far as the eye could see. This brilliant flash of light arrived with a loud, ear-splitting boom. Shards of glass from the windows blew into the alley. Boggy stood in front of his building holding his sick cat, the sound of glass breaking. He stared in a state of shock as tongues of flames shot from the windows of his apartment. He carefully lay Octavian on the ground before he ran up the two flights of stairs and unlocked the front door to his apartment. He scrambled around tiny fires and stuck his head around the corner and into the smoke-filled kitchen. He pulled a towel off a chair, went to the sink and poured water on it before putting it over his face. As Boggy turned around he saw the spot where he had left the cell phone on the counter. The wood was splintered and the cupboards above no longer recognizable with broken glass everywhere. His phone had evaporated into atoms.

He called for his other cat. "Caesar," he shouted into the flames. He knelt down by the table. Underneath it a bloodied cat sprawled out, eyes open, barely breathing. As he reached under, the flames scorched the flesh of his forearm and Boggy cried out. He crawled around, sobbing and reached under the table again until he got hold of Caesar and slowly pulled him out. With the towel wrapped around his face, he crawled out of the kitchen, stood up and ran into the bedroom, pulled out the bottom drawer of his dresser and, under stacks of old copies of the *Economist*, he grabbed his emergency backpack. Inside the backpack he had stashed: a backup hard disk drive, one thousand US dollars, and the same amount in Canadian dollars and Euro, along with New Zealand, Spanish, and Bolivian passports in various names, road maps, and three credit cards each with a different name. He unzipped the top pocket and stuffed the latest copy of the *Economist* just far enough for the title on the front cover to show. Boggy had found that tidbit of information on an obscure profiling site—no terrorist had ever been arrested with a copy of the *Economist*, and, indeed, no one but a dyed-in-the-wool supporter of the capitalistic system would ever pass through airport security with the *Economist*. Such people were automatically sent past the rectum scanning line. There was no time to backup the hard drive. It had last been backed up two days ago.

A distant wail of fire engines told Boggy he didn't have much time for anything. With the cats in the front basket, he climbed back on to his motorcycle and rode back to the vet's house. The vet looked at Caesar's wounds, "This is serious."

"Will he live?"

"I'll do my best," said the vet, who could see that Boggy, smelling of smoke and with a very nasty burn wound on his forearm, was having a bad night. "You better have that burn looked after. It might go septic. You could lose an arm."

"Doc, I'd appreciate it if you could patch me up."

"Are you in some kind of trouble, Howard?"

"I had a kitchen fire," Boggy said. After the vet treated the burn on Boggy's arm, he turned to work on Caesar. But he was too late to do anything. He pulled a white cloth over Caesar. "Sorry, Howard, there is nothing I can do."

Boggy looked down at Caesar's body, shaking his head, tears sliding down his cheeks. "Do you mind looking after Octavian for awhile?"

"It's not a problem," said the vet.

The vet stood on his front porch catching the first rays of morning light as Boggy set off on his motorcycle, backpack strapped to his back. All was a uniform white as he rode to one of the unofficial entry points along the Canadian border. The fishing-boat price did seem like too good a deal, he told himself. The man who killed Caesar would regret it. Boggy promised himself that much.

Ten Years after Errol Flynn's Death the Faragos Remember the Boss

Faragos was skin and bones, sunken eyes, dark hollows for cheeks, and thin, bony hands. He wore good clothes—Oxford blue shirt and beige trousers—but they hung on his body as on a scarecrow. He slowly opened the front door to the apartment. At first the door opened just a crack. When he saw it was Joey Balfour, he opened the door all the way.

"I brought you some snacks," said Joey. He had several boxes in a plastic bag.

He stuck his head out and looked up and down the hall before saying, "Then you had better come inside."

Mrs. Faragos sat on the sofa watching a daytime soap opera on the TV. She looked up, waved at Joey, and immediately returned to the tube. After a few moments Mr. Faragos came out of the kitchen with a tray with a separate plate for each of the pastries that Joey had given him. There was a strawberry jelly tart, another tart oozing cream from each end, a wedge of pie and an ample piece of Black Forest gateau. He set the tray on a table and pulled up a chair with his back to the television. He nodded for Joey to sit down.

"Aren't you going to offer him a glass of cold milk?" asked Mrs. Faragos.

"I was about to."

He shifted around in his chair and they exchanged one of those glances that married people exchange when they live together year after year, twenty-four hours a day: boredom, laced like a bun sprinkled with sesame seeds of regret, horror, and disgust.

"It's okay, Mrs. Faragos. I am really fine. I don't drink that much milk."

"What the boy wants is a beer," said Mr. Faragos.

Joey's crooked smile was shared between the couple. "I wouldn't say no."

"See, Mother, you don't offer a young man like Joey milk. It's an insult."

"Looking after your health is never an insult."

They seemed ancient to Joey but neither of them could have been more than thirty-five years old. After he returned with an open bottle of beer and a glass, Mr. Faragos sat down and poured the beer for Joey. "There's a certain way to pour a beer," he said. "Errol Flynn taught me how to pour it so you have just the right amount of head. He was particular about such details. Now have a look at that. See the head? That's what you call a perfect head."

"Did he ever talk about his films?"

"He told us stories you wouldn't believe," said Faragos.

Joey edged forward in his chair, leaning on his elbows. "What kind of stories? Did he ever kill anyone? Or punch someone out?"

Faragos raised his hand as if to silence Joey and then ate without greed; he chewed his food not so much with indifference but like someone working carefully, slowly, in a cottage-industry business. He left the impression that the process of eating was closer to painting flowers on a plate than to pure greedy pleasure. He rarely stopped to talk once he started on his mechanical feast, cleaning one plate, pushing it aside, and then cleaning the next plate until he was done. Once the pastries were gone, Joey looked at Faragos's gut; he would have expected to see a bulge. There was none. All that food entered his body showing no trace of where it had gone. Mrs. Faragos sat in front of a TV tray. A greasy paper plate held half a dozen party sausages; she watched the soap opera and nervously fiddled with the toothpicks stuck into the middle of each sausage. She worked the toothpicks like someone working in an acupuncture clinic. Her actions suggested she thought of the sausages as something other than a food source; she worked them as if to find the right spot, spinning, twisting, unlocking the bad energy. It was one of the longest waits of Joey's life; the Faragos, it seemed to him, were torturing him. One with her nose stuck in a soap opera, the other with his nose stuck into establishing the world record for the longest time to consume a few pastries, and all he had was a lousy beer when what he really wanted was Captain Morgan rum and Coke.

"Mother says she sometimes hears Errol climbing down the fire escape," said Faragos. He was one of those sad, childless men who called his wife *mother*. "It wasn't a fire drill. No, he was planning his escape."

Joey sipped his beer. He knew that what she heard wasn't Errol Flynn's ghost on the fire escape; she heard Joey climbing down the ladder right past their window. A few times a week he sneaked out and met up with Marty and, sometimes, with the draft dodger named Dan Harris. He closely examined Faragos's face to detect any sign of irony. There was none; the man seemed incapable of deception, just as he was incapable of gaining weight or eating at a normal speed.

"Errol was a boxer. In 1928 he boxed for England in the Olympics. He could have turned pro but he took up acting instead," Faragos said. "He loved adventures."

"What adventures?" asked Joey.

"He fought cannibals in the jungles of New Guinea. He killed a man. I think he killed several men. But what could he do? They wanted to eat him."

Joey was thinking if they ate at Faragos's rate they would still be chewing Errol Flynn's fat. Mrs. Faragos stopped playing with her food and switched off the TV. Her favorite program had ended. The talk about cannibals disturbed her. She frowned at her husband and he fell silent.

"We worked for him," said Mrs. Faragos.

"It was an informal arrangement."

"Don't you believe him," said Mrs. Faragos. "Errol certainly had *me* on his payroll." There was flash of electricity in her voice as she spoke. For the first time, she popped one of the tiny party sausages into her mouth and sucked the toothpick clean, then used it to pick her front teeth. It was hard to watch other people eat and clean their teeth at basically the same point in time.

Working for Errol Flynn had been the only employment for either of the Faragos. Like most eccentric people they had impossibly short résumés. They lived simply, avoided jobs, existed on government handouts, and waited for death without a lot of fuss. Even living with the smallest expectations required *some* money. Joey, who was still in high school, had never known adults who stayed home all day and did nothing and still had money for rent and party sausages and pastries.

"What kind of work did you do?" asked Joey.

Both Faragos snorted in a pig-like way. Mr. Faragos's nostrils flared and he coughed. For a moment it seemed like he was going to puke the plate of pastries. But he'd eaten them so slowly they were already digested by the time they hit his gut.

"We got his mail for him."

"And liquor."

Faragos nodded. "He drank a lot." He turned around. "I thought you were watching your TV program."

He blinked at the blank TV screen. Even he must have picked up his wife's interest had moved on.

"My program is over. Besides, even if it weren't, it doesn't mean I can't have a conversation," she said.

Faragos snorted again. How she could live with a man who snorted like that was beyond Joey. Why she didn't stick the toothpicks through his eyeballs and into his brain was a mystery.

"He would send my husband out with a list of books to buy. Errol was quite a reader. Dickens, Orwell, Kipling—oh, how he loved it when I read *Kim* to him."

"Before coming to Vancouver, he had been living and working in Cuba," said Faragos.

"He was a man about Havana. He knew the glamorous people. Everyone at the casinos knew Errol. He was Robin Hood and Don Juan and King Richard. Every role he played he kept on playing inside his head. Everyone loved Errol. No one could resist his charm. Don't believe what they say that he lost his looks. He matured. And was more handsome than before."

Errol Flynn's 1958 Film Venture: Havana, Cuba

With fins as big as a small great white shark's, the new freshly washed and polished white Caddy pulled to a stop in front of Hotel Nacional on Malecon. A teenager from Los Angeles sitting in the passenger's seat next to the actor, tapped on the dashboard of the car; she giggled as Errol Flynn finished humming the melody of the theme song to his film *The Adventures of Don Juan*. The locals called her Eldora, which means blonde in Spanish. Flynn liked the name and it stuck.

"You like that, Eldora?"

"I love that!" Like most teenagers she spoke in exclamation points with only the occasional comma or full stop thrown in. "Please sing it again. One more time."

He had finished a fifth of vodka by early afternoon. He could drive reasonably well after polishing off a fifth. His singing was a little rough but it didn't matter because he was in a good mood. Eldora opened another fifth of vodka. She kept his glass filled with ice and poured the vodka into it without his having to ask. An hour earlier he'd stripped and climbed into the bathtub, and bathed himself as Eldora had scrubbed his back with a large sponge and splashed water over his head. She'd washed and rinsed his hair. And she'd dried him off, kissing him as she patted all the way down to his ankles.

Also in the Caddy were Victor and an attractive young Cuban woman who was introduced to him as Garaitz, and she knew Fidel Castro from law school in Havana. They had been classmates. She also claimed to be a member of the July 26th Movement. Garaitz was a woman with lots of claims: those she made and those she said others made on her. She also said that the name Garaitz, which meant Victory, was her *nom de guerre*. Errol Flynn smiled, "I once had a *nom de guerre*."

"What was it?"

"Robin Hood," he laughed.

Garaitz didn't laugh or smile but looked straight ahead. She was still trying to get over her irritation at having been kept waiting. Victor and Garaitz had waited in the sitting room for nearly an hour while Errol Flynn finished his bath. The residual tension of the wait still burnt in the back of her throat as the Caddy pulled to the curbside next to the casino. Victor had whispered to her that Hollywood actors—the big names like Errol Flynn—marched to their own drummer and no one could ever get too upset because such people were by their nature unpredictable.

Garaitz had bristled. "It is rude. I have many things I must do." Her fiery eyes ached with hatred. "You must understand how dangerous it is for everyone."

"Please, wait a little longer. I promise he will be along." Those words echoed in her ear along with Errol Flynn's singing, laughter and dismissive humor about being Robin Hood when in fact there was a real revolution going on, and Garaitz had been sent to make arrangements for Errol Flynn to meet Fidel Castro.

Errol Flynn was unsteady on his feet as he climbed out of the car. Eldora covered her mouth with both hands and laughed. "You're a little smashed," she said.

"I am relaxed," he said. "Unless I am relaxed I can't concentrate on driving."

He stood on the pavement looking at the harbor, steadying himself with one hand on the Cadillac. His friend and business partner, Victor Phalen, got out of the back seat, where he had been sitting with Garaitz. Flynn's group stood together looking at the boats in the harbor.

"Nothing lasts forever," said Victor.

Garaitz frowned as she watched Errol Flynn's teenage companion, her lips red and her hair long and flowing, eyes bright and young, wrapping her arms around his waist and giving him a big squeeze.

"Errol will last forever, won't you, Daddy?"

"Baby, I am going to outlast the stars," said Errol Flynn, turning away from the harbor and walking towards the hotel entrance. "And I am gonna make you a star. You'll see." He glanced over at Garaitz. "I think I'll call the movie *Cuban Rebel Girls*. What do you think, Victor?"

Victor rolled his eyes. If his eyes had been dice he would have crapped out with two snake eyes. Victor was always just out of the money.

"Good evening, Mr. Flynn." The doorman held the door open. Errol Flynn pressed a five-dollar bill into his hand.

The others followed behind the actor. Managers, assistants, and staff smiled and called his name as he passed.

"Good evening, Mr. Flynn."

"Fine evening, Mr. Flynn."

"Let me know if you need anything, Mr. Flynn."

"The boss is waiting for you, Mr. Flynn."

One after another, a phalanx of hotel and casino functionaries lined up on either side like an honor guard. Eldora marched by his side, head high, clutching his hand, followed by Victor and the Cuban woman with the nickname of Victory who saw the sea of smiles open as Errol Flynn passed and evaporate as soon as they laid eyes on his entourage.

Errol Flynn walked straight to the blackjack table and sat down. He motioned for Garaitz to sit beside him. Eldora looked annoyed, a little hurt, and pouted as she stood behind him, resting her hands on his shoulders. "My mother's family comes in a straight line from an Englishman named Young. He was Midshipman on HMS *Bounty*. With Fletcher Christian they took over the *Bounty*. You see, mutiny and rebellion runs in my blood. I want to meet this Fidel Castro. Victor tells me he can arrange that." His turned his head and he nodded at Garaitz. "Victory here will help us find him." He intended it as a joke. But it was a poor joke, in bad taste and, given the circumstances of Cuba, extremely dangerous.

Batista's agents were everywhere. Errol Flynn's loud, half-drunken voice wasn't encouraging. Garaitz nervously looked around the table to see what eyes were on her. No one seemed to have paid any notice. The players were mainly foreigners concentrating on their cards. But the dealer and others floating past were Cubans. It was dangerous being with a drunk, she thought. People who worked in casinos were most likely Batista spies. Everyone knew that Batista and his wife sent around flunkies to collect a commission every day. Everyone watched everyone else in Cuba and no one could trust anyone who they suspected was on the other side.

"It's not safe to talk openly here," Garaitz whispered to him.

"Don't worry, sweetheart. You're with me. You are as safe as you'll ever be."

As he was about to continue, Frank Costello and two mobster friends came up behind Errol Flynn. "The floor manager told me you arrived," said Frank.

Errol Flynn laid down his cards and half rose from his chair. "Frank—God that's right, we have an appointment, or am I mistaken?"

"About ninety minutes ago."

"My agent in Hollywood wouldn't leave me alone. I told him, 'Sam, I've gotta go, you see, Frank Costello's waiting for me.'"

"What did he say?"

"What agents always say. It will only take a minute. But Paramount has this script and he said, 'Errol, you're perfect for it.' And I said, 'Sam, I've got an urgent meeting with Frank. Can't this wait?' And he said, 'Clark Cable wants the part. If you don't have time, that is.'"

Frank Costello cracked his knuckles and nodded. "Well, you're here now. That's the important thing. Come on back to my office where we can have some privacy."

Errol Flynn leaned over to Garaitz, "You better stay here. I'll be right back. Go ahead and play my hand." Eldora tried to follow him but one of the mob guys blocked her way and she retreated to the safety of Victor Phalen.

"What's this about wanting money for a movie deal?" asked Frank Costello, as soon as the door of the office was closed and he had gone around to the business side of a large walnut desk.

"Is this your office?" asked Errol Flynn.

"Does it matter who owns this office?"

"My partner, Victor and I are making a movie about the revolution."

"What's the story?"

"Fidel Castro runs Batista out of Cuba. That's the story."

"Fat chance of that happening. So you ain't got a story."

"What if it did happen? Fidel comes down from the mountains with his 26 July crowd and decides that casinos aren't part of his government's plan and he closes you down. And he gives you twenty-four hours to hightail it out of town. I'd say that's a story."

"The Americans would never let that happen. Get this into your Australian head: Cuba is America. Cuba ain't going any place unless we give the okay."

"A film about Fidel Castro could bring in a big audience. Let's say Batista defeats him. That's a story and a half. The two forces charge and only one is standing after the dust clears. It's a good story, Frank."

"I don't think anyone cares about Fidel Castro."

"If he thought you were his friend, it might make a difference if he wins. Making this movie covers your bets. I don't see how you can lose."

"Errol, you gotta understand something about Little Las Vegas and that's what Havana is—we play the odds. And the odds are Castro ain't ever coming off that mountain except in a wooden box."

"I am a betting man myself. I like long shots. If you go out in the street you hear a different song being sung. Batista's police are hated. They're doing more than knocking a few heads. Castro's movement gets more popular every day. You should get out of the casino and talk to some ordinary Cubans and you'll hear a different story."

"Everyone hates the cops they can't buy."

"What do you say, Frank? You want to invest in our film?"

Frank Costello cut the end off a large Havana cigar and one of the mob guys was at his side with a lighter. He leaned forward, the end of the cigar touching the flame. He puffed until a large cloud of gray-blue smoke rose. "How much you want and how much you giving in points?"

"Twenty-five grand gets you Errol Flynn and thirty points."

"Fifty points."

"Forty. And I explain to Fidel Castro that you were pulling for him the entire time."

"Deal," said Frank Costello.

This surprised Flynn who expected Frank would say, *I'll think about it and get back to you.* No one in Hollywood lets you roll into their office, ask for money and after five minutes have a stack of cash on the desk. The mob did things differently. "What's the name of the film?"

Errol Flynn had no idea and on impulse said, *"Cuban Story."* He thought it was a good idea not to mention *Cuban Rebel Girls* just in case Frank might start thinking his money could get diverted.

"When do you start?"

"Tomorrow we're heading to the mountains."

"What if you get yourself killed?"

"Then you lose your forty points and I lose sixty and get buried to boot."

Frank Costello was figuring those odds in his head as he counted out the cash. As his two stocky bodyguards with oily slicked-back hair, olive skin, and one-day-old beards, wearing tailored dark suits looked on, Frank stacked the piles of hundred-dollar bills fifty bills deep. The men like to watch the big boss counting out money. Their eyes were big and black like the wet feathers of a crow. Watching Frank with all of that money made them feel secure. Frank glanced over his shoulder at his men, licked his thumb, and counted another five Franklins, finishing the first pile. When he turned back to Errol Flynn, he thought the actor looked a little shaky on his feet.

"Hey, Robin Hood, sit down. Take the weight off. You want a drink?"

Flynn smiled. "I wouldn't mind."

He wouldn't mind, thought Frank Costello. Here was the famous actor, the great action hero, fencing master, war hero, and ship captain almost begging for a drink, coming around and demeaning himself for cash. That was the definition of power—you've got enough dough and pull to make Errol Flynn come through your door and not just ask for money. Frank had him begging for money. He was taking a chance, giving him all that cash at one time. It was a nice bet. But he wanted to humiliate him first. Show him who was boss. He liked making Robin Hood beg; it felt good.

"One more thing, Errol. I wouldn't mind a couple of scenes inside the casino. It will be good for business. Once Batista kicks Castro's ass. We're gonna want some advertisement to get the tourists coming back. So make that scene look classy. That's the image I want. You got that?"

"Great idea, Frank. I can already see the scene in my head."

"Shoot it when your head has a little less booze in it."

On the previous Monday Errol Flynn had phoned him saying he had something important to discuss. "A film deal," said Flynn.

Frank's first impression wasn't favorable, he believed that the actor was on the make. Sure he had come around the casino and all the women loved him. So what? What was he doing in Havana anyway? As far as he could tell, Flynn spent his days driving around Havana in his white Caddy with teenage girls, drinking and gambling and pretending to be in the theater business. He made some discreet inquiries after the initial phone call. All the people he approached—and that included the heavyweights—Vito Genovese, Santo Trafficante Jr and Moe Dalitz—sang from the same hymnbook: Errol Flynn hadn't been shopping any film deal around town. On the previous Thursday, Frank had invited Errol Flynn to lunch at the Hotel Riviera. Flynn drank his lunch while Frank asked him a lot of questions. He grilled not only the actor but also Victor, his partner, about the details of the film project.

His intelligence-gathering pointed out a couple of compelling elements. One he observed at first hand: Flynn was heavily into the sauce. Secondly, the theater he owned along with Victor Phalen wasn't doing so well. Meyer Lansky had it right when he told Frank, "Hey, Frank, it's fucking hard falling down the mountain when you're Captain Blood and end up on your ass as Captain Mud." Meyer had a way with words; he could cut a man off at the knees with words. He had left Errol Flynn legless in Frank's mind.

With the money counted and in five neat stacks, Frank Costello sat back in the big leather chair. "Take my advice, Errol. Don't take the money unless you intend to make the right film."

"I don't understand." A genuine look of incomprehension crossed his face.

"Let me spell it out for you. Castro's a commie. A film showing his true colors would be a good thing for everyone concerned. Americans hate the Reds. Don't they teach you anything in Australia? The last thing we Americans need is a fucking revolution in Cuba. So you sign on to show the world Castro is a goddamn thug."

What Frank Costello didn't tell him—and what he found out a couple of months later—was, like the rest of the mob in Havana, Frank had been feeding information to the CIA and to the American embassy. No one knew more than the mob running the casinos at San Souci, Sevilla-Biltmore, Commodoro, Deauville, Capri and Montmartre what people were talking about and how much Batista and his gang were walking away with commissions. If only the intelligence community had been listening to the mob, they would have known Batista was finished. What Frank had kept trying to tell Washington was that Fidel Castro was a communist. But they were the mob and no one was listening to mobsters when it came to shaping foreign policy or diplomacy. The diplomats had too much education and it made them stupid. None of the government types at the embassy, the ones who flew in from Washington, would ever admit Frank Costello knew more than some ex-furniture salesman from Michigan who sat in the ambassador's chair, except for one man. J. Edgar Hoover kept his channels to the mob through Meyer Lansky and others like Frank Costello, because he knew, as Frank always said, the FBI knew who the true patriots were. Hoover knew the educated eggheads, the types he couldn't stomach, and who could be guaranteed to fuck up American interests because, while they understood the theory, they never really understood the nature of the real interest at stake. Casinos were one large golden stake.

"I can't stop a revolution, Frank. I don't even know if Fidel can pull it off. But if he does come marching into Havana with his men, I am going to be filming it."

"You seem to like this criminal Fidel Castro. Batista should have shot him when he had him. He let him out of prison. Can you believe it?"

Errol liked Fidel because he reminded him of himself when he was in his twenties and in New Guinea and full of life, ambition and ideals. What he didn't tell Frank Costello was that he wanted to capture that missing moment of his life, that time when everything was possible and the fight for right was more important than just about anything else in life. When he was in his twenties he had real dreams and hopes and believed that a world of adventure could be had by any man willing to go out and fight for it.

Yeah, just one more time he needed to feel the rush of battle. Only this wouldn't be *The Dawn Patrol*, *The Sea Hawk*, *Another Dawn*, or *Edge of Darkness*—films about World War II where as an actor Errol Flynn acted as a war hero. Havana in December 1958 wasn't a pretend world. It wasn't a film set. This was going to be the real thing. Revolution was in the air. This time he would play himself, and he would play it for real. Real guns and bullets and bodies, and split-second decisions that would mean life or death. That was where he wanted to be—on the frontline ducking incoming rounds—it was how he wished to be remembered, an actor who became a *real*-life hero. No script or director, no one to catch him if he fell. If he could climb on to Fidel Castro's shoulders he might see the future. And to cover all bets, he'd go ahead and shoot *Cuban Rebel Girls*. He figured, if he were careful, there would be enough money to go around.

Christmas Eve 2004:
Bangkok, Thailand

Sully leaves the club with Sky and a ying who has changed out of her evening gown and is wearing a conservative, expensively tailored silk dress. Sky's mission is to escort one of the most desirable yings from the club—her off-résumé includes Robin Williams, Sly Stallone, and Roger Moore. She has a pedigree of international star appeal. She is the right woman to go to Bill Hunt's room and find another, creative way to get hold of the poster just in case that Pauley doesn't turn up. Nicknamed Gop, or Frog, this little number knows the secret combination to a celebrity's heart. Joey thinks if that charm works on guys at that level of play, what chance will Bill Hunt have? Ever watch a killer whale circle an old seal stranded too far offshore? There is a lucid moment of recognition that the old flippers don't rotate as swiftly as they used to just as the killer whale's jaws open and close. If, by pure chance, she should find the poster and come back with it, a special tip of twenty thousand baht wouldn't be a problem. She understands and smiles.

Joey is still in his formal white shirt, black trousers and suspenders sitting alone with a glass of whiskey on the balcony of his condo. His cell phone is on the table beside him. Occasionally he glances at the phone, willing it to ring. It is silent and a tiny flashing red light on the side reminds him of a tiny airport air control tower in another dimension of time and space.

Boggy stands behind the glass door for a while before he works up the courage to slide the door back and step onto the balcony. He slips into the seat next to Joey who leans forward, arms on the railing, watching the headlights of cars and motorcycles seventeen stories below. Boggy believes Joey is the eye of the pyramid on the back of the dollar bill watching and surveying its kingdom.

"How's the arm?"

"Better."

Joey takes a sip of whiskey.

"Howard, you need to start thinking about your future," says Joey.

"That's all I've been thinking about." He's picking at the new bandage that Jennifer Balfour has wrapped on his forearm.

"You need to figure out a couple of things."

"Like what?"

"What cards you are holding, how many cards you have left to draw, and what the other players are holding. You have to count and keep a lot of numbers in your head at one time and calculate the odds as if your life depends on it."

"I've been doing that."

Joey sees that Boggy's brush with death hasn't taught him much. He's not learning from his mistakes, which means he will keep on making the same mistakes over and over again. "I am not getting through to you, Howard."

Boggy is about to remind him to call him Gunnar but he is too tired, his arm throbs, he's on medication again, and he is in no mood to argue about one of those grown-up speeches that older people like to make when they don't have anything better to do. He feels Joey has been thinking about his future and has some definite plans in mind.

He doesn't have to wait long. "You are playing too many games at once," says Joey. "You can't play blackjack, poker, roulette, the slot machines, baseball and racehorse betting at the same time and do anything other than lose. Each of those games you are playing against the best players who live and breathe their game. They know their specialty. They don't get spread thin. They are focused and committed. How does this apply to you? You're out there selling posters, speculating on land, gold, stolen documents, forged passports and credit cards, inventing comic books, buying shrimp boats and God knows what else. And you are running your own Internet server and posting messages on half a dozen chat rooms at any one time. No one can keep that much shit from going sideways and tipping over."

"I've never lost any money on my investments," says Boggy.

"Boggy, someone blew up your fucking apartment. I'd call that a loss."

He tugs nervously at his beard, curling the ends into swirls. "They killed my cat."

Joey shakes his head. *How do I reach this nerdy kid?* "The first time I went broke, I lost everything. I bet the Orioles. They lost. You know what I did when I was down to zero?"

Boggy doesn't have the slightest idea that Joey has ever been broke for five seconds and is unable to comprehend the state of brokenness, but certainly has the feeling of where Joey escaped to lick his wounds. "You went home," says Boggy.

"I went home," says Joey. "I hitchhiked to Vancouver from San Diego. I was twenty-five years old. And Marty and I decided the old ways of making money which worked real well when we were eighteen weren't gonna work seven years down the road. So we adjusted to the times, our experience, and expectations, and to the fact I was totally broke."

"What did you do?"

"Marty and I opened a bookmaking operation."

"You were a bookie?" Boggy has always put Joey Balfour on that pedestal of greats—people who are famous, have had their own TV show, collect the most valuable of things, who live a legendary life of luxury in a country that isn't on the frequency wave most people are plugged into. Now, he discovers, his hero was once broke and had to become a bookie. *It doesn't get any better than this*, thinks Boggy. His nervous habit of curling his beard stops as he leans forward, eyebrows knitted together in an anxious look of doubt. For the first time since fleeing over the Maine border to Quebec he doesn't feel like a complete failure.

"I don't know if you are telling me the truth."

"You think I'd lie about being a bookie? Why would I do that?"

Boggy doesn't have a ready answer. He still doesn't have an answer after thinking about it for a moment.

"The ideal situation for a bookie is to get one hundred percent squares—or, as the British call their punters, mugs—to bet," says Joey. "The problem in the business is the wise guys. I am not talking about mob wise guys. I am talking about an entirely different type of wise guy—someone who is smart, connected, has access to inside information, or today, someone who is Internet savvy. For a bookie to turn a profit, he's got to manage the wise guys. How did I do that? I kept their limits low."

"I wouldn't take their bets," says Boggy.

This brings a smile. "You can't kick them out."

"I would."

"Wise guys then return under a different ID or they use a beard. You want to keep your enemy on the radar screen. Once you drive them underground, you have real trouble juggling the odds. Keep them where you can see them. That way once they start putting in their bets, you know it is time to change the odds. Or you bet alongside them. A wise guy bets the five-grand limit on Notre Dame and you figure he knows someone on the other side is injured, so you bet twenty grand on Notre Dame. If it were that simple, every bookie would be rich. The sharp end of the hook isn't just the wise guy. They are point five percent of the bettors. When a wise guy wants to lay down twenty bets with twenty different bookies he needs assistants. Wise guys don't run one-man shows. The best wise guys put together a team to score the big money. They are organized so everyone on the team lays exactly the same bet at, say, exactly four in the afternoon New York time. In a synchronized team effort they secure the odds. It is like a surprise raid. Pearl Harbor. But we don't live in a perfect world and that is where leakage comes into play.

The gofers, the loyal foot soldiers on the team, place bets on their own accounts, and they end up telling their friends and family, or they sell the information, and before you know it the point five percent of people in the know turns into fifteen percent and the bookie makes no profit. He ends up working for the wise guys and his cronies. You become their bank. And you get nothing out of it. At least if you own a bank you can rip off customers with a hundred different kinds of fees. If you want to stay in business, you learn to manage the wise guys, Howard. That explosion in Maine that blew up your apartment happened because you let a wise guy slip under the wire. You weren't watching carefully because an apple orchard in Penang or a Russian comic-book deal or some such wild-card play distracted you. Never forget, Boggy, that in life the real money comes from the mugs, and it is your duty not to let the wise guys eat your profits."

Joey's cell phone rings. Sky is on the other end. "Joy just got back."

He sits up straight in his chair. "And did she get the poster?"

"Not even close."

"She blew twenty thousand baht," says Joey. "But it wasn't wasted. I had to know whether Hunt had learned anything. He's smarter, wiser. That doesn't mean we can't find a weakness."

Sky is silent in the way the Joey fears most. Her signature of bad news was a particular interlude coupled with a certain way she breathed. Like the intake valve on an engine, her breathing gave away a great deal of information about the state of wear and tear.

"He told her that if she found Jim Pauley he'd give her the poster, and that it was worth one million baht. He gave her a photograph of Pauley."

"He turned her," says Joey. He laughs, seeing that of course with the right sum he could turn her. She was in business to turn and turn, this way and that way. That's what she did for a living.

"A million baht turns a lot of people, Joey."

"Do I sound surprised?"

She shook her head, thinking, *Joey almost never sounds surprised as if he anticipates what happens next, pulls rabbit after rabbit out of the hat, making it look natural.* "Ped read me the dueling part of *Anna Karenina*. It was very sweet of her. And I didn't ask her, she volunteered. Later she's reading for both of us. It's the part about how the Karenins continued living in the same house but how they were strangers. Don't be late or we'll start without you."

After he closes his cell phone, he turns in his chair just as his mother steps onto the balcony. It is like old times. He stood for hours on the balcony of the penthouse in Vancouver looking at English Bay and the ships against the horizon. There is a vaguely familiar feeling about her presence in this setting. The visuals below are different but the space high in the air suits both of them. Jennifer Balfour is unable to sleep; she can't shut off her mind, a combination of jet lag and worry. She is happy to find Joey and Boggy together on the balcony.

"I thought you boys would be sleeping. Then I saw you sitting outside. I wondered if I was having a senior moment."

Joey likes the fact that she still classifies him as a boy like Boggy. Mothers never admit that their sons grow up and, indeed, grow old. The implications are too horrible. Nothing or nobody, not even his mother, can console Joey. Her senior moments come more frequently, the white noise of the universe leaking into the space once filled by her memories, and Joey mourns the inevitable glide toward a final silence, the last strangulation of memory. Without memory, identity is lost in the void.

His warning about monitoring the wise guys and finding new mugs makes no ripple across Boggy's consciousness. He's drifting in another space, locked off, self-absorbed. The phone call tells him he should listen to his own advice. Bill Hunt is wiser than Joey remembers. Something has happened to the ex-chief of casino security in the last dozen years. He's playing at a new level. Like a heavyweight that everyone has written off as over the hill he suddenly makes a comeback. It happens. *It is time*, Joey thinks, *to recalculate the odds*. Temperance Hill had lost three races before going into the Belmont Stakes with forty to one odds. The performance of horses and boxers changes over time, as do the odds of them winning. He's been underestimating Bill Hunt.

"Mother, Boggy and I were just talking about the old days in Vancouver."

"Joey, those were wonderful days. Days for us to remember for the rest of our lives." On the table she sees a photograph of someone she doesn't know. She picks it up and examines it against the light coming from inside the condo. "Who is this, Joey?"

"Jim Pauley. He's someone I've been trying to look up."

"He doesn't look like a happy person," says Jennifer.

"Jim's had triple by-pass surgery. So he probably looks happier now."

"I don't remember him from Vancouver. And I thought that I knew all of your friends."

"He's from Las Vegas," says Joey.

"I never quite liked that crowd." She rarely used the word gangster or underworld. Trenton, Joey's father, had little problem calling people in that crowd mobsters. He watched too much television.

Most of them were businessmen. They didn't kill people or break their legs.

"Why are you looking for him?" She puts the photograph down.

Joey takes his mother's hand and gently kisses it. "It's complicated."

"Try me."

"There's a guy named Bill Hunt who asked me to help him out. I knew Bill from Las Vegas. A friend helps a friend."

"I should have guessed as much," says Jennifer. "That doesn't seem complicated at all. I am certain you will find this Jim from Mr. Hunt."

Boggy studies the photo carefully, memorizing each feature of what is a perfectly ordinary, featureless face; it is the mug of an accountant, a clerk, a face in a sea of similar faces. "Can I help find him?" asks Boggy.

Joey lets go of his mother's hand. "Boggy, you've been in Thailand for less than a day. You couldn't find a bowl of noodles on the street."

"I can try." His smile opens a sliver of a crack in his reddish beard.

"Be my guest." Joey knows this comes from an old tourists' promotional slogan, one of the many that never work to bring anything but derision. Think of a committee staffed by George Orwell and Forest Gump looking to draw in the mugs. "Be my guest," repeats Joey.

"I am your guest," says Boggy.

Jennifer Balfour cocks her head to the side. "He's right, Joey."

"Happiness on earth," says Joey.

Jennifer and Boggy exchange a glance that excludes Joey.

"And . . . ?" asks Jennifer.

"There is no and. It's only a slogan for Gunnar to remember as he's beating the pavement of Bangkok looking to reel in Jim Pauley. It was designed to make tourists feel comfortable."

"Even as a boy you would pick up strange expressions," says Jennifer Balfour. "You've not changed, Joey."

He nods at Boggy, "And neither have you, Mother."

"But I have. I know that I am forgetting things. Forgive me."

"If we could only forget the things that frighten us or hurt us."

"That would be a good forgetting. But we aren't allowed to choose. What falls away are the things we wish to hold on to the most."

Christmas Day 2004:
Bangkok, Thailand

When Sky and Gop stand framed in the doorway to his hotel room, Bill Hunt knows immediately what is going down. He knows that Joey has sent them. It is his style to send a goddess to someone he wants to impress. *She smells so good,* he thinks. He can't place the perfume; it is one of those subtle numbers, part musk, part lavender and cloves. And she has the universal sexual appeal men covet. She has full lips, Chinese eyes, slender body, curves and firm flesh hovering below the surface, everything in ideal proportion, shape and place. And she stands in front of him, wearing an understated dress concealing large breasts inside a titanium-wired uplift bra. She smells of flowers. Everything and everyone around Joey carries the scent of flowers. She has walked right off the page of a comic book he used for masturbation inspiration at fourteen. Now she is smiling at him in flesh and blood.

"Hi, Bill, I want you to meet Gop," says Sky as they stand in the doorway.

"It's my nickname and it means Frog," says Gop.

"Joey thought you'd like some companionship on Christmas Day," says Sky.

"If you want me to go, I'll go," says Gop.

"Santa Claus sent you?" Bill Hunt looks her up and down with hungry eyes. The eyes that should have been on Jim Pauley the night when he walked out of the casino with a New York Yankees' duffel bag full of cash and chips. "You're here, aren't you? Come on in." His penis is half erect as he closes the door.

Sky sees the bulge in his trousers. She glances at her watch and winks at Gop. "See you later, alligator," says Sky.

"Aren't you part of the package?" asks Bill Hunt.

"Don't be greedy, Bill. Santa sends you one beautiful package, don't get greedy and ask for two." Sky slowly closes the door, walks down the corridor and takes the elevator to the lobby where she sits in an overstuffed chair and waits for Gop.

Bill Hunt has a suite and the television is on to CNN. "You want a drink?"

Gop perches uneasily on the sofa, nervously crossing her legs. One foot does the wiggle of anxiety keeping time to a fast burst of gunfire coming from the TV. "Water is fine." She avoids looking at his face. Sky warned her that Hunt wasn't handsome, and she said, "Since when does handsome matter in this business?"

"Water ain't fine. Not in this country." He pours her a scotch whiskey from a Johnny Walker Black bottle and sets it down on the glass coffee table.

On CNN a weather map shows a cold front moving down from Canada. Bill Hunt points the remote at the television and punches a button. "Joey Balfour's another cold front that moved down from Canada. So how did you come to work for him?"

She could be a television star, thinks Bill Hunt. With her looks and the cool way she handles herself under fire. She would be good as an anchor on CNN, reading the news with that smile, her eyes drilling straight into the heart, making it ache a little. No one would care about the heartache of the world looking at her. Murder, robbery, assassination, terrorism, none of it would matter with all the men thinking what was under her dress. And she is in his room, alone, waiting, drinking his whiskey.

"Joey comes to my club. The club buys flowers from his shop. But I don't work for him. Sky works for Joey."

"Is that so?"

Street-smart, an attribute that causes Bill Hunt's balls to constrict. He loses his erection; it goes down like a balloon hit with a lit match. Bill drinks from his glass, rattles the ice, studying Gop from every angle like a pool player deciding on his next shot. "Did Joey ever tell you he had a TV show in Las Vegas? It was a big deal years ago. It's back on the air."

"He never mentioned it."

"Never mentioned it," repeats Bill Hunt. "He was famous. Now he's even more famous than before. And he doesn't mention it?"

"Not to me," says Gop.

"I've got a tape of his TV show. You wanna see it?"

"Whatever you like, Bill," says Gop. *He has the thin lips of Robin Williams and the intensity of Sly*, she thinks. But he looks much older. He has the coldness of an executioner which sends an ice storm and darkness to the depth of her soul. She downs the whiskey and he refills her glass.

Bill Hunt puts down the whiskey bottle. He walks over and removes a shiny DVD from a black case, slides it into the DVD player and a moment later there is Joey Balfour on the screen looking much younger, more confident than she has ever seen. She leans forward; it is Joey on the TV screen. He looks younger on TV. In fact, she thinks he looks younger than her. She never thought there was a time when Joey had ever looked that young. Joey's talking to a guest, someone she doesn't recognize. The camera pans to a black heavyweight fighter with a funny hat and dark glasses slouching in his chair, huge hands folded on his lap. A showgirl with a silver tray and a single martini leans over Joey's desk. She shakes her ass, then her breasts, looking back at the camera, saying her silent "I love Joey" for the audience. Then it is back to a tight shot on Joey. "Shake that bootie, shake that bootie," growls Joey Balfour. Bill Hunt turns up the volume.

"Women are iron filings to the magnet of money and power. It gives them status to be with a winner. It makes a woman feel good about herself. She wakes up in the morning and looks at herself in the mirror of a suite, and her eyes glide over to a fruit basket on the table, then to the sixty-four-inch TV set, and then finally take in the sweeping views of the city. You know what? A woman at that moment, leaning against her pillow, surveying her man and surroundings, she has no trouble telling herself that she loves this guy. She touches his hair and thinks to herself, this guy is for me. He's won my heart. It's only with a loser that a woman feels buyer's remorse. Waking up in some shitty hotel with burnt toast on a plate and empty beer bottles, and, in no time, she realizes she's made a tragic mistake. She knows at that moment that she never loved the guy, and that he never loved her. Otherwise why would he treat her like this? She takes one last look at the mess of a man and mess of a room and she walks. A week later she hears that he's won big time. He's got a suite and new car. They have a tearful reconciliation. She tells herself how could I be so wrong about such a good man? This guy really does love me. How could I deny my own deep feelings for him? And they are back together. Until his money once again goes down the toilet. Then the cycle starts over. An eternal cycle. That is the way it always works in Las Vegas. The money is the big-time hook.

"Anytime there's a large amount of cash around, there will always be beautiful women. Women pour into Las Vegas from all over the world: Poland, England, Thailand, China, and Argentina. They are drawn by one thing: *money*. This international sisterhood is like a flock of swallows flying by sheer instinct; their radar systems take them straight to the big money nest. Most of them have no education, skills or talent. But they have very good bodies. They dress well. You see them at every casino. They hover around the action. Gambling draws hookers. Gamblers and working girls are joined at the hip.

"You ask yourself, who is a hooker? In Las Vegas the line between a straight girl and a hooker blurs. Take a cocktail waitress. She gets hit on a hundred times a day especially if she's beautiful. Sooner or later one of the customers finds her price. She goes with him. The next time it is a little easier. After a while, she gets hooked on the money and the power. Rather than carrying trays, she figures out that all that upfront cash pouring in lets her elevate her position. She can buy all the things that she wants. Hookers aren't supposed to be allowed in casinos. But there's always a way in. If she blows the chief of security, guess what? She gets in. Unless she's a chippy, which is another way of saying that she's a casino hooker. She saddles up to a guy at a game table. She plays one-dollar bets and bides her time. With the skill of a pickpocket, she snags a couple of the guy's chips. If he's winning, he doesn't even notice the loss. And if he's winning big, he will likely tip her some chips for bringing him luck. A good chippy has the skill of a pickpocket and the manual dexterity of a surgeon and the morality of a politician. But the casino cameras pick up their action. The floor man waits until the mug has left the table before he kicks her out."

Bill Hunt switches off the TV. In his mind, Joey Balfour was talking directly about him. Humiliating him on air and leaving a legacy for posterity. Joey knew some of the hookers who gave Bill blowjobs to get into the casino. He'd take her in the back room and, according to his schedule, walked her down the corridor. Bill emerged five minutes later, smiling and the hooker would blow him a wet-mouth kiss. No one noticed that he was absent from the floor for a few minutes. It was a small absence. She wanted into the casino. In his mind he had two choices, getting a blowjob or turning her over to the police. It depended on whether he liked the girl. The night that Jim Pauley walked out of the casino with a duffel bag stuffed with the bankroll from the sports betting cashier, where was Bill Hunt?

Joey Balfour, a couple of days later, found out about Bill Hunt's back-room activities; he plugged into the underground mouth-to-mouth don't-tell-anyone-else news bulletin which had been working overtime to describe Bill Hunt's humping while a Bible-thumping, preaching girl from Colorado had her shot at converting him. The story was Bill Hunt had ejaculated all over the hooker's face as she recited portions of the Bible; it was Bill's way of showing authority and power that only the chief of casino security could demonstrate. It had been a biblical moment. Pontius Pilate spewing at the moment he's being asked for mercy. It was as if Monica Lewinsky had gone down on her knees in the Oval Office with a Bible and a blue dress.

The hooker, Linda Harris, came from a small Colorado town nestled against the Nebraska border. She had been a cheerleader—head cheerleader—for the school football team, which had gone to the State championship in her senior year. Her fluffy long hair, long, painted fingernails and multiple layers of makeup made her the ideal museum piece for 1980s fashion. Everyone told her she was a beauty and that she should try to make something of herself. She told Bill Hunt this as she knelt in the back room, holding his penis, shaking it from off her lips like it were a microphone.

And for his part, Bill Hunt told Linda, "I want it nice and slow. No teeth. Lots of gum action, okay? And what I mean by slow is for a long, long time. You got that, Linda?"

With his ugly veined microphone-sized dick stuck in her mouth, she looked up and mumbled, as it would have been difficult even for a world-class ventriloquist to talk normally. He stroked her long, blonde hair, and admired the way she hiked up her red velvet evening gown so that he could admire her nylon stockings and black suspenders. Every so often he gave her a smack on the ass. Linda moaned and sputtered like an old car trying to climb the side of a mountain. Bill Hunt didn't bother to look at his watch. He had all the time in the world. Linda was good, real good, and he had no desire to go back onto the floor. It wasn't his lucky night, he told himself. The Blue Jays won the World Series in six games, and he had laid a twenty-dollar bet on the Braves. The Braves were the favorite to win. So what if they were odds on to win? You back winners in life and you reap the rewards. Only favored to win and winning were two different things. He was pumped up mad at his loss and took his anger out on Linda. Every couple of seconds, Linda came up for air like a pearl diver who had stayed on the bottom just short of the time when her lungs would explode. Once, when she caught her breath, rather than diving straight back to the depths of Bill Hunt's shaft, Linda started on how the gospels said that those who were saved would watch terrible events happen to those who hadn't accepted Jesus Christ. She fumbled in her handbag and pulled out a Bible. She opened it and started to read. Bill Hunt pushed her mouth back into place. She pulled back and he kicked the Bible to the side. Then she dived down and pumped Bill Hunt's organ until she spat him out, panting. "And their eyes will boil and fall from their face, their skin will catch on fire and their flesh cook and peel from their bones and there will be nothing they can do. It will be too late to be saved."

Bill Hunt again pushed her head back on his erection with the grace of someone changing a flat tire. "All this religious bullshit isn't what a working girl should be saying. Honey, you ain't ever going to succeed in this business until you can keep your mouth firmly shut over this." He pulled out his penis, glistening with her saliva.

"My father said no man is ever too far gone that he can't be saved. And he knows because he had gone to the side of the devil. But he came back to tell the tale."

He looked at his watch. "Holy shit. Finish this off. Baby, I've got to get back to work." The hair stood up on the back of Bill Hunt's neck as he squeezed his eyes and tried not to think of hell's fire as he came closer and closer to the final exit and pulled onto the off-ramp and spurted a full load on her face. "The Bible promises eternal life to those who turn their face to Him."

"Sweetheart, this is Las Vegas. I've got a job to do. You've got to get out and peddle your ass. Why don't we leave the Bible out of it?"

Or so Bill Hunt remembers.

Bill Hunt drinks whiskey from his glass and looks around his hotel room. The night that Linda from Colorado sucked him off in the back room at the casino was many years ago, water under the bridge, only the gully has run dry, so the song goes. All he can think, as his head pounds like bongo drums is: *So what does Joey Balfour do? He sends a hooker to give me a blowjob like in the old days.* She's wearing a dress like the one Linda from Colorado, Miss Head Cheerleader, wore. Only it's not hiked up around her waist exposing her ass for a good session of slap and tickle. But it could be. All he has to do is ask. Draw her closer. He moves in on her. His face is a couple of inches away from Gop's and she can smell the garlic and olive oil on his breath. She does her level best not to gag. When he finally turns away and walks into the bedroom she exhales, half frightened, and half exhausted. She's been through worse. He is one of those guys who thinks intimidation and mind games are the best form of foreplay. She tells herself that this is a job. She can get through it. Joey has already given her five thousand baht and there is his promise of another twenty thousand baht. And she thinks about what Joey said on the DVD about hookers and money, and as with most terrible truths that everyone knows and suppresses at the same time, it makes her want to cry and laugh and her head is spinning and all she really wants is to get out of that room.

Bill Hunt returns from the bedroom carrying one of those cardboard cylinders used to pack posters. "You know what's inside here?"

She lights a cigarette and shakes her head. "No idea."

"No fucking idea? You don't lie well, sweetheart. And a hooker that doesn't lie well doesn't get the honey," he says. "Acting is lying.

Hookers act like they enjoy it. But we know they are play acting. Joey didn't send you here to fuck me, but to get what's inside this. Am I right?"

"I think I'd better go now." She smashes out the freshly lit cigarette in the ashtray and starts to rise.

Bill Hunt pushes her back. He sees the anger flash across her face as she reaches for the ashtray and he knocks it away. It bounces across the floor and shatters against the wall. "I've got a proposition for you. Listen to me carefully. I don't know how much Joey offered you to steal this poster," he tapped the cardboard cylinder. "Knowing Joey, I'd say five hundred bucks tops. I am offering you a million baht. That's something like twenty-odd thousand dollars."

"What do you want?"

Bill Hunt shoves a photograph of Jim Pauley in front of her. "I want him."

Gop looks at the photo, then up at Bill Hunt whose large frame towers above her. "What did he do? Kill somebody?"

"His name is James Elwood Pauley and he stole a lot of money from a casino in Las Vegas. That day, he ruined my life. My marriage fell apart. My wife took the kids and that was it. Her lawyer took what she couldn't carry away herself. Joey was talking about me on that tape. My old lady ran out on me after the casino cut back my salary. They said it was my fault Pauley walked out the door with a bag full of cash. I should have been doing my job. Instead I was talking to a hooker who had given me a free blowjob. Romancing her for what? I never figured out the answer to that one."

"Can I go now?"

"Take the photo of Jimbo with you. The reward stands. Find him and I'll give you a million baht. And tell Joey he can fuck himself."

The moment Bill Hunt backs away, Gop is out of the chair and at the door.

"Hey, for Joey's five hundred bucks, I should at least get a blowjob."

He unbuckled his belt and then pulled down his zipper. "Come on, baby. There is no free lunch."

A flash of hatred lights up her eyes as she stands on the razor's edge of leaving or doing what she had been sent to do. She lays down her Gucci handbag, lowers herself down and takes him in her mouth.

"Where's the soundtrack? A blowjob comes with some good moaning, doesn't it?"

Moaning, she goes down deeper until he pulls out of her, wet and glistening. He turns her around, strips down her g-string and enters her from behind. "Use a condom," she says.

"Five hundred fucks a year. I figure that's what you must do. Let's make this one special. No condom."

He feels like he is splitting her in two as he thrusts. Hitting his stride, he finishes inside her, crying out a little anguished sound caught in the back of his throat. After he moves away she says nothing, rushing to the bathroom. He hears the water running. Then the toilet flushes. When she appears a moment later, she gives him a hard, cold look.

"What about a tip?"

"Baby, you got more than a tip. You got the whole thing."

He is laughing as she slams the door behind her.

Boxing Day 2004:
Bangkok, Thailand

Boggy has a plastic bag that Jell, the maid, has prepared. Inside are two peeled hardboiled eggs, a small package of wieners, steamed rice and the skeleton of a large fish with bits of fat and flesh clinging to the bones. Outside the entrance of the pyramid, Boggy turns left and heads down the soi, and then takes another turn past the vendor who is selling wrap-around sunglasses. The vendor recognizes a selling opportunity and nudges an assistant who Boggy does not recall from the previous encounter. The red-bearded farang with the lumpy body on a squat frame ambles towards him wearing a pair of sunglasses.

"You, you. I have sunglasses for you. Not so expensive," says the assistant, a young, thin Thai teenager with a quick smile and large, clear eyes.

Boggy with his damaged arm slowly lowers his wrap-around sunglasses. "I bought these from him the other day."

The vendor blinks at him, showing no memory of ever having seen Boggy. This seems peculiar to Boggy as he recognizes every feature of the vendor from his tattooed Khmer script on his forearm to his gold incisor tooth. He blocks Boggy's path and is waving a mirror and a pair of aviator sunglasses with gold wire frames in Boggy's face. The vendor's hands flash a signed message to the assistant who nods and turns back to Boggy.

"These are very good. Not made in Thailand. No, these glasses are from Italy. How much you pay?" He flashes a calculator, which had been secreted behind the mirror. The other day the vendor is mute, today he is with an assistant who won't shut up. Boggy feels the big city is fraud-filled.

"I bought these sunglasses from him. I don't need a second pair. Can you tell him that in sign language?" Boggy gestures at his throat, tracing an incision line with his forefinger.

As on Boggy's first morning, the middle-aged Thai man in baggy trousers and a long-sleeved shirt frayed at the collar comes alongside Boggy. He smiles in recognition.

"Gunnar, good morning. Have you eaten?"

As before, the Thai lugs two large plastic bags and a dozen cats are trailing behind him, meowing and moaning, slithering around his legs, rubbing and purring.

"Why do you want to know what I've eaten?"

Daeng spreads out a newspaper and dumps part of the contents of rice and fish sauce on it. The cats leap on the food. "It's our custom. We always ask a friend: *Where are you going?* And, *Have you eaten yet?* It's polite."

The vendor leans back sensing his assistant has the possibility of a sale. Until he spots the Thai man with his bag of cat food and his mood quickly diminishes to one of gloom. He might not remember Boggy but his body language broadcasts that he knows the Thai man who feeds the cats. "Two-hundred baht only. Special price for you. Best price," says the vendor's assistant.

Boggy's Thai friend, Daeng, with a big smile, explains that the farang won't need an additional pair of fake Italian aviator sunglasses today, thank you very much. Perhaps tomorrow, though, there's always tomorrow, and *mai pen rai* or "never mind" for today. The three Thais communicate efficiently and with no conflict or fuss and the vendor, flashing his gold tooth, signs to his assistant to give up the sale. The assistant evades the band of cats and resumes his position behind the tray on wooden legs displaying his wares. He stores the cheap calculator on the tray, facing the pavement, an invitation to bargain. The vendor polishes a hand mirror, puts it next to the calculator, and then busily cleans the lenses of a pair of sunglasses. It is as if Boggy and his friend no longer exist.

Boggy clutches his bag and walks ahead, stops, turns, and waits for his Thai friend to catch up with him. More cats stream behind the Thai as he walks toward Boggy. *Daeng is Bangkok's cat man,* thinks Boggy, who counts the qualities that he likes about his new friend: Devoted, kind, regular, caring, and friendly. As he waits, Boggy scratches his burn wound under the bandage that Jennifer Balfour has so carefully plastered. But the tape is loose on one side and Boggy's finger burrows under the opening. The itching drives him crazy. He scratches too hard, drawing blood.

He squats down and opens his plastic bag and pours half of the contents into a pile on the pavement. Three cats, claws extended, spit and screech, as they dive for Boggy's offering. "I am making merit," says Boggy.

Daeng beams with pride of authorship. "Very good, Gunnar. I was reading about Norwegian fishing villages last night. They are so beautiful . . ."

His eyes are drawn to the blood dripping from Boggy's arm. "You're bleeding. I better have a look."

Boggy instinctively pulls his arm away.

"It's okay. I am a doctor."

Boggy submits his arm with a crooked smile. "I had an accident."

"I'd say a third-degree burn is a nasty accident," said Daeng.

"Are you really a doctor?"

"I am not a burn specialist, though."

"What kind of doctor are you?"

"A cardiologist."

He clicks his tongue as he examines Boggy's burn wound. "Why don't you come back to my surgery? Have you had a tetanus shot?"

"I didn't step on a rusty nail." Boggy isn't ready to tell his friend that the wound was treated by a vet in Maine shortly before he fled to Canada.

"There are many ways to contract tetanus. The bacillus can enter any wound in many different ways. If it does, then the results can be fatal," says Daeng in his doctor's voice, which carries a velocity and weight much different from his diluted cat-feeding voice.

Daeng unfolds several more newspapers on the pavement and tips over the remaining contents of his two bags and then relieves Boggy of his plastic bag, dumps the contents onto the pile, and dozens of cats swarm over the sidewalk buffet like locusts out of

Egypt. This is Boggy's third day in Bangkok and as Joey said that early morning on the balcony, he knew nothing about Bangkok. His room in his mind oscillates inside the eye of the pyramid on a giant dollar bill and the only people he knows are Jennifer, Joey, and Joey's friend Marty, and the person with Marty who might be a man or a woman, depending on how one judges the size of the Adam's apple and feet dimensions. And there is Daeng, Dr. Daeng, a heart man, scrubbing his hands in the surgery, drying them, and slipping on operating gloves as Boggy sits on a chair, his arm on a white sheet laying on top of an examination table.

"How did this happen?" asks the doctor. In his mind, Gunnar, the Norwegian fisherman, must have had a terrible accident while out at sea.

Boggy grits his teeth as the doctor cleans the wound. The needle is in a small envelope like a condom, and the doctor opens it and attaches it to a syringe. He fills the syringe and Boggy flinches as the needle pierces his skin, telling himself that he is Gunnar Brogge behind enemy lines with a mission and the doctor is part of the resistance and they are fighting together to save the free world. Nothing less, nothing more. Boggy can only keep this subterfuge before he starts to blubber and tears fall into his red beard.

"I am sorry if that hurt, Gunnar," says Dr. Daeng.

Boggy blubbers even more. "It's not the needle. It's Caesar. They killed Caesar."

The doctor remembers from the first morning, "Your cat?"

Boggy nods, taking a handkerchief from his pocket, and as he blows his nose the photograph of Jim Pauley floats right side up onto the white sheet.

Dr. Daeng looks down at the photo as if he's witnessed a subversive act. "Jim Pauley," he says.

"Exactly," says Boggy. It takes two seconds before it registers that Dr. Daeng recognizes Jim Pauley. "It is a small world."

"I did Jim's triple by-pass operation. But he's American not Norwegian."

"He's a great fisherman, and he came to my village many times. I prayed that one day I might see him again. Making merit for Caesar has brought me to him. Thank you, Doctor, for making a Norwegian fisherman so happy."

He leans forward and kisses the doctor on both cheeks.

"Jim comes for an appointment at the hospital this afternoon. I can tell him where to find you. Or I can, if you tell me where you are staying."

The eye of the pyramid, he wants to say. "Just around the corner."

"You needn't be ashamed to stay at a guesthouse," says Dr. Daeng.

Joey's five-bedroom luxury condo is as far away from a guesthouse as Caesar is from life. "It would be better if I came to the hospital. I need to get some medicine for my allergies. Dust mites, corn, dogwood, and spider's eggs. Just about everything. And I'd like to surprise Jim. I want to see his face. Boy, do I want to see his face."

"That shouldn't be a problem." The doctor writes the address down on a note pad, tears off the sheet and hands it to Boggy. "Two thirty this afternoon."

"Thanks, Doctor."

"You can still call me Daeng." A frown clouds his face as he glances at his watch. "There's been a bad storm in the South. It seems many people may have died. Every day we assume we and the world are one, and will be forever, until the day we separate from the world."

Boggy watches the doctor disappear into the crowd. For someone who isn't supposed to find a bowl of noodles on the streets of Bangkok, Boggy is very pleased with himself. He has no idea what Daeng is talking about storms and death. Feeding oneself in a strange city is sufficient comfort to block out disaster.

Selling Robin Hood to Cover Bets
October 1971:
Vancouver, Canada

Joey arranged for his own taxi before flying back to Vancouver. Marty waited at the airport in a taxi; it was to be Joey's taxi. All the paperwork had already been processed so that Joey Balfour could join the ranks of Vancouver cab drivers. That's what friends were for: to stand around at the bottom as they watch you falling head over ass and once you hit, give you the keys to a taxi.

"The Orioles should've won," said Joey.

He sounded like a mug even to himself. Should've won was like all the should've in life: should've died, should've turned right, should've gone to university, should've not married Jackie, and on and on to the bottom of the should've grave of dead ends.

"You'll get it back," said Marty.

Joey looked out the window on the passenger's side to glimpse the glistening lights from the ski lift on Grouse Mountain. High school had seemed so distant from Las Vegas and now it seemed like it was about to happen all over again. During the 1969 World Series, Joey had wagered all of his bankroll on the Orioles beating the Mets. He lost. Two years later, Joey found himself back in Vancouver and at one of the few jobs that his high-school education had made him suitable to perform. When the Mets ambushed the Orioles Joey was unprepared for the post-game world. The collateral damage destroyed his life's savings. Driving around Vancouver looking for a fare, he ran the games in that series over in his mind. Then he'd spot a fare and pull over. One evening, he picked up a fare in the financial district. A business guy, early thirties in an expensive suit, carrying a briefcase who wanted to go to an address on Point Grey Road.

Joey struck up a conversation. "Are you a lawyer?"

"Stockbroker," his fare replied.

Joey adjusted his rearview mirror and saw the guy pulling some papers out of his briefcase. The fare seemed to be a man of few words. "What stocks do you recommend?"

The stockbroker's head jerked up. "Mining companies. You ever buy shares?"

"I don't know shares. I take bets on football games and baseball, basketball, hockey," said Joey. He was winding up the stockbroker, seeing where he'd go with this line of work.

"You any good?"

Joey smiled in the rearview. This wasn't the best time to mention what happened when the Mets clobbered the Orioles. "I worked in Las Vegas for awhile. I learned a couple of tricks about how to make odds and how to make them work for a profit. Or at least how they're supposed to work. It's not that different from picking shares."

As Joey pulled up at the address on Point Grey Road—one of those fancy houses that face English Bay—the stockbroker pulled out his card and handed it to Joey along with the fare. "Give me a call. Maybe we can do business. I am a deal maker. We can make a deal."

He winked at Joey and tipped him ten dollars. Joey sat in the taxi watching his fare go into his house. Joey saw him as a scuffler—a guy who puts deals together for a living. Scufflers were guys who lived off the adrenaline rush of deals. They traveled from deal to deal like it was a commute. "We can make a deal," the stockbroker had said.

He pocketed the card, put the taxi into gear, and headed off, saying to himself, "Got to phone Marty. We're back in business." He honked the horn, rolled down the window and cried out, "We're back."

Joey and Marty had their own cubicle in the stockbroker's office. The deal was they had two hours on Friday nights taking calls from the stockbroker's clients who wanted to lay down bets on college and professional football that weekend. The office was vacant except for Joey and Marty. Joey sat in one of the high-backed executive chairs he borrowed from the managing director's office, turned in his chair as line one rang, reached over and answered the phone. Marty was on line two. Both wrote quickly as the punters who had already mortgaged their houses to buy mining shares marketed in denominations of pennies rather than dollars confidently bet the Sunday professional games.

"Number 21 bet five hundred on the Steelers. I gave him two points. We can lay it off in Vegas at three points," Joey said after he hung up.

Marty nodded. "Number 21 always bets the Steelers. He's in love with that team."

"That makes him a mug," said Joey.

Marty could lay off a hundred dollars on a horse and not blink. He might forget to check the race result for a day or two. But he had no appetite for sports betting.

"You remember that time you bet fifty on the Blue Jays. You paced in front of the TV set for two hours. You broke out in a cold sweat. I thought you were having an attack. What is it with you? You bet a hundred on a horse, it's nothing. But fifty on a baseball game and you're ready for someone to jump on your chest to start your heart beating again. It's not natural."

"I never said it was natural. I trust horses."

"How can you say that? Trust a fucking horse. Sixteen horses explode out of the gate. Anything could happen. The jockey is tired or he's taken a backhander. Or a horse gets spooked or bumped."

"I know horses, Joey. I bet what I know."

"What you don't have is confidence. That's your problem. You gotta have faith in yourself."

"Like when you went broke putting your whole bank on the Orioles? And I'm supposed to listen to you about faith in baseball teams?"

"So what do you see me doing? Working in an office?"

Marty gestures across the room. "This is an office."

"You know what I mean. A nine to five office."

The phone rang.

"Line one," said Marty. "I'll take it."

It was another regular. After writing down the bet, Marty said, "That was Number 3."

"He bet the Cowboys," said Joey, rolling his eyes.

"Number 21 and Number 3 ought to apply for the same self-help class," said Marty. "Or better yet we could open up a group therapy center."

"We could get the government to underwrite it."

"Wouldn't we have a conflict of interest?"

"We'd have another stream of revenue. There are mugs who need other ways to blow their money."

The stockbroker explained to Joey that he had a Friday facility to take bets on American football games. There were people who called toilets a facility; people who called things by such abstractions were normally afraid that using the real name of things would somehow taint them.

"Do you mind extending your facility to CFL games?" asked the broker.

"No problem," said Joey. He phoned Las Vegas but had a hard time with getting odds on CFL games as there wasn't a lot of action. To be on the safe side, Joey ramped up the odds on the principle that anyone who invested their pension money and wife's inheritance in penny-mining shares wouldn't have the brains to phone Las Vegas and find out what the odds were there.

"Line two," said Joey, picking up the phone.

"This is Larry Crammer and I'd like to place an order to buy IBM."

Joey covered the phone with his hand. "The guy uses his actual name and wants to buy real shares."

Marty took out a twenty-dollar bill and slapped it on Joey's desk. "Fuckhead," he whispered. They'd had a bet that sooner or later a real investor would phone in to place an order for real shares. Marty said, "Never in a million years. Everyone knows this broker sells only mining shit."

"Sorry, Mr. Crammer, we'd like to take your order, but we specialize only in the fast growing British Columbia mining industry. You might want to try Merrill Lynch for your IBM."

Joey picked up the twenty-dollar bill and kissed it. Joey and Marty booked bets on Friday for Saturday college games and Sunday pro games. They never knew the names of the people who placed the bet; they had numbers given to them by the broker. The pressure was from the clients on the broker who wanted a little action on the weekend, and the broker had been scratching his head, thinking of a way to accompany them without actually having to get involved in such a facility. On Tuesdays, Joey and the broker always settled up with the broker paying the difference between the winning and losing bets, or by Joey paying the broker. Usually it was the broker who paid out. The broker guaranteed the clients would pay—he pulled it out of their client account.

"Number 91 with Green Bay again," sighed the broker, counting out money. It was free information that it was time to ramp up another penny-share mining company and put Number 91 at the top of the list of potential buyers.

One Friday evening, Joey picked up line one, "I am told I am Number 17. I want to bet on the Giants."

After all of those years, Joey still recognized the voice. "Mr. Faragos?"

"I was told not to ever use my real name."

"That's true. It's just I remember your voice."

"You sound familiar yourself. I am certain I know you."

"You know me, Mr. Faragos."

"Joey? Joey Balfour?"

Chocolate Chip Cookies
in Memory of Errol Flynn

When Mr. Faragos opened the apartment door that afternoon he wore an old Mets shirt—this stung Joey a bit, he'd almost forgotten his tragic loss in betting his whole bank on the Orioles. He was also wearing a pair of trousers with the cuffs rolled up to expose his skinny ankles. Joey remembered that pair of trousers from a couple of years earlier. Once inside, Joey looked around. It was as if time had stopped. The shabby, overstuffed furniture had more dark stains—coffee and chocolate—than he remembered, and the cushions sagged more, and the yellow flowers on the throw pillows had faded almost to a pale white. The same twenty-one-inch television rested on the same cheap stand, and the framed Errol Flynn movie posters on the walls tilted this way or that. Neither of the Faragos could be trusted to hang anything straight. A layer of fine dust and cobwebs knitted *The Adventures of Robin Hood* and *Captain Blood* posters together in a freeway for spiders. Behind the sofa a walnut bureau stacked with saucers, plates, and cups featured a framed photograph of a young Mrs. Faragos in a single-piece swimming suit. She was standing with her hands on her hips. English Bay and sand were behind her. Enough cleavage promised firm, round breasts beneath. She smiled, her long brown hair caught blowing in the wind off the sea, and, Joey thought, she really did use to be a babe. He caught a brief glimpse of her in the kitchen, just long enough for her to see him but not long enough for her to acknowledge that she had seen him.

What the fuck happened to her? The answer was the same thing that happened to everyone. Mrs. Faragos had become old, stooped, addicted to daytime TV, and her face and body started to erode, sag and wrinkle. If she were a cliff, she was about to fall into the sea.

Cooking smells from the kitchen clogged the air. Mrs. Faragos again stuck her head around the kitchen door. "Joey Balfour, I am baking your favorite cookies. With lots and lots of chocolate chips."

Mrs. Faragos didn't cook or bake all that much but she had a thing about baking oatmeal cookies packed with chocolate chips. Mr. Faragos had a feeling that somewhere in British Columbia was a penny-mining company, that had as much gold inside as chocolate in one of his wife's cookies.

"And your friend, Marty, I am glad you brought him round. I understand that you boys are now stockbrokers. I always told your mother that I thought Joey had a mind of numbers."

"I didn't know you came back to live in Vancouver," said Mr. Faragos. "I thought you'd left for the States." He said this as if the United States was some distant country that took an expedition of natives to carry the necessities of life through gorges, mountain passes and over swamps.

Mrs. Faragos shouted from the kitchen. "They all come back. Who can resist Vancouver?"

"I've been back for awhile."

"I am so glad that you phoned, Joey."

He looked at Mr. Faragos who winked. He obviously wasn't leveling with the wife about his little betting pastime and was likely lying about other matters as well, such as the amount of money going into mining shares in mining activities that produced little more than new burrows for earthworms. Joey was curious where old man Faragos came up with the money he was laying down.

"I've often wondered how you two were getting along."

"Same as always," she called out, a disembodied voice carrying on a conversation.

"We like it here," said Mr. Faragos.

Then she walked into the sitting room. "You've done so well. So many of the boys in that school have ended up driving taxis." She carried a large plate piled with oatmeal cookies and put it down on a tray in front of the TV. After she looked at the plate, she sighed.

"I've not baked these cookies since last year." A tear dribbled down the side of her cheek.

"Why don't you boys sit down?" Mr. Faragos asked as he struggled to unfold an aluminum chair from a row that was stacked four deep next to the door. He positioned the chair beside the tray and then unfolded a second chair. By this time he had gotten the hang of it. The second chair was ready and put in place. Marty sat down first and picked a cookie from the plate and started to eat. Then the tears flowed down Mrs. Faragos's cheeks and she fled to the kitchen. Everyone could hear her blowing her nose from the living room; one of those honking noises like a Canadian goose defending its territory in Stanley Park. A moment later she came out with two glasses of milk and handed one to Joey and then the other to Marty who was by now on his third cookie.

Her husband sat on the couch looking as lean as ever. Joey thought they'd both aged about fifty years each. *Living in this small apartment with all the cooking smells and never getting out would age anyone*, thought Joey. Tanned their very being like a bear hide. They might have been time travelers locked forever in the sideshow in a past universe. Their clothes, furniture, the lamps, everything in their lives had come from a different era. Joey felt comfort as if he had just come home from high school and, before he had to do his homework, a neighbor had set out a plate of oatmeal cookies freshly baked for him and Marty to eat.

As he stared at the cookies, he also felt a sense of horror in thinking that none of this was real. What was real to Joey Balfour was that time had moved on. He had grown up. He no longer lived in the penthouse with his parents, he no longer had homework—in fact he never had homework even when he was supposed to because it was that kind of school—and he was basically back where he started. He drove a taxi and worked as a weekend bookie out of a stockbroker's office. He had come full circle. The Faragos were at the same place in the circle and he had this feeling he could go around and around, and each time he looked in, they would have aged a little more but nothing else would have changed.

"If this isn't a good time, Mrs. Faragos, we can come back another time," said Joey.

"Yeah, if you're not feeling well, we can go."

She shook her head, her lower lip quivering as if she might start crying again. "No, please stay. I am fine. Really, I want you to stay. It will make me feel better."

Joey exchanged a glance with Marty, who shrugged. He looked over at Mr. Faragos. He thought of the bookie operation and how Mr. Faragos was the punter assigned the Number seventeen. *Betting twenty bucks on the Giants, what a mug,* thought Joey. He couldn't help but feel sorry for the Faragos.

"You see, today is 14 October."

It was as if Joey and Marty should automatically understand the importance of that date and why it was the source of great sadness for Mrs. Faragos. "That's the day Errol died." She lifted her eyes up to the ceiling, and two stories above was the penthouse.

"She always bakes oatmeal cookies for this day. You can bet on it." Again Mr. Faragos winked at Joey. Well, he wasn't getting any odds on that not happening from what was obviously a perfect record on Mrs. Faragos's part.

"That was a long time ago," said Marty.

"1959. 14 October 1959. It seems like yesterday." The tears rolled down her cheeks. Snuffling, she walked back into the kitchen and closed the door, honked into a tissue or a towel or the sink, it wasn't clear from the outside what was going on inside the kitchen. When she finally came out a few minutes later, Mrs. Faragos had put on fresh lipstick and had combed her hair. "I am feeling better now." She had on her brave face.

Mr. Faragos nibbled on an oatmeal cookie, holding it in his spindly fingers, almost rat-like claws. "Later we light a candle and say a prayer," said Mr. Faragos.

"It's a tradition," said Mrs. Faragos. "One we never miss."

"He was good to us," said the husband, plopping the rest of the cookie in his mouth and drinking from Joey's untouched glass of milk.

"Errol had a premonition of death," she said. "When he was in Cuba he was nearly killed. A lot of people don't know he was wounded in combat. He got it in the leg. Not bad. But it caused him pain."

"That's a bit of an exaggeration," said Mr. Faragos. "The way he told it, he had a bit of a flesh wound, the size of a quarter, when a stray bullet ricocheted against a plaster wall and a piece of plaster hit him. He never made a big deal out of it."

"He was proud of that wound, Lester," said Mrs. Faragos in a fiercely loyal voice. "It was a combat wound. No question in his mind about the meaning of that wound. He bled real blood. He told me it made all the difference in the world. Between real blood and that fake blood the Hollywood stunt coordinator smeared on him, there was the difference between day and night. He said that. I remember when he stopped me reading about dueling in that Tolstoy book. He pulled the book down from my face and looked at me. He said, 'There is a big difference between men who challenge you to a duel and those who would shoot you in the back.'"

That may have been the first time Joey ever heard Mr. Faragos, AKA Number 17, being called by his first name. The initials were L.F.; Life Failure and Lester Faragos matched. The name and the initials had been tailored to fit Mr. Faragos. His entire life had been spent in Errol Flynn's shadow.

"It left a scar," Mrs. Faragos said. Then she turned to Joey. "When you were going to high school you'd come along and ask me all kinds of questions about Errol Flynn. What did his girlfriend look like? How did he die? What room did he die in? Do you remember asking all those questions?"

"Yes, Mrs. Faragos." His eyes were on her photograph and she followed his gaze. Everyone in the room stared at the photo until Mrs. Faragos broke the spell by reaching over the sofa and pulling the framed photo from the top of the walnut bureau. She breathed on the glass until it fogged over and then polished it with her sleeve.

"I was nineteen when he took that photograph." She hugged it to her chest.

"Errol took the photo," said Mr. Faragos. "She only brings it out once a year. On 14 October."

"So what happened on 14 October when Errol Flynn died?" asked Joey Balfour who had suddenly lost his appetite. He'd heard versions of the story. Each time she told it, there was a new detail.

"She is very tired," said Mr. Faragos. "It would be better if you boys came round another day. Now that I have your number, I can call you. I will be in touch."

Joey rose and for the first time noticed that the *Robin Hood* movie poster had vanished from the wall. He looked over at Faragos and back at the wall. "What happened to the *Robin Hood* poster?"

"Lester sold it to invest the money. We saw a TV show about how you should invest money. We need to think about our future," said Mrs. Faragos.

Faragos sold *Robin Hood* to bet on the Giants. *What a mug,* thought Joey.

"Late Friday afternoons are a good time to reach me," said Joey.

Marty helped himself to a handful of cookies and they left, with Mrs. Faragos sitting on her knees in the middle of the sofa, hugging her photograph.

"I always said they were weird," said Marty.

"Did I ever say they were normal?"

"Subnormal. Paranormal."

"Definitely not normal, normal. I was this close to ratting him out to Mrs. Faragos," said Joey, holding up his hand and leaving only a crack of light to pass between his thumb and finger. "Selling those posters to bet on the Giants. What a mug."

Dan Harris Repays a Debt
to Joey's Father

The following week, after they left the stockbroker's office, an unmarked RCMP car was parked at the curb in front of Marty's taxi. He'd driven a taxi long enough to spot the unmarked cars that cops used. He wondered why they even bothered. The people who couldn't spot an unmarked RCMP car were the sort of people who never committed crimes. As Marty opened the door, a tall, well-built man in a dark suit got out of the cop car and walked over to the taxi.

"Hi, Joey. I heard you were back in town."

At first glance Joey couldn't remember the face of this stranger in the suit and tie in an unmarked cop car. "Sorry, officer, is there something you want?"

"You don't remember me?"

Joey looked the officer over. He had no memory of this man.

"Remember the night you were standing around a barrel fire on Thurlow Street and you told me that you had a draft card, and I asked you to throw it in the fire, but you refused? You said you had a mission to spread the word about registering for the draft in foreign countries. I really thought that was such an incredible idea."

A big grin crossed Joey's face. "Dan Harris. What in the fuck are you doing hijacking an RCMP car?"

"Hop in. Let's go for a ride," said Dan Harris. "You can catch up with Marty later."

Marty sized up the situation. There was no percentage in arguing about whether Joey was going with Dan. That had already been decided. "Hey, I'll see you later. At the usual place."

Dan drove along Marine Drive; he swung the unmarked police car into the gravel parking lot at Spanish Banks. He got out, walked around to the front and leaned against the hood of his car and looked out at English Bay. He drew the cool sea air into his lungs. It was still daylight. In the distance, half a dozen tankers lay anchored in the bay, and a dozen or so sailboats skated along the West Vancouver side of it. Joey hadn't seen Dan Harris for years and had no idea that he'd become a cop and even less of an idea why he had been waiting for him as they closed up their book for the weekend. Joey sat in the car for a couple of minutes before getting out. Then he walked past Dan and onto the beach and squatted on a log facing the sea, watching his fog of breath curl from his nostrils. Dan Harris joined him a few seconds later.

"After I finished my PhD, I joined the RCMP," said Dan Harris.

"I didn't know the RCMP hired draft dodgers."

"As long as you don't have a record, you're fine. I was never indicted, but the charges were dropped. So it wasn't a problem. Of course I disclosed the issue."

"I didn't quite make it through university," said Joey.

"That's what I heard. You had the brains to do just about any-thing, if you wanted to that is. But you can't make someone study, or like books."

"Is that the reason you were waiting for me tonight? To tell me how smart I am?"

Dan Harris picked up a handful of sand and let it slip between his fingers. "There's a problem, Joey. I thought as we went back a long way I'd let you know what was going down and give you some advice. You can choose to take it or not. But I hope that you will take it."

"What's going down?"

"My sources tell me the broker's office is in serious trouble and has been for about four months. He's doing some crooked stuff with a couple of companies. About a month ago, we got information that there was a bookie operation working out of his office. The book runs for a couple of hours every Friday. It's a professional operation. Everyone who wants to put down a bet is assigned a number before they phone. So when they phone no names are used. They just give a number, the amount they're betting and the team they are betting on. Almost no names. About a week ago you slipped up and mentioned the name of one of the punters and he mentioned your name on the phone. Your name and the punter's are in a printout. That means that your name is part of our investigation. Next week there is going to be a warrant for your arrest. I could probably get one for Marty but why bother? You are the guy who put the operation together. You have real talent, Joey. I knew that from the moment I first met you in front of a bonfire. But Vancouver isn't the place for you to display those talents. If you want my advice, go back to Las Vegas. Establish yourself in Vegas. There are no laws in Nevada you have to worry about. If you stay in Vancouver, you are going to be arrested and you are probably going to prison. There's nothing I can do about that."

A long silence fell between them as a foghorn blasted across the water. Joey knew without being told that the RCMP had been running a wire on the stockbroker's office. Dan Harris couldn't come straight out and tell him about the wire but Joey could see it in his eyes. He could tell from the information that Dan had told him that the RCMP had been listening in on their telephone calls.

"How long do I have?"

"Until Monday."

That didn't leave much time to tie up loose ends, thought Joey. In fact it was downright unreasonable to expect him to pack up and close the book before at least Tuesday. He looked at Dan for some hint of what cards he held. Only Dan wasn't giving anything away.

"Can you give me until Tuesday? Then I can settle up."

Dan Harris was silent, throwing a couple of small stones at the shoreline. "Okay, but after Tuesday, Joey, it's out of my hands."

As Joey rose from the log, he shivered. He dusted the sand off his pants, turned and faced Dan Harris. Joey's father had been the one to argue with the department head at the University of British Columbia as to why they should let Dan Harris into the psychology department even though his undergraduate marks from Colorado had been below par.

"I guess I owe you."

Dan Harris smiled. "Let's say we are even. And say hello to your mother and father."

Joey looked over the bay at the lights in West Vancouver. It was a long, last look, and a sense of sadness filled him as he turned and walked through the sand, wondering how he was going to break the news to Marty.

Disappearing
into the Big Nothingness
of Bangkok

According to their personality profile, gamblers share a great deal in common with armed robbers, CIA agents, undercover cops, snipers, terrorists, and soldiers in combat. They possess the AFE Personality Matrix: anxiety, fear and excitement, which release chemical compounds into the blood stream that do powerful things to the body and brain, creating reactions and highs that the best drugs can't replicate.

On the third floor of the hospital, Jim Pauley sits on the examination table in Dr. Daeng's surgery, his legs dangling like a child's over the hard, flat examination table. When Howard Boggy comes into the room and offers his hand the chemicals hit Pauley's blood stream with a jolt. The rush into Pauley's system causes the blood to drain from his face. He enters the event horizon where a state of shock is a tiny step away. Time slows down. His mind concentrates on every feature of the young, bearded backpacker with long, unkempt hair. Pauley harvests each element, shaping these details, running through his memory, trying to place him from the past. He is too young to have been in Las Vegas. Is he a hit man and this is the moment of his death? Pauley's first impulse is to flee.

Boggy's smiling round face tilts to the side as he looks at the photograph he has taken from Joey's condo and at the man sitting on the edge of the examination table.

Pauley feels like he's blinded by a red flashing light and his ears throb from the automatic voice in the cockpit which screams: *Pull up, pull up*—the mutant recorded voice most often heard once the black box is retrieved from the bottom of the ocean. Not getting caught, like not crashing, is the primary and secondary goal.

The face in the photo from Joey Balfour and the face of the man sitting inside Dr. Daeng's surgery match. But, now, Jim Pauley's face is more lined, with deep wrinkles ringing the mouth and nose and eyes, and Pauley definitely has developed more pronounced dewlaps, like a tom turkey. Pauley also wears gold-rimmed glasses and has the air of slight irony as if he's remembered where he left something. It's a kind, avuncular face. Pauley looks like someone who is everyone's favorite uncle: alert, receptive, patient, and understanding. Someone you would trust with money, your wife, or your life.

The top buttons of his shirt are undone and a strip of tape covers the long puffy pinkish incision line straight down the middle of his chest.

"The doctor says this stuff is better than duct tape," says Pauley. He runs his finger along the line of tape. "It holds me together. Pull off the duct tape and my heart falls out."

"It is our inside joke," says Dr. Daeng. "Gunnar is a fisherman from Norway. He tells me that you used to visit his village over the years. I thought how nice for the two of you to meet in Bangkok."

Pauley's cheeks billow out as he tries to control his breathing. "Good to see you, Gunnar. How has the fishing been?"

"Not so good this year. Next year it will be better. But meanwhile we survive the best way that we can." Boggy's ability to assume a degree of Nordic gloom surprises even himself. Then Boggy pulls the backpack off his shoulder and unzips a flap. Pauley's heart pounds against the duct tape. Is Gunnar reaching for a gun to finish the job?

Boggy pulls out a diary. He flips to the date and writes something. Pauley lets out a long sigh, and nearly faints. A radio is playing in the corner. Reports on the tsunami indicate that thousands may have died.

"Are you alright, Jim?" asks Dr. Daeng. But it is Dr. Daeng who is not alright. The thought of so many dead makes him sad, uneasy, confused.

"I am fine. No problem. Just a little shortness of breath."

Dr. Daeng is taking Pauley's pulse as Boggy sits across the way scribbling into the diary. The doctor looks at his watch. He's counting. Slowly, the racing pulse eases. His mind wanders as he thinks of people swept away in huge waves, children, women, old and young people, their breath taken away forever.

"What are you writing?" asks Jim Pauley.

"The start of my life is from this date."

"I must leave you two to catch up. I have another patient waiting."

Dr. Daeng lets go of Pauley's wrist. "You're okay. You can go now. Don't forget to take your medicine." He walks to his desk, his ear near the radio, listening to the Thai broadcast from Phuket.

Pauley buttons his shirt, steps into his shoes and heads for the door. Boggy follows behind; he has everything of importance in his life stashed inside his backpack. They walk through the reception area. Pauley goes to the cashier and takes out his wallet. Boggy stands at the counter next to him with a bemused look, which the nurse behind the counter believes is directed toward her. She smiles at Boggy but his unfocused eyes are not registering her smile. He's thinking of the Balfours. He hasn't told Jennifer that he won't be coming back to the pyramid. He certainly hasn't told Joey. What's the point? As Pauley pays the bill, Boggy decides he has no reason to feel guilty. It is Joey Balfour, after all, who imposed a tight deadline. It is Joey who showed the faint hint of compassion. Stumbling upon Jim Pauley in Dr. Daeng's surgery gives Boggy a flash of inspiration, a way to get back into business. Boggy's luck has changed, rewarding him in a Bangkok hospital with his favorite thing in life: a chance to move ahead into a new venture. He's already thinking how to play this hand.

"Well, Gunnar, this is where we part. Happy fishing," says Jim Pauley. His hand is not offered in friendship. Both of his are firmly planted on his hips.

"We need to talk."

"I don't think so," says Pauley walking toward the door.

"Bill Hunt and Joey Balfour are looking for you."

"Are you working for them?" The adrenaline is pumping through Pauley's body.

Boggy shakes his head. "No way. I only work for myself. It's my policy."

Pauley takes another close look at the young Howard Boggy. He doesn't remotely look like a person who would be working for Bill Hunt or Joey Balfour. Twelve years have elapsed since he fled Las Vegas and the world has changed a lot. "What do you want?"

"I need your help. I want us to work together. As a team."

"You need another hand on your fishing boat?"

Boggy's nose twitches, and he laughs. "I believe I can help you."

On the evening of the great tsunami, the sun has gone down and Pauley and Boggy walk through the grounds around Lake Ratcha. Darkness folds its skirt around the lake. The lake shimmers in the light from a hundred condominiums and dreamlike images emerge along the water's edge. The casualty estimates from the tsunami have been rising ever since the appointment with Dr. Daeng. All TV and radio broadcasts are non-stop bulletins of death and destruction. By evening, Pauley has digested enough news to cause him to see the ghosts of those who are from a life lost to him. Bill Hunt's face merges into Joey Balfour's. He quickens his pace as Boggy tries to keep up. Then he abruptly stops, goes to the edge of the lake and sits down. They watch a couple of yings laughing and joking, walking and holding hands as if the world is a safe place, as if they will live forever. Beautiful ghostly forms slipping in and out of the flickering light. There are no other foreigners around the lake. In the distance there's a forest of office buildings and condos—hundreds of them—and lights in the windows with people inside eating dinner, watching television, making love, contemplating suicide, wondering whether anyone they know has been swept away in Phuket. Here and there, lights are on in the high-rise office buildings; a few people are working late at night.

Boggy watches the yings until they disappear past the tree-lined edge of the water. "Dr. Daeng shouldn't have said anything," says Jim Pauley. His bitterness constricts his throat, making his words reedy and elongated.

"I am not trying to blackmail you."

Pauley stares at the water. "That's good because I have nothing to give you."

"How can I do that? I have people trying to kill me."

"That makes two us," says Pauley.

Howard Boggy gently shoves his good hand into the water, then leans back. Pauley puts a hand on his shoulder. In the larger scheme of things, Pauley decides that he's marginally better off than Howard Boggy. Boggy appears hopelessly out of place in Bangkok. Pauley's is an old case, the trail having gone cold. Was the casino fishing for their money after all these years? Pauley tries, at the best of times, to convince himself that they gave up long ago. There are many days in a row when Pauley doesn't look over his shoulder. He knows this is self-delusion. These people never forget or forgive. Over time, though, even the most vengeful become diverted. It is an age when someone who goes against the prevailing political opinion is tracked down by people with heavy resources and dispatched to the next life. Nothing is more orthodox than theft; criminal as it is, theft is a much safer form of rebellion against the unfairness and injustice of the system.

From what Boggy has confided in Pauley, it is safe to conclude that Boggy's crime is political. His Internet campaign besmirched the fine memory and reputation of J. Edgar Hoover, an icon of law enforcement, a cross-dressing legend of the highest elevation, and with a huge building in Washington D.C. named after him. This gives Jim Pauley the comfort of the traveler who cries that he has no shoes until he sees a man with no feet. The burns on Boggy's arms are the start of what these people have in mind for him.

"Joey is serious about finding you," says Boggy. "Bill Hunt has a search party beating the bush."

"I could have been in Phuket. I'd been living there until my operation." Pauley never so much as flinches at the name Bill Hunt. He shrugs it off. His mind runs through the possibilities of a new way of disappearing. The tsunami casualties play through his mind. He could have been one of them. "Bill Hunt's been after me off and on since 1992. From day one, finding me was his passion. I am what kept Bill going for three or four years after I left Las Vegas. In those years, he thought about me last thing at night and first thing in the morning. Not his wife, or ex-wife, or kids, or mother or the new dealer at the five-dollar table he wants to screw." This is partially true. Pauley knows that Bill Hunt had given up on finding him since about 1997. Not until Pauley sells his casino chips for a heart operation does the ex-security chief go back to the trail. Monster emotions of the past are once again activated. Bill's anger is again unleashed from inside his world and into the larger world where Pauley is hiding. He knew that this would be likely to happen. He'd prepared for it. Pauley knew at the time he had no other choice. What could he do? Die of a heart attack (*ninety percent chance,* said Dr. Daeng) or die at the hands of Bill Hunt (ten percent). One plays the odds. Sell the old chips at a steep discount, go to ground and hope it all blows over for one last time.

"You don't seem too worried?"

"Bill Hunt never forgave me for getting him in trouble. I took advantage of the time he was off the floor that night. Was it my fault that he was getting a blowjob from a hooker? If he finds me, then what is he gonna do? Is he going to beat me up? Kill me? Haul me back to Las Vegas in a tiger cage and display me in the streets and then in the casino?"

"Do you plan to live the rest of your life offline?" asks Boggy.

"When you disappear with a lot of someone else's money, that is part of the package. You accept going away and never being able to go back."

"I don't know how I'd live if I thought someone was always looking for me."

Jim Pauley looks over his gold-rimmed glasses at Boggy. *He's just a kid,* thinks Pauley, *with kid-like wonder about how people learn to cope as they navigate the sharp edges ringing the world.*

"In 1992, the casino and the police weren't certain where I'd run. At the casino, it was no secret that I had a Thai girlfriend. They also knew that I would expect them to start looking for me in Thailand. The odds were in my favor once I got out of Nevada. I had better information. The casino guys knew Las Vegas. But they were out of their element in Bangkok. With ten million people in the city in those days, where were they going to start? There are thousands of rabbit-warren lanes and thousands upon thousands of cheap rooms. They had no idea where to start looking. They hired locals to find me. They came up with nothing. There was no way they'd find the place I was living in along the coast in Khao Lak. And they knew they'd never find me and this made them wise. It would have cost them more money to find me than what I stole. They ran the numbers. Once they saw the bottom line, they wrote off the loss."

"Bill Hunt didn't write it off."

"He took it personally. So I knew I had to stay *disappeared*."

"You vanished without a trace." A rare hint of admiration is in the tone of Boggy's voice.

"Bill Hunt will go back empty handed. No one in Las Vegas thinks he can find me. If he couldn't do it in 1992, how's he going to pull it off now? He's crazy."

"It might be different this time. He has something that Joey Balfour wants."

Jim Pauley pulls out some grass and lets it slip through his fingers. A ying giggles as she brushes against his shoulders in the near darkness. "Joey Balfour was big time in the old days." Again he's being less than candid with Howard Boggy. What is the point of absolute honesty with a stranger who tracks you down through your doctor with wild stories? What Pauley sees, however, like all gamblers, is an opening, a way of changing the odds in his favor.

"He certainly knows you. He wants to find you as a favor for Bill Hunt."

"Why would Joey want to do that? What's in it for him?"

Boggy watches the calm surface of the lake.

"I asked why Joey Balfour wants to help Bill Hunt. They don't play at the same table."

"They were friends in Las Vegas."

"Kid, you don't know what you're talking about. Hunt hates Joey's guts."

"I don't have any evidence Hunt hates him." Boggy squares his jaw, his eyes large and bloodshot. He pauses as a smile ripples across his lips. "But I do have evidence that Errol Flynn was murdered."

The kid lives in a universe where evidence still matters, thinks Jim Pauley. "Errol Flynn. What are you talking about? Murdered? You're crazy."

"J. Edgar Hoover agreed to use the mob to kill Errol Flynn in Vancouver on 14 October 1959. They wanted him dead for their own reasons. He took money for the film and double-crossed them. And I can prove all of this."

"Sure, kid. J. Edgar Hoover popped a movie star. I guess he didn't like his movies."

"I am not asking you to believe me."

Boggy is a little hurt that Pauley doesn't at least give him the benefit of doubt. In the depths of his hacker mind, there was no doubt that J. Edgar Hoover snapped his fingers and a lot of people disappeared. His successors no doubt kept up the tradition. Like floating a *krathong*, every year the sins were washed away by contracting out the murder of someone who was making the system wobble. *Believing or not believing isn't really the point*, Pauley thinks. Boggy sulks in a quiet spot near the water.

"The point is," says Pauley, "you should learn to stay non-political."

Boggy doesn't respond.

"An economic crime is easier. You know who's coming after you and why they want you. It's nothing all that personal. You study the tracking methods before you snatch the money. Time wears them down. After all, it's only money."

He's survived on the run for twelve years. His instincts are well developed, and, despite his heart operation, he's ready and has been ready for some time to disappear into the big nothingness of Bangkok's backstreets. He's slipped inside a black hole where the light from the outside world never seeps in. Pauley lives in a place no one could ever find; it's off the books, a room in another universe.

"My wife and my kid had a tradition. Each year we came to this lake. But that was years ago before we moved to Khao Lak. Then she went to prison. Our kid is upcountry with her folks. I haven't seen my daughter or my wife since she got out. She has no idea where I am. That's the way I want to keep it."

Jim Pauley's Wife
Doesn't Shake Her Bootie

"You find anything on Rev. Joshua Cecil?"

Marty shrugs. "I am working on it. You ever hear of the Overseas Faith Protection Associates?"

"Born-again Mafia?" Joey grins and slaps Marty on the back. "You let me know when you get something interesting on that preacher."

A peasant carries a stuffed teddy bear bigger than himself like a sack of rice. He has two smaller stuffed bears as well; he offers all three stuffed bears to Joey and Marty as they walk towards him on Soi Cowboy. Joey waves him off. Tourists are drifting in and out of the bars. Greeters in short skirts grab at farang arms and legs, trying for their quota of customers. The vendor in plastic sandals and ragged clothes sidesteps the yings and offers the same stuffed toys to a tour group of elderly farang tourists—who are graying, overweight, bunched up and moving slowly, heads moving from side to side for a quick glance as touts open the curtains to show go-go dancers who are on point, their hands clasping chrome poles. They follow a young tour guide, also a farang, holding a slender rainbow-colored oblong tube above his head like the Statue of Liberty holding a torch, waving it for his charges to follow him to the Promised Land. Not surprisingly, none of them are tempted by a stuffed teddy bear the size of a business-class seat. But the teddy-bear vendor causes a brief moment of distraction, and a moment is all that is required for a bar ying to ambush the tour guide from behind. She snatches the torch and scampers into a double shop house bar. The elderly farang herd follow the new torchbearer without missing a beat.

The tour guide makes the noble gesture of throwing himself in their path, "Stop."

But herd instinct is a powerful thing to stop. The first couple of pensioners bump into him.

"I said stop. We aren't going inside."

Slowly, the tour guide, with the hand gestures of an experienced aircraft landing specialist, brings his group back onto the flight path. Joey stops and watches. He bets even odds with Marty—a thousand baht—that the tour guide will succeed in retrieving his magic wand. In less than three minutes, two bar yings walk out of the bar on either side of a middle-aged farang who has been convinced to hold the torch above his head. The tour guide runs up and takes the torch. His herd does the equivalent of pawing the ground, waiting to be led to the next pasture. Marty hands Joey a thousand-baht note. The peasant vendor grabs at the thousand-baht note but comes up with air in his hands and two dropped teddy bears in the dirt.

"Good instincts, poor coordination," says Joey, pocketing the money.

They walk toward the Asoke end of Soi Cowboy.

"I thought she would sell it or keep it, for sure," says Marty.

He tags along with Joey. He wants to follow up information leading to the whereabouts of one Jim Pauley, heart-operation patient, gambler, thief, and wife abandoner. The information filters its way to Joey through the bamboo telegraph, winding its way through the medium of Sully's wife who claims that Jim Pauley's ex-wife works behind the counter in a curbside food stall. The information is vague. The stall might be in Soi Cowboy or it might be at the Asoke end of Soi Cowboy, or it actually could be near the underground station beside Soi Cowboy.

"She might be mobile enough to hit multiple locations," says Marty.

"Unlikely. She'd have to pay juice to the Mafia at each location. That's a lot of noodle soup," says Joey.

A farang bar owner with a glass stands behind the counter of his outside bar. He's been watching the elderly tourists disappear up the other end of the soi. He nails Joey immediately as someone who is semi-famous, a player who, if he arrives in the soi, always shows after midnight. Midnight is the equivalent of ten in the morning in Joey's twenty-four-hour cycle. The yings love a farang who eats, sleeps, and makes love on their time cycle. An eighteen-year-old ying is at her personal best at four in the morning, and Joey knows that anyone over fifty needs to climb out of bed around two in the afternoon to keep up. Hunting yings down narrow sois with a pocketful of cash brings on a rush like raising your own private militia, thinks Joey. You get to plan the war exercise and take them to your own private command center. What could be a better use of money? Joey could never find a good answer to that question.

"You missed the free food," says the bar owner. "We were packed earlier. Not a seat anywhere. It's a little quiet now."

"You know a food vendor named Oy?" asks Joey. "She's got a Garuda tattoo on her left shoulder."

"Kinky tattoos, is that the latest thing that turns you on?"

"What are you drinking?"

"Black label," says the bar owner, rubbing the two-day-old stubble on his chin.

"Make yourself a double on my tab. This is Marty. He's from Vancouver. He's staying with me for awhile."

"Marty, what are you drinking?"

"Black label."

"And what will Mr. Las Vegas have to drink?"

"Tonic and ice."

This produces a wide grin on the bar owner's face. "On the wagon?"

"I avoid wagons. This time of night is too early to drink. At three or four, okay. But midnight? I don't do midnight."

"Man, we gotta close at one a.m. You sure you don't want me to put one in a doggy bag for later?"

When the waitress delivers the drinks, they are sitting on stools with a good view of the Asoke end of the soi and halfway down towards Soi 23 end as well.

"Oy's a common name," says the bar owner. "There are three Oys in Dollhouse and a couple more in Darling Bar."

"This one sells food. She's not a dancer."

"A food Oy. There probably aren't more than half a dozen of them."

"This Oy has a Garuda tattooed on her shoulder."

The bar owner takes a long drink from the double scotch whiskey. "Come to think of it, there is an Oy who used to sell food just outside the Asoke entrance. She does a killer *som tam*, she makes it with carrots. I love the stuff. But it gives me gas. I can send around one of my girls to see if she's still there. Most of the time the vendors knock off around midnight. But who knows, you might be lucky. She might show you her Garuda and you could get naked."

Joey and Marty find Oy in an apron, her hair tied in a bun, spooning up overcooked vegetables from deep inside a crusty sludge. She works the spoon around the edges of a hospital-sized aluminum tray scraping the last tailings of the evening. Then she fills a bowl with lumpish soup tattooed with floating palm oil slicks—it all looks like prison food. Oy's stall is near the Asoke end of the soi. She's in eyeshot of her best friend who works as a go-go dancer in a live music bar. Joey listens in on the conversation she has with a customer. Oy confides in the customer as she would a best friend. The customer has the sensual, available look that silverbacks fresh in the country make promises of lifelong devotion to. She's an early thirties bar ying near the end of her playing career. *She's got to be thinking about alternatives to pedaling her ass*, Joey thinks. The new crop of upcountry players get most of the action and the old ones lurk in the shadows hopeful of a comeback. The customer's about the same age as Oy, and she's still able to climb up on the stage and dance for ten hours to disco and rock music. It's like a fifty-year-old NBA player still going on the court and sinking a three-point shot from the corner. In between dancing she hangs out at the food stall, squatting on a plastic stool in her happy coat, an inhaler hanging from one nostril.

Joey feels vaguely depressed as Oy loads up a plate of food he's ordered. She puts it down on a small card table.

Marty sits at one end looking at an identical plate. "You're not going to eat this?" says Marty.

"I like Thai food."

"But it doesn't look like Thai food."

"Thai food eaten by the criminal class. Someone should write a paper on street food and prison food. One of those thoughtful, comparative pieces. Do these people notice any difference between the food on the street and the food they get in prison?"

"Does it matter?" asks Marty.

"It don't matter."

Joey waits until the dancer unplugs the inhaler from her nose and stamps out her cigarette before calling Oy over to the table. Marty and Joey are the only farang customers—they are invisible to the dipsticks, with their hands in their pants, who stroll past the roadside tables on their single-minded mission to raid the bars of Soi Cowboy.

"Oy, I am a friend of your husband's. I'd like to find him."

She freezes, blinks twice.

"I know Jim Pauley's your husband. So don't bullshit me. Tell me where I can find him." He holds up five one-thousand-baht notes. She looks at the money. She responds with a nod of her head to confirm that this is the right ying. "He run away to Phuket. I worry maybe he died with all those people."

She stands at the table, looking down at Joey and his untouched plate.

"Phuket? Seems a lot of people are suddenly going missing in that area. A Thai wife usually knows where her farang husband is. Even when he runs away. She knows whether he's alive or dead."

Oy shrugs. "Jim not tell me everything. He wants to go, Jim goes. I don't know if he's alive. I am an upcountry girl. I live in Bangkok only short time before I meet Jim." There's something in Joey's awkward body that gives him away as someone who is uncomfortable on a stool at a roadside food vendor's stand. His friend also has a faint sense of menace; his hard, large hands and hairy forearms make her shudder.

"I knew Jim Pauley in Las Vegas. My name is Joey. Maybe he mentioned me?"

"He never talk about America. Or his old friends." She collects money from one of the tables before turning back to Joey and Marty.

Jim has never told her about his old life in Las Vegas. She knows nothing of his friends. Nor does she really want to know. Except now, this minute, as the taxi queue on Asoke moves ahead one car at a time, she realizes that Joey Balfour is the most prized of all Thai possessions: a friend of her husband. "I not see Jim for a long time. I work here every day and I look, look, and think maybe he come past looking for me."

The traffic on Asoke backs up at the light. Exhaust fumes belch from a truck packed with chickens. Motorcycle taxi drivers drift to another table and wait for Oy to take their order. Marty fans the fumes but it does no good.

"Where did you live before?"

"We live upcountry in Surin, and then we live in Khao Lak."

"In Bangkok where do you live?"

Oy shakes her head. "I have trouble and Jim go to Bangkok. He doesn't wait for me."

"I asked where you live."

"With my friend in Klong Toey." A room in a slum teeming with people inhaling doses of dust, drugs, and doom.

"He left you while you were in prison?"

One of the taxi drivers is behind the counter lifting up the lids on pots and looking inside. Oy ignores the driver's intrusion into her private area.

"Jim tells me that he sick and need an operation. I worry about him every day. I cannot get him out of my mind." She touches her head with her finger.

Jim seems to affect people in that way. Bill Hunt, for instance.

"Which hospital did he go to, Oy?"

She shakes her head and whispers, "I don't know."

"The doctor's name?"

"He not tell me."

"Where'd he get the money for the operation?"

Her eyes shift to Marty. "From a friend."

"Maybe he's staying with a friend in Bangkok," says Joey.

She shakes her head. "He not ever have any farang friends. He says they no good."

"When was the last time you saw him?"

"Six months ago."

Joey ponders the reason why Oy chooses this corner to sell food. Out of all the places in Bangkok—not to mention a thousand places upcountry—she ladles out her noodle soup at the Asoke entrance to Soi Cowboy. Thai yings rarely do something without a good reason—whether it's murder or running a food stall. "Any chance you were working in Cowboy when you met Jim? In your mind, you figure that sooner or later he will drift back to Soi Cowboy and you will be waiting for him."

She rattles a stack of plastic bowls. "Farang know too much, no good."

"That sums up the art of odds making, Marty."

"Don't take bets from wise guys," says Marty. "Every working girl knows that much."

"We have a winner at the end of the table." Joey hands him back the thousand-baht note he'd won off him earlier. He looks around the pavement. Oy returns to her job, bending over the pots and pans, fishing out the final dregs of something that had started off as eggplant in the morning; what is stuck in the depths below in the bottomless pan no longer has any resemblance to eggplant or any other known vegetable. Thai motorcycle and taxi drivers hunch over their plates eating without complaint. Oy runs a soup kitchen for them and the bar yings.

The Asoke traffic is jammed; car, truck and bus engines race as drivers, half mad from waiting at the light, ram the accelerator to the floor, pedal-to-metal. In a hatred-fueled frenzy of lane changing, the front row speeds through the green light. The peasant class slurp pulpy wet food—a goo of green with black seeds—inhale the exhaust, eat sludgy lumps, and wonder whether they can find money from some mug fresh to the city, someone who'll supply enough cash for their next meal.

"He's gone to ground, Joey. Pauley ain't gonna be easy to find," says Marty.

"Guys like Pauley are predictable. Except when they do something unpredictable like steal from a casino."

"But finding him isn't. Even his wife is clueless."

"If you were on the run, would you tell your wife where you were hiding?"

Marty shrugs. "So why are we wasting our time here?"

"Because it isn't wasted. His wife has told us a great deal."

"It was lost on me."

"That's because you weren't listening."

"Name one thing she told you that I didn't hear."

Joey looks at his watch. "I don't think Pauley was anywhere near the tsunami. If he were down there, would she be working now? She'd be on a bus to Khao Lak. My guess is that she met Pauley in Soi Cowboy. People are creatures of habit. We are predictable. We feel safe with what we know. What we don't know frightens us. That's why guys are stupid enough to remarry their ex-wives. I'd bet that Pauley is swimming upstream to spawn and die. He'd go to the place that he thinks of as home. He'd drill into Oy's head: *You don't know me. I left you. You don't know where to find me.* Day after day, until she repeats it like a parrot. She's added a new line that he's missing in the tsunami. I'm betting Pauley's living within a short distance of Soi Cowboy."

"He could take a train."

"He could but it doesn't fit the profile. When he met Oy there weren't any skytrains in Bangkok. Predictability underscores odds making. A horse that runs well on a muddy track is not something you ignore when the rain clouds unleash a torrent. Or that the Yankees have a better record in night games against the Blue Jays. The same applies to finding somebody who doesn't want to be found. Grabbing Jim Pauley will be hard; it's another long-shot play like betting on Temperance Hill. Pauley should have been caught years ago. If Bill Hunt had been doing his job, Pauley would have been caught in the casino and just about now he would be getting out of prison in Nevada. You see, Marty, betting isn't rocket science and it's not voodoo, it's a combination of both. You have to believe in magic to win. The Thais believe in magic or *saiyasat.* This is the real stuff, black magic, voodoo. It can be good or bad. The truth is, some magic drifted onto Pauley that night in Las Vegas. He is praying that his luck will come through again. I figure he's close by. The chances are he finds a way to sneak around the corner, check on his wife, then disappear again. Just a glimpse and then he's gone again. He's a guy who pushes his luck. A guy like that usually runs out of luck sooner rather than later."

Marty turns on his stool and looks around. "What do you think of Star?"

That is like Marty; he builds up a question in his mind for days, and springs it when no one is expecting it. Joey needs a full minute to connect Star with Marty's *katoey* girlfriend.

"Nice."

"Nice?" He registers a high note.

"Nice." Joey smiles as Marty stares at his fingernails.

"Is it because Star's a *katoey* that you can't say anything more than 'nice'?"

Joey's smile shows a full set of upper and lower teeth. It is the Joey Balfour smile as he watched the showgirl shaking his martini on the show.

"You thought I didn't know Star was a *katoey*? That's it?" Marty's mood swings through the gateways of anxiety, uncertainty, anger.

"I never said that."

"Why are you sounding hostile when I mention her name? And that smile. I know that smile."

Ironic, thinks Joey, *how Marty works up a good rage and then accuses me of hostility.* This is his best friend. He eases back in his seat, pauses, and waits for a moment until Marty calms down. "You know my smile?"

"'*Shake that bootie, shake that bootie.*'" His bad parody from Joey's old TV show is unnecessary, and Marty immediately regrets it.

Joey shakes his head. "I was thinking of Pauley's face when we finally catch up with him. That's what I was thinking." But he wasn't thinking about Pauley; his mind drifts to his mother and how difficult it is to accept that her senior moments are becoming senior days, and the mask of fear she wears each time memory flares out, leaving her in darkness.

In 1968 Joey Balfour Discovered the Twin Pillars of Existence

Joey's father, Professor Trenton H. Balfour, while never a household name, was well known in his field. His father's reputation in marine biology was second to none—his seminal paper on the mating habits of killer whales was turned into a book that sold almost a thousand copies. Charles Darwin was his hero and only the intervention of Joey's mother prevented Joey from being named Charles Darwin Balfour rather than Joseph Darwin Balfour. At two days old, Joey had his first compromise imposed on him. It would take him years before he understood life was a series of imposed compromises, starting when he was seventeen and living with four other people in a fifth-story walk-up in the East Village, working for the McCarthy campaign, folding leaflets, handing out leaflets, smoking dope, attending rallies, organizing a poker game in his room, phoning contributors for more money, and later in phoning bookies and placing bets, and finally being told to leave town. He once told his TV audience the main lesson of his life was learning to distinguish between asking for the right count and the fair count.

"Deal makers, gamblers, or hustlers follow the same rule. They understand that to survive they've got to settle for the fair count. That means they are happy to walk away with ninety percent. Assume ninety percent of what you deserve as the default. Take it. Accept it. Let the rest go. What's the alternative? It's saying that life owes you the right count. No one is owed the right count. Life isn't organized that way."

His father had written anti-war letters to the newspaper. His parents helped organize anti-war rallies. It was no surprise that when the time came, he agreed with Jennifer that for his son's future it made sense to start a new life in Canada. Professor Trenton discovered from his wife the details of Joey's tenure in New York City and how his son's political activities had resulted in his placement at the top of the list of young men to be drafted and sent to the rice paddies of Vietnam. Joey had dropped out of school. Once he registered for the draft it was a forgone conclusion Joey would get no deferment. The only question was when his son would be drafted. Trenton was a man who was more at home in the ocean than on land. Darwin explained everything of consequence to him. Survival of the fittest also applied to class divisions. This explained his views about Martin Gage, Joey's best friend. Marty belonged to a class located somewhere down the food chain lurking at the bottom of the sea.

Professor Balfour discouraged Joey's friendship with Marty. The supposedly firm New York Yankees deal was dismissed as one of those stories that older boys told younger boys to make them seem more important than they really were. Lying was an alpha-male ploy often found in the wild and, depressingly, such cheating and fraud often allowed the cheat to pass along his genes at the expense of the more straightforward and honest killer whale. Why couldn't Joey spend more time with Dan Harris? The first time that Professor Balfour met Dan Harris, they liked each other. Like two dogs satisfied after sniffing each other's assholes, Joey told Marty after the initial meeting. Joey had invited Dan Harris up to the penthouse to show him the bedroom where Errol Flynn had been found dead. When the elevator opened straight into the foyer and the wet bar, Joey could see that Dan Harris was more than impressed.

"I guess they don't have penthouses in Colorado," said Joey, opening a beer and handing it to Dan.

"Excellent," said Dan Harris, sipping the beer and looking around. It was unclear whether he was talking about the foyer or the cold beer or both.

They went into Joey's parents' bedroom and Joey stood at the foot of the bed, pointing. "Errol Flynn, probably one of the greatest actors who ever lived, died right there. Had his last vodka, chewed his fingernails down to the quick, had his last hard-on and sucked in his last breath. Clutched his heart and it was lights out.

No rehearsal. He just croaked. I heard the whole story from eye witnesses." Joey circled the bed before jumping feet first into the middle of the blue and white duvet. He stretched out on the bed, head to the side, stuck his tongue out and closed his eyes. "They found him like this."

He left out that the Faragos, his "eye witnesses", were certified crazy, unemployed, shiftless people, avoided by everyone in the apartment house except Joey Balfour.

Professor Balfour walked into the bedroom as Joey sprawled out on the bed, acting out how Errol Flynn was found. The professor wasn't expecting to find Joey and his new friend inside the bedroom, with Joey on the bed, arms and legs spread out. But he had come to understand that his son had an appetite for the unexpected. Joey opened one eye to find his father standing above him. He rose up on his elbows, smiling.

"This is Dan Harris. He's from Colorado and he's on the run from the draft."

Dan flushed and his face and neck turned a bright crimson. "Joey was showing me how Errol Flynn died in this room."

Professor Balfour lit his pipe, setting off a great billow of grayish smoke. "I see, Errol Flynn. Robin Hood and Captain Blood."

"It's true," said Joey. "Tell Dan that it's true."

"You must choose those whom you consider to be winners with considerable care."

A blank look fell upon Dan Harris's face.

"What my father is saying, is Errol Flynn was not a winner, and, if I think otherwise, then I'm faced with extinction and his genes as well as my genes go gurgle, gurgle down the evolutionary drain." Joey climbed off the bed and went over to the balcony, pulling back the curtains. "English Bay."

"Actors play at life," said Professor Balfour. "All of nature shows that playing at life isn't the best survival technique; unless you are . . ."

"A dung beetle and carrying your own weight in shit—everything else is considered play." Joey laughed as he watched his father puff on his pipe. He liked finishing this particular sentence and his father nodded his approval as if the lesson had stuck in Joey's mind.

Dan Harris returned many times to the penthouse—at the invitation of Professor Balfour. Joey let his friend drift into the strong tide of his father's life and scholarly interest. He knew the pull of such a tide and had fought it his entire life; he was glad to have his father's attention diverted by someone a couple of years older who could be a stand-in for the role that Professor Balfour had cast for his son, that which his son had failed to accept. Joey often found them talking in the sitting room. Dan Harris leaning forward in the chair, his father sucking on his pipe, thinking in silence before launching into another one of his lectures about Charles Darwin, the meaning of life and the hopelessness of the war in Southeast Asia. Joey sometimes squeezed himself into a chair, eating an apple, listening to his father. Not a word about Errol Flynn ever slipped from his lips. The shadow of the actor was everywhere but his father purposefully chose to ignore him, thought Joey. It had become a source of irritation for father and son, not helped by the constant storytelling of the Faragos who patrolled the corridors of the building like janky storm troopers unaware that the war was long over and that Berlin was in the hands of the Americans, Russians, French and British.

"All life has a common thread," said Professor Balfour. "The will to survive and reproduce. Everything else is secondary to those twin goals. But who survives? That is the question."

"The fittest?" asked Dan Harris.

Professor Balfour waved his pipe, trailing a wisp of smoke like a World War II Japanese Zero spiraling out of control, framed against a dark blue horizon, headed for the bottom of the Pacific Ocean. "Precisely. But it is more complex than just fitness. Survival depends on building the right defenses against predators and enemies, and adapting those defenses over time as your competitors evolve and become more clever and, to make matters worse, the members of the opposite sex become more scarce."

Joey thought about mentioning what the pimps and drug addicts called Baby Alley, a back lane a couple of blocks from their apartment building. After one in the morning, Baby Alley filled up with dozens of fourteen- and fifteen-year-olds who caused massive traffic jams as customers slowed down, looked over the wares, flossed the pretty ones, and leaned over and opened the passenger door. "Come inside, baby."

There was never anything clever at work in Baby Alley as far as Joey could see. The babies in Baby Alley wanted money; the customers wanted teenage sex. To survive was about resources, money. The main defense in a world of competitors cruising Baby Alley was to have more money than the guy in the car ahead. If his father hadn't married real money, then Trenton's competitors, according to his own theory, would have already dismembered his body and tossed it into the sea for turtles and sharks to eat, and they certainly wouldn't be living in the penthouse that Errol Flynn had rented with real Hollywood-minted money.

"The thing with killer whales," said Joey, "is they don't have money."

Both Trenton and Dan Harris went silent, turning their attention to Joey.

"They find their own way to protect themselves," said Dan Harris.

"Gangster whales shaking down other whales," said Joey.

It became heated when Professor Balfour intervened. "All life is a struggle to survive. But living the good life is more than surviving. It means getting a proper education. The beauty of a good university education is that you are equipped for life. Have you told Dan about your acceptance to Dartmouth?"

He hadn't told anyone about Dartmouth once he found out there wasn't a decent horse-racing track within fifty miles. He could hardly believe anyone would build a university so far away from a racetrack. What were these people thinking? At least they could have disclosed this difficulty in the college brochure. Who in their right mind would go to a university with no local racetrack? Trenton of all people should have understood that; they lived within a taxi ride of Exhibition Park.

"I've applied to UBC," said Dan Harris. "But I have a problem with my transcript. My old university in Colorado won't release it. And my grades weren't that great. So maybe it doesn't matter if it's released or not."

This was one of those godsent gifts Professor Trenton Balfour prayed for on a rainy afternoon: a chance to help a young man realize his dream of a university education. And at the same time, it gave him an even better chance to throw his weight around and show that his reputation and stature in the university were not limited to the study of the relationship between breeding and hunting grounds of killer whales. What Joey Balfour learned was a mixture of his father's standard Darwin lecture mingled with his experience of living on the lower eastside of Manhattan—take money off mugs before someone else beats you to cleaning out their bank account. That's survival of the fittest.

"You really got into Dartmouth?" asked Dan Harris as they waited for the elevator to come up to the foyer.

"It's no big deal. My father went there. He pulled a string."

Dan Harris shook his head. Even though he'd fled to Canada he still retained the innocent belief in the incorruptibility of American elite universities. "Not possible."

"I'll probably go to a school in Washington, D.C."

The elevator arrived and Dan Harris walked in. He turned around and faced Joey.

"And pass up Dartmouth? Are you nuts?"

"Dan, have you ever been to the horse races?"

Dan didn't say anything. He was still under the spell of Trenton.

"I can sum up my father's belief in a sentence."

"I doubt it," said Dan Harris.

"Survival and fucking are the twin pillars of existence. All the rest is just endless explanation. He likes to yammer on and on. That's what he gets paid to do at the university. But it all comes down to those two things. I intend to do both. But not at Dartmouth." This was a lesson Joey Balfour learned at his father's knee.

The elevator doors shut and Joey felt this would be the last time he would see him. But something deep inside his being whispered that someplace, somewhere that the business with Dan Harris wasn't over.

Most People's Lives Are Tragedies

Joey's plan requires an act of great patience, an ability to fight against the evils of boredom, exhaust pollution and the hawkish eyes of police patrolling the streets. The cops are looking, like the yings, to score money from the dipsticks blown out of the coughing, demented engines of Europe and America as they empty out of the bars at one in the morning; but rather than return to their lodgings, like any dipstick short on oil, they are on the street looking for lubrication. Joey walks up to a taxi at the back of the taxi queue, and motions for Marty to climb in; he slides in beside Marty and closes the door.

"Where you go?" asks the driver, eyeing the two farangs in his back seat.

"We wait, my friend," says Joey. "Turn on the meter. My friend, she's very slow. So maybe we wait a long time. No, problem, okay?" He slides a five-hundred-baht note over the seat and watches the driver's eyes grow large. *In the service industry, as a rule of thumb,* thinks Joey, *the iris dilation on the receiving end of money is inversely related to the amount of the note.* This is a night's worth of cash upfront for keeping the farang happy.

"Air-con," says Marty. "Thank God, I can breathe again."

"You remember that time when I went broke?"

"Yeah, when the Orioles lost to the Mets. And you put everything you had on the Orioles."

"At the time, I felt a bitter taste in my mouth. I promised myself that I would never go broke again."

"You kept your promise," says Marty.

"But I never stopped making large bets. What I stopped doing was making bets on bad information. I told myself I would get better information. I knew that if I was going to come back I would need to find new and better ways of interpreting. When I got back to Las Vegas after our little bookie operation was closed down, the first thing I did was hire information interpreters. Most smart people lack imagination or courage. I knew that I had one great skill. I could manage smart people. Smart people aren't smart enough to manage themselves. Most of them know it. I supplied the courage that they lacked. I figured out a way to make money from their brains and intellect. Once when I was on *Crossfire* I said, 'Betting is not rocket science and it's not voodoo, it's a combination of both. You have to believe in magic.'"

Marty wishes he had a dollar for every time Joey repeated his rocket science and voodoo saying. "You're saying Bill Hunt is using you to acquire information and then getting you to interpret it so he can find Jim Pauley."

"Regrettably you are partially right," sighs Joey.

"What's the other part that I am not getting?"

"Bill Hunt isn't seeing the big picture."

"He doesn't care about any picture other than the one that has Jim Pauley framed in it."

"That's what makes him stupid, and stupid people either undershoot or overshoot the mark. They never get the range of the target."

Marty stretches out in the back of the taxi. "What's the big picture?"

"I'd say someone has got to Bill Hunt and made a plan he couldn't resist."

"Yeah, who got to him?"

"You have to lay the information out, line it up like you would to one of those five-thousand-piece jigsaw puzzles. I want a particular poster and negotiate with our friend Boggy."

"You mean Gunnar."

"Let's call him the red-bearded Maine computer freak. What does Boggy do? He gets himself into a situation because he has too many brains cells and no one to rein him and teach him technique. That boy needs a good trainer. He gets himself straight into the face of the Feds, who may or may not have bombed his apartment. He runs to Vancouver. He looks you up. And through you, he hooks up with my mother. She needs someone in her life that reminds her of better days thirty years ago when there was nothing she couldn't pull from her memory, fresh and clear."

"You had told me about him. So I let him in. And I helped him. He said you were his friend."

Marty takes it personally, as Joey knows he would.

"So what does Boggy do? He finds out about the old apartment where I lived as a kid. Vancouver's a small place and he's a smart boy. He'd have figured that out even if you didn't help him. He gets into a conversation with the Faragos and it doesn't take him long before he has mined seriously important information. Stuff he could never have found on the Internet because it exists only in the memories of the Faragos. Then Bill Hunt turns up in Vancouver and throws money at the Faragos. He saw that rare one-of-a-kind poster and wasn't going to leave without it. How does a guy like Bill Hunt know about the penthouse in Vancouver or the Faragos or about Errol Flynn posters? The answer is he doesn't, unless someone who does know explains the possibilities."

"Boggy told him?"

Joey shakes his head, laughs and passes another five hundred to the driver. It looks like Oy is about finished washing out and stacking the trays and folding everything into what looks like a giant bin, one that folds inward like an umbrella. "No, not Boggy. More likely it was someone who had inside information. He might have followed Boggy to Vancouver. They knew Errol Flynn died in the penthouse. I said that on TV. It was no secret. But what they don't know and want to find out is exactly what other pieces of evidence might be floating around that Boggy might lead them to."

Joey fingers the business card of the Rev. Joshua Cecil. It has been on his mind for a long time. The preacher who knew an Indian tribe owned his old TV show and expected Joey to take the show off the air.

"I found out that the Overseas Faith Protection Associates is owned by an offshore company called Interfaith Evangelical Coalition."

"God seems to be working through many companies, Marty. Soon He will be doing an IPO."

"I am getting copies of lists of the board of directors. I should have them in a day or so."

Joey's impressed.

"What do you think? Was Hunt hired by some shell company being used by the Feds?" asks Marty.

"Not directly. He's working for someone. He's too well funded. Also, it's personal. Jim Pauley caused him some definite pain. Bill wants personal payback. The Feds are working a different angle. I can't figure out their game. It's not just money. Maybe if they put the screws on Pauley to plea-bargain to a lesser charge. The judge gives him a light sentence and in return he points the finger at me. He says I am the guy who cashed in a bet that was the signal all was clear, and that I got Dan Harris's niece to give the chief of security a blowjob so that Pauley could walk out of the casino and not get caught."

"Is that how it happened, Joey?"

"If you were on a jury, would you believe it? It doesn't matter that I say I never knew the bimbo was Dan Harris's niece. Who's gonna believe me?"

Marty is silent, shifts in his seat, the awkward shift of someone who is avoiding an answer, a twitching, nervous movement of hips and legs.

"Why do they want you?"

Joey shrugs, shoulders slumped forward, meaning he has no idea who they are or what they want.

A couple of Thai men in a car stop at the light; they stare at Joey. They're blabbering non-stop and the conversation is apparently about him. It is impossible for Joey to read their lips. They talk too fast and in another language. One of the men points at Joey and laughs. Maybe they find it highly amusing that two farangs sit in the back of a taxi, going nowhere, talking and gesturing. Or maybe they are part of a surveillance team; their hair is short, military or police style. They linger too long. Other cars pass them. Who do they belong to? To what team have they sworn allegiance or is it a game of watching the farangs? Joey has lost his ability to distinguish the finer points of human behavior; it is disturbing that he must assume that what is probably just ordinary behavior might be a threat, that the actors are harboring an agenda; that they are working for powerful forces unseen but always nearby. Ever since Boggy's arrival with the burnt arm in a sling, the other holding a nickel-plated gun on him, Joey's been noticing people in a different fashion. People who are waiting: are they reporting what they witness, gathering information to report later, a cell phone to their ear, their eyes on him? What does it mean? People are in the field gathering, storing, interpreting, processing and analyzing information. Everyone he sees seems to be working as part of a larger cell.

Marty stares back. "Those guys must be drunk."

"See the short hair. That means they are uniforms."

"Yeah?" asks Marty. "I don't see any uniform."

"You ever hear of the word 'clandestine'? It means officials who hide out in civilian clothes and inside civilian jobs. You don't know they're working for the government. Until it's too late and they show a badge and cuff you. No one has any idea anymore how many people go missing each year. No investigation. No follow-up. They will never return and no one cares. It is as if society has gone into one long senior moment."

The driver hits the accelerator, burns a strip of rubber. They are gone. Marty is new to the way Thais stare in an unblinking fashion, as if to decode some mystery in a farang's face or clothing or manner. The taxi driver, following Joey's instructions—this itself is a miracle in the Soi Cowboy taxi queue—signals for the taxi behind him to pull ahead. Joey watches as the other taxi moves past them; he sees the long-tooth grin of the driver, looking over his shoulder at Marty and Joey. He's laughing. A few seconds later, Oy's bar ying friend shows up arm in arm with a fifty-something farang, his shirt untucked, his hair messy; he's thumbing through a Thai–English dictionary as the ying pulls him toward the taxi. She doesn't want to hear his broken Thai. She opens the door of the taxi in front of Joey and Marty's, and throws her catch inside like a skinny fisherman hauling in a fucking huge marlin. She climbs in after him.

"I don't get why anyone's after Joey Balfour. What the fuck did you do?" asks Marty after a long silence. *He's not going to let go of this easily*, thinks Joey. There was a closet full of secrets, side deals, double-crosses, and, of course, Errol Flynn himself, the actor who was at the center of it all, who fled to Canada after he abandoned Cuba and took up with a teenage girl.

"Most people's lives are tragedies. They are either running from something or trying to run after something. They never stand still and they're tripping over their own two feet, falling down, nose in the dirt. They are like a child chasing gray pigeons in the park. You ever see a child chase a pigeon?"

Marty shakes his head, trying to imagine the scene.

"Watch the child's face as he's running after the pigeon. What you see is an exercise of determined futility. The kid never stops but the pigeon is always out of reach. When that kid grows up he chases after independence, wealth, fame, beauty, youth and respect just like he chased after pigeons that day in the park. He will never quite catch what he's after. What gives people hope is the lives of celebrities. When they see someone famous, they are looking at someone who actually caught the pigeon, their shiny-eyed smiles and wind-swept hair, perfect teeth, the way they handle themselves, their big houses, lavish parties, all of it gives a strange feeling of comfort, a release, and for a moment they can believe that life isn't tragic. If Errol Flynn can be Captain Blood and Robin Hood, I can. America is based on keeping that illusion. He made the mistake of thinking he could do whatever he wanted. That's not the deal. There is a party line to follow. You go over that line and they go after you."

"But you aren't a movie star, Joey."

"TV personality is in the same ballpark. Six months ago, an Indian chief came up with the hot idea of packaging all of the old TV shows from the casino and releasing them on DVD. The Indians and their backers got the rights from *Crossfire*, and *48 Hours*, and half a dozen old TV shows that don't run anymore, and they've launched Joey Balfour's *Gambling on Magic*."

"I always knew that show had legs. That's great," says Marty.

Joey shudders, shaking his head. "It's terrible. An American preacher showed up at the Annual Thanksgiving Ball and he ordered me to pull the show. He threatened me."

"I am checking on his company."

"And we sit in the back of a taxi waiting for Oy to pack up her pots and pans on the long-shot chance that she will lead us to Jim Pauley's rat hole."

Errol Flynn and Joey Balfour share several common traits: well-known celebrities, attractive to young women, and adored by their fans. Joey's audience is smaller but large enough to blip across the radar screen. Joey's life philosophy contains the same message as Errol Flynn's—get famous and rich, and then get out of America. Run from the place as if your hair is on fire. Not so fast—no one wins all of the chips and turns his back on Middle Kingdom. No one gets out of paradise. No one wants to leave. Everyone wants to come to those shores. That's the American message. What are the chances of hitting it big for the average mug? *Figure the odds on that race*, thinks Joey. Those odds make Temperance Hill's forty to one odds to win the Belmont Stakes closer to even. This is the horse race that keeps the entire system rolling ahead.

The traffic thins out on Asoke with only a trickle of motorcycles and taxis. Oy pushes her cart along the broken pavement towards Sukhumvit Road.

"Time to go," says Joey, opening the backdoor. He hands the taxi driver a couple hundred baht.

They stay at a safe distance as Oy walks behind her cart; her pace is slow, the exhaustion of the day makes her sluggish. It is as if her body only has enough reserves for this last journey before closing down into a long sleep.

"If I'd pitched for the Yankees, got famous, and then threw it all away to come and live here, what then?" asks Marty.

"You would have been branded a traitor, Marty."

"But I ain't an American."

"Neither was Errol Flynn. He lived outside the normal laws. He resisted control. It was his choice. He had his own mind about politics and fucking. It made them question things they didn't want to think about."

You don't let someone win the sweetest pot of all—the girls, the hero worship, the fame—and then let him thumb his nose at you and walk away as if you are nothing but a stupid mug.

She walks behind her food cart, which is mounted on bicycle wheels. At the corner of the intersection, Oy pushes the cart along a narrow path through a rabbit warren of beer bars. She threads a piece of heavy chain through the tires and wraps it around an iron bar, and slips a lock to unite the links. Her work is finished for the evening. Joey and Marty wait until she emerges out of the darkness, a weary face of someone too exhausted to sleep. They follow as she continues. She stops at one of the outdoor bars—the lights are switched off—to talk with another sleepless ying cleaning a wooden counter in the long shadows, as other vendors rattle their carts past on the uneven pavement. The ying is shaking, crying, inconsolable, lost in some private grief. Oy reaches across the counter and hugs the sobbing woman. There are no customers. Closer to the road, a couple of cops chase away anyone who looks like a customer hoping to buy one final round.

"What are they saying? Why is that woman crying?" asks Marty. "I can't understand a single thing."

They speak Thai in half whispers, their vowels swallowed by the traffic and other voices in the dark. "Her life is fucked," says Joey. "Something about a daughter. An accident. No money. Improvised misery, page after page of it. That's why she's wailing. There's no end to it. No punch line, only a siren of pain swinging around inside her head. One she can't stop hearing." *The sound of a woman wailing chills the soul*, thinks Joey. The howl of helpless, irretrievable sorrow strikes deep, breaking every language barrier.

"You said Star was nice," says Marty as the wailing continues. "But what do you really think of her?"

"You're making me crazy with this *katoey*."

Marty clenches his jaw. "I knew it. That's it. Star's a *katoey* and that's your problem."

Pushing his finger into Marty's chest, Joey says, "Wrong. It's about relationships."

"I don't get it," says Marty, stepping back. He watches the two shadowy figures moving in and out of the light. Splashes of neon flicker across Oy's face. Her friend is sobbing, head bent forward, resting against Oy's shoulder. A shudder of emotion passes between the two shadows.

Joey turns away from the two women. "All relationships are a crap shoot. Most people crap out. Dice. Women. When your bank is bust, that's it. Disaster."

More vendors crowd through the narrow passageway. "I am thinking of taking her back to Canada," says Marty, stepping aside, letting a vendor with her cart pass through.

"You're the guy who only bets horses."

The pots and pans rattle as the wheels slam over the uneven pavement. A pot falls off and bounces on the concrete, rolling next to Marty's leg. He picks it up and hands it to the vendor, who nods and continues on her way. He's been thinking about Joey's right jab about only betting on horses. Whenever Joey wants to put him down he talks about that time he bet fifty bucks on a Blue Jays game. He refuses to give Joey the satisfaction of letting it go this time. As several bargirls in tight jeans and tank tops pass by, giving Marty and Joey the look over, Marty catches Joey's eye.

"What's that supposed to mean? I only bet horses."

"Relationships are like sports betting. You'll be pacing up and down the room like you're watching the Blue Jays on TV with your fifty-dollar bet. Only this is betting the whole bank."

Here it comes again, thinks Marty. "Like you bet on the Orioles."

"And I spent my time in purgatory working out of a scuffler's office in Vancouver. It could have turned nasty. We got lucky. We got our bank back again. You can only do that so many times in life. Then you're busted for good."

"She likes me," says Marty.

"If a horse likes you, does that mean you bet your bank on him to win?"

"Star's cut. She might be a *katoey*. But she's cut. Don't say 'him.'"

"I was talking about a horse. Not Star."

The sound of the wailing lowers. Some resolution has blocked the flood of tears. There is movement in the half darkness where Oy stands. "Remember the showgirls who brought me martinis?" asks Joey.

"I remember." He had once taken one of the showgirls back to his hotel room after the show; she knew Marty was close to Joey, and she slept with him because she thought this would help her career. Marty remembers how good it had been and being used by her only added to the pleasure, as if he had any pull with Joey over the staffing of the show.

"They all liked me. But unlike someone whose name will remain unmentioned, I never hooked up with any of them."

"You never hooked up with one of them, so what? And I hooked up once. Is that what you're saying? And that makes you better than me?"

"They were for shaking martinis. They shook their bootie to increase the ratings for the show. Liking or not liking had nothing to do with it."

Oy hurries toward the main road and flags down a motorcycle. The driver pulls to the curb and she climbs onto the back. She murmurs instructions to the motorcycle taxi driver, who nods, pulls on his helmet, kicks the bike into gear, merges into traffic, turning left onto Sukhumvit Road. Joey flags down another motorcycle, and then a second motorcycle, and he tells the two drivers to follow the red Honda with the bone-weary ying, a Garuda tattoo on one shoulder, hot tears of her friend smeared on another, watching to make certain she's not swallowed up by the night. Marty grabs hold of the seat, wind in his face, tasting the sweet madness that descends upon those who follow others.

Three Women Riding the Razor's Edge

Three women flop in a low-energy state in the condo; waiting has reduced them to a quantum state. For periods that expand into minutes they collapse inside their private worlds as if stuck in a doctor's waiting room. Mostly they are happy to observe a friendly silence, having earlier talked themselves out over the impersonal, safe matters ranging from the indignity of air-travel inspections of women's breasts as possible places to hide explosives in the days of terrorism to the best place to purchase smoked salmon, and men, the nature of man, the struggles with fidelity, the festering wounds opened by the rocket fire of morality, love, hate, desire, revenge, and disappointment. They covered the waterfront out of boredom, screaming tongue-loosening fear, afraid of bad news, of loss, of death, or something changing that can't be controlled, reversed. Ped curls up, one leg folded beneath her, reading a first-edition copy of *The Razor's Edge*, her compensation payment for Sky's boob job, and Sky licks her finger, slowly turning the pages of *Elle*.

From the walls, it feels as if Errol Flynn is watching, listening, judging, laughing in response to their conversations, as the actor stares out from the dozens of framed original movie posters. They huddle under the image of a man who loved women, needed them, used them. Mr. Quattro (Ped always refers to Errol Flynn by the Italian word for four) understood the feng shui of sex, where the hands go, the direction of the legs and arms, the rituals of touching, guiding, moving, and embracing. All great actors know these closely guarded secrets about women. His hands touch the face of Barbara Stanwyck. He's a young soldier in combat dress and a

216

military hat, staring out bravely from the poster of *The Dawn Patrol*. As Robin Hood, his rakish grin and twinkle in the eye suggest little need to resort to the bow and arrow. Every available space on the wall is stacked, clustered, designed so as to accompany each of the fifty-nine original movie posters. In the movie poster from *The Adventures of Don Juan*, Errol Flynn embraces Viveca Lindfors as if leading her around a dance floor or into a bedroom. Each of the posters is framed in the heavy gold-leaf gilded frames used by museums for old masters. Throughout the condo are hundreds of flowers: roses and orchids and bird of paradise, long pieces of leafy bamboo framing the flowers in an arrangement following the patterns known only to the experts at Feng Shui Flower Shop. There is something overpowering in the color of the flowers, the scent of the roses, the sharpness of the thorns, row after row of flowers along the windows, the metal blinds open to the nightscape of the city below.

Jennifer Balfour flinches as the phone rings. Her legs are folded up beneath her as she rests on the sofa in the condo sitting room. Ped comes in with a fresh glass of Chardonnay and sits beside Sky who is still flipping through a fashion magazine, examining the models—eyes, breasts, legs, waist, thighs, ankles—with an experienced, knowing eye. They know Jennifer is talking with Joey because every couple of seconds she says, "Yes, Joey." or "Yes, son. Of course, Joey."

She puts down the phone. "That was Joey."

Neither Ped nor Sky betray surprise.

"Is he okay?" asks Sky.

"He's with Marty and they still haven't found Boggy."

Ped sips her Chardonnay. "He could be anywhere. Do they know where to start looking?" she asks.

"Joey says they will not come back without him."

Sky lays down the magazine. She no longer sees the Errol Flynn posters. They mean nothing to her. Ped's professional interest in interior design allows her to appreciate the possibility of the romance suggested in the posters. She is less confident that the military movie posters—all guns, uniforms and posturing—give the right feng shui for the guest bedrooms. The women, having waited hours for Joey's phone call, fall into despair. A general depression descends over them, as Jennifer's description of Joey's call resolves nothing. Boggy's whereabouts remain a large blank of motives, locations, and logistics. Jennifer shows no signs of going to bed. She is the senior person of the household, and both Ped and Sky are caught by their Thainess. Juniors should not mention the obvious option of turning in for the evening. It is not their role. Their role is strictly one of protocol, stay near and comfort Joey's mother and make her feel loved, important, and respected.

Boggy's fate hangs in the air. Sky tries to change the subject of why Boggy has disappeared to small talk about her last plastic surgery.

"I was never happy with my breasts," says Sky.

"No woman is ever happy with her breasts," says Jennifer.

"What Sky means is she never felt her breasts were the right shape, volume, or lift," says Ped. "Sky is a water and metal person. Nipples pointing outward are a sign of great fortune."

"Nipples pointing any direction other than at your feet are an asset," says Jennifer Balfour. "Do you think that I might have a glass of wine?"

Ped's face brightens. "Of course, I'll bring you a glass." The woman drinks as much as her son. It must be hereditary.

Sky drums her fingers on the fashion model gracing the magazine on the table. Her fingers tap the outline of perfectly formed breasts. Jennifer cocks her head, sees the nervous tic that makes Sky's eye twitch and wonders if this is the consequence of plastic surgery or fatigue or boredom.

"Ped is a famous interior designer," says Sky. "Many famous people still call and ask her to design their offices or houses."

Ped returns with two glasses of Chardonnay, handing one to Jennifer and the other to Sky. "We are in for a very long night. A glass of wine is perfect."

"Did you design the flower shop?" asks Jennifer.

Ped nods, putting down her glass on the coffee table. "Joey and Sky deserve a lot of the credit. They had such wonderful ideas. I love working with creative people. And your son is one of the most creative men I've ever met."

"Ped's modest. She's won awards for her designs. She could be working in Paris, New York . . . anywhere."

"And now she's working in Joey's flower shop," says Jennifer, a sense of mystery in her voice.

"I am content," says Ped. "And I still take on some projects for old clients."

"And Sky, are you content? I understand from Joey that you were in the music business and very successful, too."

A ruby-lipped smile flickers across Sky's face, and she gathers her shoulders, moves forward in her chair. "Very content," she says.

"Very," repeats Jennifer. She suddenly lifts her left hand nearly spilling her wine. Something has upset her and without warning. Ped and Sky exchange a worrisome look approaching alarm. "How can Joey be content with this life? Someone named Chief Black Crow or something owns his old TV show. And another thing: I have never understood why Joey would choose a career in horticulture. As a boy, I never saw him look at a plant or a flower. Now he owns a florist shop in Bangkok. And he employs two talented, beautiful women who throw away promising careers to sell roses. Do you have any idea how famous Joey was in America? And he's becoming famous all over again. He's returned from the grave of obscurity. How many get to be famous once? How many get to be famous twice? Almost zero."

"He doesn't talk about it much," says Ped.

"Before he did TV, Joey started with a radio show that ran on a fifty-thousand-clear megawatt channel right after the Dodgers' game. Two hours of air time and anyone who was anyone in Las Vegas and Los Angeles listened to Joey's show. He interviewed Archie Moore, George Foreman, Ali, George Frazier. My Joey got them to talk about themselves. He put a human face on men who climbed into a ring with the sole purpose of knocking the lights out of the other fighter. The TV people couldn't get enough of him. Some producer from *Firing Line* or *48 Hours* or *Crossfire* was always calling and begging Joey to do their show. Every time he was on, their ratings went through the roof. It took me a long time to understand Joey. It was no surprise to me when they gave Joey his own TV show.

"When he went to live in Las Vegas I could never bring myself to admit he was in that city. In my newsletter I wrote to my friends that 'Joey's working out west.' I couldn't bring myself to tell my friends what Joey really did and what city he really lived in. It seemed like a disgrace. After his first *Larry King Live* interview, my telephone didn't stop ringing. All of my friends rang. They said, 'Jenny, why didn't you tell us that your son is the most important odds maker in Las Vegas? You must be so proud.' The next year in my Christmas letter I wrote, 'Our son Joey is the leading odds maker in Las Vegas. We are very proud of Joey. You probably saw him on *Larry King* or on *Crossfire*. Larry introduced Joey as the kingmaker of professional sports betting. The king of TV interviewers is calling our son the king of Las Vegas. Trenton and I always knew deep down that Joey would be the best and do the best.' Joey had all of that. Now what does he have? He sells flowers to other foreigners in Bangkok. And he lives in a condo with his walls covered with Errol Flynn movie posters. Why would he give up his fame? I ask myself that every day. Joey had it all and he vanished from Las Vegas at the top of his fame."

"What if he didn't want it?" asks Sky.

Jennifer purses her lips. "What does Joey want?"

"Happiness, like everyone else," says Ped. Not that anyone in Thailand was finding happiness that easy to embrace. Reading *Anna Karenina* and *Madame Bovary*, Ped felt she knew the people deeply. The same people were all around her.

"And you provide this happiness to Joey." Jennifer concentrates on Ped's long finger gracefully looped around the stem of the wine glass.

"Do you know the opening line from *Anna Karenina*? It goes like this, 'Happy families are all alike. Every unhappy family is unhappy in its own way.' We take Joey's happiness very seriously." Ped lays down her book.

Jennifer studies the two young, beautiful women. "What you read is very true." She pauses as if trying to remember something, her eyes scan the walls, stopping to gaze at the movie poster of *Cry Wolf.* "Do you know why I decided to bring Howard Boggy to Bangkok?"

They shake their heads in unison like members of a synchronized swimming team.

"Joey was in some kind of trouble. In Las Vegas everywhere you turned, there were only gangsters, and someone might have threatened him. You know how envy of another man's success can poison the well of another man's happiness. That's why he's selling flowers. He dropped out because something or someone scared him. Whatever it is, he has chosen not to confide his problem to his mother. When Boggy lands on my doorstep, I think, now here's the chance to dig a little deeper into what is going on in Joey's life. Nothing happens by accident. When something comes to you it is an invitation for you to make the connection. I feel there is a connection between that boy's problems and Joey's coming to Bangkok."

This is more than a promise; it is a confession, a heart opened to Joey's key employees—if that is indeed their status—who have in their possession information she needs. Who better to explain the nature of the demons pursuing Joey than Ped and Sky? But it is painfully apparent, as she examines the faces of Ped and Sky, that neither woman has any more knowledge of the deeper, hidden levels of Joey's life than his own mother. *Whatever is buried in Joey's bottom drawer does not yield easily*, she thinks.

Canadians, Brits, Germans, Americans, Norwegians, Finns, Belgians, Dutch flock to Joey's Feng Shui Flower Shop. Word of mouth, he says. But many feel that Joey Balfour's legendary luck in picking long shots has rubbed off on his flower business. He's put together the right formula. Investigations by law enforcement agencies would never turn up anything—except pots, plants, seeds, invoices, gardening implements. Phone records divulge nothing but orders for supplies, plants, flowers, gossip, feng shui masters, fortune tellers, and employees' relations and love interest. Except for the flower shop's sideline gaming room for elite customers, which is protected by the men who play cards, Feng Shui Flower Shop is as it appears to be. Joey's business is, in fact, true. It is such a difficult leap that not even his mother can take such a step. Jennifer knows nothing about the gambling tables in the back of the flower shop. She wants to believe that part of his life is over, and Joey has said nothing to destroy this illusion.

"Why did Gunnar run away?" asks Sky.

"I refuse to call him that. I know that I forget things but I remember his name. It's Boggy. And we don't know that Boggy has run away. He has been kidnapped. Thrown into the back of a van against his will. Don't you see the pattern that is coming together?"

Ped and Sky see no obvious pattern. All they know is that Joey and his friend Marty are somewhere outside in the city, searching for something they may never find.

"Why don't you ask Marty?" asks Ped. "He's Joey's best friend."

"She's right, best friends know these things," says Sky.

Jennifer looks at her empty wine glass, holding it to the light. "Marty's like this glass. Joey pours the contents. Without Joey, it is empty. Not that Marty doesn't know anything, he knows the score but he wouldn't tell me. What he does say is rubbish like, 'Mrs. Balfour in the gambling world you don't win until you have left the table, cashed in your chips and walked out the door. As long as you keep playing, you have the possibility of winning. But you aren't a winner until you are outside the door.' He gets that claptrap from one of Joey's old TV shows. It is an insult that he doesn't think I saw Joey's shows."

Sky giggles. "I sometimes do that. Use a line from a TV show and forget where I got it."

"It's hardly amusing," says Jennifer. She's hurt and it shows as a tear forms at the edge of one eye and slides down her cheek; it is the pain that follows knowledge that at some fundamental level you are no longer thought to be reliable, as the memory can no longer be counted upon to file and retrieve the way it once did.

"I didn't mean to hurt your feelings, but it is what Joey told us," says Sky.

Ped's beautiful smile radiates as she nods, clutching the first edition of *The Razor's Edge*.

"The day he arrived in Bangkok was the first day he knew that he had won," says Ped. "Those were his exact words."

"So he isn't running away from . . ."

"Joey's never run away from anything," says Sky. "Joey loves women. All women. It's not just Ped and me that he loves. He loves the company of women and the stories he tells them. He got that from you, Jennifer. Many times he told us how you read to him as a boy and he took great comfort in hearing your voice and the stories you read. He romances women because he needs us, like he needed you, to feel safe."

Later when Jennifer goes into Ped's room, she's reading at the table. At first she doesn't hear Jennifer but something tells her that someone else's presence is nearby. Jennifer smiles as their eyes meet, "I know how you read to Joey every night. The older you get the more you understand that books are the final refuge. Whenever I have a senior moment, I go to one of my books and start to read. I can go to a place where there is never a senior moment, where everything is clear and in place."

Ped closes her book. She sees much of Joey in his mother. It touches her that she's come to her room and confided in her. "Books are the best place to live," says Ped. "You can be whatever you wish, go wherever you want, and say whatever you feel. That's what I love."

Jennifer reaches over, wipes away silent tears, and hugs Ped. "Thank you. Thank you so much. You do understand."

A Dead Man's Last Things

The motorcycle carrying Oy briefly stops at a red light. The driver looks up and down Sukhumvit Road at the traffic, calculates his chances, rotates the hand grip, full throttle, and speeds through the intersection, turning right onto Soi 22. Joey's driver hesitates. Some rare innate section of his brain reads danger until Joey finds the override button by waving a five-hundred-baht note in front of his helmeted face. The driver guns the motorcycle through the intersection narrowly missing a head-on crash with a bus full of Taiwanese tourists. Marty's motorcycle driver, like a good wingman, stays in tight formation with the lead bike. Joey hears Marty screaming as the bus comes within the length of a Singha beer bottle distance from slamming into the rear of the bike. Marty shuts his eyes, leaving his nose as the witness of his five senses to record the next crucial two seconds. The smell of metal and oil and then the after smell of burnt rubber and exhaust from the bus's wake ripples in waves across his face like a gale-force wind. The engine on the Honda whines as Joey's driver, the carrot of the five-hundred-baht note freshly imprinted in his brain, tries to find the motorcycle with Oy riding pillion. Joey leans forward, trying to spot Oy through the snarl of traffic on Soi 22 as cars, motorcycles, tourist buses, taxis, and pushcart vendors jockey for position on the race toward the Klong Toey slums.

Joey's driver—having shown his self-preservation instinct by not running a red light—goes into death-wish mode, taking his motorcycle to the pavement, honking at pedestrians and vendors to give way as he guns his chopper down the narrow tunnel lined with shops on one side and noodle stands nearest the road. By the time they return to the traffic on Soi 22, Joey sees Oy sitting sidesaddle on the back of her motorcycle. She is now behind them. Joey taps his motorcycle driver—who is drunk on pills, speed and danger—on the shoulder. He is running like a doped-up racehorse eyeing the finish line; he's no longer listening to the jockey seeking to pull him in and fix the race. Joey puts his hands over the driver's eyes. He's driving blind. It takes a moment for him to realize he can't see where he's going.

Joey shouts in the driver's ear, "Stop!"

In Thai and in English, he screams, pulls Joey's hands from his eyes, pulls over, and shoots Joey an ugly, belligerent look. Marty's motorcycle pulls up alongside.

"I am going to die," Marty moans. Terror has a face; it is the one stamped on Marty's.

Both motorcycle drivers remove their helmets and speak to each other in a rapid *Isan* dialect about how many ways they intend to cut up the two farang passengers. Joey is unworried, knowing this is a face problem that requires the cosmetic surgery of money; once cash changes hands, their face comes back to their skull, and they will smile and joke. What's the big deal that the farang put his fucking hands over my eyes? Ha, ha, ha. I got money. Ha, ha, ha. Joey likes to stuff five-hundred-baht notes into the pocket of people who lose face. Each driver smiles and they agree that farangs have a very good heart. Marty starts to lift his leg and climb off the back of the motorcycle.

"Marty, stay on the bike."

"I don't wanna stay on this bike. This guy is insane. He's trying to murder me." This is the verdict of a Vancouver taxi driver. He's shaking, his face drained of blood. He eases himself back on the motorcycle, rolling his eyes. "I really don't want to be doing this, Joey."

"Here she comes," he says as Oy's bike goes past. "Follow that bike."

"Oh, shit," says Marty, as his words fade out like a dying echo.

They follow Oy's motorcycle past a private school with high walls facing the street and turn into a dark sub-soi. High walls screen off exclusive houses, and the road snakes around right, then a sharp left. Joey and Marty follow twenty feet behind Oy's motorcycle as they travel down another sub-soi. No luxury houses on this narrow lane; the visible light is from windows and open doorways of low-slung concrete row houses. The front of the houses are jammed with vendors' carts, old wrecks, motorcycles, and accumulated junk, rusty engine casings, stripped-down pickups on blocks, and yapping dogs circling at the edge of the pavement. Deep inside a slum is the stench of canal sewage, raw turds, and plastic containers, churning in a thick sludge below a walkway. Oy dismounts from the motorcycle, pays the driver before crossing over the canal. She then disappears into one of the concrete block boxes. Wedged inside this neighborhood of Third World Bangkok are dark shadows, poverty, ruin, and squalor. Cranes, cement trucks, and high-corrugated fences around construction sites are in the next neighborhood, inside another universe. As far as the eye can see in the pools of fluorescent lights are slums untouched by development; the interior sois belong to a lost past. A human ant colony, with thousands of the people squeezed together with toilet-paper-thin walls separating them from their neighbors; roiling with hate, pain, fucking against the walls, on the floor, drinking cheap whiskey, laughing and fucking again, taking drugs, licking their wounds inside their small cells inside a giant nest.

Joey's motorcycle pulls alongside Marty's. "Now what?" asks Marty.

The neighborhood is farang unfriendly—nothing remotely inviting or notable—and that makes it the perfect place to disappear. It is no more than another honeycomb of urban decay buzzing with fatigue and fear.

"Let's go back," says Joey. He looks carefully around the lane, fixing in his mind, somewhere in this ruin, a landmark. All of the buildings run together as if smeared across a canvas, until Joey spots a tree. It is a large, gnarled tree with roots erupting out of the earth, the main trunk buckling at a twisted angle over the canal. Faded ribbons are tied around the trunk, as a blessing to the spirit residing inside, and as a warning of the misfortune to befall anyone seeking to cut it down. Joey instructs the driver to drive slowly. He needs to repeat this with offers of money before the motorcycle slows. The lane along the canal is accessible by the first sub-soi only. This is the place to wait out Oy and to confirm whether Jim Pauley is inside the building. Joey believes that he is. He would bet money on Pauley finding such a hideaway. Bill Hunt in his luxury hotel is no more than three kilometers away. But he could spend a lifetime and never find Jim Pauley in such a place.

"What are you looking for?" Marty asks as his motorcycle pulls up alongside.

"Where Pauley would go to play poker?"

"An Internet café," says Marty.

"That's it."

There were a hundred such cafés in a two-kilometer radius. They pass restaurants, hotels, Internet cafés, massage parlors, and bars. *How easy it is for a mug to disappear in Bangkok*, thinks Joey. Even if the guy on the run isn't a mug but a professional, finding the right rat hole requires determination and luck. Their motorcycle drivers slow down. The fetid smell of the klong washes over and defeats all of the other senses. But as powerful as that smell is, it doesn't stop Joey from feeling lucky; Temperance Hill money-on-the-nose, long-odds lucky. It is nearly impossible to pinpoint Pauley's Internet café. If Pauley were smart (and Joey's respect for Pauley's intelligence grows by the minute), he would shift between Internet cafés. Keep to himself, keep the volume down, the profile low, no name, no bullshit, nothing to remember him by. Another down and out farang drifts in, fires up the computer, pushes back his chair, pays his money and walks away as if he never existed. Another lone silverback, his middle-aged gray pelt glistening, leaving an impression as fragile as if he'd pissed his name on water.

When the motorcycle reaches Sukhumvit Road, Joey tells the driver to pull into the long driveway leading to Feng Shui Flower Shop. Joey's breathing hard and so is the driver. It's like they are sharing a single lung. One breathes in first, then the other, until they break through the surface.

Marty tags along, hands stuffed in his pockets, looking at the flowers as they breeze through the workout and television room. Everywhere there are flowers. The sickening stench of freshly cut flowers spreads through the air. Marty holds his nose, breathes through his mouth. "Man, how can you stand that fucking smell?" he asks.

"That's the smell of freedom and luck all wrapped into one," says Joey. There are several bedrooms running off an adjoining corridor. In the first room, Sky's bedroom, Joey peers around the corner. The room is littered with fashion and music industry magazines; glossy magazines cover the unmade bed and the side table and lie open, spines up, on the floor like large-winged birds. On the wall is a framed magazine cover with Sky in a low-cut top behind a DJ console. Marty examines Sky's face on the cover from three years ago. The plastic surgeons have changed so much he wouldn't know it was Sky unless Joey told him about the cover. Joey reaches down and picks up magazines from the bed.

"The other rooms are empty? Why? No action tonight?" asks Marty. He asks the same thing every time he comes to the flower shop. He always gets the same answer.

"Since Bill Hunt showed up, the private rooms have been closed. Ped says he has disturbed the chi."

"You don't really believe in that crap?" asks Marty.

The connection between body and spirit is something both Sky and Ped take seriously. They start the day by measuring the chi, the harmony of life forces, before they make any decision. Bill Hunt's presence has broken the life energy force.

"Why not be on the safe side?" replies Joey. "And, I could use a rest for a couple of weeks."

Two of the private rooms are exclusive to a select list of Feng Shui Flower Shop clients who wish to have a place to play high-stake games: Politicians, bankers, merchants, brokers and old, trusted friends of Joey Balfour from Las Vegas who are passing through Bangkok and want to sit in on the action. One of the rooms is exclusively for short-time activity. Where there are gamblers, there are women. The room has a king-size bed, crystal chandeliers, a lavish bathroom, mirrored ceiling, gold inlaid faucets and white marble basins. Joey is the house. The house mostly wins.

"Hunt has you running scared? You, Joey Balfour? Unfucking believable," says Marty.

"I have a bad feeling about him," says Joey.

"He's a nobody," says Marty.

They are on the same page of the racing form, thinks Joey.

"Hunt's only interesting because he leads us to his paymaster. They've invested some serious money."

"You must have some idea who's behind him?"

"Fucked if I know. That's why you're looking into the offshore angle. Maybe there's a connection, or maybe not. Go get some sleep, Marty."

With Marty out of sight, he tries to shut down his brain, but it's not happening. Alone in one of the gaming rooms, he thinks about Sky. He doesn't love her. But he likes her. Mostly he's thinking about stripping down Ped when he's fucking Sky, and when he's fucking Ped, his eyes squeeze shut and his imagination rolls out Sky shaking her new tits in his face. He rests his arm over his eyes. He can't make any sense of how his mind always loads the slide of another woman into his head from the one he's straddling. He tells himself that he is a sick fuck. It's like watching a horse race with a ticket in your hand and your head repeats a horse race from the week before. *I am a very sick fuck*, he says to himself. He tries to rationalize the situation by telling himself that betting on horses and sleeping with women are distinctly different activities, different odds, different outcomes and wholly different risks. Ripping into Sky and thinking of Ped, and shifting to images from one of the books that Ped reads in order not to come. The surefire way to stop coming was to remember eating Chinese food with Eddie the Knife in Las Vegas. Those huge, greasy egg rolls shoved into Eddie the Knife's maw. Chopping and slurping and belching in a flat, atonal melody. A performance that would stop a bull elephant from coming.

Sky and Ped flop at the condo, freeing up the bedrooms at Feng Shui Flower Shop. Marty gets Sky's room at the shop and Joey finally rises from the sofa, and walks into Ped's room, where one wall has ceiling-to-floor bookcases and each one is filled with rows and rows of first editions. Joey places her pillow against his face and breathes in. He holds his breath a long time, hoping to drive out the street and gutter smells of the slum. He glances at his Rolex watch. He phones the condo and Ped answers after the second ring.

"We are all fine, Joey. I've been reading to Sky and your mother. Not from *Anna*. I am reading to them from *The Razor's Edge*, the part where he says all big cities are alike."

"Cities are like women. They are never alike but they can be similar."

Joey still has no news of Boggy and frankly has begun not to care whether Boggy surfaces again. He wanders to Sky's room and finds Marty already stretched out on the bed.

"We will start early tomorrow," says Joey, stacking Sky's magazines on the nightstand.

"How early?"

"Seven."

"God, that is early. Maybe we should just stay up."

"The best poker starts around eight in the morning."

"How can anyone play poker at eight?"

"It's online poker. Eight in the morning here is eight at night on the East Coast."

Marty can't take his eyes off the oddly different appearance of Sky in the framed magazine. Something is bothering him. The stress shows in his shoulders and neck. He rotates his neck from side to side, and sits on the edge of Sky's bed.

"That was a nose, chin and tit job not even a year ago," says Joey looking at the photo.

"Aren't you going to phone your mom?"

"I already phoned Ped. They're reading."

Marty breaks into a broad grin. "She's something. Reading some classic to your mother at this ungodly hour. You struck gold with that one."

Joey sets his jaw, nods, sits on the bed and picks up the phone from the nightstand. Jennifer answers on the first ring. "I struck gold with both of them. Don't ever forget that. And no, we haven't found Boggy. We will try tomorrow. He's not kidnapped. First, he's not a kid. Second, no one knows he's here."

Almost everything about her son is a mystery. How did that young boy grow like a Chinese merchant sleeping at the back of his shop? He has a luxury condo and he has guests. What has gotten into her boy? But it isn't only Jennifer who is confused, unsettled by Joey; his best friend, Marty, shares her concern.

"Let's have a drink," says Joey. "There's a wet bar in the exercise room."

Marty smiles. "That's a good place to drink." He rolls off the bed and follows Joey to the exercise room.

"It pisses Sky off when I sit on the exercise bike and drink whiskey."

After pouring the last of a bottle of single malt whiskey into two glasses, Joey drops in three ice cubes and hands a glass to Marty.

"You mother is always asking me questions like why does Joey keep two girlfriends? Are there others? Are the women the reason that he stays in Bangkok? Why can't he return to Vancouver?"

His mother, he smiles to himself, would drum Marty over the head for answers. "What did you tell her?"

"I said you liked women. It was like horse racing. You could lay down as many bets on any race as you wanted. One of them had to win." Joey climbs on the exercise bike and pedals slowly. Marty's face clouds. "I didn't say anything about the special rooms at the shop. You play your cards close to your chest. That's your business. That's what I told her."

Joey climbs off the bike and drops down on the sofa, stretches out, crosses his legs, and sips his whiskey. "I know how to make the odds. Sky's strength is fashion and music, and Ped's is interior design of places and minds. They both are experts on the surface of things, they know the latest trends, they understand the nature of collectors, and they make the flower business work. Without them, there is no back-room business. In Thailand, only what one can see matters, the visible surface is everything, and the mountain underneath remains without meaning, importance, or value; beauty is the only game table drawing the powerful, respectable crowd, so you need to have an edge. A sword has two edges. A warrior keeps both edges sharp. Sky and Ped are my double edge; they increase my odds on winning."

Marty is silent for a moment. "What bet?"

"My mother thinks I walked away from everything in Las Vegas, and I walked when I was at the top. For her, once you cash in your chips, you've lost. That's the mentality that casinos love. They thrive on that belief. They promote it. The subliminal message is piped in through the music where people are playing the slot machines or poker or blackjack. 'You're a winner.' 'You must keep betting.'

'Happiness is the next hand.' 'Bliss is the next card.' Betting the horses at the Exhibition Park was another age. The players who won at poker in the Seventies and Eighties drank and smoked and they played cards as much for the status of being someone as for the money. None of these guys would stand a chance at a table in Las Vegas today. None of the players from thirty years ago who were stars in the line-up for the Mets or Dodgers would ever make the team now. The same is true for all professional sports—football, baseball, or basketball—none of the old legends could make the grade. The same applies to gamblers. Our generation had its glory. But when you know the new players are in a different league, you take your winnings and you go. And if you're smart, and know the right people, you open your own casino. It's a way to keep your hand in. And you find women who will gamble on your hand, and for a while you have the luxury of believing that nothing has changed. When you look up from the table, you know that everything is no longer the same. "

"Why is looking for Jim Pauley worth the effort, Joey?" asks Marty.

"In isolation, Pauley's nothing. But there is a chance I can use him to get Hunt off my back or at least figure out if Pauley's got something that is going to come around and bite me in the ass."

Marty nods. "Going after your business or getting personal and going after you."

"What have you come up with?"

"I'm still working through it. But Pauley's not a player. He's a nobody."

Joey shakes his head. "I'll know once I find him. You know what, Marty? It don't matter. You have to see the big picture. My mother doesn't understand but she is the first who should. All of those books she read to me as a child came with the same message: Take a chance. Go into the world and find your own story, the one that makes your heart sing. My father clued me years ago, when he was visiting me in Las Vegas. He's more eccentric than you remember. Father's biggest thrill was going out to the Salvation Army and buying a dozen shirts for two dollars each. He finds out where the main Salvation Army depot is in Las Vegas and asks me to drive him out there.

"We pull into a large parking lot and get out. Father is all excited as he slams the car door. Something has come alive in the old man. I am having trouble keeping up with him as we pass massive piles of clothes, shoes, electric appliances, tools, lawn mowers, and tables with plates, cups, and toasters. There are pathways leading through acres of discarded junk. One of those paths is jammed with hundreds of walkers. Light as a feather, the kind made out of aluminum tubing. Light, thin tubes tailor-made for the elderly who hang on to life, taking one step at a time. Using a walker, it occurs to them that the most precious thing in life is mobility. Once you can't get around on your own steam then you're gone, and they bring your walker out here to this field of walkers that go all the way to the horizon, and your family hires a brown-skinned refugee with long, bony fingers from a Third World hellhole to wipe your ass, feed you soup, and dress you.

"The walker is the last stage on that glide into helplessness. People in walkers don't feel sorry for themselves; they feel sorry for those who have reached the post-walker stage of life. I stopped and leaned against one of the walkers and I looked at my father. I thought to myself, *He's finally taught me a lesson I'll never forget. He's brought me to this place so that I can learn something about the nature of life, its meaning and how fragile it all is.* And if you walk through a field of walkers, then you are forever changed in the way you see the possibilities of your own life.

"Another thing happened on that day at the Salvation Army. It was getting late as we left the field of walkers. The sun was low on the horizon. There was a rim of fire in the distance. You could smell burning wood. My father walked down an incline, which led through another section of this vast Salvation Army field. Father looked back and told me that he had a good idea that the person at the cash register would cut us a good deal on a walker. He'd never been in this place before but he was sure they would be reasonable about price. But more than that, she would cut us an even better deal on golf clubs. We stopped on the path. Ahead of us was a couple of pieces of heavy construction equipment—an earth mover and a caterpillar tractor on muddy tracks—belching blue smoke as the drivers moved the equipment into position on the field. The tractor rumbled alongside a large open pit; inside the jaws of this monster were hundreds of golf clubs.

"Father halted and stretched his arms out like someone nailed to a cross. 'Look at that? Woods, irons, putters, drivers dumped from thousands of bags. He's dumping them in a pit.' The operator pulled a lever and the golf clubs, twisted like spider legs, fell into the pit. Father walked straight up to the operator and tapped on the window of the cab. The driver shifted the big cat into neutral and stuck his head out the window. I watched him light a cigarette and look at my old man standing on the edge of the pit and staring down. Father needed to talk to him. What we witnessed disturbed the hell out of him. You know what the driver told us? That he worked for eight hours a day with the driver of the earthmover. One dug the huge holes in the earth and the caterpillar tractor filled them with golf clubs and walkers. Every day more truckloads of walkers and golf clubs arrived. There was no end to the work. 'I can't remember the last time they sold a walker or a set of clubs,' the driver told my father. 'There ain't any demand for a dead man's last things. We've got so many tons of 'em that we have started to burn them in pits. The wood burns on the clubs but the rest bends with the heat and we bury the metal.'

"The next field over the sun slanted off the silvery top rail of walkers, flashing across the field in a matrix of rainbow colors in the hot sun. The dead had left behind their hobbies and their final means of locomotion. My father was silent for most of the ride back into town, and when I let him out I asked him if anything was wrong, and he said, 'Joey, I've been thinking what that driver said. 'There ain't any demand for a dead man's last things.' I can't quite stop thinking about that deep pit with all those golf clubs inside, all the men who held them, laughed, joked with their friends, had a beer, drove home to their wives, their dreams and hopes. All that was left of them was what we saw dumped into a common grave.'

"There were tears in his eyes. 'Do you remember that time we went to the horse races together and I asked you to help me choose a winner?' I remembered. 'And you studied the racing form. I mean you went over every horse for the fifth race, and you said, 'Dad, Geisha has always finished in the money.'

"I bought a fifty-dollar show ticket. I'd never bet more than two dollars to place on a horse. You seemed so sure that Geisha would win. Third place seemed like a safe bet. Only it was a photo finish and it seemed like hours before they announced the winner. I can't tell you what went through my mind. Pure fear was what I felt. How was I going to tell your mother that I lost fifty dollars? And then I come out to this place and look at all these golf clubs and walkers. And I tell myself, why have I always played it safe my entire life? I never took any real chances. My whole life has been one long ticket to show. The only winning ticket was marrying your mother. She was rich. It meant that I never had to worry about a job. I'd won. But had I really, Joey? What I like about you, Joey, is that you always played to win. You weren't ever afraid. I wish I had been more like you. When you're my age, you come back to this place and you remember what I said. You look out at what all these people who bet to show left behind.' Then Father broke down, he couldn't talk for a couple of minutes, walking ahead, kicking an old battered driver into a burial trench. He said he was all right and that I wasn't to say anything to my mother. He made me swear I wouldn't mention what we saw. I swore to him. A few months later I arrived in Thailand. After all of these years, Father has never asked me why I moved to Thailand."

Filing a Flight Plan
Before Going to Bed

While shadows cloud parts of her memory, certain scenes and phrases float in a brilliant light of remembrance. Jennifer might have trouble recalling the last time she had sex with Joey's father but in her mind a film automatic plays each time she thinks of Errol Flynn and Mrs. Faragos making love on the penthouse master bed.

"Sex should be pleasurable; you shouldn't have to file a flight plan before taking off to bed." Errol Flynn leaned forward in his swimming suit, sitting on the edge of his bed.

Mrs. Faragos stood in front of him, eyes cast down, blushing and grinning at the same time. His fingers interlocked with hers, and he pulled her toward him. There was something funny about his nails that distracted her attention. It wasn't that they were short; they looked like a wild animal had gnawed them. Tiny crusts of blood ringed where the nails should have been. She looked away, closing her eyes, giving no real resistance, allowing the actor to embrace her, his lips touching her bare shoulder.

The vivid moment of seduction of this vulnerable young woman was both repellent and fascinating, painting her life thereafter with brush strokes which contained elements of good luck and bad fortune mingling in a way that could never be separated. Jennifer searches for words to express these feeling to Ped and Sky.

Sky and Ped draw on their reserve strength, coming alive as they listen to Jennifer Balfour recall the day of the anniversary of Errol Flynn's death and finding Mrs. Faragos passed out in the lift. "She was crumpled in a heap like a bag lady in the corner beside the control panel. Her forehead bounced against the buttons, lighting up all the buttons for all of the floors. At first I thought the poor woman had suffered a stroke or a seizure. It was only when I knelt beside Mrs. Faragos that I could see the details of what had caused her to collapse. She was in a daze. Oatmeal cookie and chocolate chip crumbs fell down the front of her dress. Stroke victims, as a rule, don't smell of rum. I tried to lift the woman to her feet, but Mrs. Faragos was far too heavy for me and her arms flopped around like a doll's. I waited as the lift stopped at each floor. I inserted my key into the slot for the penthouse and turned it. The ride seem to last forever with this woman moaning, 'Errol, Errol, I miss you, my beloved Errol.' I thought she was saying 'arrow' as in an arrow you shoot with a bow. This increased the mystery. The lift continued until we finally stopped at the penthouse floor and the doors opened. I must admit—and I am not proud of this—my first reaction was to leave this drunken woman where I had found her inside the lift and push the down button. My conscience wouldn't let me do it. She seemed such an unfortunate woman. I dragged Mrs. Faragos into the foyer where she slumped forehead first onto the floor. She was still going on about Errol as I went to make a pot of coffee. Thirty minutes later Mrs. Faragos had begun to sober up; brushing off cookie crumbs, her lower lip quivered, and she became weepy. It was only then that Mrs. Faragos made it clear that it was Errol as in Errol Flynn that was the cause of her madness and grief."

Mrs. Faragos Reads to Errol Flynn
September 1959:
Vancouver, Canada

Errol Flynn walked into the apartment building singing the Crests' "Sixteen Candles". He stopped dead in his tracks as Mrs. Faragos wearing tight shorts and a halter top, exposing a healthy amount of cleavage, checked the mailbox. Errol hummed the signature tune to *The Adventures of Robin Hood* and pretended to check his own mailbox.

"Do you know that tune?" he asked.

She greeted his question with a coy smile. "Not really."

"It's from *The Adventures of Robin Hood*. You must have seen the movie."

Mrs. Faragos nodded, hands behind her back, toying with her wedding ring, slowly slipping it off her finger. The actor stood before her, smiling. Of course she knew who he was; everyone in the building knew that Errol Flynn had rented the penthouse from the Hong Kong Chinese owner. "You do look a little bit like Robin Hood," she said.

This delighted him. He replied with an exaggerated movie-actor bow, gesturing with his hand, a flurry of waves directed toward her, as if she were a lady. "And who might I have the pleasure of knowing?" He reached out for her hand, pulled it to his lips, and kissed it.

"We don't really do that in Canada," she said. "I should say it's not common."

Mrs. Faragos blushed, making no attempt to remove her hand from the actor's lips. *So this is what it is like to meet a famous actor,* she thought. For more than an hour she had hovered around the mailboxes, waiting for Errol Flynn to walk through the front door. For days she had planned the meeting, she had dreamt about it. Every detail had to be just right from the shorts, the high heels, the halter top (which cost more than any single other piece in her wardrobe), and the makeup. Mr. Faragos encouraged the new interest his wife had shown in her appearance. He had thought that she had finally come to her senses and understood that men wanted their wives to dress up for their husbands. He couldn't have been more pleased, even though her expenditures had exceeded their budget by a factor of one hundred percent. None of that mattered. They weren't bean counters, they were lovers on a new voyage of exploration in their marriage. Mrs. Faragos did nothing to dissuade her husband's misguided judgment of her intentions. She found his self-delusion amusing but sad.

"Have you ever seen the penthouse?" Errol Flynn asked her.

"Never, sir," she said.

"Would you like a guided tour?"

"How could a lady say 'no' to Robin Hood?" she replied.

"You must tell me all about yourself. I want to know everything about you since you were a child. Were you curious in school? Did you like and read books? What color was your mother's hair, and did your parents take you to the beach on Saturday afternoon, and buy you a dog on your fifth birthday?"

Mrs. Faragos was spinning from all of his questions. In her years married to Mr. Faragos, if she added up all of his inquiries into her background they would have been less than what Errol had asked her that first day in the lobby of the apartment house waiting for the lift to arrive from the fourth floor.

When the lift opened into the foyer of the penthouse, Mrs. Faragos stepped forward just far enough for the door to close behind her. She had never seen anything as grand as this entrance. Errol hummed "Sixteen Candles". "I can't seem to get that tune out of my head," he said. "How old did you say you were?"

"Twenty," she said. It was a white lie. But anyone singing "Sixteen Candles" was looking for a whole number that promised the youth and innocence the song promised. She had seen his girlfriend in the lobby a couple of times and knew she couldn't have been more than sixteen years old.

"Aren't you going to let me take you on a tour?" he asked.

She stood frozen on the spot not quite knowing if the young woman she had seen in the lobby was lurking somewhere in the penthouse. If she had Errol Flynn as her man, and he arrived in the elevator with someone dressed like her, Mrs. Faragos was quite sure that she was capable of inflicting some great harm. He sensed that something was on her mind and his experience with women led him to make an educated guess. "We are alone if that is what is worrying you."

"It never crossed my mind," she said.

"If you must lie, then it is important not to immediately lower your eyes. Every policeman will tell you the guilty do this quite automatically as if their eyes give them away every time. So where do we start?" He gestured with both hands like leading an orchestra. "This is the foyer. I am quite new as a tenant so I can guarantee you that this foyer does not represent my taste. I will change it for the better. You will see."

"I saw your girlfriend in the lobby yesterday. She's very pretty," said Mrs. Faragos.

He took her hand in his and slightly squeezed it; just enough pressure to suggest comfort. "And you, my dear, are beautiful." He led her into the bedroom and opened the curtains and she looked out at the unobstructed view of English Bay. The gray September weather did not dampen her feeling of awe at watching the seagulls sweeping along the tide. She counted the tankers anchored in the bay like shadowy ghosts in the mist. Behind her, Errol Flynn poured himself a double shot of gin into a glass and drank it straight down. He made a little gasp, and she turned away from the window.

"Do you like the view?" he asked.

There was only one answer to that question. "I love watching the sea. Even on a cloudy, rainy day. It is in my blood."

Errol Flynn's brow arched. "It is in my blood, too. My ancestors on my mother's side came from a small island called Pitcairn Island. One of the islanders, a man named Fletcher Christian, served on the *Bounty*, and helped organize a mutiny. I was born on an island. Tasmania. I just spent months in Cuba, another island, making a film. I've been drawn to the sea my entire life. I can't imagine not being close to the sea—waking up in the middle of the night and going to the window and opening it, just to smell the salt water."

He pulled her over to the bed.

"What are you doing?" she asked. But she knew what he was doing and she allowed him to lead her to his bed. Her body went rigid and she started to shake.

"If the sea is in your blood, like it is mine, then we will make a good pair," he said.

"Sex should mean something," she said.

"Sex should be pleasurable; you shouldn't have to file a flight plan before taking off to bed."

She no longer resisted his embrace, allowing his mouth to move along her shoulders and neck and to slip her halter top down to expose her breasts. Her wedding ring fell out of the halter top and clicked against the hard wood floor. It rolled from the edge of the bed until it struck the wall. Errol Flynn never stopped fondling Mrs. Faragos's breasts as they both watched the course of the wedding ring. When it finally fell over, Mrs. Faragos stopped breathing, a sense of horror etched on her face.

"I can keep a secret," said Errol Flynn. "The question is whether you want to keep a secret, too?"

She blinked, searching his eyes for some indication of exactly what he intended.

"I've never done anything like this before," she said. "I've always been faithful to my husband. He's the only man I've ever been with. I married him when I was nineteen."

He slowly rotated her nipples as she spoke. She never looked down as if refusing to acknowledge what he was doing.

"Married only a year?"

He's very quick, she thought.

"But if you are attracted to someone and they are attracted to you, is there a crime in acting on that attraction?"

Her mind didn't work fast enough for him. She knew there was an answer but as he pulled down her shorts, she glanced over his shoulder at the sea. The gulls, ever so gracefully, patrolled the beach. A storm front was gathering rapidly and one by one the tankers disappeared into grayness. His tongue worked over her breasts and belly. His mustache felt prickly on her stomach as she arched back on the bed. She was almost afraid to touch his body—almost but not entirely. Her hands resting on the bed came in contact with his leg. She felt a scar, and outlined it with her fingers. Now it was his turn to moan and she liked the feeling of power his desire gave her. As he entered her, she saw that his eyes were squeezed tight, his mouth drawn, as if he were in some other place, another time, and with another woman. He worked himself into a sweat, reaching over to drink another glass of gin, smiling and then closing his eyes again as if a coal miner going back to the pit for another shift. When he finally finished, he rolled off her, panting, and smelling of gin. He made no effort to hold her, or touch her afterwards. She turned on her side, propping up her head on her hand, studying him. She reached down and touched the scar. This time she could see the patchy red botch of a recent wound.

"I was wounded in Cuba," he said without opening his eyes.

"You were shot?" Her eyes wide open, examining his flesh for evidence of bullet wounds.

"When you find yourself under fire on the frontline, then anything can happen. I saw men killed and wounded. It was unlike anything I ever saw in Hollywood. Cuba was the real thing. No director yelled, 'Roll 'em' or 'Cut' or 'That's a take, Mr. Flynn. You can go to your dressing room.' What happened wasn't in anyone's script. That was terrifying but at the same time I felt totally alive, and involved in something larger than making a movie. I'd experienced real war. Do you have any idea what I am trying to tell you?"

Here was a man whom she had just met and didn't know except for his movies and they had just made love. And what does he talk about? His war wound. If that is what you could call it. "Can I have a glass of water?" she asked.

He broke out laughing. "That's what I love about the young. They have not the slightest idea of death or the horror of war. All they know is when they are thirsty or tired or bored. This attitude makes waging war ever so much easier."

Errol climbed out of bed, disappeared into the bathroom, then emerged wearing a bath towel tied around his waist and holding a glass of water. He sat next to her. Mrs. Faragos had wrapped the sheets from the bed around her. She took the glass of water and drank.

"What I mean to say is, why don't we find a way to be happy?"

"What do you mean?"

He got up and stood looking at the sea. "I am not sure. What I think may be possible is an arrangement. You see, I am new to Vancouver. I really know nothing about where to find things. And frankly, I really don't have the inclination to learn. I'd rather be on a boat out there. On the bay." He poured himself another drink and was getting slightly drunk. "So it is like this. What if I offered you and your husband a certain sum to help me?"

Mrs. Faragos's teeth chattered from the cold and the uncertainty. "Help you do what?"

"Run errands, for instance. I need someone to go out and buy books and liquor and other supplies. I am always running out of something. And, yes, of course, to check my mailbox, and you could arrange to have my bills paid. Yes, yes, that's it. I need someone who can provide me with a certain degree of comfort and who can see that I am not disturbed by the day-to-day things that I find quite maddening. Am I making myself understood?"

"You want to pay me money?"

"Yes, I want to pay you."

Mrs. Faragos nodded. "That means I am hired?"

"Darling, you've already completed your first audition. But for this role, you must also read." He placed *Anna Karenina* on the bed and opened it to a marked passage. "Now let me hear you read this in a clear voice."

Mrs. Faragos looked down at the passage and blushed.

"Read it," he said.

She did as he asked, "'For anything to be undertaken in a household what is essential is either total discord between husband and wife or loving harmony. When their relationships are vague, neither one thing nor the other, it is impossible to do anything at all. A great many families stick it out for years in the same old ruts hated by both husband and wife, simply because there is neither out and out strife nor harmony.'"

When she looked up from the book, Errol Flynn was fast asleep on the bed.

Jim Pauley's Bad Feng Shui

It is six thirty a.m. when Joey's driver stops the car beside the fountain. Following behind his car are two vans with Feng Shui Flower Shop stenciled on the side panel. Both vans are freshly washed and polished and the drivers climb out, walk to the back and two workers inside the back of each van work with their driver unloading flowers. Sky and Ped sit in the back of the car, watching the workers stacking the freshly cut flowers alongside the fountain. Hundreds and hundreds of flowers perfumed the courtyard. Sweet, fragrant, transitory scents carried away by a light breeze. Smells that bring all of one's sense alive with feeling and possibility. There is holiness and a divine quality in the presence of such beauty. And also glimpse of tragedy, for in days, they will be dying, and ignorant people will fail to see their own link to death as they pass the flowers.

Exotic shaped petals some tapering to sharp spikes while others unfolded lush centers like a spiraling galaxy in deep space. Long stem, short stem, thorns and brambles and foliage collided in a rainbow of prime colors. The arrangement cast a mystery, a subtle drawing of pleasure, luring the hand and the eye—to touch, to behold, and to preserve. The flower arrangements along with feng shui are a navigational device, a magical compass guiding customers through their daily world of supernatural surfaces, conflicts, obstacles, and dangers, delivering them safe, whole and secure. In this world ripe with superstition, Joey is king. A dozen other vans fan out through the city. The drivers and workers in Feng Shui Flower Shop gold and blue overalls know their routes by heart; delivering fresh flowers to the high-rise office towers, the luxury apartments, restaurants, and nightclubs. Ever since the tsunami, the flower orders have skyrocketed. None of the employees have slept for two days filling orders. Most in demand are funeral wreaths.

The new customers, like the old ones, share a reverent belief that the principles of Feng Shui Flower Shop, through a combination of merit acquired in the previous life and merit creditably earned in this life, has harnessed an ancient wisdom. The terrible power of the tsunami has at the same time reinforced the desire to restore the forces of harmony and nature. The place of flowers is as important as the flowers themselves. No one at Feng Shui Flower Shop does anything to dissuade their customers; indeed, quite the opposite, they do all within their power to bring the miracle of feng shui to their customers. They wanted flowers and magic. Joey Balfour wants flowers, magic, and two back rooms where professional gamblers can play. The alliance of interest forged between them is as unbreakable as the glue between money and belief.

Sky and Ped are true believers, and the power of such faith (such true belief cannot be faked) is evident for all to behold from the moment they carefully photograph the interiors, measure light, distance, air flows, diagram the axis of each room (laying out the north, south, east and west points), map the corridors, the door frames and entryways.

Working for hours, appearing as the sun rises and departing after the sun sets, taking their readings and making notes. After accumulating all of the data, Sky and Ped draw elaborate charts for each room showing what flowers, what color of flowers, and what placement for each room would be best feng shui. The customers don't want complicated flow charts, PowerPoint presentations, and simulation of light and balance in animations, they want flowers to honor the dead whose numbers have grown to the tens of thousands.

The old customers whisper to others that something inexplicable happened to their bottom line after the deliveries started. The day of the first delivery is the one traceable event to explain their new prosperity. The specific details of arrangements for fresh flowers from Feng Shui Flower Shop become the secret competitive weapon in the Bangkok expat and Chinese community. Sky and Ped's evaluations are treated as company trade secrets. Employees are fired should they breach the security guarding the feng shui for the flowers. Even their accountants are forced to admit in obscure footnotes to financial statements that profits and good fortune occurred once they signed a contract with Feng Shui Flower Shop. The business blooms. As with all such lovely blooms, in the shadows await those wishing to pluck the flower and possess it themselves. The whispers have reached the ears of the relatives of the dead in the South. The phones never stop ringing.

Joey slides into the back of the car with Ped and Sky while Marty stands close to one of the vans and watches the workmen carrying flowers from the fountain and into the shop.

Jennifer sleeps in the condo wondering why her famous Joey boy has given up the gambling business to run a flower shop. Joey would like to explain to his mother but has trouble finding the right words. What started as a cover for his secret gambling operation in Bangkok has taken on a life of its own. Joey has thoughts about how this leap happened. If you use a beard often enough, it's no longer just a beard. It becomes who you are. Just as Sky and Ped were first hired to front for Joey's back-room operation and finding the finer choices of working yings, one day something weird happened: the working yings began to hold less and less interest, and Sky and Ped, his twin beards, emerged as a perfect fit for talent, sex, conversation, reading, and business.

"With all the foreigners killed in Khao Lak, we can't keep up with the orders," says Ped. There are black rings under her eyes.

"Ease up. You're working too hard. We have some other things to take care of," says Joey.

"Joey, we're gonna lose people unless we can hire more staff," says Sky.

"Hire them. There's something else. What is it?"

Sky says, "Your mother is worried sick over Boggy. She's reliving your youth through him."

"That kid can't take care of himself. She has every right to be worried. Except for one thing. Boggy isn't someone she should be wasting worry time on."

"Agreed. I don't like the way he used your mother to come to Bangkok," says Ped.

He likes that Ped has x-ray vision when it comes to people. Joey doesn't much like the way Boggy latched on to his mother the way a parasite finds a host in order to feed and survive. Marty taps on the window and Joey presses the button to make it silently roll down. "We're discussing business, Marty. But that is over." He eyes Ped and then Sky, who take his glance as the signal that they are dismissed from the car. The door opens and Sky emerges first. She walks into the shop without turning around. Ped leans over the door and looks in at Joey.

"Are you really looking for him, Joey?"

"I owe it to my mother," Joey says.

Ped's smile turns into a fun grin. "You owe her everything." A wall-to-wall library of the world's classics in literature had not altered her view on motherhood, the Thai default perception of the role and place of mothers could never be altered.

And this from a Thai ying born and bred in a mother-goddess culture. How the times are changing, thinks Joey. His little business has contributed to the Frankenstein-like grafting of Eastern and Western ways of thinking. Genghis Khan meets Bill Gates and empires are formed. Marty climbs into the back seat and closes the door. Ped watches them as Joey tells the driver where he wants to go. It is seven in the morning. Joey figures that Jim Pauley, if he's living in the slums behind the canal, will be emerging for online poker. He reaches under the seat and finds the nickel-plated handgun placed exactly where he asked Ped to place it. As the car circles around the flower-shrouded fountain, Joey rolls down the window and blows Ped a kiss. She stands, shaking her head, hands planted on her hips. Joey slips the handgun into his pocket.

"You gonna shoot him?" asks Marty.

"I am not going to shoot him," says Joey. "That's my feelings for the moment. Feelings can change."

Marty turns Joey's words over in his mind. "Then, why are you packing a gun? For a change of feelings? Is that it?"

"Because he might try and shoot me. I make the odds eight to one."

"About the same odds as a relief pitcher hitting a homerun. Even a roll of the dice has a one in six chance of a number coming up."

Joey nods and thinks about the dice rolling. "More like ten to one he has a gun. And thirty to one he would try and shoot me. But sometimes the long-odds horse wins a race. It is wise to be prepared."

The tinted windows of Joey's car make it impossible for anyone to see who is inside. Staring at the window is like looking into one of those two-way mirrors the police use inside interrogation rooms. All of the powerful and rich people in the city ride around in tinted-windowed cars. One-way mirrors on a city of suspects. Joey's driver follows his instructions through the spider web of sub-sois until they roll to a stop thirty meters from where Oy climbed off the motorcycle and walked on a series of planks over the canal to the shack with a corrugated roof on the other side. Chickens under a domed basket made of bamboo scratch in the dirt. A couple of mangy dogs scratch their ears and necks. A food vendor lights the charcoal in a small open grill. People walk in the street in ragged shorts and tank tops, blowing their noses, lighting cigarettes, spitting up buckets of yellow phlegm. The neighborhood buzzes with the life and activity of a rural village dropped into the heart of Bangkok. Other cars—mainly beat-up green and yellow Toyota taxis—pass as they wait. When Pauley finally emerges on the gangplank he's wearing a baseball cap backwards, as if he's a teenage ghetto kid, and jeans, running shoes and a Singha beer T-shirt. The jeans are loose fitting like he's lost a lot of weight, and his face is drawn, gaunt, lined as if someone had melted the flesh into furrows.

"That's him," says Joey.

Marty leans forward. "That guy looks eighty years old."

"If you just had open-heart surgery, you'd find your candle had burnt way down."

Marty reaches for the door handle but Joey stops him. "Wait."

"I thought we were going to grab him."

"There's no hurry. Let's see where he's going."

Jim Pauley climbs onto the back of a motorcycle taxi. Joey's driver puts the car into gear and follows a safe distance behind. A taxi wedges itself between the motorcycle and Joey's car. *Perfect,* thinks Joey.

"He looks real beat up," says Marty. Pauley gets off the motor-cycle, hands the driver some notes, and walks slowly away; he's skin and bones, cheeks hollowed out, his eyes haunted.

"He's going to work, Marty."

Thirty minutes after Jim Pauley disappears into the lobby of the short-time hotel, Joey studies the feng shui of the hotel. He gets out of the car and walks the length of the drive and surveys the grounds. The earth and metal elements are in conflict. Marty stands at his elbow. "Jim Pauley's made a mistake. He picked a short-time hotel with only one way in and out. If he had done that in Las Vegas, they would have caught him. He must be getting sloppy living in the tropics." Joey turns and walks back to the car.

"Jesus, Joey, let's just close whatever deal you're gonna make."

Joey looks over his shoulder, first directly at Marty, and then turns around and looks at the short-time hotel. It is a rundown shell of a hotel. He wants to let Jim Pauley run with the line a bit longer before he tugs on the pole. "We have all the information we need, Marty. Let's give him a little time to let him make some money. That will put him in a confident frame of mind. We know where he lives so we can always find him. And we know where he plays poker."

"In the back of a short-time hotel. What are the odds of that?"

"The odds are closing in on one hundred percent. That means we own him."

Finding Your Level
and Beating the Odds

His eyes open slowly in a strange, windowless room with a sink with a leaky faucet. Boggy experiences a moment of panic. Have the agents who blew up his apartment in Maine tracked him down in Bangkok? Have they drugged him, transported him to a facility on the Cuban coast, and incarcerated him with hundreds of other men who are confined in small cells? He dreamt of leg irons, torture racks, pyramids of human flesh, with cameras flashing and snarling dogs. He smells plugged toilets and vomit and stale beer. His injured arm throbbed as a guard beats him. He pleaded for the guard to stop hitting his arm but his protest brought more blows. "Renditions" is the word circling in a loud moan throughout the cells and torture rooms. It's the unofficial way, the off-the-books way, the way of Judge Dredd, his cellmate explains to him. "You've been rendered. Render unto Caesar what's Caesar's."

Someone outside pounding on the door woke him. He remembers as he rubs his eyes that this isn't Cuba; he's inside a small, sparsely furnished room in a short-time hotel. Jim Pauley, who lives in a secret location nearby, has recommended the room. After leaving Lake Ratcha, Jim had taken him along a shortcut into the sub-soi that led to the short-time hotel. For a silverback like Pauley—the Discovery Channel image of an old ape with a silver streak running down the length of its back, hands clutched into fists, beating its chest, and claiming dominion over his harem—he moves with an alert eye, waiting for a younger challenger. Like his jungle cousin, Jim Pauley's savvy and instincts instilled him with survival skills. He has the right combination of suspicion and doubt, a quick reaction time, and an ability to see that in the adult world most people lacked a rapid response system. Boggy lifts up his wrist and squints at his watch. It is seven thirty a.m. This is his usual close-down time. When he switches off his computer and feeds Octavian and Caesar before dropping into bed.

"It's Jim," says Pauley from the other side of the door.

He gets out of bed and walks over and opens the door; Boggy sleeps in what he normally works in, a T-shirt and underwear. He paddles back and sits on the edge of the bed, a vacant expression on his face. He yawns, one of those full-mouth yawns that bends to the outer hinges of the jaw.

"Last night you said you wanted to sit in while I played online," says Jim.

Boggy rubs his eyes. "I do. But, I thought that professionals played poker at night. Late at night."

"It is night where we are going to play. And I am not looking to play professionals. I want to make money, not lose it."

Over a hot cup of coffee in the hotel coffee shop, Boggy watches the waitress feeding a cat. There is a slight catch in his throat as his thoughts drift to Caesar.

Pauley gears up psychologically for the game. "The idea is to catch the after-work crowd. They're tired after working all day at some job. Playing online poker is all they have to look forward to. It's the only action they have all day. But with this tsunami in the news it might keep people away. I am going to try and you're welcome to watch."

In the corner a TV screen shows home-video footage of huge waves sweeping away furniture, cars, and people.

"Joey Balfour said that a nine to five office job has the same effect as a frontal lobotomy after a few years. It doesn't make for good poker players."

Pauley nods and watches the TV. "That sounds like something Joey would say."

Joey hadn't said much to Boggy about his TV show other than it was many years ago. He did say something, though, about the audience for this TV show. It was as small now as it was in the beginning. Joey sat on the balcony after Jennifer left, and described the audience: The hospice for the post-lobotomy cases with no other place to go. A horde of mugs living in the shadows, without a real life, feeling (if any feelings are left) depressed, numb, bored, looking for action, as they watch him and a celebrity guest tell stories about winning long shots. That is their dream, their hope for salvation. So the mugs log on and play online poker and dream of the big kill. They have as much chance winning big as the man in the witch's black cloth with wires snaking out of his arms, standing arms raised like Christ without a cross in Abu Ghraib prison.

After Pauley finishes his second cup of coffee, they walk into a small, empty Internet room with four computers on tables. "At night you can't get a computer. The girls are online begging money from boyfriends. After they kick out their last short-time john for the night, they drag their asses into the back room and sign in on their free email accounts," says Jim Pauley.

Other than a morgue, few places are as quiet as a short-time hotel at eight in the morning. Except for the waitress and a cat, no one or nothing else surfaces. The tables in the restaurant and the Internet room next door are empty. Motorcycles scream up and down the soi behind. Jim Pauley sits at a computer, logs in on the Empire site and finds about a thousand punters at five hundred and ten tables. He picks a three-dollar table and a six-dollar table. Boggy looks over Pauley's shoulder at the computer screen as he plays three separate hands. He moves swiftly between the three-dollar and six-dollar tables; it isn't long until thousands of gamblers from all over the world fill a thousand tables, looking at their hands, laying down their bets. Pauley wins a hand of Texas Hold 'em. Then, fifteen minutes later, wins another hand, and then loses one in the next moment.

"I make about twenty-eight dollars an hour," says Pauley, leaning back from the screen. "That doesn't seem like a lot. But it goes a long way in Thailand."

"What happened to all the money you stole in Las Vegas?" Boggy shudders to think of all the deals he could have closed with that kind of money. He'd have millions and millions from that nest egg now. What has this silverback done with the mega bucks?

"I lost most of it when the Thai stock market crashed in '97. I made a couple of big bets on shares and lost. The shares still haven't recovered. The rest of the money?" He shrugs his shoulders, looking at his cards online, "Well, it melted away on living expenses, visa runs, moving around money. Sometimes I found a poker game going in an upcountry back room. Places like Korat, Pattaya, Hua Hin, where old farts go to retire and die. But such guys don't have much money. And out of those who had money, more than a few were pretty good players who figured out that living in Thailand was a whole lot better than living anywhere in America. I couldn't beat them. They were as good as some of the players in Las Vegas. What saved me was Internet poker. By then, most of my money was gone and I was back living from day to day. Doing the best I can to get by."

Boggy is deflated. He wants to like Pauley. But he's a fool. Or very unlucky. Or both. Again he thinks of how Pauley has blown a small fortune, and what he could have done with it. The options he could have secured on Malaysian apple orchards, the e-gold contracts he could have locked in and swapped for Brazilian coffee, which he knew from an internal memorandum posted by a disgruntled employee, was about to explode in price. Such knowledge without funds is a constant source of depression for Boggy, when he's not worrying about being followed by American agents.

Pauley admits his greed got the better of him in 1997 and nearly pushed his head below the surface. "I had made well over a million in early April 1997. The money just kept growing. Every day I told myself to get out. A little voice in my head said, 'Pauley, bail out.' I intended to sell all holdings and repay the casino. End of June in that year, and I was down to my last five grand. My greed taught me a lesson. Stay at your level. Don't go to a table to play a game you don't understand or have enough information to play. I violated all of the rules Joey Balfour used to go on about on TV. Howard, none of us are as smart as we see ourselves."

By nine thirty a.m. Bangkok time the floodgates are open; thousands of people slump in front of their screens, shoulders hunched, scratching their balls, placing one more bet, playing one more hand in the never-never land against the unseen who are just as fucked up as they are, wives screaming at them to get a life, come to bed, talk to the kid, talk to them.

"Professional poker players live on the edge," says Jim Pauley. "Most of the professionals are socially dysfunctional. I know one guy who used to play in Las Vegas. He got a straight A in statistics and a D in history. He'd stay up all night reading about statistics and fall asleep in his clothes. In the old days, to make a living in poker you had to do three things: you had to win, then you had to collect what you'd won and finally you had to be able to walk out with it. The great thing about playing online is the last two things no longer apply."

Pauley's spill reminds Boggy of Joey Balfour, as it should, since it comes undigested from one of Joey's old TV shows. Pauley is another in a legion of acolytes spreading Joey's mission.

Jim Pauley smiles as he wins a hand, and stops to sip his coffee, his eyes on the screen. His free hand hovers above the keyboard. He's up eighty-four dollars and it is only ten a.m. His life is small-time in every way, thinks Boggy: the Internet game room, the short-time rooms that smell of musty sheets, paint peeling off the walls, his world of whores and poker, a world with only the possibility of small wins and losses. No question, though, Pauley is getting a kick out of winning the small-time bets and watching his money accumulate. This is the same guy who once knocked off a casino for hundreds of thousands of dollars, taking his pleasure and satisfaction in money for a bowl of noodles. He's adjusted like an old whore to getting by with the proceeds of the occasional daily service of a loyal customer who doesn't know any better.

"Joey Balfour had this great cable TV show in Las Vegas for years. He once had one of the all-time great Texas Hold 'em players on his show. Will 'The Red Baron' Madden. The Red Baron said all great players are world-class romancers. Take a table where you've got three professionals beating the brains out of a tourist from Iowa. The tourist excuses himself from the table to take a toilet break and one of the guys follows him to the bathroom. The tourist is all depressed and ready to fold for the night. The wise guy stands next to the tourist; they are pissing in the urinal when the wise guy tells him that he's been up against some bad luck. But a streak of bad luck isn't so important if the player is really good, and he thinks the tourist is a good player. That's what the Red Baron called romancing the weak link at the table. The tourist comes out of the bathroom thinking he's good and he doubles his bets. The first rule of poker is, to win, you have to romance the sucker." Pauley sighs, shakes his head, "But like a lot of things in the real world, it doesn't work as well as it once did. Too many people are wise."

Boggy wants to know why. "So the romance has gone out of the game?" he asks.

"No, not altogether," says Pauley. "The problem is Internet poker. How can you romance someone you can't see? Who is the guy at the table? You have no fucking idea. You're looking at a computer screen, a piece of equipment. You don't have a chance to interact with the other players. You can't figure out how to get to this weaker player and romance him into doubling up his bets and losing his car and house. Online poker you play blind because you can only read the cards. You can't read the other people at the table."

Around noon a ying in shorts and flip-flops, with chicken-bone-sized arms and legs, walks into the room and flops at the next computer. She logs on to her email account and is no two-finger wonder, instead she types like a pro. In less than a minute, she's checking her email. She looks away from the screen to Boggy who's staring at her. She smiles, causing small sinkhole dimples to appear at the corners of her mouth. Her smell is of lavender, beer and cigarettes. No makeup and unwashed hair make no difference as Boggy's heart rate increases. Jim Pauley glances over at her.

"Hi, Apple." Pauley greets her, looks at his cards, and increases his bet. "You look tired this morning. Late night?"

"Hi, Khun Paul."

At last Boggy knows Jim Pauley's street name, the one he's hiding under.

Pauley's looking at Boggy. He knows why, too. He wants to know if Boggy has registered his street name. Like a good poker player, Boggy's face remains unchanged, placid, his eyes returning after a moment to the young woman.

"Do you work here?" asks Boggy.

She shrugs, yawns, and blinks two or three times as if accessing some database buried deep in her brain. "Yeah, sometimes I come here." She avoids the word work. The young woman has an air of pride. Her movements suggest a business-like gravity. She arrived, like Pauley did, with a purpose—to place another bet, to make money, to collect winnings from the week before.

"Apple's what you'd call freelance."

"I work freelance," says Boggy.

"A cat burglar and jeweler are both in the gem business. But one is freelancing. You can guess which one Apple is," says Pauley as he looks away from the screen. He allows himself to get distracted and loses the last hand; a bad bet, losing the pot to a Broadway straight draw.

It is a reminder to Pauley why he stays at the three-dollar and six-dollar online tables. He often thinks about moving up a level or two but at each level the competition is tougher. It is harder to win. On Joey's TV program, he once had an English poker player everyone called Galaxie. This guy used to play a mean game of cards. Joey interviewed him about poker and about his fight career. Galaxie told Joey how he had boxed on his team at a public school in England. After a few months of training, Galaxie was the school lightweight-class champion. No one in his school could touch him. He won every fight. Then he moved up a notch with boxing competitions at three or four other schools. Again he won his fights. Galaxie thought he was good enough to turn pro. His first professional fight was in London. He climbed into the ring and within one minute of the first round he had been knocked out. Galaxie never saw the punch. One of those bad beats on the chin out of the blue. He remembered being on his back, looking up and seeing the ceiling spinning and feeling that something had been dislocated inside his head.

"The guy who landed the punch on Galaxie, what happened to him?" Joey asked him.

Galaxie laughed and clapped his hands. "That's the best part. Nothing much ever happened to the career of a boxer who knocked me out. He fought forty professional fights. Lost thirty-seven matches and won three. I was knocked senseless by a loser. But at that level even a loser can make you see stars." In his professional career, the man who caused Galaxie to see the stars went on to lose most of his professional fights. Galaxie said, "Each level up it gets tougher and tougher in boxing. But it don't stop with boxers. It's the same for poker players, hockey and baseball, singers, golfers, politicians, field and track stars. And hookers. Everyone has to find their level and make the best of it."

Jim Pauley has found his level: three-dollar and six-dollar online tables.

He logs off and orders a beer.

"You want something to drink?" he asks Boggy.

"Coke, thanks." His eyes are drinking in Apple.

"How about you, Apple?"

"Coffee," she says not looking up from her inbox.

Apple's trolling for cash deposits, SWIFTs, electronic transfers in her inbox messages; she knows more about banking than a Zurich money launderer. She's in the zone of total concentration. Pauley admires the skills of a pro. She opens and closes the messages like a professional gambler studying each hand, figuring which one is the best one, placing her bets, calling the hands of men trying to bluff her. She flits back and forth between two of the messages before narrowing her choice down to one, and then sets out to reply to her suitor. Apple reminds Pauley of a mechanic he knew in Las Vegas—not a car mechanic, a card mechanic. Nevada had a certain tolerance for killing people. But it had none for cheating. If you got caught cheating in a casino, you were going to do time. Pauley knew the rules of the game when he walked from the casino with the cash and chips. He never thinks of what he did as cheating. Cheating was what one guy he knew did in card games. He was a mechanic. He got caught dealing a second card. He cheated the house. He went before the court with no prior record. It didn't matter. The judge sentenced him to a long prison term, saying, "The convicted stands before the court as a man who has cheated for the house, cheated for himself and cheated for others. That is a hat trick. It deserves a substantial amount of time in the penalty box." Pauley knows the story's been embellished over the years, but it doesn't take the sting out of the judgment.

Apple strikes Pauley as a ying who is at the top of her game; she is full of dreams, and plans, and options as if the road to riches has opened up to her and will forever be open. He sees from the way Boggy is drinking her in, how easy it is to find a constant source of new mugs in the ying game. His dopey eyes are innocent and hopeful, as if this ying deserves a better life, as if she is someone he can rescue. Bar yings, the better ones, have highly developed skills in romancing the sucker. They do it for a living. It is a marvel, thinks Pauley, watching her typing away to a punter in Berlin or New York, worming her way into his heart, making him show all of his cards, while she sits back and decides which hand is the one she wants to play. *Boggy is blind*, he thinks. *He can't see what is going on in front of him. No wonder he's on the run. Boggy is doomed.*

"What happened to your arm?" she asks, playing the sympathy card.

"An accident," he replies.

"Does it hurt?"

"Not so much."

"Where are you staying?" Apple asks, after she clicks the send button on a message asking for the immediate deposit of five thousand baht.

Boggy's head cranes forward. "I am staying here," he says.

Her face grows cloudy. She checks her watch, pushes back her chair, waves to Pauley and leaves.

Boggy turns to Pauley, "What'd I say?"

"You told her the truth and she decided not to play at your level."

Apple does what Pauley advises every ying to do but most never understand the importance of the lesson—ask a punter one question: where are you staying? Is it a guesthouse, a flophouse, a rundown short-time hotel or a suite in a five-star hotel? When that ball is in play she immediately knows if you're in the big-league stadium or some small-town football field. As a rule of thumb, a punter pays half the cost of his room for a ying. Apple knows this because her friend "Paul" taught her the formula. Knowledge is power and power is money. Apple also knows this and worships Paul for taking her under his wing. She has no regrets kicking back twenty percent of her winnings, although she cheats him on what she discloses, and he knows and accepts this.

"In picking the right ying you have to play the odds," Pauley says, as they are back in the restaurant and his lunch of rice and chicken is set before him. "You need information before you make any bet otherwise you don't know the odds of winning. That's why the smart money gambles on making nice, nice to the mamasan. She's the one with the best information. Of course, no matter what, you never play the equivalent of no-limit poker with a bar ying. You put up some money on the gamble and when it's gone you walk from the table. No-limit poker and no-limit ying poker are the best ways of going broke. With a ying, especially one like Apple—whoever mentions price first, loses. Did you see all those emails she had in her inbox?"

"You should see my inbox," says Boggy.

"Do you have a regular column of men waiting every day to wire you money because they are in love with you?"

Boggy wrinkles his nose and digs into a hamburger.

"Okay, I take that as a 'no' but that's Apple's mail. She doesn't get junk mail. So when you decide to bet on someone like Apple, you have to calculate the odds. When the bet is two thousand baht you need information before laying down the bet. If you take a ying just by looking at her, it is like betting just by looking at the horse five minutes before race time. That's not a bet based on information, it's based on gut instinct. Why is it a man can understand this about a horse but not about a woman?"

Boggy grins as he finishes eating the last bite of the greasy hamburger. He has no answer for Pauley. He's young, on the run, in a strange city and has no idea what Pauley is talking about. He's in love with a ying named Apple. He wishes he could consult his friend Dr. Daeng who has a compassionate heart and could advise him what to do next.

"Women like Apple should never marry. At best, men are their temporary allies as they advance along the front, capturing prizes and defeating rivals. They find victory not in marriage but in showing their family and everyone in their village that despite all the odds they beat the casino. They beat the house by getting the house to build them a mansion. That's big-time face."

Boggy didn't expect such a speech from Jim Pauley. Not this silverback who lives in the shadows. This avuncular, quiet, determined man with stories of card tables, hiding places, and close calls with casino thugs looking to get him. Jim Pauley has evolved an insight that allows him to measure another person and calculate their intentions. What Boggy hears is not the Las Vegas street-smart voice, or the wounded voice from 1997; instead, Boggy hears a deeper voice, one that he imagines Pauley only occasionally allows to escape into the larger world. When Pauley reads Apple's reply to Boggy, a voice he doesn't recognize bubbles to the surface, a voice of warning, a voice that says loud and clear that life teaches only a few people how to read another person's hand, it teaches even fewer the intentions of the person holding the cards. When that person shows an intention, they have already played their hand. Apple has shown her cards to Boggy and, for the life of Pauley, he can't understand why this young man, who is apparently on the run, wants to risk betting against that kind of hand.

The Probability of Shooting Jim Pauley

"Money is the solvent that removes the stain of class, race, status, gender, nationality, and education. Underneath is a single smooth polished surface of life with all friction removed; a life that glides along a monorail of pleasure, influence, and power. The Declaration of Independence considered the pursuit of happiness but what it really meant was that the pursuit of money gave everyone the equal right to buy their piece of happiness. You can handicap the odds of winning money, and you can handicap the odds of finding happiness. This is why Americans get out of bed in the morning. The problem with the probability of things happening is a gambler pays for each chance. The greater the odds, the greater the probability you will lose before your chance to win comes around. The bigger the odds, the more likely you are to lose. Even with a forty-nine percent chance of winning, if the person you bet against has more staying power then it is absolutely certain that over time you will lose. You will lose everything."

Joey Balfour opened his final TV show with this observation. Over a million people tuned in to watch Joey's swan song. They hung on his every word as he did a wrap of his eight years of broadcasting, naming the celebrities who had appeared on his show, the long shots that had won at the racetrack, and the professional football and baseball teams that had done the most to overcome the odds and win championships. Joey spoke from the heart about chance and probability, the margin of error between winning and losing, and the part of the human spirit that made men and women take risks with their earthly goods. They shared a common bond;

they wished to ride that monorail of winnings into a new and better life, one that some day would make them a "somebody." Joey's final TV show from Las Vegas was ranked as the most popular of the new DVDs of Joey's collected programs. It occupied a zone somewhere between self-help, evangelical inspiration, with tips, pointers, folklore interspersed with rational, logical methods on how to go about handicapping the odds in poker, dice, blackjack and horse racing. As the camera fades out on Joey, a showgirl is shaking her bootie.

Marty watches the familiar sight of Joey working out the odds on a string of independent events. Like the old days at Exhibition Park in Vancouver, Joey is handicapping the probability of events. He taps his pen on the notepad. This goes on for some time.

"The odds are better than even that Hunt will whack Pauley," says Marty.

Joey doesn't look up from his notepad. "I am thinking of events first. Then odds. That's the order you factor in odds making. And the number of times something happens. The more times someone tries to kill you the more likely over time that they will succeed."

Joey includes his highly successful feng shui flower business as one of those long-shot plays equal to his bet on Temperance Hill in the Belmont Stakes. The vision had been a way to launder money from the gambling operation. Now it makes a large amount of money on its own. Being the last man to see Jim Pauley was another fluke. Finding him in Bangkok once he had found Jim's wife, Oy, became a two to one favorite to win. Thai yings never stray far from their farang husbands. They have a built-in husband locator that works better than a GPS system in tracking the coordinates of vanished husbands. As Joey and Marty sit in the back of the car, Joey is running the odds with a string of possible bets he has made with himself. What are the chances that a competitor of Feng Shui Flower Shop is seeking to knock Joey out of the market or make a hostile takeover of the business? Or that local casino people don't like Joey cutting into their operations in Bangkok and so want to eliminate the competition? He ranks the odds of the two business reasons equally as four to one or batting average of a big-league catcher. There is a personal reason to consider. Bill Hunt traveled to Bangkok to settle an old score and to heal his long-time wounded pride, and to avenge his public humiliation at the thieving hands of Jim Pauley. Joeys thinks the odds are longer: one in nine. Why nine to one and not, say, four to one? Had Hunt started his search hours after the theft, rather than years, his probability of success would have been higher in finding Pauley. The long lapse in time diminished the probability of locating his target. It doesn't make sense to Joey that Hunt has waited twelve years, an entire cycle, a turn of the wheel, to launch a campaign to find Pauley. And where did Bill Hunt get the money to finance the purchase of the rare movie poster from the Faragos (indeed, how did Bill Hunt of all people have the slightest clue about where to find them)?

Joey books the odds as five to one that Boggy and Bill Hunt have some prior connection. And what are the odds that someone inside a government agency is trying to eliminate Boggy because he has been snooping around and collecting evidence of a government-sanctioned hit on Errol Flynn? Joey decides he doesn't have sufficient information. Therefore he leaves a question mark beside the odds box drawn on the notepad. What are the odds such authorities are using Boggy as a cut out, and their real intended target is Joey Balfour? It isn't as if Joey is living underground. He is in plain view. They can nail him anytime.

But the conspiracy theory is always seductive and seduction usually causes gamblers to make wildly wrong subjective assessments of the odds. For fun, Joey marks down the odds that the government is somehow trying to harm him as one in six. The same odds as any number from six to one coming up with a fair toss of the dice. That seemed a safe number as it likely applies to most citizens in most situations. The addendum adds to his subjective evaluation, and increases the odds to five to one in his case.

What are Bill Hunt's intentions once he has Jim Pauley standing in front of him? Kill him? Beat him up? Force him back to the States for trial? The Statute of Limitations would have run on the heist so Joey carefully draws a line through the last option. Beating the living daylights out of Pauley appears a disproportionately small coin to drop for all the trouble Hunt has gone to; the costs are too high for the goal of inflicting a beating, and that makes Joey put the odds of a beating at eighteen to one—call it the long-shot equivalence percentage. But killing Pauley works out as justifying the full invoice for all of the related expenses, closes the account once and for all on Pauley's crime, and allows personal justice to score a win while officially looking the other way. Once Pauley has been turned over to Bill Hunt, the odds of Hunt murdering Pauley are, in Joey's mind, around two to one once given the chance at a clear shot. Fifty-fifty chance is a high risk of being murdered. With those sort of odds working against Pauley—and presumably anyone stupid enough to get in the way—a prudent odds maker would want to reduce his odds of getting caught in the crossfire, so carrying a handgun is an odds equalizing opportunity.

Jim Pauley emerges first. Boggy walks a couple of steps behind then quickly catches up until he is side by side with Pauley. Both men talk as if they are old friends. Though Joey knows (or thinks he knows) this is not the case. Gambling brings a strong bond between players who are on the same side. This confirms Joey's bet that Pauley has been playing Internet poker; Boggy would not have been a player who could have defeated him or from whom he won money—the latter case does not inspire friendship or idle conversation such as Joey witnesses from the back seat.

"That's both of our boys," says Joey.

"Boggy has made a new friend," says Marty.

Joey waits until they are one foot away from the car and then opens the door and steps out into the path of Jim Pauley.

"Hi, Jim, it's been a long time."

Pauley stops, his eyes bulging out. He has the start of a wattle under his chin, which wiggles as he walks; it's like watching a Thanksgiving turkey on the way to the table. At some point it dawns even on the dumbest turkey that it has been walking straight to the slaughter house. Pauley tries his best to control his uneven breathing. He wipes his sweaty palms on his jeans. "Hi, Joey. I heard some Indians took over your old TV show. That's something."

"Climb on in, Jim. We need to talk."

"I'd like to talk, but I've got an appointment," says Pauley, his voice breaking.

Boggy stands nearby, squinting with the sun in his eyes.

"Your appointment can wait, Jim."

"Can't we arrange something later this afternoon?" Pauley's pleading makes his knees weak.

Joey shakes his head. "Let's get this over with, Jim."

The driver opens the door on the passenger's side. "Get in, Boggy," says Marty.

Boggy does what he's told without a whimper. Joey takes the handgun from his pocket. He's wearing a surgical glove on his gun hand. "Pauley, don't make this difficult. Just get into the fucking car."

Marty gets out of the car, walks around and helps Pauley climb into the back seat. He slides in beside Pauley, leaving Pauley in the middle between himself and Joey. It is like old times, the way Joey and Marty communicate, divide up the labor, decide the next move as a team with nothing more than a glance. The air-con is cold enough to make Pauley's teeth chatter; his lips turn blue. He hunches down, squeezed in the middle, looking ahead as the driver pulls out of the entrance to the short-time hotel.

"How'd you find me?" asks Pauley. He eyes Boggy, feeling a burning on his face and throat, sensing that Boggy has betrayed him.

"Forget about that, Jim. Let's catch up on old times. The last time I saw you was in Las Vegas."

"I paid you twenty grand."

"Good memory."

"I never took you for a bounty hunter, Joey."

Joey laughs and sticks the gun into Pauley's ribs. "Buddy, you are in some deep waters. I hope you've grown gills since the last time we met."

Pauley starts to blubber about recovering from open-heart surgery and how he's still not a hundred percent and he's not feeling all that hot, and if Joey could ease up with the barrel of his gun against his chest that would be much appreciated. Boggy turns around in the front seat and stares at Joey. "And you, Gunnar, you are in the same boat. The two of you are the catch of the day. All I've got to do is deliver you up to Bill Hunt and then my fishing days are finished."

Pauley's shaking, pale faced, eyes pinpoints, his skin prickly with sweat and goose flesh. He looks like he's about to enter a state of shock. "Hunt?"

"You haven't forgotten your old chief of security at the casino the night you took a walk?"

Pauley is silent.

Joey pauses and looks him over. "Bill's got the memory of an elephant. And he wants one thing. Guess what that one thing might be?"

"Isn't there some way we can square this, Joey?"

"Jim, you need to understand that what you did is something that no one in Las Vegas has ever forgotten. Square it? How can I do that? How can anyone do that? You know the answer. You made your play, you chose a game that can't be squared."

"Bill Hunt will kill me," says Pauley.

Boggy, turning around in the front seat again, can't take his eyes off the handgun. A flicker of recognition registers. He knows this gun; he has pointed it at Joey. Pauley's desperation hits Boggy hard, and he repeats what Pauley already has asked for: "Can't we find a way to settle this, Joey?"

Joey ignores him. The kid from Maine with the half-fried arm isn't in any position to settle anything. He's an online merchant who dreams of small-fry deals out of tiny African and Southeast Asian countries most people can't locate on the map.

"I bet with Marty that the odds of Hunt killing you were even. Let me put it in a positive light. That means you've got a fifty-fifty chance of not getting killed. If you gave the casino back the money, then the odds would be increased in your favor. But I have an idea that the money is long gone."

Pauley looks down, slowly shaking his head, shuffling his feet. But there is no place to run. His look of defeat is absolute, like a condemned man being led to the place of execution; Jim Pauley appears to accept his fate. Boggy has done enough deals with Joey Balfour to know that Bill Hunt must have something that Joey wants and he's willing to trade Pauley in order to get it. The car idles on Rama IV Road waiting for a light to change.

"This is about the holy grail of all Errol Flynn posters," says Boggy. It is hardly a stab in the dark. Joey's obsession with those posters is how Boggy built up a profitable little business. A little furrow of sweat appears on his brow. "It's connected to Cuba."

Joey's voice is a whisper: "It was signed by Errol Flynn, 'To my comrade and friend, Fidel Castro.'"

Boggy's eyes grow misty. The possibility of possessing the ultimate Errol Flynn poster makes him a little dizzy. Even he would hand over Pauley for such a poster.

"If you know so much, which movie?" asks Joey.

"*Edge of Darkness*," says Boggy. "It's in perfect, mint condition. I thought that it was probably a fake. There are so many weird schemes driven by fast-talking online shills selling heavily discounted counterfeits; but you can't be sure unless you are an expert. So you take a chance. You lay down a bet that it's real, laying off odds that it isn't. Unless you are somebody like me who really knows the merchandise, then the odds change. I can tell you if it's real. You know that I can. There isn't a fake that can fool me."

"You're good, Boggy, real good. Do yourself and Pauley a favor and tell me exactly how you got this information," says Joey.

Boggy prides himself on knowing every poster ever signed by Errol Flynn and this one does not register. Joey responds with the degree of interest that Boggy assumes would come from learning about such a poster. Joey's cold steel coolness shows a determination and discipline that even Howard Boggy believes is outside the realm of ordinary behavior. He has a new respect for Joey. A florist in Bangkok ordering rare original movie posters isn't exactly a high scoring card. Joey Balfour's picks up all kinds of new points with Boggy.

"What if I told you what really happened that night in Vancouver in the penthouse?"

The blank expression drawn over Joey's face is spoiled by a smile. He can't help but show a flicker of interest.

"The night that Errol Flynn died in your penthouse. Though 'technically' in 1959 it wasn't your penthouse."

"How could you possibly know what happened in 1959?" Joey already has the image of Mr. and Mrs. Faragos hanging out in the hallway in his mind.

Pauley leans forward, shaking his head. "What's this got to do with me?"

"Shut up, Jim," says Joey.

Pauley slumps back in his seat, head down, muttering under his breath.

"Mr. Faragos told me the story," says Boggy. "Mr. Faragos also told me about Bill Hunt. I know how much he paid for the poster."

"I am not buying it, Boggy. Not yet. Maybe not ever."

"That's because you didn't know how Mr. Faragos had been selling the posters for years to finance his gambling."

Joey Balfour's demeanor suggests he's been knocked into cold silence. His eyes half close, his head bows as if in prayer. He can no longer clutch onto the belief that Boggy's bluffing. Boggy's hand is a straight flush and he's laid them on the table.

"Can I say something?" asks Pauley.

"No," says Joey. "Shut up, Pauley."

"Hunt paid Mr. Faragos five thousand dollars for the poster."

"That's nothing for such a poster. It's an insult."

"Not to Mr. Faragos it wasn't. Five grand was a lot of money to them. But he didn't tell Bill Hunt about Errol Flynn's last day in the penthouse. Mr. Faragos said that he's not told another living soul. He had promised Mr. Flynn that he would never talk about that last day. The fact he never told you means he was telling me the truth. Maybe you never asked him about Errol Flynn's last night. Or you didn't ask him in the right way."

"It's the last poster he would have parted with. He didn't know you. You were a total stranger."

"True. But I showed him something that made him change his mind."

"What?"

"The J. Edgar Hoover letter." The original letter. The letter they were after when they fire-bombed Boggy's apartment and killed Caesar. Joey visualizes Boggy unfolding that letter and handing it to Mr. Faragos, who slips on his reading glasses, his lips moving as he reads each word.

"What did he tell you?" The back of Joey's neck tingles.

"If I tell you, will you let Jim go?"

Pauley takes a big breath. "Are you going to kill me?"

"What do you think?" asks Joey.

"He doesn't know. That's why he's asking you," says Boggy. "It's a fucking reasonable question, don't you think?"

"You're not in a position to make the odds," says Marty. He nods at the gun that Joey holds.

"What Marty's saying is if you can get better odds from someone else, then take your business to him," says Joey. He nudges Pauley with his elbow, and continues. "How did you get yourself a patron? It certainly can't be your charm, Jim."

"If you are going to kill me, can't you just do it?"

"No one is going to kill you," says Boggy.

"Boggy, you're pushing against a rope that you might need later. Ease off. There are some places you don't want to go," says Marty.

"It's okay, Marty. He spends too much time in front of a computer screen. The kid has a story. I think we ought to hear him out before we phone Bill Hunt."

"Swear it, Joey." Boggy is wild eyed, pinching at his beard, pulling it down, clenching his jaw; he looks like a red-bearded animal ready to charge over the front seat. Joey's driver pulls him back with a sudden motion that takes Boggy by surprise.

Joey smiles and with a slight shrug takes his oath. "I swear I'll play fair and straight. No cheating. No card up the sleeve." He holds up his hand as if he is back before the grand jury when he was asked to swear on the Bible before he had to say what Eddie the Knife had told him in the ten minutes before he'd been gunned down.

"I want you to swear that if you go back on your oath you will have seven years of bad luck," says Boggy. "That settles it for me."

"What's settled?" asks Pauley.

"Jim, none of this is your business," says Marty.

"Joey Balfour is holding a gun on me and none of this is my business?"

"That's what I said," says Marty.

"Do we have a deal?" asks Boggy.

Joey looks at Pauley and then at Marty, who nods, "We have a deal."

"But you didn't say the words and swear it," says Boggy.

Marty raises his brow. "Boggy what are you talking about? Swear? Get a life."

Joey raises his hand and rolls his eyes. "I, Joey Balfour, swear an oath of seven years of bad luck that after you tell me the full story about the Castro movie poster I won't harm Pauley."

Joey is curious why Boggy would care whether Pauley lives or dies; it doesn't make sense. But the one lesson he's learned dealing with Boggy is that his chaotic, unpredictable style, dark mood and murky business plan mean that he could actually have some mystical sense of honor rolling around inside his brain, breaking like waves against the side of his skull. Boggy closes his eyes.

"I don't think you mean it," says Boggy.

"I swear I won't harm Pauley," says Joey again, holding up his hand. Of course, if Marty happens to pull the trigger and Pauley gets in the way of a bullet that is hardly a breach of his personal oath.

"Remember," says Boggy. "Seven years of bad, terrible earth-shattering luck if you breach your oath."

Joey exchanges a glance with Marty that says, "This kid has watched far too much television."

Boggy Enters Mrs. Faragos's Bedroom

Mr. Faragos had pure white hair, soft and silky and thin like that of a baby. It was combed and parted along one side. The face was deeply wrinkled, especially around the eyes, and he had waddles like curtains at his throat, and when he lifted his chin the flesh firmed up around his neck. Lester Faragos sat in his favorite chair, arms on the armrests, with a sparkle in his eyes. They were a clear blue—smiling eyes that lit up the moment Boggy spoke the name Errol Flynn.

Boggy switched on the mini tape recorder. Joey sat back, glanced over Pauley at Marty, who nodded. They recognized the voice immediately. It was Lester Faragos.

"I not only knew Errol. I worked for him. So did my wife. We were both in his service."

It was the way that Mr. Faragos chose the word 'service' that suggested a bond that wasn't of the usual employer–employee relationship.

"Service?" asked Boggy.

"We were—," and he paused, licked his lips and a wide smile caused the wrinkles around his eyes to close, making him look half-Chinese. "We were companions. She sometimes read books to him.

"If a man has only one wife—or, in theory, he should have only one—should she stray, then it ought to be with an Errol Flynn. Why shouldn't she have fallen for him? What woman wouldn't find an internationally famous action hero desirable? We both loved that man. As for me and him, we liked each other immediately, Errol and me. He once told me the story of his time with Castro in Cuba. He made a movie about it. He made two movies about Cuba. Errol came here with strong views about the rights and wrongs of Cuba. He believed that Castro was a savior, and his revolution was just and right. Cuba had needed someone to sweep the path clean of the dirt Batista had left."

Boggy noticed the bedroom door was ajar. From that room came an aroma of macaroni cheese and a sickly smell of unchanged sheets in a closed room that was never aired. A small, weary voice mumbled. None of the words were coherent. As hard as Boggy tried he could not make sense of the jumble of sounds. Mr. Faragos, his head cocked to the side, half turned in his chair as if trying to hear what was being said from the person in the bedroom. On the table next to him was a TV dinner with the foil peeled back. The macaroni cheese was untouched. Some flies struggled over the sticky terrain. They were laying eggs, and hatching a whole new generation of baby flies, which would burrow into the dinner.

"It's a friend of Joey Balfour," Mr. Faragos shouted. "My wife and I were very fond of Joey."

"His mother told me," said Boggy.

"He also knows Jennifer Balfour," shouted Mr. Faragos. "Why don't you come and say hello to my wife."

Boggy wasn't prepared for what happened next. Mrs. Faragos lay in bed with lit candles on tables surrounding her; the warm candlelight dancing off her face, flickering shadows crossing her forehead, closed eyes, and nose. She breathed slowly like someone in a deep sleep. She was motionless except for the occasional twitch of her mouth as if she were trying to bring forth words to describe the parade of images passing through her consciousness. Whatever those words were, they came up like bubbles from the deep that broke as they hit the surface leaving only the slight twitching around the lips as evidence that anything beneath existed. Joey's mother had discussed both of the Faragos with Boggy. Her assessment of Mrs. Faragos stuck in Boggy's mind. Jennifer had said that she was like a three-hundred-year-old red wood. You count the rings to determine the age of the tree, and each ring etches the condition of nature, the full history of the life of the tree. Anyone with some training could read the tree's life and know the periods of plenty and the periods of want. In Mrs. Faragos's case, Jennifer said she saw only one big, fat engorged ring in all of her years and that ring was encircled by many small, diminished weak lines so faint that to read them all required a special microscope of imagination and sympathy. The rain that had fallen in her life that one year had been enough to nurture her.

"I was telling Joey's friend about Errol."

Mrs. Faragos's eyes flickered and a slit opened as she looked up with a faint smile on her lips. A dry, wispy voice, slow and patient, came from her throat. "I thought I heard you say something about Cuba."

Mr. Faragos nodded; leaning forward he took his wife's hand in his own rat-claw hands. "Yes, I was about to tell him about Cuba and Errol."

She smiled. "That's a nice story. I like the way you tell it."

The Last of the Romantics
12 October 1959:
Vancouver, Canada

"I am one of the last of the romantics. Fidel Castro is another. There could be another one out there, Lester. But I am damned if I know that person, and I've kicked around a lot of places and I am sure I would have met him," said Errol Flynn. Lester Faragos pulled a new fifth of vodka from the bag and set it down on the table next to the actor. It was ten in the morning and the bottle of vodka from the day before was empty. Flynn opened the new bottle, his hand shaking as he poured three fingers into the glass and drank it down, then refilled the glass. A long, mournful sigh came from his lips like a balloon deflating. He tapped the vodka bottle with his thumbnail, reached over and gave Mr. Faragos a playful punch on the shoulder.

"Do you understand what I mean by being the last of the romantics?"

Mr. Faragos was a simple man of few needs and even less education. He admitted he only had a vague idea of what it meant to be a romantic.

"The world winds down if there are no romantics. If we are down to the last of the romantics, then the world stops, like a grandfather clock that hasn't been wound."

He drank from the glass again and belched. The long rupture of alcohol in Errol Flynn's guts lasted a couple of seconds. Then he continued, "They thought that I was pro-Castro and Hollywood needed to be sent a clear message: You can run but you can't hide. I borrowed money from the mob to make a film. They thought it was going to be an action adventure film like I am known for. It was action already, with lots of real-life adventure thrown in. What they hadn't liked was that Fidel was my buddy and I stuck up for him, and showed what he and his men were doing by getting rid of Batista. Well, the mob were good pals with Batista and his crowd. Batista's wife sent around her own mob of gangsters to the casinos every night to pick up a commission in cash. Everyone was doing swell in those circles. I made certain we had shots inside the casino just like Frank asked for. But that wasn't good enough. They thought they were buying a pro-Batista film. I have to admit, that was why it started out. Then I started to dig into what was really happening.

"The problem was everyone but Batista's cronies lived dirt poor, and if they opened their lips the secret police came round at three in the morning and dragged them away. And after they were tortured, the police shot them. The torture sessions were to get information about others who shared the crony's opinion that Batista's crowd wasn't a swell group looking after the greater interest of the country. There was this unwritten rule that you weren't supposed to talk about the off-the-book activities of the secret police.

"Once Castro marched into Havana, it didn't take long for the boys in the casinos to find out that Castro intended to close them down. They squealed like stuck pigs. They got onto their contacts in the government and complained. Can you imagine that? The mob and the government saw eye-to-eye on Castro. It didn't take long before the FBI and CIA started making noises that Castro was a communist. It didn't matter to them what Batista had done. That was just the cost of doing business. He wanted social justice. Batista's people had killed thousands but no one was interested in those murders. And they didn't much like that Castro had his own views about what business he wanted to do in Cuba, and the Americans didn't much like his economics.

"Frank got steamed when he found out I used his money to shoot a second film. When he heard about *Cuban Rebel Girls* the word came down that for my own good I'd better get out of Cuba. I wasn't going to cheat him. You don't cheat the mob. I know that. I let word get back to Frank that he was in for the same cut on *Cuban Rebel Girls*. But he'd gone quiet. Didn't want to talk to me. I don't like it when people like Frank refuse to talk to me."

Errol Flynn pushed himself up from his chair and held on to the railing of the balcony. He inhaled the air, held it, exhaled and repeated the exercise three more times, before turning with his back to the sea and looking directly at Lester Faragos.

"Lester, what I am about to tell you must be kept a secret. Can you keep a secret, Lester?"

"I guess I can."

"Secret-keeping isn't about guessing. It's about a man making a commitment and then keeping it no matter what. Are you up to keeping a secret?"

Mr. Faragos scratched his head and nodded. "I'll keep your secret."

The actor relaxed as if a weight had come off his soul. "The mob isn't happy with my film about Cuba. Like I told you, I used their money for a second film, *Cuban Rebel Girls*. Helluva title, don't you think? We used some of the same footage from the documentary. That made Frank and his boys mad as hell. And J. Edgar Hoover isn't putting me up for any Freedom medals either. I still have my friends in Cuba and they got a message to me. It's not the kind of message any bloke likes to receive. In Australia we normally get a trial before a death sentence is handed down. I gather the same thing happens in Canada. You can never be certain whether such information is reliable. I've had enemies all of my life and I've out-fought and out-lasted them all. This time I'd be a fool not to take the threat seriously. I'd been warned in Cuba. That's why I left in a hurry. The mob ordered a propaganda film and I disappointed them. I've had my share of critics. Every actor does. But this time I've got on the wrong side of the wrong people. But I am working something out. There are some like-minded people in Hollywood who want the rights to my film. They're coming up to Vancouver for me to sign the papers. Once they distribute it around the country, I should be okay."

"What if the deal doesn't work out?" asked Lester; as someone who'd never had a deal work out in his life, it was a natural question.

"In that case, I am in a real jam."

"With the Mafia?"

He looked at the sunlight on the bay and smiled as if something in the sea amused him.

"Can't you go to the police?" asked Mr. Faragos.

Errol Flynn took another long pull of vodka directly from the bottle. He winked as he exhaled. "And tell them what? I think the mob's sore at me?" he asked. "I had a fortune teller in Cuba tell me that 1959 was a dark year for people in show business."

Errol Flynn walked back into the bedroom, opened the wardrobe and removed a cylinder, took off the lid, and pulled out a movie poster for *Edge of Darkness*. He unrolled the poster and called Mr. Faragos in from the balcony. "Come and have a look at this."

Mr. Faragos appeared beside the actor and looked down at the poster. "I've signed it for Fidel. You've got me thinking. You know, nothing is ever certain in show business, and this deal might fall through. So if something should happen to me, I want you to keep this poster a secret. Then I want you to see that it's delivered personally to Fidel. I promised him the poster and a man likes to keep his promises. Can you promise me this, Lester?"

He looked at the poster, then at the actor, wondering to himself how he could ever finance his way to Cuba and deliver the poster to Fidel Castro. He and the missus had never left the West End of Vancouver. It was as if the world dropped into an awful void beyond English Bay, boiling with oil and tended by flame-spitting dragons. What was he letting himself in for? The threat of violence had been spelled out in perfect images but the hair on the back of Lester Faragos's neck stood on end as the actor talked about the mob and the FBI. Errol Flynn, though half drunk, had never appeared so agitated and determined. His happy-go-lucky manner had vanished and in its place was an anguished desperation that took Mr. Faragos back on his heels.

"I promise, Mr. Flynn," he finally said.

This perked up Errol Flynn. He appeared to be greatly relieved. He rolled the poster up and slipped it back into the protective cardboard cylinder, using the heel of his hand to pop the lid tightly into place. "Come over here, I want to show you where I hide them. There will be other items in this hiding place. Including an amount of cash that is sufficient for you to go to Cuba and return. In the closet are a lot more posters. I want you and your wife to have them if something should happen to me."

They walked out onto the balcony and Errol Flynn knelt down near the railing and pushed his hand hard on the floor. He climbed onto a table facing the wall. Below where the fire escape came down, a section of the wall protruded by half a foot. The false section of wall had been invisible to the eye. No one would ever have expected to find such a hiding spot. Flynn put the cylinder inside the drawer that he pulled from the wall and then closed it. Mr. Faragos didn't breathe for a moment. He had no idea that the Hong Kong Chinese owner had built secret compartments in the building. The presence of this space made his mind reel. How many other such places might there be in the building? Perhaps there was such a compartment inside his apartment.

"Clever, isn't it?" said Errol Flynn. "I discovered it quite by chance."

What he left out were the details of the discovery that only Mrs. Faragos knew. Flynn had discovered it by accident one evening when he was making love to Mrs. Faragos on the floor of the balcony. His knee had moved to the edge of the railing and had tripped a switch. He'd looked up and seen that a section of the wall had moved. He'd pulled himself out of Mrs. Faragos. "What's the matter, Errol? You never done that before."

"Nothing, sweetheart, just a little preoccupied. Why don't you go inside and get dressed and go out into the sitting room? Better yet, go down stairs and have your husband buy another fifth of vodka. My daily supplies are running short." He playfully spanked her bare ass. She rose to her feet looking confused and a little angry. "I don't think you should be treating me like this, Errol."

"Let me have a few hours to think through some things. Then we can pick up where we left off."

She picked up a novel from a bedside stand; her hands were trembling. "I could read to you."

"I am not in the mood for a reading," he said.

He waited until she had dressed and stormed out of the room. He had pulled a bath towel around his waist, climbed onto the table and examined the secret drawer. Inside was a loaded pistol, a Canadian passport that he opened to find an unsmiling, white shirt and tie Chinese male in the photograph. There was a small box and it contained two bars of gold. No cash, only gold. *The Chinese knew the value of exchange when it came to making a clean escape*, he thought.

The night of his death, Errol Flynn had been drinking steadily all night. Mr. Faragos had been in and out of the penthouse, delivering bottles. The last time he came back to the building there had been two strangers in the lobby. Men in suits were the ones Errol Flynn had expected from Hollywood. One carried a briefcase. They looked like bankers or accountants or ordinary professional types. They wore hats like Bogart with the brims pulled down over their eyes. The two brushed past him. One stopped and slammed Mr. Faragos against the wall.

"Who are you looking at?"

"No one," he said, so scared he couldn't swallow.

"Let's get out of here," said the other man.

The man holding Mr. Faragos let go and the two walked out the door. Half an hour later, the ambulance arrived. The lobby was filled with medics and police and Errol's girlfriend, her face wet with tears, walked behind the gurney with Errol Flynn stretched out on top.

"Heart attack," said one of the medics when Mrs. Faragos ran up to the actor.

That was the official story. The verdict the authorities had written on the death certificate. Mr. Faragos knew better. They had slipped something in his drink. The government had all kinds of secret drugs that made it look like someone had had a heart attack. Certain kinds of drugs left no trace. That was Lester Faragos's theory. The doctor who did the autopsy examined the body and there was nothing to suggest foul play, no concussion, bruises, broken bones. So he wrote down heart attack. That was an educated guess for a doctor in 1959. But someone who was a born athlete, who spent a life on sailing boats, just didn't keel over at fifty from a heart attack. Lester was convinced that the movie actor Errol Flynn was killed because of the propaganda film and his friendship with Castro. He was too popular for this world. Kids looked up to him, stood in lines to watch his movies. If Errol Flynn said Castro was okay, then the kids would have thought Castro was a hero, too. Who was Lester

Faragos going to tell? Who would listen to him? So he kept quiet. Four years later, after Lee Harvey Oswald whacked the president of the United States, Mr. Faragos remembered thinking about what Errol Flynn had said regarding the connection between the mob, the FBI, the CIA, and Cuba, and there were hints of the relationship that bubbled to the surface but never came to anything.

Year after year, Mr. Faragos thought of his promise to deliver the movie poster to Fidel Castro, and then he thought about how he could do this. He was a little person. No one was going to drive him from the airport in Havana to Fidel Castro's office so he could hand over the poster. So he left it where Errol Flynn had hidden it, safe and secure, and waited for some sign that he could find a way to honor his promise to the actor. It became easier to use the money in the hiding place for their day-to-day expenses and Mr. Faragos's weekly football bets. There had been a lot of money in the safe. Two weeks before Boggy showed up at Faragos's apartment, Mr. Bill Hunt arrived at his apartment door and said that he'd had a meeting with Fidel Castro, and Castro told him about how an actor named Errol Flynn had made the only decent documentary about the revolution, and how he often thought about this man. Castro said that Errol Flynn had once promised him a movie poster of a film that Fidel was particularly fond of but somehow the actor, being a Hollywood type, had never followed through.

Boggy Replays the Tape Recording
28 December 2004:
Bangkok, Thailand

Joey Balfour knew the Faragos as well as he knew his own family. From the description of the couple, he was convinced that Boggy had indeed met them, and no doubt had been witness to one of their long conversations down Errol Flynn's memory road. They were lonely people desperate for someone to listen to their stories. He was less certain whether a number of details in the story were partly invented by Boggy.

"I've listened to your story," says Joey.

"You believe me, don't you, Joey?"

Joey's smile conveyed neither belief nor disbelief. He had a poker player's smile. "Let's say, you tell a good story about the Faragos, but I want to hear that tape again."

Boggy reaches into his backpack and Joey stiffens as he leans forward with the gun. "Careful, Boggy."

"I'll play it as many times as you want. It's my proof."

"What else do you have in there?"

"It's just a tape recorder."

Joey lowers the gun, believing that Howard Boggy has been street-smart enough not to pull something dangerous. Boggy knows how to hedge his big credibility gap that he knew would arise once he played the tape and told Faragos's story. Young and ambitious, Boggy proves another attribute that Joey admits he had glimpses of before: a cautious, careful, calculated approach to a possible moneymaking situation. He must really have something the government wants. Joey orders his driver to pull over and stop the car. He nods for Boggy to continue removing the tape recorder, which was smaller than a cell phone, from his backpack. It was an instrument used by professionals for secret taping. Howard Boggy coming to Bangkok suddenly makes sense to Joey Balfour. He wants the signed poster and figures if he can get it before Joey Balfour, then he has something valuable to bargain with. It is like the second half of a pirate's map marking hidden treasure. He claims to have a J. Edgar Hoover letter strongly condemning Errol Flynn as degenerate stock from a degenerate bunch of rebels from Pitcairn Island, and he's put it together with Errol Flynn's film in Cuba and the poster signed for Castro—it is the trail of evidence that lends support to the murder of the actor. Add the tape of Faragos's recollection of the day of Errol Flynn's death, and there is a case to answer.

Deeds in the Name of the Lord

Bill Hunt paces across his hotel room, stops at the mini-bar and makes himself another drink. He looks at his watch, picks up the remote, points it at the television and a BBC reporter appears inside a makeshift morgue. Hundreds of people are looking for relatives, friends, children. Pictures are posted on a bulletin board. Survivors with a haunted, passive expression sit on the floor, trying to make some meaning out of why they are alive and their friends are dead. A ten-year-old blond boy with piercing blue eyes looks for his parents whom he last saw in Khao Lak. There is no word whether they have survived. The count is now over forty thousand dead. The number impresses the Rev. Joshua Cecil, who, with one finger on the page of the Bible, looks up at the television.

"We will defeat the forces of evil," he says. "We act out of righteousness. Our deeds are in the name of our Lord, and He anoints us with His wisdom and power and grace."

At first Bill Hunt doesn't respond as he continues to listen to the report. He's shaking his head as the camera pans over the site of the explosion. "Balfour said he would call an hour ago."

Whatever destruction is playing itself out along the coast from Indonesia to Thailand to India doesn't distract Bill Hunt from his mission; that is why he has the job, and the confidence and support of his employer. Joshua Cecil has been reading passages from the Bible for the last hour and a half. Images of natural disaster in Asia are replaced with tongues of fire rising from the shattered remains of a truck on a street in outside the green zone in Baghdad. The droning of his voice has Bill Hunt seeking refuge in the latest terrorist act in Iraq as a reprieve. Passing time is difficult when the only distractions are watching the wreckage of a car bomb on television and listening to Joshua Cecil who only stops long enough to lick his fingers before turning the page.

"It would be so much easier to hire someone to hit Balfour."

Joshua Cecil slowly closes the Bible. "Mr. Hunt, what is easy is not always just. And what we require is not Mr. Balfour's death which might well make him a martyr. That serves the devil's own purposes. Our goal is not to make Joey Balfour a larger-than-life hero but to discredit him together with his associate Howard Boggy. The pair will be transformed, as others before them, into another pair of career criminals who cheat, consort with whores, and murder. Who will believe them once they are exposed? Who will follow them? When a house of cards falls, no one can ever believe it was ever a house."

Hunt is being paid well and he has no cause to pass judgment on his employer's motives. If the business plan requires Joey and Howard to become pin-ups for the evilness of the world, it is fine by him. What isn't right, though, is that nowhere is there any real interest in having Jim Pauley repay his debt. Nothing can make Bill Hunt forget that Jim Pauley's theft caused the failure of his marriage and the loss of his job. His world collapsed. The bottom line is unfinished business, and no amount of Bible reading can ever convince Bill Hunt to turn the other cheek.

"Are you getting cold feet, Mr. Hunt?"

Hunt glances up from his drink, glaring at the preacher. "I always finish the business I am assigned to do, Rev. Cecil."

"Even if you don't fully agree with all of the details of the assignment?"

Bill Hunt is silent for a moment before he nods. "I have no reason to disagree. It doesn't concern me whether Joey Balfour is dead or living in disgrace. Either way, it closes the books. I don't care much about Boggy other than he's in the same game as Balfour and what comes to him is what he earns by dealing with the likes of Joey."

Joshua Cecil weighs each of Hunt's words, nodding as he listens, like a teacher looking for some mistake or fault in the student's lesson. "Then everyone will be happy."

The hotel phone rings. Hunt lets it ring two more times before picking it up. "You have Jim Pauley?" Bill Hunt's eyes are on the preacher. "That's good. I'll bring the poster. When and where can we meet?" He scribbles notes on a piece of paper. "No, I don't know where it is but I can find it."

"I'll send around a car for you," says Joey. Beside him is Marty and Jim Pauley. Howard Boggy leans over the front seat of the car. "What are you planning to do with Pauley once you've got him?"

"What's it to you?"

"I am curious. I might want to lay down a bet."

"That's between him and me."

"You two gonna mud wrestle? Winner takes all?"

"This ain't remotely funny, Joey."

"Bill, I am thinking you two can find a way to work something out."

"Keep out of it. If you want the poster, back off and put him on the phone. I want to hear his voice."

A thin film of sweat appears on Jim Pauley's upper lip. Like any man who has recently undergone major heart surgery, Pauley looks beat up, pale, thin, with deliberate, almost slow-motion actions as if everything still hurts. The stress of sitting wedged between Joey Balfour, who holds a gun, and Marty, who looks large enough to have played professional baseball, makes the blood drain from his face and his skin feel clammy.

"This is Jim," he says, his voice raspy and timid. He looks grotesque, like someone humiliated and tortured, forced to talk but has nothing to say.

"Pauley, is that you?"

"It's been a long time." He pauses, and wets his lips. "I am real sorry, Bill."

"He don't look so good," says Marty, as Pauley slumps against his shoulder.

Joey takes the phone from Pauley's hand and he offers no resistance. "You've talked to him. Bring the poster."

Boggy stretches forward from the front seat and pushes open one of Pauley's eyelids; the pupil is a pinhole. "He's having a heart attack. We need to get him to the hospital. Like now."

Joey takes a closer look at Pauley who slumps forward. No question about it, Pauley isn't faking it. He's in the midst of a major episode and this is a trailer for what looks like a build-up to dying in the back of Joey Balfour's car and he's still holding the gun on a man having a heart attack. That is manslaughter in most civilized jurisdictions, and a potentially expensive headache in Thailand. He orders his driver to go to a hospital on Soi 1, off Sukhumvit Road.

Boggy corrects him with the address of Jim Pauley's hospital.

"How do you know that hospital?" asks Joey.

"That's where I first met him."

His estimation of Boggy's knowledge, skill and talent is accelerating at the speed of light. Joey knows from experience that the biggest mistakes are made from underestimating people and information; bad information, and wrong bets are the formula to ruin.

Marty is loosening Pauley's shirt.

"Give him the kiss of life," says Boggy.

Marty makes a face and looks at Joey. "You heard the kid, give him the kiss of life."

Joey dials Bill Hunt's hotel. Joshua Cecil picks up the phone and gives his name. Joey is taken back at first, "Glad I got you on the phone, reverend. I've been meaning to ask you a couple of questions."

Joshua Cecil slowly sits down and ponders whether to hang up. "What kind of questions?"

"I collect Errol Flynn posters. And I keep track of the prices. It's a hobby. Harmless, fun, absorbing," says Joey. "A little like religion."

This is a random walk, thinks Joey. For a moment, the phone goes silent. Joshua Cecil is a heart beat away from hanging up.

"I am afraid I really can't help you," says Joshua Cecil.

"That's too bad. I had some conflicting reports on an Errol Flynn poster sold in Vancouver. Someone said they received five grand. And Bill Hunt tells me he paid twenty something grand. Now I find that just very interesting, don't you? In fact you might call it a miracle. Like Jesus that time when he fed the multitudes with a few fish and a couple loafs of bread. The numbers don't add up, so what does a man do? It comes down to a matter of faith. You have to convince yourself that these little contradictions don't matter."

After the conversation ends, Joshua Cecil goes out of the room and finds Bill Hunt waiting for the lift. "That was Joey on the phone. There's been a change of plan."

Vengeance Is Mine Sayeth the Lord

The nurses patrol the entrance to the ICU. No one gets inside the unit without first changing out of their street shoes and into a light green, thin surgeon's gown, slippers, and paper cap. They do this in a small room just outside the unit. The changing room has lockers and a shoe rack. They undress together. Joey, Marty, and Boggy look like astronauts in the puffy gowns and surgical masks as they stand around the bed looking at Pauley. Jim Pauley lies motionless on the bed. He's curled up, facing the curtain on the left side of the room. A divider curtain gives privacy between his bed and the one next to him. A teenage accident victim with massive head injuries lies in the bed on the other side of the curtain.

Boggy sneaks a look at the young man, shaking his head, "The kid next door isn't gonna make it," he says.

The ICU room smells of alcohol, cleaning and body fluids. Glittering chrome-plated machines, their digital numbers bouncing in rows along a series of small panels announce the current state of each patient's chi. The machines measuring the energy force are positioned alongside Pauley's bed. An IV feed coils above the bed and the plastic tube disappears into a vein in his left arm. Another transparent tube is attached to his nose. Pauley is breathing, eyes closed, tucked under a sheet in a bed with heavy metal railing. Pauley's doctor wears a white coat and a surgical mask. He carries a clipboard and makes notes from the various dials on the machines that surround Pauley. The doctor scratches his chin as he stares at the digital number display pulsing on the machine closest to Pauley's bed. He motions for Boggy to follow him. Joey and Marty take this as a general instruction to follow the doctor.

They pass through the airlock area that separates the ICU from the changing room. The doctor removes his mask.

"Gunnar, you were right to bring him here."

A wave of shock rolls through Joey Balfour's consciousness. He does a double take, blinks, and looks again. Joey knows this man. He's seen him almost every week for a couple of years. "Khun Daeng?"

"Khun Joey. I didn't know you knew Gunnar and Jim?"

Joey thinks, *How is it that Howard Boggy, who knows no one in Bangkok, who has only been in town for a matter of hours, walks out the door of the condo, wanders down the street around the building and happens to befriend the local cat man of the neighborhood?* It has never occurred to Joey that Daeng has a job outside of feeding stray cats. In his mind, Daeng is a street person. He has no other life apart from feeding stray cats. Joey's speechless; his mouth hangs ajar as he tries to find words to reply to the doctor.

The fact that Joey and the doctor recognize each other unnerves Boggy. His natural paranoia nurtured by a life defined by online game-playing, makes Boggy pause. *Is it possible those two are planning something unexpected and unpleasant?*

"I didn't know that you knew my house guest," Joey says.

"I had no idea Gunnar was your guest."

"*Was* is the right word," says Boggy. This leaves a hint of friction in the air.

"I had no idea that you were a doctor. You never told me."

"Somehow we never talked about our occupations," says Dr. Daeng. "It never seemed important."

Joey neglects to divulge the potentially embarrassing information that for more than two years he's been handing over to Daeng three thousand baht as a monthly stipend to pay for the food and medicine for support of the neighborhood cats. He assumes each time that he meets Daeng that he is an unemployed person, a Bangkok equivalent of Mr. Faragos, who wanders around undertaking assignments that no one else willingly volunteers to perform but upon which a community of people depends. The apartment house in Vancouver springs to mind.

"Is Jim going to die?" asks Boggy.

The doctor sighs. "I can't say. He may pull through. Then again, he may not. He seemed so strong at his last check-up." Boggy sees no point in sharing the information with Joey and Marty that he was present at Pauley's last check-up. It is one of those private moments between Daeng and Boggy.

"How bad was this heart attack?" asks Marty.

The doctor nods. "If you hadn't brought him here, he'd be dead now."

A soft humming noise from one of the machines fills the void of silence.

"Stress," says Boggy. "That's what caused it."

"That is always a possibility. Or it might be that it is his time," says the doctor.

"I didn't think doctors were supposed to say things like that," says Joey.

"There are a lot of things doctors aren't supposed to say. Mostly we call those things the truth. But I find that most farangs like to hear the truth. There is comfort in knowing what can happen next," says Dr. Daeng. He washes his hands in a basin and wipes them on a towel. "I'll return in the morning." Dr. Daeng makes an indirect political point. Official news that a tsunami was likely on the way hadn't been released, and, some were saying, it had been suppressed out of fear of broadcasting bad news that would hurt the tourist industry. Withholding the truth had resulted in the death of the very people whose money was valued so dearly. And the toll continued to climb.

Boggy and Joey are thinking the same thought: *After he feeds the neighborhood cats, he will look in on Jim Pauley, check the machines, the tubes, the hoses, the temperature, and make more notes.*

Walking down the hallway from the ICU, Dr. Daeng passes a farang who appears lost.

"Is this the ICU?" asks Bill Hunt.

The doctor nods, wondering how many more friends Jim Pauley has. He never seemed like a man who would attract a lot of people to his bedside. Pauley seemed like a loner. He smiles to himself. He's happy to be wrong about his patient. His next thought is: *Khun Jim's friends must have a good heart to see their friend in such circumstances.* He directs Bill Hunt to the ICU. He watches him disappear down the corridor, thinking of the surprise on Joey's face when he had discovered that he was a doctor. It was one of those rare moments that he will always treasure. He fully expects he's seen the last of the monthly stipends to feed the stray cats. That is the way of karma. He will make do. He also asks himself, as he enters the parking lot, how it is that farangs have good hearts but are poor judges of the hearts of others.

The next person Hunt meets is Marty Gage who stands in the middle of the corridor, arms at his side, as if looking down home plate waiting for the catcher to signal him the pitch that he wants to throw. They recognize each other behind the funny green gear, slippers, and masks.

Hunt stops a foot in front of Marty who is not giving way. "Where's Pauley?"

"You got the movie poster?"

Bill Hunt taps the cardboard cylinder, held under his left arm.

"Mind if I have a look?"

This is not the place to cause a disturbance, Bill Hunt thinks. "You sure Pauley's here?"

"Positive."

Bill Hunt removes the movie poster and holds it out while Marty takes a look. "Where's Joey?"

"He's inside the ICU with Pauley and the others. He's expecting you."

Marty moves to the side and lets Bill Hunt pass. Hunt is level with the ICU entrance when he turns and looks back at Marty. "Setting up the meeting in a hospital is a good one. You just never know who you end up seeing in hospitals."

"Like you never can guess who you end up working for," says Marty. "What goes around comes around."

Bill Hunt frowns and twists the cardboard cylinder under his arm. "What are you talking about?"

"You remember the name Linda Harris? She's an old friend of yours."

He's caught Hunt flat footed, off guard, and Bill Hunt walks back towards him. "What are you talking about?" asks Hunt. He blazes with a high-octane mixture of anger and surprise.

"I did some digging and I found out that you are working for an outfit called Overseas Faith Protection Associates. That company is wholly owned by another company called Interfaith Evangelical Coalition, or IEC, as they call themselves. Take a wild guess as to who is on the board? Someone you'll remember from the old days in Las Vegas. An ex-hooker named Linda Harris. You spent some time with her the night Pauley took a hike with the casino's cash and chips."

Bill Hunt had thought of Marty Gage as another of Joey Balfour's flunkies. "You get this from Joey?"

"Joey got this from me," says Marty.

A look of disbelief clouds Bill Hunt's face. Hunt is someone who is short on knowledge and shallow on wisdom which means his perception of things is usually scraping the bottom of the barrel. "Sure thing, Marty."

Marty knows this look—he's seen it on the face of many others who think that Joey Balfour walks on water. He accepts this assumption as a source of strength. He has tracked down the security outfit and the parent company IEC from public corporate records and obscure faith-based websites on the Internet. When he found out that Linda is an executive at IEC, he knew that his prayer had been answered. There is some reason in the universe.

By the time Bill Hunt appears in the ICU, he has had enough to time to think about what he should do now that Joey Balfour knows the corporate and personal history of his employer. He decides it makes no difference and walks out into the common area. At the far end he spots Joey Balfour, even though his face and head are covered. He would recognize Joey if he were hiding under a blanket from the way Joey's shoulder slopes to one side, the slight turn of his head.

"You set this all up for me?" asks Bill Hunt.

"It's not a Halloween party, Bill."

"Where is Pauley?"

Joey moves away from the end of the bed. "That's him."

From the shell of the man in the bed it could be anyone. "That doesn't look like Pauley. I was just talking to him. What's he doing hooked up to machines?"

"He's had triple by-pass surgery and a heart attack. What do you expect him to look like?"

Bill Hunt leans over the bed and tries to match the face on the person whose head is turned to one side on the pillow with the man who worked the sports betting bank at the casino a dozen years before. Time has not been kind to Jim Pauley.

Joey looks at the cardboard cylinder under Bill Hunt's arm. "You got the poster for me?"

Bill Hunt continues to stare at the man in the bed. "It's not Pauley."

Joey walks over to the side of the bed, slowly lifts Pauley's right arm, and rolls up the hospital gown. "You see that tattoo?"

On his upper arm is a heart-shaped tattoo with the word "Linda."

"You know what Linda that's referring to?" asks Joey Balfour.

"The deal was Pauley. Not a vegetable called Pauley," says Bill Hunt.

Joey shakes his head. "You got that wrong, Bill. Our deal was I deliver Pauley and you deliver the poster. There was nothing said by anybody about what shape Pauley had to be in. It makes it easier, doesn't it, Bill? You can take your time, sit down on the edge of the bed, and do what you were going to do anyway. No fuss or struggle. Or you can wait and see if Mother Nature makes the hit for you. What I see is that I've delivered you a better hand than the one you expected. You're not worse off. You're better off. So what's your beef?"

Boggy sits hunched over in his chair beside Pauley's bed. He's glaring at Bill Hunt, his fists balled up, the fingers white, waiting for Hunt to make a move for the bed. But Bill Hunt's attention remains on the tattoo. He ignores Boggy entirely. Joey decides the point's been made and carefully lowers Pauley's arm and pushes it under the sheet.

"She didn't tell you about the tattoo, did she, Bill? What were the chances of you finding it? Four to one? Ten to one? It was a risk unless of course she knew it didn't matter anyway because you weren't coming back from this assignment."

Now it is Bill Hunt's turn to look pale and like he's about to do a belly flop onto the floor. He grips the end of the bed. The cardboard cylinder drops and bounces on the floor. Marty Gage, who has crept up behind Hunt, leans down, picks it up, and lays it on one of the machines that are keeping Jim Pauley alive.

"Your problem, Bill, is that you take too much on faith, on what things look like on the surface. Marty finds out among other things that your employer was a major contributor to the last presidential campaign through one of those Christian network pacts. I bet they haven't invited you to any of their prayer meetings. The parent company is big on global prayer meetings. We ought to look at the situation from Linda's point of view. In other words, why fund the purchase of the poster, your five-star trip to Thailand, not to mention your fee? Is this Linda Harris's way of providing you with a chance for personal atonement? Linda is a born-again type, right? Maybe she only wants to save your soul. Her company is big on the salvation of souls. Maybe she plans on a joint rapture of just the two of you. But I doubt that; she invested too much money to save one lost soul. Could it be that Linda still holds a grudge? When Pauley walked out with the cash you thought nothing about dragging her name through the mud with the casino personnel and the Las Vegas police. Of course, he left Linda high and dry as well."

"Linda was working with Pauley that night?"

"Revenge or salvation? What do you think motivates most women?"

"That was years ago," says Bill Hunt. "It's not Pauley so much as you, Joey Balfour."

"Marty, tell Mr. Hunt what we know about IEC funds."

Marty removes a printout from a folder and flips through a couple of pages. "IEC funneled funds through the PACs that paid for ads against gay marriage, abortion, gambling, and promiscuity. One of their directors is ex-White House, another is ex-Defense Department. Joey Balfour blinks across the IEC radar screen about a month after the DVDs of the old TV shows are selling. Chief Black Crow's casinos are filling up with customers. Fifty thousand DVDs were sold in the first three months. But Joey sees none of the money as he has no residual rights. From their point of view the world occupied by Joey Balfour and Errol Flynn is a world of whores and pimps. They are Satan's spawn. Letting Joey become a folk hero is something they will use all of their resources to prevent happening."

"It just so happens that doing God's work is also settling an outstanding debt Linda Harris has been working to clear for many years. Both God and women move in mysterious ways," says Joey.

"But to kill Joey Balfour would only make him a greater hero, larger than life," says Boggy, who gets up from the chair. "The best way to remove Joey as an icon is to discredit him. Turn Joey Balfour into a thug with blood on his hands."

Could this kid have wiretapped his conversation with Rev. Joshua Cecil? thinks Bill Hunt. *Or could he be just plain lucky?*

"Linking Bill Hunt to the murder would tie up the loose ends. Settle the outstanding debts," says Joey.

Bill Hunt is starting to sweat under his mask. "You're reaching for a door that ain't there, Joey."

"Joey's a symbol of something Linda's people hate and fear," says Marty. "Not all gamblers fail. Not everyone goes broke. A middle-aged man like Joey keeps attracting and maintaining a stable of young women. And there's Linda Harris, middle-aged, someone no one would think about fucking, nursing a twelve-year-old wound inflicted by Pauley, Hunt, and Balfour. No wonder the woman went deep into religion. She's a perfect convert. *Vengeance is mine sayeth the Lord.* Looking at the background of IEC, I'd say there is a good chance they have more than unofficial government help. You know this business about renditions?"

"You're talking tunes for fuck's sake," says Bill.

"No, I am talking about grabbing people and letting some Third World place give them a work over. Bamboo under the fingernails until they sing like a bird. That's why it is called a rendition. You got to get with it, Bill. You see, IEC and these guys who snatch people in the middle of the night make a good fit: The puritans inside the government and their counterparts who crossed over to IEC. Those boys see things in the same way. It's all in the Bible. Renditions are ours, sayeth the Lord. The IEC has good sources of information. Weren't you the guy who once said, 'One hand washes another?' So you have people helping each other out. Are they planning an off-the-books operation? You got to see where people have a mutual interest. Whoever is behind the operation in the government retains deniability. Call it outsourcing. A private firm is assigned the dirty work. Think of what's been going down in Iraq, Iran, Cuba, Afghanistan, and now Thailand. You are on the payroll of seriously committed people, Bill."

Joey unrolls the movie poster and examines the handwriting. He's seen enough of Errol Flynn's handwriting to believe that this is indeed a signed original.

Joey looks up from the movie poster as Marty finishes. "Marty's left out someone." He nods towards Boggy at Pauley's bedside. "That kid over there. His name is Boggy. He's another troublemaker they want out of the way. You knew that? Or have your Christian brothers and sisters kept a few secrets from you?"

Boggy bends his head forward like he's looking around a corner. The mere mention of his name makes him force a grin to mask the grim, hollowed-out boy-man, who is thinking about that maggot-filled macaroni cheese TV dinner in Faragos's apartment. Wherever he travels, ever since he left Maine, his journey has been from one bedside to the next, one face after another locked into a strange expression of near death. Pauley's hospital room makes his head spin, and his arm throb; he knows the people around him have gathered solely for the purpose of making him sick.

"That's Boggy, the kid with the red beard," says Joey. "He's an Errol Flynn movie poster expert. *The* expert, so he likes to remind me. But he doesn't stick to selling posters. Boggy's a curious man. That means he's been busy getting his nose into other people's business."

Boggy leans into a bedpan and vomits.

"That's it, kid. Let it all out."

Joey turns back to Bill Hunt, his face filled with disgust. "He's come up with a connection exposing one of those old deals between the mob and the FBI. Ain't that right, Boggy?"

Boggy retches again and the room is still. An alarm is set off and a nurse rushes in and checks Pauley. They wait until she's through checking the dials like an air traffic controller looking for a near miss. The digital numbers flash a deep crimson red. Pauley's heart is pumping through some tough turbulence. The nurse eyes each of them one at a time as she reaches down and picks up the bedpan. No one points the finger at Boggy. The only one with a mask hanging around his neck is Boggy. "Put on that mask," she barks at him, then she turns and walks away.

Boggy slips on the mask; the change in air circulation causes him to gag. He can only hold it long enough for the nurse to leave the area.

"Boggy believes that Errol Flynn was murdered in Vancouver," says Joey. "Before the same people in government found God, they used the mob to outsource some of their business. Faragos saw two men leaving the apartment house the day of the murder. He thought that the guys were from Hollywood coming to buy the rights to *Cuban Story* and *Cuban Rebel Girls*. That's what the Faragos said. I've never known the Faragos to lie outright. Boggy tells me that he trolled the Internet looking for more evidence, when he had some major trouble in Maine. Tell Bill that's right."

Boggy hangs over a fresh bedpan, but nothing comes out. He has the dry heaves.

Joey shakes his head. "Boggy survives with a burnt arm and a weak stomach. He couldn't help adding more insult to the injury by playing his harp over the injustice suffered by the men arrested on Pitcairn Island. They are charged with statutory rape. The funny thing, Bill, is that that is exactly the same charge Errol Flynn faced in LA in 1943. The statutory rape charge put Flynn on the FBI radar screen. You know the expression 'In like Flynn' came from Errol Flynn's acquittal on the statutory rape charge. Tell Bill how a light went on in your head."

"I thought it strange." Boggy's voice is a wisp of squeezed air.

"You'll be okay, kid. Now where was I? Yeah, the kid likes that sort of connection. Seeing that Flynn is related to people on Pitcairn Island he starts another campaign. None of this is sensible. It's bad for business. It's bad for his health. So Boggy finally comes to his senses and skips to Bangkok," says Marty.

"I don't care about the kid," says Bill Hunt. Here's a man who knows what he knows and doesn't want anyone confusing him.

"Hold on a minute, Bill," says Marty. "Boggy's part of the deal."

"He ain't part of my deal," says Bill Hunt.

"He's part of the deal for your people. That's what Marty's saying. They are looking at a different hand to the one they dealt you. In the time it takes to recite the Lord's Prayer, it occurs to them that they are holding four high cards—Hunt, Boggy, Pauley, and

Balfour. Three of whom just happened to be in the casino the night of Pauley's theft."

"What are you saying?" Bill Hunt pushes his mask away. The edges of the mask have left deep marks on his cheeks.

"That the people you work for are happy. They got these four men who everyone on their side agrees should no longer interfere with the good work of global prayer meetings by tempting the faithful."

"Let's get out of here," says Marty. He helps Boggy off the floor and slides the bedpan under Pauley's bed.

Playing the *Mutiny on the Bounty* Game

In the hospital canteen, they pull two tables together. Boggy and Marty sit at one and leave Joey to babysit Bill Hunt at the next. Marty breaks out a deck of cards and deals a poker hand, and includes Boggy in the game. A tray of hot, black coffee arrives. Bill Hunt pops a pill into the back of his throat, throws his head back and swallows a mouthful of coffee to wash it down. "Goddamn, that coffee is hot."

"Coffee's supposed to be hot," says Joey.

Bill Hunt shakes off the pain and stares across the table at Joey. Something in the boiler room of his memory and conscience gurgles and bubbles to the surface; something that has been bothering Hunt since they left Pauley in the ICU all hooked up to the machines. One face keeps looking up at him, his pants around his knees, her lips around his erection.

"What did Linda think I was going to tell the cops, I'd been abducted by Martians? I had no choice. I had to tell the casino and cops what really happened. It was bad enough as it was, but at least with her to back me up I was pretty much in the clear. The first thing they thought was I had something to do with it. But I didn't have anything to do with Pauley's heist."

"Women aren't always rational," says Joey, pouring milk into his coffee, then stirring it with a spoon. He looks up at Hunt. "Or haven't you figured that one out?"

"You're saying that Linda Harris is on some board and that this board is somehow connected with the people who hired me?"

"You didn't know?"

"I didn't know," says Bill Hunt.

"She set you up before, so how can you be sure she hasn't set you up again, Bill?"

"What do you mean she set me up before?" His voice drops an octave.

Joey has him, and he reels him in as the fight goes out of Hunt. "Pauley has a tattoo on his upper arm. It's one word, 'Linda', and before you say the world has a couple of million Lindas, you might want to think of the possibilities of meaning for this tattoo. For instance, it is for Linda Harris. He had a thing with her. They planned the heist together. Her job was to get you off the floor. When she turns up at their meeting point, Pauley isn't there. He's dumped her. The way I look at it, Bill, you aren't the only one nursing a grudge about Pauley."

Bill Hunt stares at his knuckles, taut and white, and his jaw is moving. Nothing like watching an ex-security chief slowly crunch through a mixed bag of new information, processing it like a cow chewing grass.

Joey leans back in his chair and enjoys the show. The man seated in front of him isn't the old Bill Hunt from Las Vegas: cocky, self-confident, a tiny piece of Nazi-like authority stitched into his mentality, strutting around the casino, glad-handing the big shots. The Bill Hunt sitting across the table is a different kind of man, one metamorphosed into a more shallow, uncertain person—edgy, paranoid, distrustful, and belligerent. The veins in Bill Hunt's neck throb to some unheard two-beat tempo. He's loosened the top two buttons on his shirt. Sweat drips down his neck, dampening his collar, and he's tapping his fingernails against the side of the coffee cup. He's not tapping Christmas carols.

"I report to Joshua Cecil. He ain't ever mentioned Linda Harris. All I've got is your word on this, Joey. And given a lot of things that have happened, I am not certain I can trust what you're saying. Or what your friend Marty Gage found snooping around on the Internet."

"Joshua Cecil and I had a little talk," says Joey.

"Like most preachers he likes to talk," Marty adds.

"He's the same guy who crashed the Annual Thanksgiving Ball." Joey remembers the preacher's hot, intense face across the table. The glint of hate in his eyes as he rose from the table and stormed off.

"You met him?" asks Bill Hunt.

"He didn't say anything about knowing you. But who you report to and who you work for can be two different people, Bill," says Joey.

This is an observation that causes Bill Hunt to push his lower lip out, almost turning it inside out, before he raises the coffee cup and takes a long swig. "Joshua told me about the Faragos and Errol Flynn in Vancouver," he says, looking happy with himself. "That's how I knew to go there."

"I've met this guy. I can't see him knowing where to find Canada on a map. What is more likely is it comes from another source. I see a Harris family Christmas in a little town in Colorado. Dan Harris, her father's brother from Vancouver, is in town. They are all settled in, nice and cozy, drinking some nice Christmas non-alcoholic punch, and Linda confides in her uncle about what happened in Las Vegas the night Pauley walked. She probably didn't tell her uncle that she was holding Bill Hunt's dick in her hand when Pauley ran. But I am certain that he guessed. I know Dan Harris. So does Marty. He's a stand-up guy who'd comfort his niece, and say, 'Hey, I know Joey Balfour. I remember when he was in high school in the West End.' He also knew a lot about the Faragos. Linda's uncle is a member of the RCMP. Those are Canadian cops, Bill. Dan once gave Marty and me the heads up on a problem we might have in running a bookie operation from a stockbroker's office. He had some information about me and the Faragos. He had that information, Bill. He knew about the Errol Flynn connection. It wouldn't take much to put that together. Not for someone bright like Dan. He gave Linda something that she could work with. She only needed the opportunity. And she found the right time and place."

"Why are you telling me?"

"Linda knew about the Errol Flynn movie posters from her uncle. You didn't just turn up at my old apartment house asking for a poster left behind by Errol Flynn. You gotta admit someone inside knew the score."

"Joshua Cecil knew." This observation makes Bill Hunt scratch his head.

"Where'd he get that information from? China?" Bill Hunt is watchful but he's calming down. The color returns slowly to his face and he asks for another coffee.

"You ever see *Mutiny on the Bounty*?" Joey asks him.

"I've heard of it," says Bill Hunt. His coffee arrives and he drinks.

This is good, thinks Joey Balfour. *He's open, he's receptive, listening.*

"Errol Flynn played Fletcher Christian. And Fletcher is the officer who leads the mutiny against the captain. Errol Flynn was a distant relative of the real Fletcher Christian. It's a fact. Fletcher Christian and his men left Captain Bligh and eighteen others in a boat. Then they sailed the *Bounty* to Pitcairn Island. They settled in with a dozen Tahitian women. They burnt the *Bounty* so no one could accidentally discover it. Or they didn't want the day to come when they started to feel homesick, looked out at the bay, saw the *Bounty* and started to think about sailing home. Once that ship was gone, they were in for the long haul. Their descendants are still on that island."

"So what's this got to do with me, Joshua Cecil, and Linda Harris?"

"I am inviting you to play the *Mutiny on the Bounty* game," says Joey.

"I never heard of any game called that."

"People play it on a regular basis but they don't always know that is what the game is called. When you are up against some authority like the captain of the *Bounty* who is crazy and out to destroy you, you have a choice: you go along with that authority and hope for the best, or you start a mutiny and take the ship. That's the choice you have. You can keep going ahead with your security firm employer and hope for the best, or you can join us."

"That makes you Errol Flynn?" asks Bill Hunt. His mocking tone draws the attention of Boggy who is about to say something until Marty grabs his wrist, and whispers, "Play your hand."

"What do you know about Joshua Cecil?" asks Joey Balfour.

"He works for the security firm that hired me."

"The card he gave me says he's a preacher. Something's not right."

"People can put anything they want on a business card," says Bill Hunt.

"You got that part right, Bill. I made a couple of calls to some old friends in Las Vegas. Joshua Cecil has been in the security business for a long time, it seems. He works as a fluffer. The guy who goes into a crime scene before the police arrive and makes certain that any evidence that could incriminate someone really important like a rock star or a politician is removed. The really experienced guys like Joshua can bat left or right handed."

A long silence follows as Hunt's face twists with horror at his sudden recognition of trouble, like a sailor in the crow's nest spotting a storm front closing in fast. "What's that mean, Joey?"

"A fluffer can either clean a crime scene or go to the next step and plant evidence in a crime scene. If it is a good job, the cops pick up the planted evidence—thinking it's good evidence—and they use it to nail the target of the plant. Everyone goes to bed happy. The rock star gets to sleep in his own bed that night, and some mug who leads a useless life takes the fall."

"So he was a fluffer? So what?"

"Think about it. Joshua was sent to do what he does best."

"And I was sent to do what I do best."

"The assignments aren't mutually exclusive, Bill. Linda Harris means to close the books—on Pauley, and you, and me. That's one, two, three outs. The inning is over when three men are out." Joey glances over at Boggy. "Taking out the kid is doing her bit for God. Giving some other people Boggy helps her pay them back. Let's call them the official connection. It all fits together. What all of this means is you've got to make a choice. You go downstairs and finish off Pauley. If that is what you're supposed to do, go ahead. Then you have your follow-up plan. You plant evidence connecting me and Boggy to Pauley's death."

Joey sips his coffee, deciphering from Bill Hunt's face how he's processing the information that is slowly sinking into his skull. At what point does a man switch from supporting Batista to Castro? When is the decision made to join the rebel cause? It's the *Mutiny on the Bounty* game, and Bill finds himself playing it even though he doesn't want to. He has no choice. It was the same for Errol Flynn when he found himself filming in Cuba, using mob money;

there was a defining moment and he had to make a choice. Go with the money or go with the heart. Errol Flynn never stopped playing Fletcher Christian and played him right to the end.

"You're thinking about Pauley," says Joey Balfour.

Bill Hunt nods.

"Think it through, Bill. Pauley's not alone in the ICU. Nurses and doctors are everywhere. How are you going to kill him and make it look like I was the killer? The hospital records show that I brought Pauley to the hospital in my car. I could have driven around in traffic until he died. So if I were to put down a bet it would be that your Joshua Cecil, once you tell him what happened, is going to go for plan B. Bill gets killed and Joey gets framed for the murder. Who you gonna trust? A fluffer who works for Linda Harris? Or Joey Balfour who has an escape plan mapped out?"

He can see from Bill Hunt's eyes that he is sitting on the edge. It is the biggest decision that Bill Hunt has ever had to make. Joey understands that this isn't the time to rush him. It is the age-old dilemma of being between a rock and a hard place, whether to play fair or to cheat. Bill Hunt doesn't want to believe that he's been set up and that he's been part of the security firm's plan from the beginning. He can see Joshua Cecil as a fluffer. But why did he sit around reading from the Bible? Clean-up guys might have religion but they don't spend all their free time with their nose in the good book. Hunt's head hurts; he's confused, angry, trapped.

It makes perfect sense. Joshua goes in after a hit and eliminates all evidence of anyone important who was at the scene of the murder. Like God, he wipes away the guilt, the sin, and the damnation. Joshua's plan is straightforward: kill Jim Pauley and do the reverse of the usual fluffer job of eliminating evidence; his job is to plant evidence that implicates Joey. He will take the fall for Pauley's death and Bill Hunt has done his job; his employers are happy and they shell out a fat performance bonus and hire him for future jobs down the road.

Marty puts down his coffee cup. He's been keeping quiet, letting Joey do all the talking. Joey's good at that; he always was, and that was what made him a TV celebrity.

"Joshua Cecil is one of those fundamentalist types. The way I see it, those people are born-again fluffers. If you can fluff dinosaurs from the geological map, cleaning up a murder scene is a piece of cake. This preacher is the guy I'd hire for the job," says Marty.

Joey grins. *That's my boy*, he thinks to himself. Marty doesn't say much but when he says something, he's obviously put some thought into it. Joey's mind moves like a film, he sees the unfolding lesson of Fletcher Christian who wins the support from the crew. He must show altruism.

"Why would Joey Balfour help me?" asks Bill Hunt. "It don't make sense."

"I can avoid a loss," says Joey Balfour. "And if you come to work for me, I also have a gain. We can help each other stay one step ahead of them. The way I see it, we both benefit. Take a hard look at the cards you're holding, Bill. Think about the future. Does your employer have any need for you after you finish this job? What is your comparative advantage as far as Joshua Cecil and his people are concerned? I'll tell you how I read it: close to zero. Do you really believe you fit into their prayer group?"

"What do you have in mind for me?"

"Security. You can handle security."

It all comes down to a matter of real intentions and who you can trust. Bill Hunt turns that over in his mind. It is never a good time to walk across the quarterdeck from the captain's side to join the mutineers. "I don't know."

"There is never a perfect time or perfect conditions, Bill," says Joey Balfour. "What do you think Linda Harris has in mind for you? She's gonna get her company to install a pew with your name on it at the front of a church?"

"She thinks you helped Pauley get away," says Bill Hunt.

"What do you think, Bill?"

Hunt looks down at his own hands, shifts in his chair. He pushes his cup of coffee away. It has gone cold. He's lost his appetite and starts to get up. Bill Hunt and Joey stare at each other waiting for the other to blink first.

"I had the chance to ask Joshua how much he paid for the poster. You know what he told me?"

From his reaction, it looks like Bill Hunt has stopped breathing. He's holding his breath. Hunt eases back into his chair, as if he knows Joey Balfour is holding him over the deep end of the pool.

"Twenty-five grand is what he told me. Boggy, can you play back the bit on the tape?"

Boggy takes his tape recorder from his backpack. He replays the part when Faragos is talking about the price of the poster. Self-interest and self-preservation were always the best ways for the Fletcher Christians of the world to convince their crew to desert their posts and join the rebels.

Bill Hunt slowly starts to breathe again as he explains what the incriminating evidence is and where it should be planted. Boggy and Marty slide their chairs in closer as his first words turn into a flood exposing Captain Bligh's plans for disposing of an entire crew.

To Every Thing There Is a Season

Joshua Cecil's voice hits a high note as he looks up from the TV. Biblical images of the massive destruction in Phuket and Phang Nga coil across the screen as the television news feeds new footage of the horror. Joshua Cecil sits on a chair in front of the television with his Bible, talking. "These are the days when dark clouds gather for the end of times. The Armageddon hovers at the horizon. Locusts swarm in Egypt, tsunamis rock Asia, mega earthquakes, floods, neighbors killing neighbors, death without end on a scale that tells us that the arrival of our Lord is upon us."

Bill Hunt watches as Joshua opens the Bible, licks his fingers, carefully pulling back one page after another. He stops, finds his place, and starts to read from Ecclesiastes, "To every thing there is a season, and a time to every purpose under the heaven: a time to be born, and a time to die; a time to plant, and a time to pluck up that which is planted; a time to kill, and a time to heal; a time to break down, and a time to build up . . ." He looks up at Bill Hunt and looks at him long, and hard with cold, searching eyes. "Do you believe?" he asks.

"I have a job to do," he says, looking at his watch.

"What you are seeing on TV is a sign from the Lord. You must do His work, and do it well. Now go," says Joshua Cecil.

As Bill Hunt leaves the room, he turns over in his mind the passage Joshua Cecil read. He remembers it from Sunday school. This passage from Ecclesiastes sticks like a broken record in his head: ". . . a time to be born, and a time to die . . ." *Joe Balfour's friend Marty Gage has pegged Joshua*, thinks Bill Hunt. A born-again fluffer is among the most powerful forces a government can employ, and their faith changes them, leaving them without doubt and sure of their mission. Once they lock on target, they never take their finger off the trigger. Joshua Cecil loves the death on the screen. He slaps his knees and shouts hallelujah; he's not faking his feelings; death and destruction affirm his faith, they fill him to the core, and the solace he finds in his faith keeps him strong. In his mind, he will win paradise.

Bill had rehearsed the back-story, repeating it to Joey over and over, before he found himself face to face with Joshua Cecil and the dress rehearsal was over and he had to give a convincing performance. Joshua was a hard man to lie to; it was as if he could see through a man and tell whether he was leveling. If it hadn't been for the tsunami pulling Joshua's attention away, he's not certain he could have pulled it off. As he spoke to Joshua about the meeting with Joey Balfour, he could hear Joey's voice in the back of his head, coaching him, line by line, word by word, image by image, the way a film director works with an actor.

"Joey delivered Pauley like he said he would. But there was something that went sideways. Pauley's in the ICU hooked up to life-support systems. He's got nurses and doctors crawling all over the place. I saw him with my own eyes. Jim Pauley looked like he was already dead but he still has some life in him. I got no choice but to wait until he gets out. If he gets out of the hospital."

Joshua Cecil accepted the reasoning that Joey's Good Samaritan act of taking Pauley to hospital made it difficult to believe that he would then turn around and kill the man he'd rescued.

"Even in the Bible the Good Samaritans aren't killers," said Bill Hunt. This had been one of the lines Joey had asked him to memorize. It worked.

The fluffer, doctor of divinity, and corporate employee, Joshua Cecil said, "That is why we always have a plan B."

What was Jesus's plan B? thought Bill Hunt.

"We never intended to harm Balfour physically. Our desire is his total disgrace. We want the world to know this man's true colors. A whoremonger, a liar, thief, and traitor. Such a man is hardly a hero. Who will watch his TV program then? The answer is, no one. He can go back into his hole in hell. Never forget, that on the road to salvation the temptations are many. And men like Joey Balfour offer a powerful image to the weak who look up to such evil men."

"What about plan B?"

The sermon style suited Joshua Cecil as a prelude. "I am getting to plan B."

He carefully explained to Bill Hunt the details: plant a quantity of nasty, disgusting kiddy porno, along with links to Errol Flynn and the Pitcairn Islands on the Feng Shui Flower Shop computer hard drive. "Place the photos in the office drawers and bookshelves and coffee tables. And place copies in the gambling rooms that Joey Balfour runs in the back of his shop. We have email print outs. You'll find pages and pages, which describe lurid sexual acts with children. You are to hide them with the photographs. They also go in the bedrooms and the other rooms, too."

Piece by piece Joshua showed Bill Hunt each document, paper, photo until he excused himself and went to the toilet and vomited. When he returned to the sitting area, Joshua Cecil was waiting, his eyes darting along the photos and his perpetual smile wholly unaltered. More TV footage of tsunami devastation played in the background. Was the preacher's smile mocking him? Had Joshua seen through his deceit and half truths?

"All of the evidence establishes that Joey Balfour is a pedophile and that Pauley, Boggy, and Marty Gage are part of this international ring. The Thais will be happy to break his illegal gambling operation. We will be happy to have him off the air. It is a superior plan, don't you agree, Bill?"

Hunt had to admit the plan gave Joey Balfour's passion for collecting Errol Flynn movie posters a new meaning.

"Balfour has worshipped an actor who was once charged with statutory rape and died with a teenage girlfriend at his side. He has followed this false idol and deserves his fate of everlasting damnation." Joshua finished with a broad smile. There was no doubt in his mind that planting the kiddy porno at Feng Shui Flower Shop was morally justified. "Killing Pauley, to be frank, was never my first choice," said Joshua Cecil.

Joey was right, thought Bill Hunt. *If killing Pauley wasn't his first choice then who had wanted Pauley dead?* However one looked at it, all roads came back to Linda Harris. But with Pauley in the ICU,

Joshua got to do it his way. If that was the case, then Linda Harris wasn't in charge of the job anymore. If she was out of the picture it could mean that Joey Balfour was wrong. In that case, he should do his job and let Joey Balfour get what was coming to him. Why should he get personally involved? It flooded back as Joey's answers rang inside Bill Hunt's head: *Because the people you work for will betray you. You are not one of them. You have no future with them. You will be discarded. If you are going to be betrayed, then you must find your allies and a safe place to stand for the moment of battle. Make no mistake, Bill. They are using you.*

When Bill phones Joey later, he notices how calm Joey's voice is.

"Are you using me, Joey? Because if you cross me on this, I'll . . ."

"No threats, Bill. You've already crossed to the other side. You are one of us. We'll play this hand out together and everyone is going to walk away without a problem."

A Time to Keep Silence,
a Time to Speak

Night fell hours ago. Bill Hunt rides alone in the back of a taxi with a tight knot in his gut. Nothing settles his stomach. He punches another stomach pill from the tinfoil wrapper, pops it into his mouth, cocks his head back and swallows. He has a case of gamblers' nervous superstition, angels and devils enveloping his mind. He knows what he must do but finding the will to do it is another thing, another dimension. The windows of shops along Sukhumvit Road are mostly dark; metal gates are pulled down over the entrances. He notices the driver watching him through the rearview mirror; the driver is on Joey Balfour's payroll.

Bill Hunt's taxi stops on Sukhumvit Road. This is the defining moment. The driver waits. Bill Hunt taps the briefcase, then opens the locks and dumps the full contents of the briefcase onto the back seat. In place of the hard disk drive, printouts, and photographs, Hunt fills the briefcase with five identical Bibles: King James Version. He lowers the top of the briefcase, secures the locks and without saying anything gets out of the taxi. Standing on the broken curb, he watches the taxi pull into traffic, the red taillights disappear into a sea of other taxis. He walks past the police kiosk at the Soi 22 intersection, and continues walking until he comes to the small lane turning into the compound of shops.

The entryway to Feng Shui Flower Shop is dark, deserted. The buildings at the front are lit up with advertisements for luxury condos featuring coffin-like shaped swimming pools on the balcony. He stops and looks over his shoulder at the traffic on Sukhumvit Road. He checks his watch and looks up at the sky. There is a full, yellow moon shining and the light illuminates the fountain in front of the shop. The fountain gurgles enough for a skinny stream of water to rise half a foot from the surface of the pool. He shifts the briefcase to his right hand. The Bibles are heavier than the kiddy porno package.

He stops at the front door. It is locked and he takes out a jimmy and slides it between the door and jamb. After a moment, he pops the lock and pushes open the door to the overwhelming fragrance of flowers. On the counter of the shop are bowls of fresh flowers for which Bill Hunt has no name. White and red flowers with enormous, fleshy petals and evocative pulpy stems studded with seeds. He stands directly in front of the hidden cameras. The telephone rings. Hunt jumps, his heart thumping in his chest. He lets it ring six, seven times and then picks up the phone, stares at it, but doesn't put the receiver to his ear. He waits until it stops ringing and the room is again silent. He opens the briefcase and goes into the bedrooms and puts a Bible on the nightstand beside the beds. Then he goes to the office area and places another Bible on the keyboard of the computer. Finally, in the television and workout area, he places a Bible on the seat of the exercise bike. As he's coming out of the office area, he hears voices at the front counter. He switches off the light and crouches down onto the floor.

"Mr. Hunt, we advise you to come out with your hands up."

It is an American voice.

"What do you want?" asks Bill Hunt.

One of the suits has a shaved head, and wears horn-rimmed glasses; his ears are too big for his head. He looks like he was the class clown until one day some great sadness fell upon him, and he never smiled again. His partner, about ten years older, is bigger, head, body, and shoulders, like an ex-marine or boxer; he has closely cut reddish hair and a thin mustache. Hunt figures he's wearing contact lenses. The senior suit has the alert, angular look of a Jack Russell terrier who has cornered a rat. The suits are dark, two-hundred-dollar suits like the floor guys in the casinos would wear.

"The Thai police have a warrant to search this place. Please come out very slowly," says the senior suit.

Bill Hunt closes his eyes and wishes he were somewhere else. Anywhere but in Joey Balfour's Feng Shui Flower Shop. He rises to his feet and slowly walks out to the counter area, his hands over his head. There are two Americans in suits and several uniformed Thai police. The phone rings again. The Americans and Thais look at the phone.

"Can I answer that?"

The American suits look at each other.

"Answer it. Take down your left hand only and do it real slow."

This time Bill Hunt answers the phone. It's Joey Balfour on the line.

"Hi, Joey. Your shop is crawling with cops," he says, looking at the pair of farangs. He extends his arm, offering the senior guy the telephone. "It's the flower shop owner. He says that he wants to talk to you."

The senior suit takes the phone and puts it to his ear. Not a moment after saying hello, Joey is talking to him, man to man, and after a moment, the ex-marine looks like someone is holding a bayonet at his throat.

"If you are not out of my shop in five minutes I'll have my friends from Tonglor Police Station showing up. It won't play all that well for the American embassy. If you think this is a bluff, you are mistaken. You can phone Colonel Chumpol at Tonglor Police Station. I can give you his number. He is a personal friend. I said there might be a break-in. He is waiting for my call."

Joey Balfour places a bet that Joshua Cecil is getting his logistical support from the embassy, and they would bring in cops from the special branch, officers who are assigned to work with embassy officials. Renditions require logistical support. A whole line of command is behind the men standing in front of Bill Hunt, and these frontline guys are left with the decision of how to proceed.

"Mr. Balfour we have probable cause to believe you are running a child pornography racket. We have a search warrant for your shop. We advise you to come here immediately or the police will be sent to arrest you."

"What evidence do you have?" asks Joey Balfour.

"Jenkins, check the bedrooms," says the American who appears to be the senior of the two, and who holds the phone.

He comes back in under a minute carrying two Bibles.

"What the fuck is this, Jenkins? A joke?"

"That's all there is on the nightstands. I checked the rooms. They're clean. Nothing. Zip."

"Excuse me," says Joey Balfour. "Could you tell me why the possession of the Holy Bible is evidence of a pornography racket? Read me that passage. You're fucking around in my shop and how many people are dead in the South? I think people in Washington might be asking what the fuck you were doing wasting time collecting Bibles out of my shop when Americans are missing in Phuket. Or am I missing something? The embassy can expect to hear from my lawyers. What is your name, sir?"

The American puts down the telephone without giving his name. He stares hard and long at Bill Hunt. The two Americans disappear. Hunt hears them next door on the computer, opening and closing files. After ten minutes, they emerge.

"You didn't do your job," one of the Americans says.

"What was my job?" says Bill Hunt.

The Thai police are confused, circling around the flower shop, picking up, and sniffing flowers, waiting for some clarification. None of them want to make a decision. This is an American detail, it's up to them how to play it. The Thais eye the two Americans who huddle, shouting under their breath. Suddenly they are gone. The door is wide open. The Thais follow them. The Americans stand in front of the fountain arguing. One of them jabs his finger at the front door and the other American is cursing. Finally the senior official tells the Thai police that there has been some misunderstanding and apologizes. He follows the apology with a deep *wai*.

Bill Hunt stands behind the counter, his hand on a stack of Bibles. *Saved by an act of God*, he thinks. There is a bookmark in each Bible and in the identical place. He opens at the place of the mark. Bill Hunt clears his throat and reads the underlined passage: "To every thing there is a season, and a time to every purpose under the heaven: a time to get, and a time to lose; a time to keep, and a time to cast away; a time to rend, and a time to sew; a time to keep silence, and a time to speak; a time to love, and a time to hate; a time of war, and a time of peace."

As he lays down the Bible, the senior American glares at him, clenching and unclenching his jaw. "You can still change your mind."

Bill Hunt shakes his head. "I don't think so."

Later that evening, Joshua Cecil hands his passport to an official behind an immigration clearance counter at Terminal 1, Don Muang Airport. The official flips through the passport, and slides the front page through a reader. He looks up at Joshua, and then turns in his chair and calls to another official who walks over and the two of them look Joshua up and down. The preacher is in the computer. There has been a tip-off. Thai immigration has been alerted to check Rev. Joshua Cecil's briefcase. It takes a few minutes to remove a small computer handy stick, one that holds half a gig of information. It is hidden in a small compartment in the lid of the briefcase. When they put the handy into a USB port, they go to the pictures folder and open it. On the stick are hundreds and hundreds of photographs of naked children. These are not pretty pictures. The expressions on the officials' faces don't change, but eyebrows raise as the Thai officials huddle around the computer screen. When a senior American embassy official arrives at Don Muang Airport, Joshua Cecil is in the lock-up, hands on the bars of his cell.

"It's going to be difficult," says the official.

"How much?"

"Fifty thousand dollars," says the official.

"I don't have the money."

"We'll see that you get a good lawyer." The official is looking at his watch. He's on night duty, and his cell phone hasn't stopped. The number of Americans missing in Phuket is growing by the hour.

Joshua Cecil shakes with rage. "I don't want a lawyer. I want Linda Harris to get me out of here. Do you know who I am? Do you know who you are dealing with?"

"If you want us to contact someone on your behalf, please give us the contact details. I am afraid I must go now. We will be in touch."

A Time to Be Born,
and a Time to Die

Boggy and Marty share an office, each sitting at computer terminals, tapping on the keyboards, eyes on the screen. A calico cat, curled on Boggy's lap, stretches out its front paws and yawns. Next to him, on a third computer, Pauley is online, cleaning up at a three-dollar and six-dollar table in a poker room. Boggy and Marty are at the beta stage, testing a new generation of Feng Shui Flower Shop software.

Bill Hunt comes into the room, "Has anyone seen Joey?"

Hunt arrives from a security office located in an office building near the flower shop, and Feng Shui Security and Investigations has many of the same clients. He has continued to monitor security at Feng Shui Flower Shop and its grounds. So far he has discovered no evidence of wires or surveillance. He's taken considerable pride at installing new levels of security at the flower shop, the condo, and in Joey's personal life. But no one is easing up, believing that it is over.

The day before Marty had said, "Earthquakes happen in intervals. In between, when everything is quiet, the tectonic plates continue to slide. It's not only earthquakes that do this."

The others had nodded.

The gambling regulars still come in their chauffeur-driven luxury cars on Tuesday and Thursday nights, parking in the same place as always. On the surface, little has changed. What bubbles below the surface remains less of a mystery than a long silence before a new rumble occurs. Ever since Joshua Cecil's people used the cover of the tsunami to broker a deal for him to leave Thailand, Bill Hunt has been waiting for IEC to open a new front. Joey Balfour's old TV program continues to grow in popularity. In most of the four hundred and eleven Indian reservation casinos in America, Joey Balfour is a local hero. He was featured in *Variety* as a lost celebrity. His photo was taken for this feature with Chief Black Crow, and Joey is wearing an Indian headband.

"Joey hasn't turned up," explains Marty. The boss is being interviewed by CNN about risks, odds, and probabilities. He's being interviewed live about the last big earthquake and how the experts had predicted another big tsunami, but not a wave higher than a kick boxer's foot hit the shore. He is asked about the probability of a third big earthquake, the day of the final end, and Joey has a way to explain this that viewers love. There is a TV in the corner but no one is watching. It is another Joey Balfour slick-as-cow-spit performance.

"Do you believe in acts of God?" the CNN reporter asks.

Joey smiles into the camera, "I play the odds. As far as I can see, no one has ever figured out what hand God's holding, so it's hard to know what acts are His and what acts aren't."

Joey told all of them as they assembled at Feng Shui Flower Shop on the day Joshua Cecil left Thailand, "They will try again. Like all true believers, they hit and run, wait, and try again, believing that their divine destiny guarantees a winning hand. The more times you play, the more chances you have of winning. All gambling is based on counting. What you need to watch are the cheats. They look for a shortcut. To win, you need resources larger than the house because at the end of the day the house always wins. We are the house. We will win."

The CNN interviewer frowns into the camera. There are December 2004 images of beachfront hotels in ruins, bodies in the debris, and rows and rows of coffins. The new earthquake disappoints by producing low numbers of casualties, all of them in Indonesia, only there is no one as colorful as Joey Balfour available. Re-running the old stock photos injects some drama into the broadcast.

"What are the odds of the next big tsunami hitting Thailand?"

Joey Balfour smiles into the camera.

"About the same as Temperance Hill winning the Belmont."

The interviewer's smile fails to mask his perplexed expression. "What's that mean in terms of the weather?"

"An earthquake is a long-shot odd. And so is a tsunami. But long shots can win. Professional gamblers don't put all of their money on a long shot. They play the odds. You only have to win a little more than fifty percent of the time to keep your bank flush. The ideal situation is you have information from the past that lets you predict what will happen in the future. You lay your bet down in the present. With Mother Nature you want long, long odds on a disaster happening. We have no good way of knowing what she will do next. Mother Nature doesn't have to play by the rules; she creates and changes the rules whenever she wishes. We have to live with that. What I know is gambling, and neither the house nor a smart punter bets against Mother Nature."

As Bill Hunt watches Joey Balfour on CNN he knows that he's talking to Linda Harris, and he wonders if she's listening.

A Time to Break Down,
a Time to Build Up

Resting against the pillow, he turns his head as Ped stretches out with a book open on her lap. Sky sits up on the other side, leans forward, painting her toenails. In his mind, Joey is making a list of places to travel, expeditions to a beach or mountain top. For days he's kept away from Feng Shui Flower Shop, away from his usual haunts, he's confined to his condo, where he watches Dr. Daeng in the street below feeding the cats. He reminds himself that he's won a battle but the war will never end, the knives will always be out. He looks at Ped and she begins to read the final passages of *Anna Karenina*. Sky looks up from painting her toenails. She's ready to listen.

"'Well, and what about the Jews, the Moslems, the Confucians, the Buddhists—what are they? He thought, putting himself the question that seemed to him dangerous. Surely these hundreds of millions of people can't be deprived of that highest blessing without which life has no meaning? He started pondering, but corrected himself at once. But what is it I'm asking? he said to himself. I'm asking about the relationship to the Deity of all the diverse beliefs of all mankind; I'm asking about the general revelation of God to the whole universe with all of its cloudy nebulae. Then what is it I'm doing? There has been revealed beyond question to me personally, to my own heart, a knowledge unattainable by reasoning, and I'm obstinately trying to express that knowledge by means of reason and language.'"

Joey's eyes open, and he pushes the book down so that Ped stops reading.

"What Tolstoy's saying is no one can explain magic," says Joey. "And anyone claiming a monopoly on knowing is selling something."

He looks up at the *Cuban Story* movie poster opposite the bed.

"Mr. Quattro had magic," says Ped.

"But his luck ran out."

Sky moves across the bed, reaches over, picks up an envelope and removes the hundred-dollar note that Bill Hunt had given her. She rolls back over the bed, holding the note high, and lets it go. The hundred dollar floats onto the bed between them. No one says anything for a long time. "I am betting this is our lucky day," says Sky.

"You've been reading the *Book of Change*," says Ped. She knows Sky's look of confidence after immersing herself in feng shui.

She is as calm and happy as someone who has found something to hold on to. Raindrops strike the window outside. Sky climbs out of bed and opens the blinds. Joey and Ped join her at the window watching the lightning. Cracks of thunder peal in the distance. The flashes of light against the sky disappear one after the other. No one says anything as they watch the rain come down in sheets, closing in the world, isolating them atop of the needle. The sound of the rain is the sound of chi flowing, enveloping them. They gaze at the sky.

"What is magic," asks Sky, "but a space where harmony balances."

No one expects such profound observations from Sky. Joey leans forward and kisses her on the brow. "That's good, Sky," he says.

"True magic is never forgetting. That's what your mother taught us," says Ped. Jennifer's problem with forgetting certain memories had become less frightening than the possibility of a larger void of forgetfulness, which would swallow up a lifetime of books, stories, folklore, and legends, all the hours of reading to her son, the possibility that they would be lost, forgotten, as if they never resided in her mind.

Joey worries about the place his mother is traveling to. He reaches over and strokes Ped's cheek, and then brushes the hair away from Sky's face, only to find she has tears in her eyes.

"'That we appear and vanish like lightning, and that for a brief moment we are alive, that is truly magical. And before we disappear altogether we leave the sound of distant thunder. What power we have is small. What we know even smaller. But the odds are we reappear somewhere else, another time, another place.'"

Ped fluffs up her pillow, positions it against the headboard, and finishes reading *Anna Karenina* and, as she closes the book, Sky is asleep, her hair feathered over the pillow, her perfect body moving as she breathes. Joey doubts the incontestable meaning of goodness. Not in Tolstoy's world, not in his world. It is enough to settle for the chance of doing good, the chance of making the right bets and beating the odds, one day at a time. He meets Ped's gaze, as she waits for the magical feelings to pass from beyond the book resting on her lap. Her hand touches his and he leans forward to kiss her. A tear drops onto his hand and it belongs to her. Joey brushes the back of his hand against her cheek. He embraces her, rocking her, as if to comfort her.

"I am afraid they will take you away," she says.

Joey kisses her again. "They had their chance. It's passed. The game is over. They will find someone else."

She believes him and is soon asleep in his arms. He climbs out of bed and goes to the window and watches the storm. He smells the rain outside and remembers the penthouse in Vancouver. He wonders what Mr. Quattro had racing through his mind in those last minutes as he looked out at the rain over English Bay, when that rolling blanket of darkness came for him. For a moment, he must have known they had cornered him in a place designed for escape but, rather than flee, he stood his ground and let those forces take him far away.